Plantaૃ Tuaor Queen

The story of Elizabeth of York

Book I of the Plantagenet Embers Trilogy

Plantagenet Princess, Tudor Queen

The Story of Elizabeth of York

Samantha Wilcoxson

Plantagenet Princess, Tudor Queen

The Story of Elizabeth of York

By Samantha Wilcoxson

ISBN10: 1511803312

ISBN13: 978-1511803311

Printed in the United States of America

For men who fought for a king they had never laid eyes on.

For women who kept homes ready for men that would never return.

For Lancaster.

For York.

For Elizabeth, a Plantagenet Princess who became a Tudor Queen.

Family of Elizabeth of York

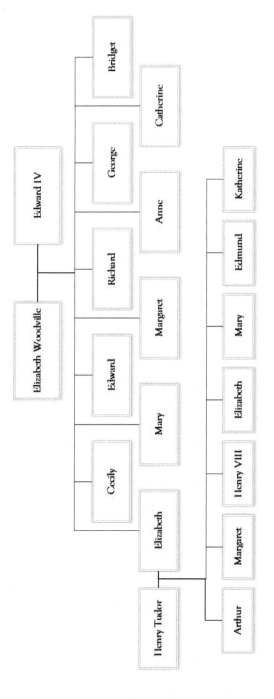

November 2, 1470

Elizabeth's lips were firmly set in a pout as she glared out the window of Westminster Abbey. She should be rejoicing, as the rest of London was, for the birth of the wailing baby boy. But her stomach was churning like the Thames below being pelted by icy rain on the other side of the glass. After three girls, beautiful girls undoubtedly but still only girls, her father had his first precious boy.

She watched various attendants file up and down the stairs of the abbot's lodging that had been graciously turned over to the woman whom Yorkists still considered the Queen of England, Elizabeth's mother. The fact that Margaret of Anjou claimed that title for herself meant little to them. They were confident of the return of their golden Plantagenet King, Edward IV. Elizabeth twisted the skirt of her dress in her hands, careless of the wrinkles she was creating, and prayed that they were correct. How she missed her father!

When the Lancastrians had paraded their frail claimant to the throne, Henry VI, through the streets, Elizabeth had been shocked that this man inspired people to fight for him. To her, he looked more like a poor traveling friar or tutor than a mighty king. Certainly her father would return from exile and rescue his growing family from sanctuary. At least, she hoped so.

She wondered if he would still love her now that he had a son.

"Princess Elizabeth, would you like to meet your baby brother?"

Elizabeth looked up at Jayne, one of her mother's young servants. Elizabeth's eyes normally danced with the mischief typical of a four-year-old, but today Jayne saw more fear and concern than a child's eyes should. Elizabeth slowly released her hold on the crumpled dress and took the soft hand that Jayne held out to her. As she stood, she reminded herself to hold up her head proudly with its crown of coppery blond tresses. She was still a princess, after all.

Elizabeth looked up into Jayne's face as they proceeded up the worn stone steps. Jayne, still only a child herself, exuded gentle kindness, leaving Elizabeth feeling comfortable to ask, "Is my mother so very happy?"

Crouching down to Elizabeth's level Jayne said, "Of course, she is happy, my lady." She saw Elizabeth's face fall slightly and continued, "Not only because she has a lovely new baby, but because she has such a wonderful eldest daughter to help her with him."

They continued up the final few steps and paused before a large carved wooden door.

"Are you ready?"

Elizabeth took a deep breath and straightened her back. "Yes, I am ready."

Jayne hid her smile at the miniature picture of her mother that Elizabeth made. She held open the door for the little princess to enter.

Elizabeth's eyes widened at the scene before her. Certainly she had been invited to see her younger sisters upon their births, but she was almost five years old now and noticed more of her surroundings. Her gaze took in the hunchbacked midwife with stringy, dark grey hair. She was bent over a pile of bloody rags and a basin containing what looked like an animal's stomach. Finally, Elizabeth turned enlarged eyes toward her mother lying in bed cradling a small bundle.

She walked toward the bed, keeping the proper pace as her mother had taught her, hoping to earn the queen's favor with her maturity and grace. However, Queen Elizabeth, for whom little Elizabeth had been named, did not even reward her daughter with a glance until she had reached the side of the bed. Elizabeth Woodville sat up with her glorious hair arranged around her. The color of corn silk, the queen's tresses were her pride and joy. Elizabeth craned her neck to peer at the little face held close to her mother's breast.

"Elizabeth," the queen said with a satisfied smile. "Meet your little brother, Prince Edward."

"He is quite red, mother." It was out before she could stop herself. So much for acting like the perfect princess in her mother's presence.

But, the queen just laughed. "As all new babies are, my daughter," she assured her. "Even you, as lovely as you are now, looked much like this when you were first delivered."

Elizabeth wrinkled her nose in distaste. "Really, mother?"

The queen patted the bed beside her, and Elizabeth finally relaxed as she climbed up next to her and settled herself in the plush bed coverings.

Her mother whispered as if they were conspirators. "Yes. In fact, most babies are just a little bit ugly for the first few days, but then they begin to improve dramatically."

Elizabeth tried to contain a giggle as she leaned over to examine the young prince more closely. Her mother accommodated her by pulling back the layers of blankets confining him. As he was freed, the baby boy flailed skinny arms and legs and scrunched up his face which reddened in frustration. Elizabeth raised an eyebrow at the unimpressive specimen and looked up at her mother.

"You are right, mother. A little bit ugly."

Elizabeth jumped as Edward released the wail that he had been saving up breath for, but her mother only laughed again.

"He is fine, just unhappy about being disturbed," she said as she nonchalantly handed the baby off to his wet-nurse. Contented suckling sounds almost immediately replaced his cries.

Without the baby between them, Elizabeth felt she was being too familiar sitting on the bed with her mother, so she stood.

Looking around the room for something to focus on besides her mother's face, she asked, "Father will be quite happy, will he not?" She tried to sound casual, uninterested.

"He will be very happy, Elizabeth. Your father will always love you, but every king needs an heir," the queen stated in a tone that welcomed no nonsense.

Elizabeth met her mother's eyes and said, "Yes, I know. I will go say prayers for my baby brother now." She turned from the bed.

"Come visit again tomorrow, Elizabeth," her mother said as she walked away.

At the door, Elizabeth turned and curtseyed saying, "I will, my lady mother. I look forward to seeing how the Prince's looks improve."

~ ~ ~ ~

The next morning Elizabeth was awoken by coldness in her toes that was creeping up her thin legs. She pulled her feet up into her bed coverings and tried to force sleep to return to no avail. Sighing, she peeked over at Cecily and Mary and was happy to see that they also were awake. Their little blond heads were close together as they played at some private game. Elizabeth pulled her covers around her and moved toward them for their companionship and warmth.

"Did you see the baby prince yet?" she asked her sisters.

Cecily, who was not yet two years old, was quite certain that she was the baby but certainly no prince. "I'm a princess!" she corrected in her childish lisp.

"Of course you are," said Elizabeth with the maturity of a four year old who has already been made a big sister three times. "But our lady mother has another baby, Prince Edward."

"I want to see!" exclaimed Mary, who had recently celebrated her third birthday.

"We will see him today," Elizabeth assured them. "But I will tell you a secret."

She waited for her sisters to lean in as she savored her higher knowledge.

"He is just a little bit . . . . well, ugly."

The girls burst into fits of laughter that brought their nursemaid, Matilda, into the room to see what they were up to. She smiled at the vision of the three York princesses snuggled up together.

"And what is going on in here, my ladies?" Matilda asked.

"Bess said the baby is ugly!" Mary announced.

"Mary! That was to be a secret!" Elizabeth was horrified that her confidence had been so casually broken, but Matilda just smiled knowingly as she stepped up to the pile of blankets and little blond girls.

"You may find that he looks more handsome today," she said. "Babies do recover quickly."

"When can we see him?" Mary demanded.

"We must wait for your lady mother to call for you," Matilda reminded them. At their disappointed sighs, she added, "Let us go and find some bread to break your fast," knowing that food was certain to distract them, even from the excitement of the new prince.

As the little girls ate with a speed that indicated hunger tempered by noble manners, they continued to talk about their new brother. Cecily asked, "What about Papa?"

"Our father," Elizabeth corrected her, "will certainly want to see him as soon as possible." As she said it, she prayed to God that it were true. Would her father return soon?

"When will he be here?" asked Mary, certain that her older sister was the source of all answers.

"We must ask our lady mother when we see her today,"

Elizabeth said because she hoped for an answer just as much as the younger two.

Soon, the queen did call for her daughters. They ran giggling up the stairs but were stopped on the landing by Matilda, who reminded them to compose themselves before the queen and prince. When they walked into the room with Elizabeth first, followed by Mary, and finally little Cecily toddling behind, they were a picture of royal decorum.

"Good morning, lady mother," Elizabeth said as the three curtseyed, Cecily almost falling over in the effort.

"Good morning, my beautiful daughters!" said the queen as she beckoned them to come forward.

The girls had exhausted their capacity for self-control with their greeting and hurried to the bed to see their brother.

"Oh, Bess! He is not so ugly!" Mary exclaimed with her trademark candor.

Elizabeth blushed and refused to meet her mother's eyes until she heard her laugh. "No, he is certainly more attractive than yesterday," her mother agreed. Elizabeth looked up and her mother kissed her forehead and gave her a knowing smile. "Bess, you will be such a big help to me with your brother and sisters while we are here."

"Here" meant in sanctuary. Living in the abbot's quarters of Westminster Abbey instead of one of the royal palaces.

"How long will we be here?" Elizabeth asked. Three pairs of innocent eyes in various shades of blue locked onto their mother, and their chattering stopped as they waited for the answer to this question.

The queen lifted her head and looked down at them as though she were sitting on a throne rather than reclining on the abbot's bed. "Your father the king will remove us from this place as soon as he possibly can. Warwick will not be able to stand up to him now that he has a son and heir to fight for."

She said it with such confidence that the girls did not doubt her in the least and began gazing out the windows several times a day to watch for their father's livery.

February 11, 1471

Little celebration would take place on this day despite the fact that it was Elizabeth's fifth birthday. Her mother had seemed so certain three months ago that her father would be rescuing them, but here they were still in rooms that felt increasingly cramped with food that was nothing compared to that of the royal kitchens. To a five year old, "soon" meant long before three months had gone by. Where was her father?

She was disconsolately sitting at the window, no longer really watching, but sitting there as a course of habit. Maybe her father would surprise her for her birthday. She could not make herself excited over the possibility. After all, if he hadn't shown up for tiny Edward, she doubted that he would show up for her. She had heard her mother talking to her grandmother, Jaquetta Woodville, Lady Rivers, about a host of people with names that were familiar without understanding the real reasons why her father could not come home.

She had heard that the Earl of Warwick was supporting old Henry VI as King now, but didn't understand why. Had he not fought with her father? Were they not cousins? How could there be so much confusion over who was king? Elizabeth was confounded by the events swirling around her.

She was roused from her reverie by her two half-brothers, Thomas and Richard. They were all that remained of her mother's first marriage to the Lancastrian knight, Sir John Grey. She could see that some of their darker coloring must have been inherited from their father, but both were just as handsome as any son of Elizabeth Woodville would be expected to be. The boys bounded up to her holding out a lumpy, poorly wrapped package.

"A present for you, Bess!" they exclaimed together.

Forgetting her depression, she wiggled down from the window

seat to see what the boys had managed to bring to her. Lavish gifts were no longer the norm for the royal family after the long months in sanctuary, and she wondered how they had come up with one.

She eagerly took the package from their hands, forgetting her manners in her excitement, and pulled at the twine bow holding the scrap of fabric in place. "Oh!" she said softly as two bright oranges rolled out of the wrapping.

Elizabeth felt tears come to her eyes as she remembered just a few days earlier when a basket had arrived from a local merchant with a note encouraging them not to be dismayed. York supporters had not forgotten them. The children had torn into the fruit like starving animals. She had thought it gone, but her brothers had saved the last and most precious of the fruit for her.

"They look wonderful," she said as she craned her neck to look up at each of them. "Thank you."

Richard, who was ten years old, was a fun and slightly mischievous boy. His hair was dark and eyes brown, apparently taking after his father. Sir John Grey had been killed in 1461 at the second Battle of St. Albans fighting for Henry VI. Woodvilles were all staunch Yorkists now that Elizabeth Woodville was Edward's queen.

Thomas, at sixteen, was too old to be considered a child, but his mother had insisted that he, too, flee with the family to sanctuary when Edward was forced into exile by his former friend and ally, the Earl of Warwick. The rugged, blond haired boy was straining for self-control in the confined quarters and had enjoyed occupying himself with plans to entertain the girls this day.

"You are very welcome, my lady," Thomas said as he bowed and extended his arm to her. "Now if you will come with me to enjoy the day's festivities."

Elizabeth giggled before composing herself to mimic her brother's seriousness. "That sounds delightful, my lord." She placed her small hand upon his arm and allowed him to escort her into the next room where her sisters were already sitting on pillows waiting for the show to be put on by Richard and Thomas. They clapped as the three of them entered, and Elizabeth realized that the boys must have been planning this for days, knowing that she could use some cheering up. She kissed them each on the cheek before taking her seat.

Richard set a circlet that had been fashioned out of twigs onto her head and one of his own cloaks on her shoulders. Then Thomas announced, "Let the tournament begin!"

Thomas and Richard retreated to opposite sides of the room where they hoisted their makeshift jousting equipment and climbed onto broomstick destriers. Elizabeth was touched that Thomas, who was certainly too old to play this way, was doing it solely for his half-sisters' amusement. The girls cheered uproariously as the boys jousted and dueled enthusiastically before them. When, at last, the boys stepped forward to bow before their sisters, Elizabeth put on her most royal princess countenance and posture in place of a crown. She rose and complimented them on their knightly bravery and aptitude.

"Thank you so much for putting on this show for us today," she added more informally.

She was enveloped in a group hug with her siblings. Though she was momentarily happy, she couldn't help but wonder where they would be when her next birthday arrived.

April 1471

Elizabeth's mother never tired of reveling in the plans that her father would be making when he returned. If he returned. As for the little girls, they only dreamed of running through fresh grass and picking wildflowers. The betrothals and alliances that might be made upon the return of the king were still quite beyond them.

Surely, a suitable match would be made for Elizabeth, but she thought little about it. The queen did not seem to have any doubts about Edward's return to England and its throne, but as the months dragged by, Elizabeth began to wonder if she would ever see her father again. She often caught herself staring out the window, daydreaming about people whose lives were moving on as they sat in the same rooms day after day.

The reverie was broken when a flash of movement caught her eye. She sat faithfully in the same window seat as she had every other day for months now. The adventures of her imagination flitted away like a shadow. She peered through the window, attempting to discern through the rain, the never ending rain, what had stolen her attention. It was a young man dressed as a page who looked vaguely familiar.

Once he was given entrance, he announced that he was in the service of Cecily Neville, Duchess of York and Elizabeth's grandmother. Excitement rose from deep within her. She was aware that her grandmother would only send a message to her mother if she absolutely had to. Even at only five years old, the snippets of speech and condescending looks her grandmother aimed at her mother had not gone unnoticed.

The queen hastily passed baby Edward to Matilda and grasped the note from the dripping messenger. She tore it open as though it contained the Holy Grail, and rightly so for it contained the message that Edward, with his brother Richard, had landed at

Ravenspur two weeks earlier.

Hurriedly replacing her almost maniacal look with one more suited to a queen, Elizabeth's mother formally thanked the young man and invited him to dry himself by the fire. Immediately forgetting him, she turned to her daughters and announced, "Your father will be here soon!" More quietly she added, "To reclaim his family and his kingdom."

In the days following this momentous visit, the queen regained her zeal for life and applied that passion to ordering her children and servants to complete an endless list of tasks in preparation for Edward's arrival. Rooms must be cleaned, trunks must be packed – for certainly they would not be remaining here for long, and the girls must be made presentable to stand before the king. Elizabeth did not even mind her mother's short temper, for her father would arrive any day now!

Rumors came to them in the coming days, and it was more frustrating than ever before to be trapped in sanctuary. This place they had fled to for their safety felt like a prison, and they were never more anxious to leave it than when their rescue was close at hand. One day, the boy who brought their bread from a loyal Yorkist baker whispered that Edward was headed for London with his army. George of Clarence, Edward's brother who had helped send him into exile when he joined Warwick, had defected back to Elizabeth's father, putting the Lancastrians into a more difficult position.

Warwick had ordered the people of London to close the city gates to Edward. The queen still seemed outwardly confident that he would be welcomed, despite Warwick's command, but Elizabeth saw the fine lines racing away from her eyes and caught the slouch of her shoulders when she thought nobody was looking.

Would London hold for Henry VI or shove him aside for Edward IV?

It was Holy Week and Elizabeth spent much time on her knees, beseeching the Lord to be with her father and uncles. Her mother often found her in prayer and would join her briefly before returning to tasks that she found more practical in preparation for the return of her king. On Maundy Thursday, Elizabeth heard cheering erupt out on the street. She ran to her window seat but could not ascertain if the praise was for her father.

"My sweet Elizabeth," she heard a deep, masculine voice behind her say.

Fountains of joy burst within her, and she turned and jumped down from her ledge only to stop short. Her father was embracing her mother, and it was to her those precious words were directed. Struggling to control the blush she felt racing across her cheeks, she fell into a curtsey as she had been practicing since hearing of her father's return to the country.

Soon, she felt his large, calloused hand on her chin. "Is this beautiful young lady truly my little princess?" her father asked.

She rose with the pressure of his hand and solemnly responded, "Yes, father."

"Then come here and kiss your father," he exclaimed, grabbing her around the waist and swinging her up into the air.

Elizabeth squealed happily and felt relief flood through her. Her father had returned and did indeed still love her. Her slender arms circled his neck and she held on as though she were afraid he may change his mind. "I missed you so," she whispered in his ear.

"And I missed you, my darling Bess."

She closed her eyes and drank deeply of the scent and feel of being in her father's arms. Her mother would insist that he take a bath, but Elizabeth didn't mind that he smelled like horses and sweat. He felt strong and solid as the Tower of London.

"And who are these lovely ladies?" he asked, and Elizabeth was dismayed that she was going to have to share him with her sisters.

"Oh, father, you know it is Mary and Cecily," she said without releasing her grip upon him. When she peeked at her sisters, she saw that Mary looked in awe and uncertain while Cecily looked purely terrified.

"Surely, you remember our father," she admonished her sisters.

Edward shifted her to one arm while reaching out with the other as he stooped down to the little girls' level. "Their father has been gone a long time for ones so young," he whispered to Elizabeth. "They are not yet as quick and mature as you."

She grinned and was willing to allow her sisters to share in their father's affection after hearing this.

"Good day, father," little Mary said with a clumsy curtsy.

"Ah, that's enough formality, isn't it?" said Edward. "Come here, my Mary."

Mary overcame her uncertainties and threw herself into Edward's waiting arm. Cecily looked like she was struggling to decide whether or not to join her sisters with this man she did not remember.

"Father, you stink!" said Mary as she pulled back and wrinkled her freckled nose at him.

He laughed deeply and loudly. "I'm sure that I do," Edward admitted unashamedly. "I'd be willing to wager that your mother has disappeared to order me a bath, and a well deserved one it is, too." He kissed Mary on the forehead and released her. Elizabeth still clung to his other side with no plans of releasing him until she had to.

"Cecily...." He reached out to her as he said her name, but Cecily dissolved into tears.

"Cecily!" Elizabeth shouted. "How could you treat our darling father so?" She looked to him in apology for her small sister's offense.

"There now, it's quite alright," he said as he detangled himself from her grasp. "She will be happy to be with her father in no time." He looked to his wife standing in the doorway to the next room. "It appears that now I am to be bathed."

The queen smiled in a way that Elizabeth had not seen since they had taken up residence in the abbey.

"Mother, you must speak to Cecily," Elizabeth commanded, but her mother motioned to Matilda to comfort Cecily before closing the door behind her and her husband.

Elizabeth approached Cecily and Matilda, who was attempting to wipe away her tears. "Now why would she let Cecily misbehave that way? Certainly father has servants to help him bathe."

"Certainly, he does," Matilda admitted with a smile, but she did not seem surprised that Cecily had not been reprimanded.

Later, an uncommon amount of time later for something as simple as a bath Elizabeth thought, Edward and his wife rejoined their cluster of girls. Elizabeth and Mary settled on his lap, while Cecily sat nearby. She had dried her tears but continued to look uncertain of this giant of a man, who everyone claimed was her father.

The queen smiled at her husband as if they shared a secret as she slipped from the room. That is when it hit Elizabeth. The Prince! Her father had his little Edward and would no longer care that Elizabeth was his oldest child because she was a girl. Sure enough, her mother reentered the room with a small bundle and a satisfied smile.

"Here is your son," she said.

Edward deposited the girls on the floor as he rose from his seat. Slowly, as if he was a little afraid – but that was silly, this man who had taken on armies from the age of sixteen could not be afraid of a newborn – he approached his son.

"My love, you have given me everything a man could desire," he said as he gazed at the baby boy.

17

He wasn't that remarkable, thought Elizabeth. Though she had to admit her baby brother was much cuter now than he had been that first day. Her father would not be as impressed if he'd seen him then.

Edward kissed his son and his wife in turn before moving his eyes back to his daughters who seemed to be eagerly awaiting his judgment of their brother.

"What a blessed prince he is, too, with three lovely sisters," he said happily as he put his hands out to them.

Elizabeth was the first to fling herself into his arms.

"You will be a wonderful help teaching our little prince how to behave, will you not, Bess?" her father asked.

"Of course, father," she responded, seriously adding, "But he does not do much besides cry and eat."

Edward grinned. "I'm sure you are right. Please let me know when he acquires more notable skills."

Elizabeth nodded and smiled as she laid her head on his shoulder. He understood, and he loved her.

As they all sat together as a family for the first time in six months, Elizabeth focused on the feel of her father's strong, warm arms holding her while conversation swirled around the room.

Her brother, Thomas, had many questions about where Edward had been and what he was going to do next. Young Richard seemed in awe, not only of his step-father, but his older brother as well. It was overwhelming to Elizabeth, this talk of who would side with who and how they were all related. Reveling in the warm fire and feeling of security, her eyelids drooped and her chin slowly drifted down to her chest. She just hoped that her father would stay right where he was.

It was not to be as Elizabeth wished. The next day, servants hustled about moving the last of the queen's and princesses' things from the abbey to Grandmother Cecily's London residence,

Baynard's Castle. Even more were scurrying in preparation for Edward's army to move out to meet that of Margaret of Anjou, known to the Lancastrians as Queen of England.

~ ~ ~ ~

How Elizabeth longed for peace, not because she was aware enough to be concerned about the thousands of soldiers who would be barbarically throwing themselves at one another, but because it would mean more visitors and freedom. The idea that men were out there preparing to die either for her father or in an attempt to steal his throne was still too far beyond her comprehension.

A line of wagons piled high with the queen's and her children's things made their way to the duchess of York's castle nestled into place on the bank of the Thames. Elizabeth tilted her head back to see the top of the hexagonal towers and high turrets. The huge stone complex looked like it would stand forever and gave her a feeling of security that she had not felt in the months spent at the abbey. She closed her eyes as the sun warmed her face and wished that she could lie in the grass enjoying the contrast between the cool ground and the heat of the sun. The jolting of the carriage brought her from her reverie and she saw her grandmother's servants lined up to assist with the family's things.

Soon she was settled into a lovely set of rooms with her sisters. Baby Edward, of course, had his own private suite with a fleet of caregivers from wet-nurses to rockers to laundresses. Duchess Cecily had welcomed them kindly but formally. Elizabeth didn't think her grandmother knew how to be informal and affectionate. She wondered how her father had learned to be warm and jovial. For the first time, she wondered what had happened to her father's father, whom she had never met.

Matilda came in with Mary and Cecily in tow. With their father back in London, they saw less of their mother. The joyous family reunion they had enjoyed when he first returned was a flash of familial harmony and togetherness that was quickly extinguished.

"Lady Elizabeth, are you practicing your lute?" Matilda asked.

Elizabeth slid the instrument off her lap and pushed it aside with disdain. "Not really," she replied.

Mary came stomping in and demanded, "Why is our father leaving again?"

Three sets of curious eyes locked onto Matilda as they were each very interested in the answer to this question that only Mary dared to ask.

The nurse crouched down and the girls huddled around her as though they were a part of a conspiracy.

"Your father goes to defend his right to be King."

"That's nonsense! Of course he's the King!" Mary exclaimed.

"Yes, love. I know he is," Matilda assured her. "But Margaret of Anjou fights for her son's right to inherit more than her husband's right to hold the throne. She must fight for her husband to benefit her son."

"But our brother, Edward, will be King," Elizabeth said in a slightly questioning tone.

"He will," Matilda said with certainty. "Because your father will defeat these murderous Lancastrians once and for all!" The girls were used to outbursts such as this and none of them thought to wonder what had turned their soft-spoken Matilda so vehemently against King Henry.

"Why do they fight father?" Mary asked. Elizabeth was quite glad that she had.

Matilda sighed. "Well, that is a very long story, isn't it? And too confusing for little girls." She looked at each of their expectant faces and decided to try. "When your father became king, some people believed that it should still be King Henry VI no matter how unfit he was to rule. Your father's father, the mighty duke of York, had put forward his own claim to the throne before he died, showing that he was rightful heir going all the way back to Edward III."

"But why does our uncle Warwick fight with them?" Elizabeth asked.

"The earl of Warwick is anxious to have as much power as he can possibly possess, and has decided that any king will do if he is holding their reins," she said slowly as if trying to be sure that she answered correctly, if not completely.

"How could the wrong person be king?" Mary pressed on.

"Yes, how?" Elizabeth added, ignoring Matilda's raised eyebrows.

"Well, this is a better question for one of your tutors than for me," she huffed. "But it started with Henry IV taking the throne from his cousin, Richard II. That got the crown going along the wrong branch of the family tree. Nobody worried too much about it until our King Henry started acting addled. Then your grandfather, Richard Plantagenet, decided it was time to advance the lines of the other sons of Edward III."

She examined the little faces gazing at her own. Could they really understand? She wasn't sure that she did.

"So, our family should have been kings all along." Elizabeth stated.

"I suppose that's true," Matilda agreed, though she was not sure it was. She dared not point out that if their grandfather had been king, Elizabeth Woodville would probably have never managed to marry their father.

"And our father will prove again that he is the rightful king!" Mary cried out in obvious repetition of exclamations made throughout the castle.

Smiling as she groaned to straighten up, Matilda agreed, "That he will, my little ladies. That he will."

For days after this conversation, Elizabeth had pondered what it all meant. Why had people not wanted her father to be king? She had seen the dreary, fragile Henry and couldn't imagine him making a better king than her powerful, handsome father. As for Queen Margaret, she was not nearly as beautiful as Elizabeth's own mother, and she had borne only one child compared to her mother's six (if you counted Thomas and Richard, and she supposed she must). If her family also had the clear lineage required, why did the people fight?

She wondered if sometimes men actually enjoyed having something to fight about.

~ ~ ~ ~

As they waited for news of her father, Elizabeth's mother appeared more in the nursery. The pinched look that had been etched into her face during their time in sanctuary was replaced by a more confident, peaceful one, but Elizabeth was certain that fear still loomed behind her eyes.

"Father is the greatest soldier in all of England, is he not?" she asked her mother.

The queen blinked as though she were being shaken from a dream. "Certainly, he is. None can begin to compare to your father on the field." She stated it as she said everything, as though there was no room for debate.

"Then why do they fight him?" asked Mary.

"Because they are sentimental idiots," blurted the queen.

"Will father win?" Elizabeth asked in a voice barely above a whisper.

"Yes." The queen straightened her back and tilted her head back ever so slightly, giving power to her husband's troops through her own regality.

At that moment, a page rushed in and bowed low before the girls' mother.

"Yes, what is it?" she demanded.

"Pardon me, your grace," he said without completely straightening. "A messenger from the king has arrived."

"Have him brought to my chamber immediately," she ordered as she swept past the boy without waiting for a response.

When the girls heard cheering in the courtyard, they kneeled in prayer to thank God for the news that nobody had bothered to give them yet.

Tidbits of news were gathered by Elizabeth as she eavesdropped on conversations people assumed that she was too young to be interested in. Her father had defeated the traitorous Warwick at Barnet. She knew that she should be happy. Richard Neville of Warwick had executed her grandfather, Richard Woodville, and uncle, John Woodville. He had hoped to kill her father, but part of her was still sad that cousin fought cousin in these battles.

With the disadvantages her father had faced at Barnet, everyone at court said that it was God who had given him victory as the rightful king. Elizabeth thought that it all must be over. Then she heard that Margaret of Anjou and her son, whom some people called Prince Edouard and others called Edouard of Lancaster, had landed on England's shores to attempt once more to restore his father's throne.

It was difficult to embroider, practice her lessons, or even to eat, knowing that her father was out there, fighting for his kingdom and his life. Her life seemed too ordinary for something so important to be going on. She tried to keep herself occupied with Cecily and Mary as they awaited messengers from the battlefield.

On May 6, the news came. Edward and his army had crushed this final Lancastrian challenge at Tewkesbury two days earlier. Margaret's son, Edouard, had been killed in battle, and Margaret taken prisoner. Elizabeth wondered if the sometime queen would be allowed to join her husband in the Tower.

Certain that there would be peace now with both Warwick and Margaret defeated and Henry's heir dead, Elizabeth found more energy for her daily tasks and was enjoying assisting her grandmother with an altar cloth she was working on when another exhausted looking messenger was ushered in. Cecily Neville had a proud, aristocratic face that may have at one time been beautiful. Her auburn hair was pulled back severely, emphasizing her clear blues eyes that quickly took in all around her. Though she was strict, she was not unkind, and Elizabeth enjoyed their time together.

"What is it?" demanded the duchess.

"Rebels are approaching the city."

"Rebels? What rebels are left?"

"Fauconberg," he replied breathlessly. "With an army of almost 20,000. The mayor suggests that the royal family," he tipped his head toward Elizabeth, "move to the greater security of the Tower."

Elizabeth did not know who this Fauconberg was or what this latest enemy had against her father. She looked at her grandmother questioningly. This lady, who had faced much stronger opponents in her long and tragic life, looked barely perturbed by this latest threat.

"Thank you. You may find sustenance and rest in the hall."

The messenger bowed and accepted his dismissal.

"Who is Fauconberg, grandmother? Does he want to be king, too?"

Cecily snorted in a quite undignified manner. "No, he is simply causing trouble. Sometimes men have no idea what they will actually do if they are victorious in their ridiculous quests!"

Elizabeth scrunched up her face doubtfully. Surely, this man must have some objective, and men must have their reasons for following him. She had no time to consider it further or ask additional questions as her grandmother had moved on to ordering servants to prepare for a move to the Tower.

The city of London refused to open its gates to Fauconberg's army, despite his assurances that they had no intentions of ravaging the townspeople. Their only goal was reinstating Henry on the throne. In the Tower, Elizabeth could hear evidence of the attack on London Bridge and smell smoke of burning buildings.

Elizabeth's uncle, Anthony Woodville, had joined them at the Tower and assisted in its defense. Anthony, Lord Rivers since his father's death, was handsome and intelligent. His stories kept Elizabeth in rapt attention for as long as he was willing to tell them. An able soldier like her father, Anthony was even more passionate about intellectual pursuits and had a library larger than any Elizabeth had ever seen.

When news of Edward's approaching army sent Fauconberg into retreat, Anthony pursued them. With breathtaking quickness, Fauconberg was captured and executed. Elizabeth heard the news and breathed a sigh of relief. Surely there was nobody left to take up the fight against her father.

She was correct.

With no one left to fight for King Henry VI, he died in his rooms at the Tower on May 21. Elizabeth heard that his death had been ordered by her father to avoid any further uprisings, but she chose to believe the official statement that he had died of melancholy following the death of his only son and heir.

April 1483

Elizabeth dreaded entering sanctuary again, especially since she was less than convinced that it was necessary. She was no longer the little girl who worshipped her beautiful mother, but was now an intelligent young woman wondering if her mother wasn't making everything worse. As if things could be worse, when her father was dead.

On April 9, just days short of his 41st birthday, Edward had sickened and died after a damp day of hunting. It seemed lacking in honor for a man who had gloriously led troops and reigned over the greatest kingdom in the world to meet death because of cold and wetness, though she supposed that the extra weight he had put on in recent years didn't help either.

Maniacal screaming and the sounds of scurrying came from the room she was about to enter. She took a deep breath and lifted her chin, preparing for the onslaught before pushing the door open. Her mother was in the middle of the room surrounded by open trunks haphazardly filled with gowns, jewels, and gold plate. A cloud of disarrayed silvery blond hair flew around Queen Elizabeth's head as she barked out orders to the stooped men and women around her. Elizabeth was the calm in the middle of the storm.

"Mother, surely this is all unnecessary," she insisted. "Why are you so sure that our uncle Richard means us harm?"

"You are a young fool!" her mother retorted. "Your dear uncle has kidnapped your brother, and you would like to sit here embroidering while he comes for the rest of us?"

Elizabeth refused to raise her voice. "It can hardly be considered kidnapping for him to take custody of Edward. After all, father did name him Lord Protector."

The queen snorted as though she had never heard such idiocy.

"Your father put too much faith in his brother of Gloucester. I will not be making that mistake, and you are coming with me."

"Of course, I will do as my lady mother pleases," Elizabeth allowed. "But I feel that we are creating undue conflict when we should all be preparing together for my brother's coronation."

"If there is a coronation," her mother mumbled.

"Why would you say that?" Elizabeth asked, feeling some of Mary's bravery at the moment. If only Mary were still alive, she thought. She would be bold with mother and possibly more able to convince her of her folly. If only her father had not suddenly died! That strong true prince – how could he be taken from this world so unexpectedly and so young? The loss of those she loved weighed heavily on Elizabeth's slender shoulders.

Her mother stopped short in her chaotic movements to look Elizabeth in the eye. "Richard has . . . . taken custody of your brother. He has arrested my brother and son. Do you think this is simply so that he may come to London for the crowning ceremony?"

Elizabeth wasn't sure how to answer for her uncle's actions. Why had he arrested her uncle, Anthony, and her half-brother, Richard Grey? His motives were not clearer to her. She was just more willing to trust in him because her father always had.

"I will go see to my own packing," she said and left the room.

~ ~ ~ ~

By the time Richard, duke of Gloucester, and the newly declared Edward V had entered London, Elizabeth Woodville and her other children had once again entered sanctuary at Westminster Abbey. Elizabeth had reclaimed the window seat that had been hers as a child. More than enough time was now available to think about the past and about where the future would take her.

Continued efforts to convince her mother that Richard was simply fulfilling his role as Lord Protector had fallen on deaf ears. When Anthony Woodville and Richard Grey were executed for treason on Richard's orders, Elizabeth made no further attempts to discuss it.

Elizabeth remembered the fun-loving yet shy Richard, and wondered what treason he could have possibly participated in. Many hours were spent in prayer, not only because there was little else to do, but because Elizabeth truly felt comforted when she gave up her troubles to God. She wished for the opportunity to speak with her uncle. Her father had trusted Richard with his armies, large portions of his country, his life, and his heir. For these reasons, Elizabeth was hesitant to not trust him, but her mother's ranting was starting to take root. Whispered rumors and the unmistakable truth that he had ordered the killing of her beloved half-brother made her mind a fertile ground for doubt. Maybe her father had made a mistake.

Once again she wished for Mary's comforting presence. Elizabeth's younger sister had been carried off by illness not a year before their father. Mary would not have been afraid to ask the difficult questions and probably would have marched right up to the duke of Gloucester and asked him exactly what his intentions were. But Mary was gone and would no longer speak the words Elizabeth only dared to think.

She also couldn't help but selfishly wonder what this would all mean for her. At seventeen, she was at an age for marriage and had almost been given to the Dauphin of France before he had humiliated her by choosing to break their betrothal and make his promise to Margaret of Austria. To be put aside for a mere child! Elizabeth was happy to not have to leave her home country, but the offense still stung her pride. Who would her brother, now that he was king, marry her to? Or would it be the decision of her uncle

Richard?

For weeks Elizabeth dwelled on these questions bouncing around in her mind, not solving any of the mysteries that assailed her.

Elizabeth's father, her sister Mary, and her half-brother Richard Grey, were all dead. Her younger brother, Richard, duke of York, born three years after Prince Edward during much happier times, had been allowed to join Edward at the Tower of London. That left Elizabeth with her increasingly unstable mother, and four younger sisters for comfort and company. She longed for the day that she would be able to leave this place and the gloom of her mother's paranoia.

June 1483

Crushing news was delivered to the family, burying Elizabeth's hopes ever deeper. An act of Parliament had declared the children of Edward IV and Elizabeth Woodville bastards. Proof was brought forward in the person of Bishop Robert Stillington, who professed to have performed the betrothal ceremony of Edward and Lady Eleanor Butler. Eleanor was the daughter of John Talbot, Earl of Shrewsbury. She had died in 1468, so Stillington alone was able to give testimony in the case.

With this came evidence that Elizabeth's mother may not be as paranoid as Elizabeth had previously believed. Richard of Gloucester, claimed the throne for himself, as his bastardized nephews were ineligible for succession. Rumors found their way to Elizabeth's ears that he was hesitant to accept this role, but it had been pushed upon him by the council. In the end he had accepted. Elizabeth was astounded and decided that she had nothing to lose by confronting her mother.

As she strode into her mother's room, she felt the steel in her spine convert back to willow. Elizabeth Woodville, dowager queen of England, no longer shone with the beauty that had enabled her to ensnare a king. Darkness circled her eyes, and her smooth skin seemed to have aged upon hearing the announcement that she was nothing greater than one more of King Edward IV's mistresses. She held a wiggling little Bridget and would not let go of this last child they had created together. Elizabeth eased herself down next to her harried mother and gently took her arms, releasing her grip on the energetic toddler. Bridget happily scampered away while her mother stared into space not seeming to notice.

"Mother?" Elizabeth took her mother's hands in her own and noticed that the aging process had not spared them. The queen had so carefully kept herself youthful, but just a few months of neglecting her routine was telling. "I must know if it is true."

"Oh, Edward," the older Elizabeth sighed. "I don't know."

The fact that her mother had not adamantly denied the story was evidence enough for Elizabeth. The rumor could be true. If her father was not truly married to her mother and she was a bastard, so was her poor little brother who had been raised to be king.

"What will we do now? We cannot remain in sanctuary forever."

The queen, who had schemed all her life to improve the station of her family, seemed out of plans. She lifted her eyes only for a moment before giving her daughter an almost imperceptible shrug.

"I will see if I can arrange for a doctor to visit, mother. You seem not at all yourself, and you still have your children to think about. Even if we are all bastards."

She stalked out of the room, knowing that she had been harsh, but no harsher than her mother had been with her plenty of times before. This was their reality now, and they must decide how to proceed.

The doctor who was called upon did seem to brighten the former queen's outlook. Elizabeth wasn't sure that her mother had actually been ill, but was thankful for his ministrations anyway, up until the moment that she understood her mother's reasons for improved spirits.

"Elizabeth, I must speak to you at once," her mother demanded.

Elizabeth removed herself from the grasp of four year old Catherine to follow her mother from the room. Cecily, who was now fourteen and longing for freedom even more than her older sister, took charge of their little sister.

When Elizabeth entered her mother's room, she noticed that the dowager queen seemed to have regained her regal bearing. Though she would never look young again, Elizabeth Woodville

32

had salvaged her confidence that bordered on arrogance.

"What is it, mother?" Elizabeth asked.

"I have wonderful news for you!"

Elizabeth felt her insides begin to churn.

"What is it?" she repeated.

Her mother stood and took both of her hands.

"A betrothal for you, my darling!"

Elizabeth freed her hands and turned away, wishing for the hundredth time in the past few months that she could escape.

"A betrothal? How could you have negotiated a marriage while we remain self-enforced prisoners?" She spun on her mother. "And with who?" she added almost as an afterthought.

Keeping her smile firmly in place, her mother approached Elizabeth again and placed her hands on her shoulders. "With Henry Tudor, my daughter. He is Lancaster's final red rose, and the two of you will unite the warring factions."

Elizabeth could not believe what she was hearing. She melted and was thankful for the bench within reach. She shook her head to remove this disheartening information from it to no avail. Her mother had betrothed her to the enemy of their family.

"How could you?" she demanded. "What do you mean warring factions? Father crushed the Lancastrians and Henry Tudor is in exile!"

Vomit threatened to rise in Elizabeth's throat as her mother replied. "Your father is no longer here to keep him in exile though, is he?" She looked very pleased with herself, and Elizabeth wondered if her mother was only happy when she was scheming.

"You plan to rebel against your husband's brother, the man he named Protector of the Realm?"

"It is the only way."

"But Edward is the one who should be king, if not Richard. Do you think Henry is going to invade and then hand the crown over to my brother?"

"Edward is dead."

She said it with such certainty, yet complete calmness. Elizabeth had heard the rumors, of course. Her brothers had not been seen at the Tower for weeks, but to assume them dead and be prepared to replace them. Their own mother!

"How can you say that? Surely my uncle has simply had Edward and Richard moved to some more appropriate residence."

"Do you hear yourself? You naïve girl!" The former queen stormed around the room as if looking for something on which to take out her anger, her dress stirring up the rushes and dust on the floor.

"Do you hear yourself?" Elizabeth whispered, forcing her mother to calm her movements in order to hear Elizabeth's soft voice. "You calmly state that your sons are dead at the hand of our uncle, the king. Yet you do not mourn them, but look for a way for me to supplant them with this creature Tudor."

Raising her hand and her face flushed, Elizabeth's mother stopped herself short of actually striking her child. Elizabeth surprised herself by standing firm before her mother's threatened violence.

"Once again, I know the truth from what you do not say rather than what you do." She rose to leave the room and narrowed her eyes at her mother, daring her to stop her. "You did not deny father's precontract, and now you do not deny that you scheme against your own sons to replace them with their sister, only because you hope for more power for yourself that way."

Elizabeth rushed from the room without waiting for her mother to respond.

~ ~ ~ ~

On Christmas Day, 1483, Henry Tudor stood in the cathedral at Rennes to declare his promise to marry Princess Elizabeth of York.

When Elizabeth heard of this, she increased her efforts to convince her mother that they should leave sanctuary. How could they plan a rebellion against Richard, and truly against her brothers, without making a better attempt to discover the truth? She was determined to be back at court, and invitations for them to return were not in short supply.

March 1484

Richard stood in front of the mayor and aldermen of London. They looked expectant, relishing the embarrassment of their king. Wringing his hands and twisting his rings, Richard cleared his throat and forced his hands to be still at his sides. No one would guess from looking at him that this was the brother of Edward IV. Thin and wiry, where Edward had been towering and muscular, Richard could hardly have looked less like the king that every person in London wished hadn't died. Looking more like their father, Richard duke of York, who had attempted to take the throne three decades earlier, Richard III made a public proclamation.

"I do solemnly vow, as the King of England and follower of the Lord Jesus Christ, that I will watch over and protect the daughters of my brother, the late King Edward IV. Should the Lady Elizabeth Woodville choose to remove her family from sanctuary, I will see that they are provided for as fits their station and that suitable marriages to gentlemen of the realm are arranged."

When he was done speaking, he quickly turned and strode away from the distasteful scene while two of his men left the hall to take the news to Elizabeth Woodville.

The dowager queen gave in to her daughters and brother-in-law after squeezing this public promise from Richard, ensuring her family's safety and well-being. The girls were relieved and overjoyed that they would soon be free and wearing beautiful gowns, eating delicious food, and flirting with handsome men. Elizabeth was as anxious as her sisters to rejoin the world but did not speak of her exiled groom-to-be.

Richard greeted them upon their return to court. Elizabeth remembered him as seen through the eyes of a child, for he had spent much of his time ruling the north of England for her father rather than in London. She had more memories of her father speaking of his faith in Richard of Gloucester than of the man himself.

Seeing him now, she was impressed by the man as well. He could not be more different than his brother, she admitted. Where her father had been a giant among men, boisterous, and fond of flirtations that were happily returned, Richard was much smaller in stature, darker in coloring, and more reserved. If she looked closely, she could discern the twisting of his spine that gave him a slightly lopsided posture which he kept well hidden with expertly tailored clothing. His form was deceiving though. She knew him to be a battle hardened warrior who had never been defeated on the field. She examined more closely the firm, lean muscles that were visible beneath fine fabric, and then blushed with the realization of what she was doing. A quick glance around reassured her that no one had taken notice.

"Lady Elizabeth," he said to her as he took her hand. "I am delighted to have you and your sisters at court." He gave her a slight bow and she could detect some auburn glinting in his dark hair giving evidence of his Plantagenet blood.

"Thank you, your grace," she murmured with an expert curtsey.

As Richard formally greeted her sisters and mother, she watched him closely. Determined to decide on her own whether he was a man to be trusted or was the murderer of her brothers, she looked for clues that would give him away. He was shyly demurred to by her sisters, besides Cecily who flirted with the eagerness of a young woman kept too long in sanctuary. Richard took no note except for the slight upturn to one side of his mouth.

When he reached her mother, he politely bowed and kissed her hand as though she were still queen. She, on the other hand, stood stone-like, giving no acknowledgment that he was the current king. After some attempts at conversation, he turned to Elizabeth again, perhaps finding her the most receptive to his efforts. She curtseyed low before him once again.

He raised her up and held his arm out to her. Laying her hand lightly on his arm, she ignored the look her mother was attempting to dissuade her with and allowed herself to be led to the gardens while servants attended to her luggage. Jayne, who attended to Elizabeth now rather than her mother, followed closely behind, as did several of Richard's attendants. Elizabeth was determined to make an unbiased judgement of her own of this mysterious uncle who had been revered by her father but despised by her mother as they strolled into perfectly manicured gardens.

Scents and sounds of spring and new life filled her with hope and joy for the future. Green buds popped out everywhere she looked, and early color from daffodils and crocuses splashed across the ground. The fertile smell of warm, damp earth filled her nostrils as she closed her eyes and filled her lungs.

"You enjoy the season as much as myself, I see," said Richard, breaking her reverie.

She felt her face heat up as she cast a sidelong glance at him. "I do, but I would be grateful to be outdoors in any weather after these past months."

"That is understandable," he paused. "You do know that I have desired your presence at court all along?" he asked, and Elizabeth felt that he meant her in particular. He had a way of looking at a person that made her feel as though she was the most important person in the world. She wondered where the peculiar shade of green of his eyes came from, as neither she nor any of her siblings shared it.

"Of course, we received many invitations," she admitted. "I am sorry that my mother was so distrustful." Did she sound like an ungrateful whelp speaking of her mother this way? "I am most pleased that we can be here with you now."

"Yes, well, it is certainly more comfortable for your family here, and my wife, Anne, is anxious to see you again."

Had he purposely mentioned his wife, Elizabeth wondered. She found herself grasping his arm more firmly and standing more closely as they ventured down the green paths, but surely she had not been obvious. She was just now realizing how she had missed male attention during the months she had spent cooped up with her mother and sisters.

"I look forward to greeting my aunt as well," she said. "And to speaking more with you." She had not forgotten her quest to discover the truth about her brothers, but did not feel comfortable bringing them up quite yet.

"Of course. You and your sisters may join Anne and I at the high table for supper."

"We would be honored, your grace." She could not blame him for excluding her mother who would likely have balked at the invitation anyway.

He raised her hand not quite to his lips and said, "I must attend now to less pleasant matters. Excuse me."

She watched him walk away before continuing a long walk in the gardens, treasuring her freedom as thoughts and feelings that were even more conflicted than before coursed through her mind.

~ ~ ~ ~

At their first ball since leaving sanctuary, Elizabeth and her sisters reveled in the food, music, and festive atmosphere of the court. Those who were less generous with their analysis of them thought they were flirtatious, just like their mother, but those who knew them to be pious young women saw their joy at being a part of the world they had missed for precious months.

Dancing with the handsome duke of Buckingham, Elizabeth

momentarily forgot the reasons that she had given her mother for returning to court. She was lost in the moment as her lovely new aquamarine colored gown swayed elegantly, giving her the appearance of dancing upon waves of the sea. Henry Stafford was married to her mother's youngest sister, Katherine, so he was not a viable suitor, but he was a marvelous dance partner likely to earn her glances from more available noblemen. She gave little or no thought to Henry Tudor.

"You must be parched. Let us have some wine," Henry said as the dance ended and another prepared to begin.

"That sounds wonderful."

As they left the room for the cooler garden area, the duchess of Buckingham joined them. Since she shared her sister's famous attractiveness, Katherine had no need to be jealous of her young niece and embraced her enthusiastically.

"I am so happy that you are here, Bess!"

"So am I," Elizabeth replied with a smile. "This evening is beautiful!"

"And so are you, Princess," said Henry returning with wine. "Almost as lovely as my wife," he added handing a cup to his wife as he placed a kiss on her cheek.

"Oh, Harry," Katherine said as she playfully swatted him away.

Elizabeth hid her smile behind her wine goblet. How she longed for someone to share her life with as Katherine and Henry had each other. They had been married since they were children and had the close relationship of those who had grown up together.

"What young man do you hope to share the next dance with?" Katherine asked as she eyed the prospects.

"Oh, I don't know," Elizabeth sighed as she scanned the crowd. "I am simply happy to be here." Her happiness was somewhat diminished by the thought that her betrothal meant that she shouldn't be considering the marriageability of any of the young men around her.

"Well, I am certain that plenty have their eye on you," her aunt assured her.

After dancing with several eligible bachelors, as well as a variety of extended family members, Elizabeth fell asleep content and free from worry that night.

~ ~ ~ ~

Elizabeth did not frequently get to spend time with her uncle and the opportunity to ask him about her brothers had not presented itself. Those at court seemed content with his rule, and she had to admit that he seemed more concerned with governing and justice than her father had been. She heard no rumors of mistresses in the palace, as she was embarrassed to admit had been the case with her father.

She was picking an arrangement of flowers for her sister, Anne who was not feeling well, when she sensed someone approaching.

"Lady Elizabeth, we meet again to enjoy God's great creation."

She turned to see Richard holding out a white rose to her.

She smiled. "A white rose of York."

"Of course."

"Anne will love it," she said as she added it to her basket.

"Is she still not feeling well?"

"I do not think it is serious, but the flowers will cheer her." Elizabeth was touched that a man with as many responsibilities as Richard would concern himself with the health of her eight year old sister.

"Do let me know if she requires anything else."

"Certainly. Thank you, your grace."

"How is your mother?"

She examined his face for guilt but only discerned slight

irritation.

"My mother is becoming accustomed to her new circumstances."

Richard's laughter surprised her. "Spoken like a tactful princess!" He let his hands glide along the small pink flowers of a dogwood bush before saying more seriously, "She has had a difficult time. It was not my intention, but it was necessary."

Elizabeth kept her own focus on the flowers, though she wished she could examine his face and force herself to be bold. "She has not done much to make her burden easier. You have cared for us well since we left sanctuary. She could have done so sooner."

"Well, your mother and I were never the best of friends," he said with a wry grin, once again exposing a sense of humor beneath his solemn facade.

Elizabeth wasn't sure what to say. She was old enough now to know some of what was said about her mother, and to know that at least some of it was true. She still was completely unclear about the man she was speaking to. Part of her was undeniably drawn to him, but then she would think of her brothers or uncle Anthony and feel compelled to draw away.

"I'm glad that we can be friends," Richard said.

Elizabeth looked up at him, and a warm feeling deep within her momentarily chased away her doubts. "I am glad too." She felt the heat rising to her face and searched nervously for words.

"Tell Anne that I pray for her healing," Richard said, seemingly oblivious to Elizabeth's embarrassed silence. He dipped his head to her briefly and walked away.

Elizabeth watched his confident stride as he purposefully moved toward his attendants waiting for him at the garden gate. It brought a smile to her face to notice him pause and gently touch a perfectly formed early bloom before carrying on. It wasn't until he disappeared from her sight that she realized that she had missed the opportunity to ask him about her brothers. She angrily tossed the flower in her hand into her basket while mentally admonishing herself for her imprudent behavior.

A few days later, she was summoned to her mother's rooms. Even without knowing of the missed opportunity, the former queen was attacking her daughter for being too fond of King Richard.

"Mother, you are being ridiculous!"

"You are affianced! Yet you throw yourself at the married man who murdered your brothers!"

Elizabeth's face felt hot and her throat tight with anger as she retorted, "This again! I will never marry Henry Tudor! Richard would never even let him set foot in England, and you are a fool for believing otherwise."

The slap that her mother placed on her cheek echoed through the chambers and left a dark, wine-colored stain on Elizabeth's pale face.

"You cannot win with words, so you will choose to beat me. So be it, but remember that I am no longer a child."

The two Elizabeths glared at each other, considering their next words.

"You cannot love him," the older insisted causing the younger to look away.

"He is my uncle, of course I love him."

"Ah, but I do not refer to familial love . . . . this you know."

"He is a married man."

"And you are a foolish girl."

Anger flashed in Elizabeth's eyes momentarily before dimming. She was being a foolish girl, but she could not seem to help herself. Her heart and mind were at war whenever she was in Richard's presence.

"You do not know what you speak of," she whispered.

Her mother seemed willing to give up her anger as well. "You think not? I was once a young girl as well."

"I desire only to learn about my brothers."

"You are convinced that he has not had them killed."

"How could he? You know how loyal he was to father. To kill his nephews, it is incomprehensible."

"Maybe." She must not let herself hope. Tudor was their salvation now.

"I will ask him directly."

"You will ask him if he has killed your brothers?" her mother asked skeptically.

"Of course not! I will simply ask where they are residing that I may visit them."

"Hmmm, you make it seem quite straightforward."

"Sometimes an uncomplicated solution is the best one."

Before Elizabeth was given another chance to speak to Richard about the fate of her brothers, he had left on progress with Queen Anne.

April 1484

Elizabeth was surprised how much the absence of Richard seemed to affect her. She was not dishonest enough to deny that she had feelings for him that she should not, but she felt somewhat more empty than expected when he was gone. They had enjoyed just a few garden walks, evening dances, and shared meals, but her feelings for him had grown as had her faith in his good intentions toward her family.

Her doubts withered and she became confident that her brothers had been whisked away to a safe haven where supporters of Richard could not do him the favor of eliminating them and enemies couldn't make them the center of rebellion. She did miss them and wish to visit them, but was no longer assailed by thoughts of murder and usurpation.

Sitting in her room with Cecily, they worked on embroidery which she found tedious but relaxing.

"When do you think uncle Richard will return?" Cecily asked as though reading Elizabeth's thoughts.

"I certainly don't know," Elizabeth answered more tersely than necessary. Uncertain of her own feelings, she was uncomfortable having them guessed at.

Cecily glanced at her with a raised eyebrow. "Did you see Anne before they left? She is thin as a willow branch."

"Yes. I think she makes herself sick with worry when she cannot have their son with her."

Cecily nodded. "She will be happy to see Edward soon when their progress takes them to Middleham."

"I do wonder why they have not brought him to court."

"Maybe he is not healthy enough for the trip," Cecily guessed.

"Do you think he is as ill as that?"

"Maybe not. They could be overly protective since he is their only child."

"One child in over ten years."

"It is sad is it not?" Cecily asked, considering her own large family.

"Anne does not look like she will carry more."

Cecily gave Elizabeth another sidelong glance. "No, not likely," she admitted.

Both sisters tended to their work without speaking for a few minutes, Cecily wondering if Elizabeth desired to be Richard's next queen, and Elizabeth wondering the same.

"What of our brothers? Try as I might, it is difficult to ignore the rumors that are not so quietly whispered."

Elizabeth sighed, "You have been speaking to our mother." She stabbed the needle through the fabric with increased intensity. "I am determined to ask Richard about them as soon as he and Anne return to London."

Cecily's eyes widened. "Is that wise?"

Elizabeth looked at her contemptuously. "Of course, it is wise." She threw her work in the basket at her feet so that she could pace the room. Her gown swirled around her and stirred up the rushes on the floor. "Why on earth would Richard do anything to harm our brothers? Clearly, he has moved them somewhere secretly to avoid rebellion, nothing more."

"I pray that you are correct, dear sister." Cecily remained calmly in her seat, attending her own project.

"You will see. And mother too."

"I'm sure you're right, of course. I would not want conflict between us over something that cannot be proven one way or another."

Their mother came into the room stopping any further conversation on the sensitive subject. The look on her face was indescribable. Even to her daughters, who knew her well, it was impossible to determine if it was a look of sadness or victory, worry or contempt.

"What is it, mother?" asked Cecily. Setting aside her embroidery, she stood to grip her mother's hands.

Elizabeth stopped her pacing and felt a weight in her stomach that portended bad news.

"Edward is dead," their mother whispered with a mad gleam in her eyes.

The girls exchanged a look of concern.

"Yes, mama," Cecily said, reverting to the affectionate term not used since toddlerhood in her distress. "We know that father died. He died a year ago."

This seemed to shake their mother from her inner thoughts. "No, no! Edward. Richard and Anne's Edward!" She said it almost with joy. The corners of her mouth were being forced not to turn upwards. "Richard's heir is dead."

"Oh no!" Elizabeth fell back into her seat as she thought about how this would affect Richard and poor Anne, who was such a devoted mother that she had hated being in London and away from her son, even if it meant being queen. She was also old enough now to realize the delicate position this left Richard in as a king with no heir to follow him.

Cecily was still staring at her mother, mouth agape. "Are you absolutely certain, mother?" In her nervous state, she was shaking her mother by the shoulders. "Who told you this?"

"A messenger from Middleham looking for Richard and Anne," the former queen said as she tore free from her daughter's grip. "Why are you looking at me like I am insane?"

The girls exchanged another look, silently asking each other what scheme their mother was already hatching in her head.

"Are you alright, mother?" Elizabeth asked. "I know that Edward was your nephew and named for your husband." She hoped these reminders would keep her mother on her best behavior.

"What?" Their mother looked back and forth between her two daughters. "Of course, I am alright. I barely knew the boy who was prepared to take the place of my own children. Richard will have to name one of you as his heir now."

"One of our brothers, you mean," Elizabeth said.

"Yes. One of your brothers," she said in a humoring tone, as though she addressed someone lacking intelligence. She turned and left the room.

When she disappeared, Elizabeth and Cecily found themselves in each other's arms.

"Poor boy! Gone, just like our Mary!" exclaimed Cecily.

"What will Richard and Anne do now?" Elizabeth whispered into her sister's soft, silvery hair.

Cecily pulled back enough to look into Elizabeth's eyes. "I truly do not know."

Over the coming weeks, news reached Elizabeth's ears that Richard and Anne had been devastated, not only by their son's death but by the fact that neither of them had been with him in his final moments. She also heard the whispered judgment that Richard had been cursed when he took the place of Edward V and was now being punished with the loss of his own young Edward. Elizabeth was more determined than ever to find out the truth about her brothers, but Richard had yet to return to the city.

He and Anne held an elaborate funeral for their precious son at Middleham before they reluctantly returned to court.

September 1484

The King and Queen had reentered London without celebration, rather quietly and cloaked in black of mourning. Even those not close to her began to whisper that Anne looked unhealthy and gaunt.

Poor Anne. Poor Edward. Was it worth it, Richard? Elizabeth longed to ask him. She yearned to ask God if these tribulations were truly his judgement upon the usurper king or if it were simply fortune's wheel turning.

Anne kept to her own rooms and was rarely seen after their arrival. Richard was visible but not approachable as he scurried from paperwork to council meetings, and from dinners with ambassadors to overseeing the creation of a new and fairer method of trial by jury. He entrenched himself in his work to distract himself from his buried son and withering wife.

One of the few times he allowed himself time to relax was when he went riding, so Elizabeth determined to approach him then. Despite her concern for him in his despair over his son, she was becoming impatient to learn the fate of her brothers.

She rose early and had her horse made ready, not caring if her ploy was obvious to the servants she was forced to include in her plan. Seeing the indiscreet glances some of them gave her as she ordered her riding clothes and saddle made ready, she knew that they had things on their mind besides a murder inquiry. Did they think her so shallow? She admitted that Richard stirred something within her heart, after all he was the king, a powerful, handsome, intelligent man. But that would not matter if she discovered that he had mistreated her brothers.

Waiting on a bench near the stables, she practiced her words in her mind for when he appeared.

"Good day to you, Lady Elizabeth."

She had been so lost in her own thoughts that she had not noticed of his approach.

"Your grace," she said as she stood and immediately fell into a perfect curtsey.

"Please," he said with his hand on her elbow. "You mustn't be so formal in private." He smiled at her, and she had to force herself to remember her mission.

"Are you going for a ride? It is a beautiful day." She followed his gaze up at the blue sky with only a few puffy clouds and took in a deep breath of cool, autumn scented air.

"I am. I would be honored if you would join me." He used the hand on her elbow to guide her toward the stables.

As they entered, he addressed a groom, "Please have the Lady Elizabeth's horse made ready. She will be accompanying me this morning."

"The lady's horse is already waiting for her," the groom responded with a curious look at Elizabeth who turned her face away to hide her blush.

"Indeed?" Richard would reveal no more than raised eyebrows at this news in front of spying eyes and listening ears. As if he had expected this news, he simply assisted Elizabeth onto her sleek brown courser before leaping into his own saddle.

Soon they were trotting toward the forest, leaving speculative whispers in their wake. Instead of giving them mind, Elizabeth took joy from the small creatures that scampered away from their path and birds flying from trees causing rustling of branches and some falling leaves. They were deep in the forest where the sun could not quite reach the ground through the rich green canopy when Richard turned toward her and broke the silence.

"You wished to speak to me."

Now that her opportunity was served to her on a golden platter, Elizabeth couldn't find her words. Suddenly unsure of herself, she wondered if he would be offended by her inquiry or if he would wonder why she hadn't asked sooner.

"You were waiting for me, that much is clear. What is it, Bess?"

His use of her name that only family employed, loosened her tongue. She took a deep breath and forged forth. "I was hoping that you would allow me to visit my brothers." She wanted to hang her head and hide her face as she waited for his response, but she forced herself to look him straight in the eye and examine his reaction.

He hesitated, and Elizabeth felt terror rising in her. Darkness seemed to deepen beneath the thick trees. The realization hit her that she had ridden out to the middle of the forest with the man her mother accused of killing her brothers. What if she was right?

"I am afraid it would be impossible."

Elizabeth backed and turned her horse, preparing to flee. Though her throat constricted her voice to a whisper, she would not abandon her mission.

"And why would it be impossible, my lord?"

Richard seemed to shake himself from inner thoughts, taking in her aura of fear. His posture slackened, and just for a moment his eyes closed and lips clamped tightly shut. When he looked at her again, his face was accusing, yet somehow also sad. "I thought, of all people, that you trusted me, Bess. Yet you look as though you are afraid that I may be possessed by demons."

She forced herself to be calm and narrowed her eyes in examining his face. Fine lines were etched there that she swore had not existed a few months ago. He seemed hurt rather than angry.

"Why would it be impossible?" she repeated.

He edged his horse closer to hers, and she controlled her urge to cringe away. She sat confidently upon the back of her favorite horse in a way that revealed her Woodville heritage. Not encouragingly approachable, but as proud as her mother, she awaited his response without shifting.

"Bess, how would I hide your progress to the north? It would be evident to all who search for the boys that you go to visit them." He had a pained expression on his face as though he needed her, of all people, to believe him. He held a hand out toward her, pleading with her to understand.

Relief flooded through her body, and the features of her face softened, lessening her resemblance to the dowager queen. "You are hiding them."

"Of course," he said. "You do not believe the vile rumors?" He looked as though he wanted to pace and yanked on his confused horse's reins instead. "I suppose you believe that I am poisoning Anne as well." His lips formed a thin line as he clenched his jaw to keep from saying more.

"Poisoning Anne?" Elizabeth eased her horse toward him, her fear gone and sympathy replacing it.

He released his grip on the reins and took a deep breath, slowly releasing tension from his shoulders and jaw.

"That is the latest rumor to explain Anne's failing health. In my haste to marry someone more capable of providing me with an heir, I am poisoning her." He shook his head at the thought that he would murder the woman he had fought so hard to marry. His eyes seemed to search the woods for a solution.

"Oh, Richard. I'm so sorry." She had not heard this rumor and realized how sheltered she was in her position as illegitimate princess. "Is Anne fairing so poorly?" She nudged her horse to close the gap between them.

He nodded. "God help her, she is. I know nothing more that can be done for her. She wastes away and coughs up blood, though she tries to hide it from me. I am no fool."

"No. Nobody would accuse you of that. And nobody who knows you would accuse you of being a murderer either."

She had moved close enough to lay a comforting hand on his

arm. He glanced at it and seemed to make a decision not to say more. He could not bear to see the hurt and humiliation on her face if she knew that some people believed that he was poisoning Anne in order to marry her. She looked at him in utter trust and innocence that he was sure he had never possessed, even at her age.

"I am sorry that I cannot take you to your brothers. It is safer if they remain in hiding."

"I understand. Would it be possible to write to them? It would give my mother such comfort."

He sighed, and Elizabeth wondered if any man upon becoming king was ever pleased with the way it turned out.

"Write your letters and I will see if I can have them discreetly delivered."

"Thank you, your grace. I will keep you and sweet Anne in my prayers."

"God is the best help for her."

Deciding he would find little comfort in the woods this day, he led the way out of the clearing. Richard and Elizabeth rode back to the stables in silence, each lost in their own thoughts.

December 1484

Elizabeth walked toward Anne's rooms wondering how she would find the frail queen. Since her forest ride with Richard, she had seen him only in public and had not been able to ask him further about her brothers or Anne's health. Richard and Anne did all they could to present a normal face in court, though few were fooled. All whispered that she was dying. Those who were kind said it was of the wasting disease, others poison.

An attendant opened the door for Elizabeth, and she found Anne up and dressed, sitting with some embroidery. Elizabeth was pained by the way Anne's dress hung limp on her thin form. Her seamstress could not take her dresses in quickly enough to keep up with the queen's shrinking body.

Elizabeth curtseyed before her. "You wanted to see me, your grace."

"Yes. Please, sit next to me," Anne said with a smile. Anne had once been a beauty who captured the heart of young Richard before he was even duke of Gloucester. Her beauty had been devoured by cruel illness and left her looking haggard at twenty-eight. Her once shimmering hair was now listless and dull, yet her face was still open and kind.

Sitting next to Anne, Elizabeth fidgeted with her trailing sleeves. She was not used to sitting with nothing in her hands.

"Do you see the fabric on that bench?" Anne asked as she nodded toward the other side of the room.

Elizabeth stood and crossed the floor to examine it. As befitted a queen, it was soft purple velvet that felt luxurious under Elizabeth's fingers.

"It is beautiful. Is it for your Christmas gown?"

Anne nodded. "And yours, if it meets your approval."

Elizabeth rubbed the fine fabric through her fingers, and

imagined what it would be like for her and Anne to present themselves dressed to match, showing their love for each other. Surely that would quiet the rumors that caused the blush to rise to Elizabeth's cheeks when she heard servants whispering of it. She returned to Anne and knelt at her feet.

"I would be honored, your grace, but surely it is too great a privilege for me."

Anne placed her small, white hand beneath Elizabeth's chin to raise her eyes to meet her own. "I can think of nobody who I would rather honor. It brings me joy to see your youth and beauty at court. My own sister was taken from me. I would love to share this moment with you."

"Of course, your grace. Thank you for thinking of me."

When the day came to wear their matching gowns, Elizabeth wondered if it had been a mistake. Gossipmongers refused to let go of the story of Richard's plan to replace poor Anne with her. The fact that she was his niece and he had been considering various marriage matches for her seemed to make little difference to them. Elizabeth was beautiful. Men wanted her and assumed that Richard did as well.

She walked into the great hall and her eyes roamed the room until they fell on Anne. Now she was sure it had been a mistake. Elizabeth was not vain, but she knew how she looked in her gown with her bright copper hair falling in curls and winter flowers entwined into the thick locks. Anne looked as though she had aged ten years since the public had last seen her. Her auburn hair looked dull and brown, and bones protruded anywhere her skin was exposed. In comparison, Elizabeth looked young, healthy, and – possibly most importantly of all – fertile.

If there had been any hope of Anne providing Richard with another heir, it was extinguished by her presentation at the Christmas festivities.

Elizabeth hoped that those in attendance also took note of the loving concern on Richard's face as he looked down at his diminutive queen, and the gentle way he kept his hand on her arm or waist.

As those near began to take notice of her presence and turn with appreciative exclamations, Elizabeth determined to enjoy this evening without concern for rumors, mysteries, or the continuation of Richard's dynasty. She held her head high and smiled, accepting the compliments of those crowding to be near her. Taking her hand or touching her arm to gain her attention, several men fought to be the one she settled her eyes and interest on. Though she danced with many of them, she was disheartened to realize that none of them particularly captivated her interest. She kept finding that her eyes were following Richard as he moved through the room. When she danced with him, she felt as if she were floating on a wispy summer cloud. She couldn't keep herself from wishing that he would hold her more firmly, then feeling guilty when her eyes met Anne's and the queen smiled lovingly at her.

When Elizabeth took a rare moment to herself to rest on a window seat, she discreetly watched Anne and wondered if she should approach her to show their solidarity to those in attendance. Anne was trying to be jovial, but her stooped shoulders and pale face were evidence of her weakness.

What did Anne think of the way her life had turned out? First married to Edouard, Henry VI's son, while her sister, Isobel, had been married to George, Richard's brother, did Anne think about her father's skillful play at putting a daughter on either side of the civil war, one married to a Lancastrian and the other to a York prince? She seemed to be a more than dutiful wife. Was she happy with Richard? Why had she given him only one son?

Elizabeth shook her head of the pointless meanderings and stood, determined to join Anne in the face of those who assumed them to be enemies.

"Your grace," Elizabeth said as she swept into a deep curtsey.

"Bess," Anne said with a hand on her arm to raise her up. "I knew the purple velvet would suit you to perfection!"

"You flatter me, your grace. It is your beauty that shines this evening."

Anne dismissed the compliment with a wave of her hand. "I am pleased that you escaped your suitors long enough to visit with me. Join me in that alcove." She directed Elizabeth to a quiet spot.

As Elizabeth took the proffered seat she wondered what picture her and Anne must make to their audience. They could be considered nothing less, the partygoers who were giving them sidelong glances and more obvious stares as they whispered behind hands or drunkenly exclaimed that Richard had both his women in attendance. How did Anne tolerate it?

"Your grace, are you feeling well? Can I get you anything?" Elizabeth prepared to stand and attend to Anne's wishes as soon as she was seated. Anne's soft touch on her arm kept her in her seat.

"Bess, I am perfectly fine and waited on by overly eager ladies as it is. I wish only to speak with you."

"Certainly." Elizabeth placed her hands in her lap and forced herself to be still.

Anne smiled. "First, you can relax." She put a small hand on Elizabeth's. "I am as aware as you are of the talk, the looks, and the rumors. I have no fear that you wish to replace me or that it is my husband's desire."

Elizabeth looked down at the small hand on hers. Even in this minor detail, Anne's poor health was evinced in the protruding bones and paper thin skin compared to Elizabeth's soft, smooth flesh. Anne moved it to direct Elizabeth's face toward her own.

"Look at me, Bess," she said with intensity. "I know you walk around in a cloud of doubt about your brothers, fear of rumors, and concern for your future. I can assure you on all accounts. Your brothers are kept safely in the north. I pay no heed to gossip and neither should you. As for your future," she added this with a twinkle in her eye. "I happen to know that Richard is considering a good match for you."

"Truly?" Elizabeth grasped Anne's thin hand in both of her own. "I do feel that my life is so aimless, leaving me too much time for ungodly anxiety."

"Yes, my dear Bess. I hope that he will be speaking to you soon on this matter."

"And my brothers?"

"I know that they are safe."

"Praise God," Elizabeth whispered. She silently thanked God for Anne and her strength to give support to one it would be so easy for her to condemn. "Uncle Richard has certainly found a treasure in you, your grace," Elizabeth said with a smile.

Anne patted Elizabeth's hand and noticed more than Elizabeth guessed of the aside whispers and sidelong glances the two of them were receiving. "He will take good care of you."

"Oh, thank you, Anne!" Elizabeth leaned over to envelope Anne in an embrace. Her joy was somewhat diminished as she felt Anne's delicate frame, even smaller than expected under the layers of flowing, rich fabric. She was careful to remove any look of dismay from her face before pulling back. "I look forward to speaking to my uncle. Thank you, again."

With the corners of her mouth slightly upturned, Anne watched as Elizabeth rose and left the queen with her thoughts of just who would end up marrying the beautiful princess.

Elizabeth, too sweet, or maybe too naïve, to believe just how many people present were picturing her as England's next queen, spent the next few moments daydreaming about who her uncle would match her to and whether she would get to remain in

England or be married to a foreign noble. At least she would be saved from her mother's proposed match for her to Henry Tudor.

She decided to step outside despite the cold in order to clear her head of the competing thoughts racing around her brain and to walk privately where she would not feel so much on display. The gardens were desolate and frozen. No longer did the smell of wet earth and greenery permeate the air, but she still took pleasure in the quiet calmness of the bare branches and browned grasses. Taking a deep breath of cold, clear air, she looked up to the heavens and wondered what God's plan for her life would be. She was too old to be at the court of her uncle with her mother and sisters. She needed to begin a family of her own and was anxious to hear her uncle's plans to this end.

With a sigh, she pulled her mantle tighter around her and allowed her mind to turn over her past broken betrothals. Her father had certainly had plans for her, but whatever his hopes had been had died with him almost two years ago.

First he had promised her to George Neville when she was a small girl. Now that she was old enough to understand such things she marveled at her father's confidence that he would eventually be presented with a son. Planning to marry his oldest daughter to a relative of Warwick's was just one of the many moves made in an attempt to appease the ambitious earl. This plan had been disposed of, and George Neville had gone to God shortly thereafter.

A second and more impressive betrothal had been made to Charles, Dauphin of France. More appropriate for the firstborn of the King of England, this planned marriage had been greatly celebrated by both of her parents. Elizabeth's mother had dreamed of the day her daughter would become the Queen of France and required that all in the household refer to Elizabeth as Madame la Dauphine. Her father had insisted upon the best of schooling for her in English and in French to prepare her for the duties of queenship.

When Charles was instead married to the daughter of Maxmilian, Holy Roman Emperor, in December 1482, it was a crushing blow. Followed so closely by the death of her father, it almost seemed that Elizabeth's troubles had truly begun that day she was informed that she would hereafter be addressed as Lady Elizabeth.

With her father dead and her brothers missing, she had only the marriage prospect proposed by her mother to consider. Thank God her uncle had thought of her!

"Bess, what are you doing out in the cold?"

Her sister's voice broke her reverie and she gladly turned to walk arm in arm with her toward the palace.

"I just needed some time to myself."

"It is rather loud and chaotic inside," Cecily said with a smile that indicated she didn't mind the noise or crowd at all. "Anne has retired for the evening."

Elizabeth took a slow, deliberate breath before speaking. "I fear for her health, sister, though I would not say it to any but you."

Cecily squeezed Elizabeth's arm. "She did not look well this evening despite her ladies best efforts to put forth a painted countenance and padded dress."

"You knew her dress was padded?"

"Surely you guessed as well."

Elizabeth shook her head. "Not until I embraced her and felt the thin bones beneath."

Cecily turned toward her and grasped both arms. "Bess, you are too innocent and optimistic! All see that the queen is dying. The only question remaining is if our uncle intends to have you replace her."

Elizabeth pulled away. "Not you, too, Cecily!"

Not easily offended, Cecily took hold of her sister again. "Yes, me, too. Bess, you must look at things as they are. Think about them from Richard's point of view. His wife is dying. He needs a son. He also happens to have a beautiful young woman of royal blood in need of a husband residing at court. Surely you are not so blind that you cannot see his love for you."

"He loves us as his brother's children!"

"As long as you keep convincing yourself of that, there is no point in us discussing it further," Cecily said, releasing her.

It was Elizabeth's turn to reach for her sister. "I do not want to argue. You are my best friend, but you are allowing rumor and gossip to color your thinking."

"And you are allowing your better nature to veil yours."

"Why would Anne be such a good friend to me if any truth were in such tales?"

"Because she wants you to know that she understands and does not blame you. She desires you to feel no guilt when she is gone. She would do anything for Richard."

Elizabeth stopped short and pulled her sister closer. In a harsh whisper she asked, "Do you truly believe that? You believe Richard intends to marry me?"

Looking deep into her sister's eyes, Cecily whispered back, "I do."

When she lay in bed that night after several more hours of merrymaking, Elizabeth was still sifting her sister's words through her mind, recalling her look of intensity and absolute certainty. She knew that she should be offended by the idea of her father's brother intending to take her to the marriage bed, but the idea was far from repulsive to her. As she drifted into sleep, her dreams were formed of images of her fingers in his dark hair and his firm arms wrapped around her.

Elizabeth counted her blessings when the next few days did not bring her into close contact with Richard. She knew that she would not be able to hide or explain away the blush that rose to her cheeks when seeing him brought her nocturnal thoughts to the forefront of her mind in the light of day. Feeling guilty and ashamed, she sought out her sister's company instead. They spent the afternoons walking in the gardens, examining fabrics to make choices for new gowns, and carefully avoiding mention of their Christmas conversation.

February 1485

Watching Anne's health decline, Elizabeth couldn't help but be reminded of others who had gone to God. Mary and her father especially invaded her thoughts at this time. She smiled as examples of Mary's candor flitted through her memories.

"Oh, Mary," she sighed to herself. "If you were here, you would just march right up to our uncle and demand to know his intentions." The picture of her sister, who would always be fourteen years old in Elizabeth's mind, forcing the king to reveal his plans made her laugh out loud. The lonely sound echoed around her empty rooms. No one had a need to call on a bastard princess, and she was alone with her morbid thoughts.

Her father, so strong and invincible. If only he had truly been so! If he were here now, his musical laugh would cheer her, and his skill for putting all in order would relieve her fears for the future. Most likely she would be married by now if it weren't for his untimely death. Then thoughts of marrying her uncle would not have ever occurred to her.

Then there were the little ones, a sister named Margaret who had lived only a few months during Elizabeth's sixth year and a brother George. George, named for her father's brother, George of Clarence, had lived just two years before proving that the plague could not be held back by riches or royal status. Elizabeth's parents had consoled themselves with the fact that they still had two sons, Edward and Richard. Elizabeth wondered if she would ever see them again or if they would live out their lives in hiding.

Still she felt sympathy for Anne and frequently visited her. Anne now kept to her rooms with no pretending toward normalcy. Elizabeth provided a listening ear, her own stories when Anne tired of talking, and prayers when nothing else seemed to help. She loved Anne, though she would not object to replacing her in the king's bed. Elizabeth knew that none besides Cecily would understand her conflicted feelings and confided them only to her, finding comfort in the fact that Cecily insisted that Anne knew and understood as well.

A tentative knock sounded at the door.

"Yes, come in," Elizabeth said as she cleared the ghosts from her mind.

"Hello, sister," Cecily smiled as she floated into the room. Elizabeth envied her lightheartedness that made her radiate beauty.

"I'm happy you're here to save me from my dreary thoughts," Elizabeth admitted as she embraced her younger sister.

"Ah, you worry about Anne."

"She seems too wasted to last much longer."

"True." She took a breath before continuing. "Another issue is bothering me."

"What is it?" Elizabeth asked, examining her sister for signs of distress. Never did Cecily's concerns reach her face.

"Have you had any letters from our brothers?"

Elizabeth shook her head. "I have sent several, but have yet to receive a reply."

"Does this not worry you?"

Standing and walking to the window, Elizabeth considered a moment before responding. "Both Richard and Anne have assured me of our brothers' safety." She turned back toward Cecily. "There is the difficulty of taking letters and supplies to and from them without it being made clear where they are residing."

"Yes," Cecily said doubtfully. "But bringing a letter back should not be complex once one is delivered. Surely our Edward would write even if Richard is too occupied with more recreational pursuits."

Elizabeth knew her sister was correct, but also did not believe that the king and queen would lie to her. She shrugged. "I don't know what else to say. Where do you believe they are kept?"

"I'm wondering if their bodies do not reside beneath the Tower grounds," Cecily whispered.

A quick intake of breath was Elizabeth's only response.

"Do not be offended, Bess!" Cecily beseeched as she reached for her sister's hands. "I have supported you in everything, but why does he hide the truth of our brothers from us?"

Still slowly shaking her head, Elizabeth mumbled, "I do not know."

Cecily persisted. "Why did he declare us illegitimate, yet hide them away? And he is still willing to marry you for your claim to the throne!"

"Cecily, no!"

"I think you must carefully consider whether you should trust and accept this man."

"Do you not think that it is often at the forefront of my mind, Cecily? One moment, I believe myself in love - there I have said it - and the next, I wonder if he shouldn't be my most despised enemy. I am surrounded by conflicting rumors, advice, and evidence!"

Elizabeth had taken up pacing but now stopped short before the window and stared out at the cold, wintery landscape that did little to cheer her. It took only seconds for Cecily's arms to find their way around Elizabeth's waist. She held her tight with her head rested on Elizabeth's shoulder.

"I apologize, Bess. I only want what is best for you."

Elizabeth loosened Cecily's arms just enough to turn and return the embrace. Tears had sprung to her eyes, so she buried her face in her sister's hair.

"Will nothing ever be certain for us? Are we to live our lives wondering what happened to our brothers, if our uncle is our savior or our nemesis? What if I am expected to marry him?"

"Is it not your wish?" Cecily asked, shifting enough to see Elizabeth's face.

Elizabeth let out a long sigh. "Sometimes there is nothing I want more." She gave her sister a stern look that told her this should go no further. "Other times, I believe that I am as naïve as our mother accuses me of being."

"And I have not made it easier on you. I am sorry, Bess."

Cecily loosened her hold on her sister to search within the folds of her dress for something. "I almost forgot. I have not heard from Edward or Richard, but I do have a letter from our brother, Thomas."

"From Brittany?" Elizabeth pulled Cecily to her bed where they pulled the hangings to further block out prying eyes. "What is his news?"

"I know it only adds to the confusion that he has gone into exile with Henry Tudor." Cecily glanced at Elizabeth to see her reaction to the mention of her betrothed, but she had been long trained to not allow her emotions to reach her face.

"And?" Elizabeth prodded impatiently.

"It seems that an invasion was attempted in October."

Elizabeth gasped. "An invasion that nobody felt fit to tell us about."

"They came on the heels of our uncle of Buckingham's rebellion. Apparently the armies were supposed to have been coordinated. Henry could see that the plan had failed and decided not to land. Richard continues to attempt to convince those around him to turn him over."

"I still cannot see why Harry, of all people, turned against Richard. Were they not the closest of friends?"

Cecily pressed her lips tightly together and wrinkles of thought lined her forehead. "I just don't know, Bess. Sometimes I feel as though there is so much going on that nobody is telling us."

"And our only remaining brother has chosen to side with Tudor."

"Well, after Richard was executed with our uncle Anthony..." Cecily let the thought trail off. There was no need to continue. It was one of the events that still pierced Elizabeth whenever she started feeling too strongly for Richard. How could he have had them executed?

"What else does Thomas write?"

"Not much, of course," Cecily continues. "He would not give away Tudor's plans or name the many who have joined him. He expresses joy that you are to be joined to Henry."

Elizabeth forced herself not to roll her eyes. "Do you believe that I should be considering it, Cecily? Marriage to a man our father kept in exile over one he trusted with our lives?"

"I do not believe that it will be your choice."

~ ~ ~ ~

On March 16, Anne died as an eclipse of the sun left Englishmen wondering if it were the sign of new beginnings or a curse upon their land. The official story released was that Anne had fallen asleep in her husband's arms and peacefully slipped away. Elizabeth knew that it had been much more dramatic and less romantic with Richard shoved aside by physicians as they attempted to keep Anne from asphyxiating on the blood that she continuously coughed up.

Tears slid down Elizabeth's cheeks matching the pace of the rain running in rivulets down the thick, blurry glass of the window in her chamber. Forcing other consequences and decisions away for a few days of mourning, she thought only of the sweet, small girl who had been destined to be queen. First as the child-wife to the Lancastrian heir, then as beloved consort to an unexpected Yorkist king, Anne had lived briefly, but for greatness. Had she regretted any of it?

She thought of Anne's auburn hair, lustrous and thick when she first joyously married Richard, dull and thin the last time Elizabeth had spoken to her days before her death. Anne's small hands had held her own, just as they had at Christmastime. Frail and aged compared to Elizabeth's, yet it had been Anne's hands patting hers in comfort and love. Her brown eyes had become watery with fever, but had never lost the glow of intelligence and awareness.

Elizabeth would miss Anne as much as her siblings and father who had welcomed her to heaven.

~ ~ ~ ~

In the days following Anne's funeral, Elizabeth began to wonder if all the gossip had indeed been just that. Her uncle Richard had not sought her out and seemed devastated by the loss of his wife, though she had been withering away for close to a year. Cecily had not wished to speak of it since they still had no word from their brothers, no reassurance of any kind that the letters that they were writing were actually reaching the hands of the boys. Without being able to pour her heart out to her closest confidant, Elizabeth felt neglected and alone. In desperation she went to her mother.

"Lady mother," she said as she swept into a curtsey in front of the former queen.

"Please rise, child," said her mother in a tone that evinced more impatience than affection.

"I have come to see how you fare since Anne's death. I know you were fond of her," Elizabeth said as she rose and moved to sit near her mother.

"Of course I am fine. I have survived much deeper wounds than the loss of a sister-in-law."

Though her voice was harsh, Elizabeth detected softness in her mother's eyes that indicated that she did mourn Anne Neville, despite her desire for people to think otherwise. Feeling somewhat guilty for not visiting her more often, Elizabeth grasped at her mother's hand and attention.

"I am truly glad that it is not a heavy burden for you to bear. You have been through too much already."

Elizabeth's mother seemed taken aback by her daughter's kindness. It took her a moment to form her next words.

"Anne was a lovely girl. I do believe that she and Richard had always loved each other in some way."

"Mother! Even when she was married to Prince Edouard?"

With a knowing smile on her face, her mother answered, "Maybe especially then. Lord knows that we are not usually blessed enough to marry for love. I am sure that Anne was thankful for her years with Richard."

Elizabeth couldn't remember her mother ever speaking so positively about her uncle and decided that it was a good time to speak of her feelings.

"I can understand how Anne felt."

Her mother sighed and patted her hand. She looked at her daughter who was as beautiful as she had been at that age. It did not seem vain to her to acknowledge her own beauty. The girl could have any man. Why would she choose Richard?

"You are betrothed to Henry Tudor," she quietly pointed out.

Pulling her hand from her mother's grasp, Elizabeth stood and paced to the window, willing herself under control before speaking. "Must you continue to insist upon that nonsense?" Turning away with her hands reaching toward the heavens as though praying for divine intervention, Elizabeth took another moment before turning back to her mother. "Don't you see? Henry Tudor will never be welcome in England. Will never amount to anything! Why would you have me chained to him when I could marry for love and be queen?"

The lines at the corners of Elizabeth Woodville's eyes deepened and her lips grew thin. "What of your brothers? Do you have not a care that this man you claim to love has murdered them?"

Elizabeth closed her eyes and took a deep breath. Her mother still believed this to be true. Cecily was starting to believe it, too. The rumors still flew around the kingdom that Richard had put his nephews to death to secure his hold on the crown. She could not bring herself to believe it. Her father had trusted Richard, and so did she.

"I do not believe that they have been murdered."

Rather than responding in anger, Elizabeth's mother simply looked tired. "I will not argue this case with you any longer. God will choose the victor, and therefore your husband, when Henry invades this summer."

Elizabeth ran to her mother and threw herself on the floor at her feet. "Mother, you know of invasion plans? We must go to the King at once!"

"Surely he knows. The man employs spies and does not require information from me." She dismissed further comments with a wave of her hand. "Of course Henry will attempt to take the crown. It is what his mother, Margaret Stanley, insists is his destiny. While I do not share your love of Richard, or your trust in him, I am willing to wait and support the victor of God's choosing."

There was no point in saying more. After a rushed and shallow curtsey, Elizabeth hastened from the room with golden hair and flowing fabric trailing behind her.

~ ~ ~ ~

Three days later, trunks and crates were scattered through Elizabeth's rooms with servants scuttling about to fill them with her belongings. She had rushed to Richard to inform him of what she had heard only to find out that her mother was correct. He knew. He was spurred into action by the fact that news had reached her and that her mother was planning on welcoming Tudor with open arms should he miraculously be successful. He decided that she and her unmarried sisters would follow her brothers north.

She blinked tears from her eyes as she watched her gowns being carefully folded and packed. Had she been foolish to think he would propose marriage? Elizabeth wondered if Richard believed that she, too, was planning to lovingly welcome Tudor. She hoped that she never had cause to meet the man in her life!

The one bright light in this forced exile, for she could see it as nothing else, was that she was likely to be able to visit her brothers soon. Though she did not know exactly where Richard had set up their residence, she knew that her party was being sent to Sherriff Hutton. Her cousins, the children of Richard's brother George, the young Earl of Warwick, and his sister, Margaret, would be joining them. She hoped that they would not be such a distance apart that she must still be kept from her brothers.

A knock at the door broke into her thoughts of the boys with red-gold hair like their father's.

"Yes, who is there?" Before the question was asked her sister's head peeked through the doorframe.

Elizabeth quickly stumbled around the scattered obstacles to embrace Cecily. "I am so glad to get to see you before I leave!"

"And I would not let you leave without a proper farewell."

Tears stood on Cecily's cheeks when Elizabeth released her hold on her. "Cecily, whatever is the matter?"

Not able to stop the flow of tears, Cecily gave them free reign and stooped to seat herself on the closest trunk. She held up her hand to indicate that she needed a minute to compose herself. Elizabeth waited impatiently, wringing her hands as Cecily struggled with her emotions.

"I am afraid that I will never see you again," Cecily finally admitted. "Like our brothers."

"Oh, Cecily!" Elizabeth pulled her younger sister and best friend into her arms with a firm grip. "You have nothing to concern yourself with! I am going with a full escort and our cousin of Warwick." Cecily had recently been married to Ralph Scrope and would not be joining her unmarried sisters on their journey north.

"It is true that he is not sneaking you away from London as he did with Edward and Richard, but I cannot help but be frightened. I love you so, Bess!"

Squeezing her even tighter, Elizabeth replied, "And I love you, more than anyone else, my sweet sister." She freed her grip enough to look into Cecily's eyes that were shining with tears. "I promise you that there is nothing to fear. Tudor's planned invasion will amount to nothing more than a minor headache. Then I hope that I and our brothers will be able to return to court."

"You really still believe him don't you? I admit that I thought the worst when I heard that he was sending you away with Edward. After all, our cousin of Warwick has the strongest claim to the throne after our brothers."

Elizabeth did not admit aloud that she had not thought about it quite that way. Maybe Cecily and her mother were right and she was being too trusting. It was too late for doubts.

"I have no concerns whatsoever," she stated firmly. "I will return once this threat is crushed." Attempting a lighter tone, she added, "We can hardly have Henry Tudor succeeding in abducting me and forcing me into this insane marriage he has proposed!"

Cecily did not smile but did seem somewhat reassured. She

placed a kiss on her sister's cheek. She hoped that it was not for the last time. "Thank you for your confident words, Bess. God go with you."

Elizabeth did not let her moment of doubt linger. Soon she was travelling through the countryside, taking deep breaths of cool air filled with scents of greenery. During the trip she found herself drawn to her young cousin who reminded her of her absent brothers. Edward of Warwick proved to be a delightful traveling companion, and they took advantage of the opportunity to get to know one another better.

At other times, her thoughts strayed to visions of the wedding that she hoped would take place once Richard had dealt with the Welsh milksop.

~ ~ ~ ~

Sherriff Hutton finally appeared in the distance, its four strong towers standing like sentinels at each corner. Elizabeth's fingers clasped Edward's arm as she leaned over to point out their new home to him.

"There it is, Edward! Sherriff Hutton. Of course, you must have been here before." Sometimes Elizabeth had a difficult time connecting this docile cousin to her memories of her blustering uncle George, his father. He had matched her father in looks but never in personality. His scheming and betrayals had finally ended in his execution in 1478. At the time she had been too young to question her father's decision. Now, as she looked at the profile of her cousin, she wondered if she could ever order the execution of a close family member.

"I have," Edward replied. "I think so." He wrinkled his forehead in thought. Edward was ten years old, but Elizabeth was sure that her younger siblings had been more advanced in their thinking at that age. Of course, Edward had been somewhat neglected since being left an orphan at three years old, an orphan that everyone chose to forget had the strongest claim to the throne.

"No matter," Elizabeth assured him with her arm around his thin shoulders. "We shall enjoy our time here until our uncle Richard comes to collect us." She squeezed him to her, bringing a smile of contentment to his face and crinkling the corners of his eyes. "I cannot wait until we can explore the grounds! What do you look forward to, Edward?"

This time he required no time to think. "The stables!" He looked at her with such happiness in his bright blue eyes that she wondered when was the last time someone had asked him what he would enjoy. "Do you think they may have puppies, Elizabeth? And I would love to ride out on a pony. Could I learn to brush the horses when they come in from riding?" he asked in a whirlwind of excitement.

"Well, it's not a typical pastime for one of noble blood," Elizabeth laughed. "But I'm sure that we can find a kind stable boy to take you under his wing."

Edward chattered on about the adventures that he and Elizabeth would have together until their caravan pulled into Sherriff Hutton's courtyard. The opportunity to give her love and attention to another young person clearly in need of a friend was a salve to Elizabeth's emotional wounds.

After settling into her rooms, Elizabeth sought out Edward. Did she enjoy his company because he reminded her of her own younger brothers or because she felt he must be a something like her father was as a child? A little of both, she decided.

"Edward, shall we go on an adventure?" she asked him with her voice filled with the promise of excitement.

"Oh, yes, Elizabeth!" he exclaimed jumping down from the alcove bench he had been seated on. Spindly legs carried him quickly to her side and reddish blonde hair fell into his eyes when he gazed up at her.

She brushed the hair from his face and leaned down to be eye to eye with him. "You must call me Bess since we are cousins and such good friends."

A smile full of joy and crooked teeth was her reward. He took her hand and they strode toward the courtyard.

"Shall we ask first about the kennels or the stable?" she asked him.

"Hmmm…" Edward wrinkled his freckled nose when thinking, and the action pulled at Elizabeth's heartstrings, for it reminded her so much of her brother of the same name. "Puppies! Let's see if there are puppies!" Having made his decision, he released her hand to run in the direction that seemed likeliest to him to contain the kennels.

Laughing, Elizabeth gathered her skirts to quickly follow him.

"You must have the nose of a hunting dog yourself!" Elizabeth said after finding Edward seated on the kennel floor surrounded by a litter of puppies. "Found them right away, did you?"

"Look at this one, Bess," he said holding up a wiggling brown pup that took the opportunity to lick Edward's nose. He giggled and held the tiny dog to his chest in unabashed pleasure. "This one is my favorite."

"And how have you decided that already?" Elizabeth asked as she attempted to crouch down to his level without ruining the fabric of her dress.

"She likes me," he stated simply.

Elizabeth reached out and ruffled his silky hair. To take happiness from life's simple blessings. If only more people could be as easily contented as Edward.

Upon reaching her bed that evening, Elizabeth meditated on the young earl of Warwick. Was he a naturally happy and simple little boy or had the lack of love in his life made a pup's kiss an exorbitant act of affection to him? She was determined that he would never again feel that none cared for him.

Their weeks at Sherriff Hutton went by quickly as the cousins enjoyed the summer weather and many places to explore. Their days became filled with riding on the moors, finding hidden nooks in the castle, and playing with Edward's dog – for the little brown pup had fallen in love with Edward as much as he had with her that first day. Any other adventure the two could imagine was explored until they fell into bed in exhaustion each night.

Only when Elizabeth had a few quiet moments to herself did she remember that she had hoped to visit her brothers while in residence in the north. She still did not know exactly where Richard had sent them, only that they should be close. She wasn't sure who she could ask now that she was here. Who would Richard have confided in?

She resolved to make the time special for Edward, until such a time as she could obtain information about her brothers. The chapel at Sherriff Hutton was a place that they frequently visited to pray for the success and health of their uncle Richard. News took days to reach them, when anyone remembered that they were there and may like to hear of it. Elizabeth heard that there were rumors of Henry Tudor attempting to land on English soil. Of her uncle's public denial that he had any plans to marry her, she was not informed.

August 1485

Edward found Bess on her knees in the chapel. He did not wonder why he found her there more often as the weeks turned into months but simply took a place at her side as he said his own silent prayers: keep King Richard safe, give his sister Margaret good health, and let him stay here with Bess as long as he can.

Elizabeth crossed herself and stood, still gazing at the crucifix on the altar. Dear God, please grant your servant Richard victory and send him here to gather us, she prayed. Edward mimicked her motions without the tension and worry that covered Elizabeth's countenance.

Sounds of horses and chaos in the courtyard filled their ears as they turned to leave the chapel. Excitement lit up Edward's face as he had no thoughts of the riders possibly bringing bad news. The gladness that Elizabeth expressed was forced, but Edward didn't notice.

"Wait!" she said grabbing his hand when he made to run down the corridor. "Let's observe from here." She directed him to a narrow opening that looked down upon the courtyard. She peered at the banners and emblems on the men's horses, but the lack of wind left the banner unfurled and she couldn't quite make out the small medallions. The colors were not Richard's.

She felt as if an anchor had been dropped into her stomach as one of the banners caught enough breeze for her to recognize it as that of Henry Tudor.

Elizabeth turned so that her back was against the wall and slid to the floor with a moan.

What did this mean? Richard defeated? Impossible!

Edward knelt next to her, still oblivious to the reason for her distress. "What is it, Bess? Whose men are they?"

His face was all innocence and trust. Elizabeth looked blankly at him and wondered when her tears would fall. The crushing weight inside her made her question her ability to stand.

"Oh, Edward," she whispered. "They are men of Henry Tudor." Her words felt false to her own ears, and Edward furrowed his brow upon hearing them. Elizabeth gazed into space, not certain what she should do or what had happened. Were Henry's men here to abduct her and force her to fulfill the betrothal promise that her mother had made? Where was Richard?

"I can sneak down and listen in," Edward said. Before she could stop him, he had scampered away.

After a moment she realized that eavesdropping was likely her best chance at receiving complete information. She could not wait for one of the men to decide when and how much to tell her. The hidden alcove Edward would spy from was known to her as well. She forced herself to her feet and hurried after him.

Tudor's men seemed in high spirits, not like men on the run from the king they had betrayed. Elizabeth clenched her hands in the fabric of her skirt in an attempt to keep them from shaking. She was sure that she would not like what she was about to hear.

"We are here to escort the Princess Elizabeth and the Earl of Warwick to London," a man Elizabeth did not recognize stated. He looked dirty and worn, but not distressed.

"On whose authority do you make such a request?" asked the warden of Sherriff Hutton who certainly recognized the Tudor emblems.

"On the authority of King Henry VII!" exclaimed the man proudly. He scanned the courtyard as he made this declaration, daring anyone present to declare their dissention.

"King?" Elizabeth whispered, immediately realizing what the announcement inferred.

"But uncle Richard is king," Edward pointed out in his childlike way. What would this mean for Edward, with the

Plantagenet blood in his veins?

"He was," she managed to whisper before the tears finally came.

She held back a whimper as the men carried on.

"King Henry VII?" questioned the warden. He was in the precarious position of needing to appear loyal to whomever held the most power.

Tudor's man took a step closer to the warden and made a point of looking down at him. "His grace, Henry Tudor was crowned on the twenty-second of August at Bosworth Field after the defeat of the usurper Richard of Gloucester."

Elizabeth could not listen to more. She ran from her hiding place careless of who saw her or knew what she had overheard. Richard dead! If Henry was king, she would be forced to marry him. She ran on ignoring the shouts following her out of the courtyard. She ran out onto the moor feeling the long grasses whip around her ankles. She wished that she could run away from Sherriff Hutton, away from England. Away from Henry Tudor.

Her mother would be pleased.

A stitch formed in her side and she fell headlong to the ground with tears streaming down her face. The life that she thought she was going to have flashed before her eyes. Life with Richard. She sobbed and tore at the headpiece that had become loose, pulling it from her hair and taking her anger out on it as she shredded it in her hands. Her unbound hair spilled around her in the grass, but she paid no heed to the weeds it gathered as she thrashed in misery. She would be allowed only this one unguarded moment to vent her agony before the inevitable return to the castle where she would be expected to be the tactful princess.

Speculation on how Richard had met his end flashed like cruel visions through her mind. He would have gone down fighting, of that she was certain. But how could things have gone so wrong? She prayed that he had not been treated dishonorably and had died quickly in battle. She was sure that was what he would have wanted. She received little comfort by believing it was true. How could it matter when he was gone? She tried to thank God for welcoming Richard into the heavenly realm, but only succeeded in being angry that he had been welcomed there too soon. God had taken so many of the people she loved.

The tears that she thought would never stop truly only lasted a few minutes. Her hands ran over her face, wiping away tears and massaging the puffiness around her eyes. She did not know what she should do, only that she had to return to the castle. She and her sisters, along with Edward and Margaret, would be expected to welcome Henry as their savior. She must find strength.

She determined first only to find the strength to stand. Then enough to return to her rooms. Maybe then she could pack her things. She must take one step at a time, and maybe by the time she reached London she would be prepared to be introduced to her prospective husband.

Her first steps returned her to the Sherriff Hutton chapel where she begged God for the courage to face her future.

September 1485

The fall weather was unusually warm and pleasant for travel. Elizabeth was angry that it was. How dare the sun still shine and birds still sing when her life was turned inside out? She couldn't adjust to thinking of Henry Tudor as her betrothed rather than her family's enemy. Her mother had warned her that she was being foolish and that Henry was her future. If only she had listened. She would have been prepared. She wouldn't feel like her heart had been ripped out of her chest.

Elizabeth reminded herself that she did not know what Richard's feelings towards her had been. It was difficult to know how to mourn in the midst of wondering. Had he been fond of her as his niece or loved her as his future wife? Now she would never know. Replaying the conversations that she'd had with Richard in her head did not help. She wished that she had pressed him, but she had been afraid of rejection and embarrassment. Never had she considered that she would not see him again this side of heaven.

And what of her brothers? Would she ever discover where they were hidden or if they were even alive?

Her cousin, Edward, guided his pony to be near her. He was smiling and enjoying the day with the ease of a small child. Elizabeth wondered if he was the lucky one, unencumbered by daily worries and stresses. Edward of Warwick would never learn to be a soldier or a king, but he was happy with what God had given him.

"Give me that feeling of contentedness, Lord," Elizabeth quietly prayed.

"Bess, will we stay at Baynard Castle with our grandmother when we get to London?" Edward asked. He looked at her with such trust and confidence in his eyes. If only he knew that she was more worried about their future than he would ever be.

"That will be the king's decision," she said in a more clipped tone than she intended.

Edward didn't seem to notice. "Imagine, Henry Tudor being king."

He said it like it was inconsequential, as one would comment on someone wearing a color not suited to their skin tone or rank, not the way one of the few remaining York princes should regard the Tudor usurper.

"It is difficult to imagine," Elizabeth agreed. "But we must give him the full respect he deserves."

Elizabeth worried that Edward would make improper remarks about his royal family, not realizing the precarious position he would be in at the Tudor court. Would people rally to Edward as the York heir? Surely not, Elizabeth answered her own internal question. If any loyal Yorkists remained, they would flock to John de la Pole. John was twenty-four and had been Richard's heir after his son's death. He would make a more attractive rallying point than the simple-minded Edward.

Would Henry be safe on his throne? She didn't know. She had thought that Richard was.

"Edward, do go and gather those wildflowers in the field," she requested. "Then I will show you how to weave them together into a crown." The only crown the boy would ever wear, she was sure.

~ ~ ~ ~

London was a blurry shape in the distance. Elizabeth still wasn't sure that she was ready for what she must face, but she had been given little choice. She wondered if Henry would greet her as soon as her procession entered the city. Was he anxious to meet her or did he share her concerns about their match. She was eager to see her mother and would listen to her wisdom this time.

Conversation among the travelling party quieted, and

Elizabeth pretended to be taken in by the scenery as they plodded on toward London. The city she formerly considered home when it was under her father's rule now felt like a foreign land to Elizabeth. It was ruled by a Welshman who had been living in France and Brittany. It was a foreign land.

If only her father had not died.

Their party approached the northern gate of the city and Elizabeth began to wonder what reception they would receive. Henry would likely not be happy with an overly exuberant welcome for the York children, but the people still loved Elizabeth and her sisters for the sake of their father. She couldn't expect the lively crowds that used to line the streets for them, and she was uncertain what she should anticipate. She lifted her chin and straightened in her saddle. Whatever would come, she was still a princess.

Soon a crowd formed around their caravan, though it was not as large or energetic as what Elizabeth had become accustomed to. Everyone in London seemed to share the desire to not offend their new king.

"God bless our York queen!" one man bravely shouted.

Elizabeth was flattered, but also afraid of what punishment such opinions could incite. She focused her attention on directing her ladies to hand out coins to the peasants who were pressing in to gain what reward they could. The sight of children in dirty, torn clothing caused tightness in Elizabeth's chest as she imagined what their lives must be like in the grubby hovels throughout the city. There were worse destinies than being queen to the wrong king, she decided.

"Bless you, little one," she said to one little red-haired girl. The small child appeared to be only eight years old, but had calluses from years of work already on her tiny palms.

"God be with you, your grace," the little girl whispered in awed response.

Elizabeth gave her own troubles over to God as she concentrated on serving those who had so much less.

~ ~ ~ ~

Elizabeth, with her sisters, mother, and cousins, was given rooms at the Palace of Westminster. It felt odd to stay in rooms besides those for the royal family. Though they filled some of the finest rooms available, it was still clear that they were guests and supplicants. After a few days to settle the large family and get gowns, bedding, and other necessities unpacked, Elizabeth had not yet heard from Henry Tudor.

"Cecily, I am so thankful that you are here with me," Elizabeth said to her sister as they occupied themselves with sewing.

"Of course I am with you, Bess," Cecily said matter-of-factly. "You need me."

"I'm afraid I will always need you."

Cecily smiled. "Have more confidence in yourself, Bess. You are going to be Queen of England!"

Elizabeth sighed. "Yes, I suppose I am."

The look Cecily gave her spoke volumes about what Elizabeth had left unsaid.

"I know that you had thought of attaining that position differently . . . ." It was all she dared say. Everyone in was afraid of appearing too fond of Richard in the eyes of his successor.

"I was foolish. A child," Elizabeth stated firmly, lifting her chin in false confidence. She heard her mother's voice in her own words.

"Maybe," Cecily admitted. "I pray that you will be blessed and happy."

Elizabeth allowed her chin to fall as she glanced sideways at her sister. "I pray for us all," she said quietly.

They both worried that no word had come to them from the

new king beyond beckoning them to London. "Maybe he has changed his mind," Elizabeth whispered to Cecily.

"Surely not. He has many responsibilities to attend to. It is difficult work to usurp a crown," she added wryly.

"Cecily! You know that Henry's men watch carefully for those who speak against him."

Cecily regretted her words when she saw the fearful look in her sister's eyes. She placed her hand on Elizabeth's arm. "You're right, sister dear. I apologize for my outspokenness."

"I do not mean to admonish, Cecily, but what would I do without you?" Elizabeth shook her head and abandoned her work to lean in more closely. "To think that he has dated his reign from the twenty-first of August."

"In order to brand many good men as traitors." Cecily laid aside her own fabric and gazed toward the window.

"You are thinking of Lord Scrope," Elizabeth said. "I'm sorry, Cecily. I have been selfish with my own concerns."

Hastily retrieving her work, Cecily said, "It is of no concern. The King has decided that my marriage is to be annulled."

Elizabeth's gasped and waited for Cecily to offer more information, but she had firmly clamped her mouth shut. "I was never certain why Richard married you to someone beneath you as Ralph was."

A single tear traced along Cecily's cheekbone. "Because I asked him to allow it."

"But why? And why didn't you tell me?" Elizabeth was shocked. She had thought that there were no secrets between her and Cecily.

Cecily kept her eyes on her work as she replied. "Because he loved me, and I felt that I could grow to love him." Seeing the confusion on Elizabeth's face, Cecily continued. "I had no desire to be sent away to be the Plantagenet bride of a foreign prince. England is my home, and I have no desire for politics."

The sisters shared a knowing look. Their family had been embroiled in political upheaval and war for their entire lives.

"Ralph was sweet and safe," Cecily finished in a whisper.

"I'm so sorry," Elizabeth said, pulling her sister into an embrace.

"You've no need to apologize, Bess. It is simply fortune's wheel turning."

"I prefer to think that God is the one in control," Elizabeth countered.

With a small sigh, Cecily responded, "If God is in control, he seems not very fond of England."

"Lady Elizabeth?" The call came from a servant dressed in green and white, the new Tudor livery.

Elizabeth beckoned him forward, her stomach suddenly in knots. "Yes, what message do you have for me."

"Your presence is required at Coldharbour House. His grace the King and his Lady Mother would speak with you."

It did not pass either sister's notice that no part of this was worded as a request.

"Of course, I will be in attendance as soon as possible," Elizabeth replied.

The servant stood for a moment as if he expected to see evidence of her preparing to leave. Elizabeth lifted an eyebrow toward him.

"You are excused," she said in a voice of authority that she copied from her mother.

As the man left, she whispered to Cecily, "Best that we not let them forget that we, too, are royalty."

Cecily smiled and wondered if it wouldn't be better if they just let everyone forget.

Elizabeth and Cecily approached the home of Henry Tudor's mother, Margaret Stanley, with heads held high and their ladies trailing behind them. Despite her uncertainty, Cecily did not hesitate to support her sister.

They were led to a great hall and greeted by an unexpected person.

"Mother! What are you doing here?" Elizabeth asked. She had seen little of her mother since returning to London.

"I'm here to help you of course," she said as she placed a kiss on her daughter's cheek that felt as light as a butterfly.

Elizabeth looked at her mother's face which was still beautiful though there were lines around her eyes and creases of tension in her forehead. Was it better to have her mother, who was infamous for her scheming, here with her? She turned her gaze to Cecily. Her eyes wide and worried, nobody need guess that Cecily thought their mother was a detriment.

"What is going on, mother?" Elizabeth asked.

"Your betrothed is anxious to meet you." The former queen took her daughter's arm and began pulling her across the room that bustled with courtiers.

"So, he is still my betrothed?"

"Of course! It has been my sole concern since Henry ascended the throne."

That seemed such a positive way of saying since her uncle had been killed and his crown usurped.

"Thank you, mother."

Elizabeth's mother took her firmly by her upper arms and gazed intensely into her eyes. "You will be queen. Do not ever doubt it."

Digging down to bring her own confidence into her response, Elizabeth replied, "I do not doubt it."

"He needs you," Elizabeth Woodville continued as she released her daughter's arms and guided her more gently to the other end of the room.

Elizabeth looked quizzically at her mother but dared not voice her question.

"He knows as well as the rest of England that he has less than a drop of royal blood. He needs yours."

The right of conquest would only take him so far. There were York descendants with a better claim: John and Edmund de la Pole, Edward of Warwick, Elizabeth's brothers . . . . what of them? She shook the question from her head. She needed her wits about her when she met the man who was now king and was to become her husband.

"There he is," her mother said as she subtly gestured to an ordinary looking man standing with Margaret Stanley. Elizabeth knew Lady Margaret from her days as her mother's lady-in-waiting. How odd that their roles had been reversed.

Henry Tudor was only slightly taller than Elizabeth with little of the swarthy Welsh handsomeness that she had expected. She couldn't help comparing him to Richard, and Henry did not fare well. Where Richard had been strong in a lithe sort of way, Henry looked thin and almost ill with pale, gaunt cheeks. She tried not to imagine Richard's dark good looks as she took in Henry's dull hazel eyes. The slight cast in his left eye caused her to be uncertain what his gaze focused on. His dull brown hair had only a slight glimmer of the auburn that so defined the Plantagenet family.

She thought of her father who had been handsome, fit, and commanding in his presence. There had been no need to point out who was king when her father was in the room. Henry Tudor did not look powerful among his court. He eyed each person in wariness and distrust.

"Your grace, the Princess Elizabeth," her mother introduced her, and Elizabeth dipped into a deep curtsey. He seemed to forget for a moment that he must ask her to rise, but she greeted him with a smile regardless of his social ineptness.

"Your grace," she said in a shy, submissive tone, keeping her eyes downcast.

"I have looked forward to this day for many months," Henry said as he took her hand and placed it on his arm. She was surprised by his soft, pleasant voice and the sincerity in his tone.

He guided her away from their mothers. Elizabeth glanced back and saw that her mother took joy in this. His did not.

"I, too, am happy to meet you," she said. She hoped it was adequate, not being able to overstate her excitement. She couldn't push from her mind the fact that she had hoped this day would never come.

He led her through those gathered for the feast laid out by his mother with little effort. Each person stepped aside and bowed to him – or was it to her – as they passed. Finally, they reached a door leading to a garden. It was bare and brown in its fall phase, but Elizabeth could see that it would be beautiful come summer.

"Ah, this is better," Henry said once the noise was muted, and he smiled at the relative quiet of the outdoors.

"Yes, it is," Elizabeth agreed, remembering meeting with Richard in the garden at Westminster in its summer warmth and beauty. She told herself that she must stop comparing the two men. Richard was dead, and she would be Henry's wife.

"Are you comfortable in your rooms?" he asked.

"They are adequate for our needs, yes." Elizabeth admonished herself for her rudeness, but she despised being treated as a guest in the palace that she had called home for most of her life.

Henry glanced her way and considered her response. "I hope to see more of you."

"I would enjoy that as well."

"Would you?" he asked, facing her.

"Of course, your grace," she said, not meeting his eyes.

Henry touched her chin and lifted it. "None of that," he said. "I have everybody saying, 'yes, your grace' now. I desire honesty between us. You are to be my wife."

Elizabeth studied his face more carefully. Yes, he was thin and pale from his recent hardships, but a hidden strength was evident. His eyes shone with the same determination that had led him to land on English soil and attack a king who commanded armies that dwarfed his own. The tilt of his chin dared anyone to question his right to be sitting upon England's throne. He was younger, but more serious, than Richard had been. It had initially made her think that he looked older, but seeing him up close, she realized that his face had youthfulness that some time with less stress would increase.

She took his hand and felt the roughness of hard work. He had lived a life that included privileges of court but also times of hidden exile. This is where God had placed her and she would put forth her best effort.

"I apologize, your grace. I was concerned about your feelings toward me as well."

A smile lifted one side of his mouth, and he almost appeared charming. "Just Henry, please."

"As you wish, Henry." She forced herself to smile back.

~ ~ ~ ~

The outbreak of an illness worse than any London had ever seen kept Elizabeth from further audiences with the new king. Some, who were well at breakfast, were dead before nightfall, and each household was terrified of letting it in. Any who could stay at home did. Even Elizabeth sent away local servants, keeping with her only those she was closest to, those who had come with her from Sherriff Hutton.

Whispers spread as quickly as the sweating sickness that Henry Tudor had cursed England. His foreign mercenary troops must have carried this plague with them as the path of death seemed to follow them from Milford Haven, where Henry had landed, to Bosworth, where Richard had died, and finally to London.

"It is a curse from God that we allow this usurper to be anointed when we have royal heirs at hand," Elizabeth heard one of her ladies whisper.

And who would they have crowned? Edward, who was a simple-minded youth, but a Plantagenet son? John de la Pole, Richard's nephew and heir? For not the first time in her life, Elizabeth wondered if the people enjoyed having something to fight about.

Pushing the rebellious thoughts and rumors from her mind, Elizabeth focused on doing what she could to help those affected by the sweating sickness. She forwarded extra money to the priests who were charged with caring for the sick and their families. Since she had been forbidden from leaving the palace, she put her time and talents to sewing simple clothing that could be distributed to poor families who had lost their means of support.

She did not see Henry, but heard that his coronation would be delayed. She was thankful, for the thought of thousands of people gathered together with this illness lurking among them made her stomach churn.

No word arrived regarding her wedding.

October 1485

Henry's coronation was scheduled for the thirtieth of the month. Elizabeth tried to push away her fears caused by the fact that he was being crowned without her, without even naming a date for their wedding. Those who supported him due to their love of her and his promise that they would be wed began to lose patience. Elizabeth was frequently found in her private chapel on her knees, attempting to give up her worries to her God.

As she rose from the altar on a chilly October morning, she turned to find her mother waiting to speak to her.

"Mother, you are welcome to pray with me," Elizabeth invited.

Elizabeth Woodville's lips curved in a smirk, but she joined her daughter before the altar. Returning to her knees, Elizabeth begged God to help her converse civilly with her mother. She knew that her mother had the best interests of the family in mind, or at least what she thought was best for the family. Rising together, they each crossed themselves and bowed briefly before the gold crucifix before turning to leave.

Elizabeth's mother did not waste time on pleasantries. "I've spoken to Margaret about the wedding plans." She also did not waste effort on titles for her former lady-in-waiting, despite her present position as the king's mother.

"I'm sure Henry is busy with plans for his own coronation," Elizabeth said, wondering why she felt the need to defend him when she shared her mother's concerns.

"You are too understanding, daughter. He hurries to crown himself with no mention of marriage to give people the impression that he takes the crown by his own right."

"I suppose he does, as the victor at Bosworth," Elizabeth struggled to keep her tone indifferent.

Her mother was not fooled but carried on. "The sickness

decimating the city does not help his case. Those brave enough to say so preach that it is God's judgment on Tudor's usurpation."

"Mother, you must not speak that way. As you have said yourself, he is king and will be my husband. No benefit is obtained from considering what-ifs or past desires." Elizabeth turned to face her mother and saw a new respect in her eyes.

"You have truly grown up," her mother said with a smile. "I am glad that you have accepted Henry."

"I have no choice but to accept the future that God has laid out before me. His wisdom is greater than mine."

"You are devoted to your God and will be devoted to your king. It is as it should be. You will make a good queen, my daughter."

Not able to completely bury her own curiosity, Elizabeth asked, "And what did Lady Margaret have to say about the wedding plans?" She was surprised that she felt any peace about moving forward with Henry. God seemed to have put tranquility in her heart about the path he had placed her on.

"She said that you and Henry would benefit from additional time to get to know each other."

Mother and daughter shared a look that spoke volumes. Both knew what could happen to royal betrothals given enough time.

~ ~ ~ ~

Henry's coronation was as splendid and glorious as the world had come to expect from English monarchs. Surely that was Henry's point. If he looked enough like a king, the people would be bound to accept him as one.

Elizabeth and her sisters were part of the long procession that wound through the streets displaying their support of the new king. Yards of Lancaster red cloth adorned the path they walked along, and Elizabeth couldn't help but compare it to the color of blood.

How much blood had been shed between Lancaster and York to get them to this place where the man wearing the crown had little of either?

Some men and women with more royal blood followed Henry today. Elizabeth and her sisters, Edward of Warwick and his sister, Margaret, and John and Edmund de la Pole, were all receiving curious looks as the crowd seemed to be wondering who would be the next cousin to revert to bloodshed. Since Henry IV took the throne from his cousin Richard II, the Plantagenet family had been battling each other for the crown that would soon rest upon Henry's head.

Outwardly, Elizabeth was nothing but supportive, and she pushed away any discouraging thought that came to mind. "God grant me peace," she whispered as she arranged her face to meet the probing crowd of onlookers. She would encourage the country, her country, to accept this man in any way she could for the sake of reconciliation.

Henry was splendidly clad in a purple gown with cloth of gold trimming that gleamed in the sunlight. He would overwhelm them with his majesty and the richness of the presentation. Then he hoped England would love him. The procession of noble men and women made their way from the Tower to Westminster Abbey amid trumpets blaring, heralds announcing the approach of the King, and people shouting in loyalty. Looking at this moment in time, it was easy to believe that Henry was beloved.

Red roses had been hurriedly painted on shop fronts, embroidered on gowns, and planted in courtyards. Banners fluttered in the wind as though God himself was showing his support for the beginning of the Tudor dynasty. Elizabeth wondered where all the white roses had gone.

Henry knelt before Thomas Bourchier, Archbishop of Canterbury, under the soaring arches of Westminster Abbey. The hundreds in attendance became almost eerily quiet. Were they waiting for a sign, some indication from God that Henry Tudor was blessed and war would be no more? No flash of lightning or thunder crash gave signal of a curse, and Elizabeth sighed in relief that Henry had been so encouraged throughout the day. If she could not have her own desires, she simply wanted peace.

At the moment the crown was placed on Henry's head, he sat on St. Edward's Chair where the kings of England had sat for their coronation since 1308. The large chair was carved out of dark wood, and Henry seemed rather small sitting in it. A tingle raced through Elizabeth's body as she thought of the history of the Coronation Chair, where her father, Richard, and almost two hundred years of kings coming before them had sat.

Edward I had the chair built so that it had a compartment for the Stone of Scone, which had been captured from the Scottish. The placement of their coronation stone within the English coronation chair indicated England's sovereignty over Scotland. Henry would undoubtedly have to defend his kingdom against the Scots that he supposedly ruled.

That day would be thought of later. For today, Henry was victorious, cheered by his people as he took the crown in his own right. Whether through conquest or his questionable royal blood, Henry VII stood before all those in attendance as King of England.

November 1485

A wedding was being organized. It would be beautiful and magnificent, as was only proper considering the circumstances. Margaret Stanley seemed both insistent that she should be in charge and somewhat unhappy that the wedding would be taking place. The bride would be beautiful with her long, blond hair and voluptuous figure. Dressmakers had thronged around Lady Margaret's rooms for the opportunity to be considered worthy of outfitting such a gorgeous subject. The groom, with his dark brooding face, held Welsh charm that people accepted as handsomeness.

The couple was Katherine Woodville and Jasper Tudor.

Katherine still had her share of Woodville allure. She was twenty-seven years old, and, like her older sister, her beauty seemed not to fade with passing years. Her first husband, Henry Stafford, had been duke of Buckingham under Elizabeth's father. As talk of Katherine's wedding flowed around Elizabeth, she remembered dancing with the aristocratic Stafford. He had been so handsome and devoted to the lovely Katherine. Elizabeth had hoped to find that kind of love with someone, had thought she might with Richard. Now, they were both gone.

Through a course of events that Elizabeth still did not understand, Henry had been executed for rebelling against his onetime friend and confidant. What had made him rebel against Richard? Elizabeth considered asking Katherine, but didn't think the time was appropriate. It probably never would be. Lost in her own selfish world at the time, Elizabeth had not considered what had been Stafford's motivation.

The thought crossed her mind that others had also betrayed Richard at Bosworth Field, making it possible for him to be defeated. Why had so many left his side when they were most needed? Perhaps there was too much that she didn't know.

She was consumed by the fact that the fate of her brothers remained a mystery. Did those who had turned against Richard have knowledge of events that would tarnish her memory of her beloved uncle?

Katherine was marrying Jasper Tudor, the new king's uncle and closest friend. He was in his mid-fifties, but was healthy and fit from the constant activity of conspiring with Lady Margaret to bring their golden boy to the throne of England. Without Jasper's help, Henry never would have been able to raise troops, plan an attack, or fight the winning battle. Elizabeth wasn't sure whether to thank him or hate him.

Elizabeth was lost in thoughts of this complicated family tapestry when she realized that someone was repeating her name.

"Yes? Sorry, Aunt Katherine, I was just thinking of you."

"You were looking quite contemplative," Katherine said with a smirk. "I hope that you were not pondering too carefully. It is what often gets your mother in trouble."

Elizabeth laughed. Katherine was more willing to take life as it came to her. "I was just thinking of the paths that we all took to get here," Elizabeth admitted, hoping that wasn't saying too much.

Katherine's smile faded slightly, "Ah, then you were having serious thoughts."

The faraway look on Katherine's face told Elizabeth that she was thinking of Henry Stafford, and that she did still love him. But did she think him treasonous? She dare not ask.

"How are the arrangements coming along?" she asked instead.

"Oh, wondrously, of course," Katherine sighed as she lowered herself to a stool near Elizabeth. "As you know, the Lady Margaret is more than capable of arranging all of our lives and events so that we may sit back at our leisure."

Elizabeth grinned at Katherine's lighthearted disrespect for the king's mother. "She is very ambitious and driven," she admitted.

"And soon will be planning your wedding." It was a statement but held a slight tone of question.

"I believe so," Elizabeth ventured. "What have you heard of it?"

"Elizabeth, you should not have to ask others whether your wedding plans are being made," Katherine admonished. "You must stand up for yourself. It is a wide gulf between keeping yourself from being trampled and being overbearing."

Smiling again at her aunt's insight, Elizabeth admitted, "I do hope to avoid the reputation that our mother has earned. People do not see that she only does her best to protect her children."

Katherine laid a hand on Elizabeth's smaller, softer one. "I understand your concerns, but you must force Henry to make a decision."

"And how does one force a king to make a decision?"

"Seduce him, of course!"

Elizabeth felt heat rushing up to her cheeks. "I couldn't."

"Don't shake your head at me," Katherine insisted. "I'm not saying to lay with the man. Of course not. But make him desire you as a woman and as a queen. Your innocence is one of the reasons that he will."

Elizabeth looked her aunt in the eye, considering what she said. "You think that I am being too submissive."

"You will need to learn to enforce your will a little if you are to be the daughter-in-law of Margaret Stanley," Katherine said grimly.

"What of your will?" Elizabeth asked in an attempt to take the focus off of herself. "Are you happy to be marrying Jasper?"

"Such a question!" Katherine exclaimed, but she patted Elizabeth's arm as if to comfort her. "Jasper is a fine man and in favor with the king." She paused but saw that Elizabeth wanted more than an analysis of Jasper's political appropriateness. "I believe that we will be able to please each other."

It was not the love that had shone in her eyes when she had looked at her Harry, but it would have to suffice. Elizabeth was determined to accept her own fate with the same resolve.

On the seventh of November, Katherine and Jasper said their vows, and a celebration worthy of the king's most valued ally commenced. Wine seemed to flow in unlimited quantities, and there was enough food to make Elizabeth wish that she could be there to see the leftovers handed out to the poor. A feast would be enjoyed by all this day, and she felt free to enjoy herself for the first time since Henry's accession. She was determined not to concern herself with her own future for this one day. This day belonged to Katherine.

Laughing and dancing with the flush of activity and wine upon her cheeks, Elizabeth felt as though the last few months could be forgotten. More than ever before, she was ready to accept this new life. Henry joined her, and she was able to smile up at him with genuine happiness. He seemed pleased to see her so.

"I would speak to you, my lady," he said to her as the musicians ended a lively tune.

"Of course, your grace," Elizabeth said with a tilt of her head. Her hair was starting to fall in wisps about her face from the complex arrangement it had been pinned into.

"Please, call me Henry," he reminded her as he placed her hand on his arm.

"Yes, Henry. I'm too out of breath to think," she said with a smile, and he grinned in return.

"It brings me joy to see you so happy," he admitted as he directed her to a quiet alcove and motioned to a servant to bring wine. "I understand that times have been trying for you."

Elizabeth frowned, not wanting to think about anything but this moment. She looked into Henry's eyes, hoping to see his soul revealed. "I am happy right now and hope to remain so."

"I apologize," Henry said with a shake of his head. "I should not impose unpleasant memories on you as I comment on your pleasure. Forgive me."

"Of course, I do, Henry." She saw a gleam of copper in his eyes that she had not noticed before. The cast of his left eye did not distract and horrify her as it had when she had first laid eyes on him. In fact, she thought that she remembered hearing that King Edward I had a similar characteristic. "There is nothing to forgive you for," she added, boldly laying a hand on his arm. "You are a thoughtful king."

"And you will make a beautiful queen," he said as he lifted his hand to trace the outline of her jaw. "So beautiful."

Elizabeth felt a fluttering inside that she never expected to feel with Henry. It was the wine. She knew that she had consumed too much and it was fueling feelings that she did not truly have. Then she remembered her aunt Katherine's words. Elizabeth looked across the room at Katherine, the vision of a happy bride dancing with Jasper Tudor. Only Elizabeth would have guessed that she was still longing for Harry Stafford in her heart. But Harry was dead, as were so many they had loved.

Henry was waiting, and she lowered her eyes and looked up at him through her lashes. "Am I truly to be your queen?" She felt blood rushing to her face and hoped it would be masked by the flush already there from the dancing and wine.

"You do not doubt it?" Henry seemed legitimately shocked by her inquiry. "It has always been my plan to make you my queen, even when I doubted my ability to make myself king."

"I should never have doubted you." Relief flooded through her, and she suddenly realized that this was what she wanted. For the sake of her country and her family, she wanted this marriage and would have to let go of her memories and past hopes.

"I will try to give you no further reasons to." He leaned close to her and she could feel his breath on her neck. It tingled down her spine and made goosebumps pop up on her arms. He placed the lightest of kisses on her warm cheek. "You will be my queen, Elizabeth."

~ ~ ~ ~

Elizabeth was on her knees in her private chapel. Despite the majesty of Henry's coronation and the almost royal wedding of Katherine and Jasper, Elizabeth knew the city of London to be suffering yet from the sweating sickness. Only this morning, one of her pages had been missing and she wondered if she would see him again. The work within these seemingly safe walls went on, but Elizabeth desired to do more.

She rose and crossed herself, bowed before the golden crucifix, and returned her prayer beads to their place at her waist. Her savior on the golden cross seemed to stare back at her asking how she would help his people. It was many moments before she moved her eyes from his gleaming metallic ones. When she strode from the chapel, it was with purpose and a plan.

Glancing about her rooms, Elizabeth pulled Jayne aside and asked her to recommend someone to assist her.

"It must be someone who keeps quietly to herself so that few would notice her activities," Elizabeth insisted.

"What is it you are proposing, your grace?" Jayne asked in a suggestive tone.

"Not what you are thinking, Jayne," Elizabeth said with a grin. "It is a mission of mercy, which I would ask you to participate in but your absence would be noted."

"And yours will not?"

"No, because I have you to cover for me."

"Very well," Jayne acknowledged. "Emma. She would be

perfect."

Elizabeth looked to the young woman in question. She knew her to be pious and devout, if somewhat shy. Even her small frame, light brown hair, and sad brown eyes attracted little attention.

"Emma, would you attend me a moment?" Elizabeth asked as she stepped close to her, not wanting the others' curiosity aroused.

Emma looked up in surprise but responded, "Of course, your grace." She quickly put aside her embroidery, an altar cloth, Elizabeth noted. Emma followed Elizabeth to her room where she was directed to a large trunk. "What would you have me do, my lady?"

Elizabeth took Emma's hands in her own, surprising the shy girl even further. "Emma, I would like you to be my partner in a little scheme that I have planned."

A small smile touched Emma's lips, but she was afraid of York schemes and was surprised that Elizabeth would take after her mother in this way.

"What sort of scheme?" Her eyes were downcast and she wondered what she was doing questioning the woman everyone knew to be the next queen of England.

Elizabeth laughed and squeezed Emma's hands. "This is just why you are perfect to be with me," she reassured the timid girl. "It is God's work, and I would have you to help me above any other."

A new light came into Emma's eyes. "That sounds wonderful, my lady."

Elizabeth pulled Emma to sit by her on the trunk. "We will have to be slightly dishonest in order to complete our mission," she admitted, "since we are not allowed beyond the castle walls due to the sweating sickness." She paused to gauge Emma's response. She looked determined and unafraid to do what Elizabeth was asking. "I would like to take food and clothes to those who are unable to leave their houses, coin to the many who have lost their men, and especially prayer to those who are suffering."

"Of course, my lady."

Elizabeth was encouraged by the admiration she saw in Emma's eyes. Formerly, she had looked at her with the standard respect due to her rank, now she looked at her with the mutual esteem of a sister in Christ.

"I will need you to choose two pages who are trustworthy to carry the goods that I would deliver," Elizabeth continued.

Emma nodded in agreement.

"I would like to leave immediately following the midday meal. We are unlikely to be missed during that time."

"We will be ready," Emma said with a new confidence in her voice. "Thank you for thinking of me, my lady."

They exchanged a look of mutual admiration and camaraderie in their conspiring before silently moving away to their individual preparations.

That afternoon, the two women met again in Elizabeth's room and Emma smiled at the modest gown that Elizabeth was wearing. "Wherever did you find it?" she asked.

"I've not only lived in palaces," Elizabeth said. In her mind she was picturing herself at Sherriff Hutton wearing this dress as she and Edward ran through the grasses of the moors with his puppy chasing after them. She forced the thought away to focus on the task at hand. "You have found reliable boys to assist us?"

"Yes," Emma nodded as she adjusted Elizabeth's hair and gown. "My cousin, Alfred, and his friend. I've not met the friend, but Alfred vouches for him. Alfred is a devoted Christian," she said by way of reassurance.

"I trust your judgment," Elizabeth said. "The goods are in a small pull-cart just outside. They know not to wear their royal livery?"

"Oh, yes. Do not worry, my lady. The right hand will not know what the left is doing."

Elizabeth smiled at Emma's application of scripture. "Let us be gone then."

The women snuck down a little used stairway to an even less used exit through the palace wall. There was Elizabeth's cart stacked high with goods. She and Emma had each placed purses heavy with small coins around their waist and under their cloaks. They smiled at each other conspiratorially as they closed the door behind them. They were in forbidden area now.

Two young men of about fourteen years of age stood near the cart, and Elizabeth knew them to be Alfred and his friend when Emma embraced the taller of the two. Their familial relationship was not at all evident in their appearance, Alfred's golden blond head already six inches above Emma's dull brown one. His blue eyes glittered with excitement over being involved in a quest both secret and honorable. He broke from Emma's embrace and stepped forward.

"My lady, Princess Elizabeth, I am honored," he said as he knelt before him.

"Be blessed," she said raising him up. "I am pleased to share this day with you. Thank you for helping us."

"We wouldn't miss it!" he exclaimed, sounding more like a boy now than a man. He motioned his friend forward. "This is Francis," he said. "Also trustworthy and a servant of Christ."

Francis came forward more awkwardly and knelt silently before Elizabeth.

"God's blessings," she said with a light hand on his dark locks. He examined her with intelligent eyes, and she knew that he took in more than he spoke. He reminded her of Richard, but she refused to think of that just now.

He rose and said, "God be with you also, my lady."

"We are off then," Elizabeth said. She led the way with Emma walking close beside her. Alfred and Francis followed, pulling the heavy cart.

Emma did not ask how Elizabeth knew where to go. Sometimes it was evident from the sadness that seemed to emanate from a home that was little more than a shack. Eventually, children began approaching them on the street as word of their good deeds quickly spread ahead of them. Elizabeth and Emma each shared a blessing with those they approached before filling their arms with food, clothes, blankets, and some coin.

Elizabeth knocked on the door that she knew to be the home of her missing page. It had not been easy to obtain the information or the goods that she distributed this day, but the smiles on the faces of the dirty children, worn out housewives, and ill husbands filled her with joy and satisfaction. She prayed for the boy within the small wood frame house as she waited for the door to open.

A woman who couldn't be more than thirty but appeared twenty years older cracked open the door. "What is it?" she demanded. Then her eyes widened at the party on her step. Even in her least fancy gown, Elizabeth was clearly of noble blood. "You don't want to be here, my lady!" she exclaimed in fear. "We've got the sweats!"

"I understand," Elizabeth said. She put forth a hand as if to touch the woman, but, seeing her cringe away, she withdrew it. "How is young Edwin?" she asked.

The woman's eyes filled with tears. "I'm afraid he is not long for this world, my lady."

Elizabeth gestured to Alfred and Francis to bring forth a sack of goods. "I would leave you with these items as they may help. Could I see him?" she asked. She heard the gasps of those around her, but she felt that she must encourage the boy and pray at his side.

"Oh no, my lady! It wouldn't be right, even at the best of times, for you to enter such a place as this," Edwin's mother insisted.

"Scripture tells us that there is indeed a time and place for every activity under heaven," Elizabeth countered.

Edwin's mother didn't know how to respond to this without sounding like a heretic. Emma came to her rescue.

"Surely it would be acceptable for me to see the boy. I am sure that Princess Elizabeth just wishes for a prayer to be said over the boy." She glanced at Elizabeth for approval and received a small nod.

"Well, I don't know." The poor woman was overwhelmed with the circumstances surrounding her.

Emma took the bulging sack from her cousin. "I will bring in these goods that Edwin is in need of."

Relenting to the need to open the door further to allow in the parcel, Edwin's mother also accepted Emma into her home. Emma glanced back at Elizabeth with her eyes full of confidence and joy that Elizabeth had never seen in them within the palace before closing the door gently behind her.

Elizabeth watched the door for a moment. She closed her eyes asking God to bless this house before turning to Alfred and Francis.

"Let's canvass these houses," she said gesturing to the area surrounding Edwin's home. "For others in need while we await Emma's return."

"They are likely all in need," said Francis as he gazed at the ramshackle homes surrounding them.

"You are right, of course," Elizabeth admitted. "Let's prepare a sack for each."

By the time they had packed and delivered goods to the ten closest houses, Emma emerged from Edwin's home with an aura of peace about her.

"How did he appear?" Elizabeth asked.

"Not well," Emma admitted. "But I do believe he was

encouraged by my presence and your gifts."

"Then this has been well worth it," Elizabeth whispered.

"Yes, it certainly has been," Emma agreed.

Three days later, Edwin was back at his post in Elizabeth's household. One of his first tasks was to deliver a letter, handwritten by the princess. She regretted to inform Emma's family that their daughter had died of the sweating sickness.

December 1485

Westminster Palace was in a flurry of preparations once again. Henry Tudor had begun his reign with celebrations that almost felt staged to remind the people of his majesty on a monthly basis. Dressmakers, bakers, musicians, and a swarm of others rushed through the castle with the hope of their work bringing them into the king's favor. Though still in mourning for Emma, Elizabeth was pleased that one of the events that would soon be taking place was her marriage to Henry.

While being measured and fit for the perfect gown, her mind still drifted away to the families she had seen that day with Emma. How many had died? Had they really made any impact? Was Emma's sacrifice to mean anything?

She had certainly felt so. Though she lay suffering and dying, Emma had seemed at peace with the work that God had given her during her short life, and she was prepared to meet him. Elizabeth had not been permitted to visit Emma and had managed to sneak away only once to beg her forgiveness for her part in bringing the illness upon her.

"Don't be ridiculous, your grace," Emma had said.

"Emma, I feel as though it is my fault that . . . ."

"That I am dying?" Emma finished for her, and Elizabeth bowed her head, not wanting to face the truth. "It is alright, my lady. I go to meet our God and will welcome you one day."

Tears filled Elizabeth's eyes and words would not come. She sat quietly holding Emma's hand until she fell asleep. Saying a blessing over her for the last time, she returned to the castle and never saw her again.

Elizabeth was shaken from her memories by her sister's approach.

"My beautiful sister!" Cecily exclaimed as she firmly embraced her.

"How wonderful to see you," Elizabeth said. She was glad that Cecily seemed in good spirits despite Henry's annulment of her marriage to Ralph Scrope. It was a topic that would be left unmentioned today.

"I see that you will soon be queen," Cecily said as she eyed the preparations going on around them.

"To be Henry's wife," Elizabeth corrected. "Henry has decided not to have my coronation as part of the event."

Cecily's eyes widened at the news. "Not to be crowned? What does he mean by this?"

"I am uncertain," Elizabeth admitted.

"It will be his mother's doing, I can assure you."

Elizabeth raised her eyebrows to her sister. "It matters not," she assured her. "I will be content with being his wife and eventually a mother. The ceremony is unimportant."

"Surely, you do not believe that," Cecily insisted. "It is an insult for you to not be crowned. He has already postponed the wedding long enough to send the message that he claims his throne by his own right."

"It is only insulting if I chose to be insulted," Elizabeth insisted. "I will not look for trouble where none need exist. I am certain that he will have me crowned when the time is right." She looked at Cecily's doubting face and desired to lighten the mood. "Maybe that will be next month's ceremony."

The sisters laughed together, and Cecily did not bring up Elizabeth's lack of crown again.

~ ~ ~ ~

Elizabeth and Cecily sat together as the Yule log was dragged into the palace. The men had felled a huge ancient tree in order to

114

have this log that was as wide as Elizabeth was tall. It was large enough to be lit tonight and remain burning throughout the twelve days of Christmastime. No less than ten men struggled to pull it into place as the court fool cart-wheeled around them singing his own irreverent Christmas songs. The looks on some of the men's faces revealed that his antics were not appreciated, but he seemed not to notice.

Conflicting feelings were at war within Elizabeth. On one hand, she wanted to be happy and excited for the wedding plans being made at this very moment for her to be joined with Henry. On the other, her lonely sister Cecily stood next to her with no further word of who Henry planned to match her to. He had annulled her marriage to Ralph Scrope but not yet indicated what he had in mind that had made the annulment necessary. How she tried to give Henry the benefit of the doubt, but there were so many doubts.

"Shall we spend tomorrow evening with mother and Cat and Bridget?" Elizabeth asked Cecily.

"That would be nice," Cecily said in a way that made Elizabeth wonder if she even realized what she was agreeing to.

"Maybe we should ask Margaret and Edward, as well. I have not seen much of our cousins since arriving in London," she added.

"They would like that," Cecily agreed absently.

"Are you quite alright, sister?"

Cecily focused on Elizabeth's concerned face. "I apologize, Bess. Yes, I am fine," she said. "I only wonder what our first Christmas together would have been like."

Elizabeth nodded and placed a supportive hand on her sister's arm.

"It would not have been grand, and we would not have been surrounded by groveling courtiers. It would have been wonderful," Cecily ended in a whisper.

"I am sure Henry has an ideal match in mind for you," Elizabeth said, hoping it was true.

Cecily blinked away the tears that had filled her eyes making them bright blue in the dim light. "I'm sure he does. Someone politically appropriate and distantly related, not just a man who will love me simply as a woman."

"Oh, Cecily," Elizabeth whispered as she wrapped her younger sister in a loving embrace. "I will do all I can to find out, though I know little even of my own wedding plans."

"At least you know they are being made," Cecily said after forcing a false smile onto her face. "Thank you for trying. Any news would be greatly appreciated."

"Be strong, dear sister," Elizabeth said, still holding firmly onto Cecily's arms. "God will not give you more than you can bear and he would have you cast your concerns onto him."

Cecily sighed. "Of course, you are right, Bess. I do not stand as firmly in my faith as you do. Thank you for your support and encouragement. Henry is a lucky man."

"He is king."

"That is not what makes him blessed."

The next evening, Elizabeth was excited to be hosting her family for an intimate meal away from the main hall. She directed servants to place a table and chairs within her own rooms that would accommodate the seven of them and double checked the menu that she had settled on to ensure that everyone's favorites were accounted for. Certain that everything was in place, she spun around cheerfully, eager for her guests to arrive.

"Bess! Bess! We're here!" announced five year old Bridget before entering the room.

Elizabeth was ready to scoop her up into her arms when the girl rambunctiously ran into the room. "Oh, Bridget! How I have missed your smiling face," she said after a warm embrace. "I am very happy that you are here."

"And so is Cat and mama," Bridget added unnecessarily for their mother and sister were standing directly behind her.

"Then I shall greet them," Elizabeth said with a final squeeze. "Cat, you are a beautiful young lady," she said as she reached for her second youngest sister.

A blush rose on the pale cheeks of six year old Catherine. "Thank you, Bess."

What happens to us between five and six years old that causes girls to all of a sudden grow up, Elizabeth wondered. Then again, Cat had always been more subdued than Bridget who seemed to find joy in every occasion.

"Mother," Elizabeth said in greeting with a bow of her head.

"Dear daughter," her mother responded more warmly and leaned over to hold her daughter close. "I am happy to be with you."

"And I with you, mother," Elizabeth whispered, surprised by the show of affection.

Soon, Cecily, Margaret, and Edward had arrived as well and they sat down to a meal like that enjoyed by many families throughout London. For a short time, they could forget that they were the remnant of the York family.

"Margaret says that you are going to be queen," Edward stated.

A smile tugged at Elizabeth's lips. "Yes, cousin, I will marry the king next month."

"How is it that Henry is king?" Edward asked. The table grew quiet in response to the innocent question.

Elizabeth took a deep breath before answering. "Well, Edward, you were with me when we heard the news that Henry's troops had defeated our uncle Richard's. That is how Henry is king."

"But isn't our cousin, John, Richard's heir," he paused and looked thoughtful. "Wasn't I?"

"You mustn't speak so," Margaret admonished. "I'm sorry,

Bess."

"Do not feel you need to apologize," Elizabeth assured Margaret. "I know that you look out for your brother and you are a wonderful caretaker." Then she turned to Edward. "Yes, John de la Pole was Richard's heir, as were you at one time. However, since Richard lost the battle at Bosworth, it is through that defeat that Henry has taken the throne."

Edward scrunched up his face in thought, but clearly couldn't straighten it all out. "Alright, Bess."

"I know you do not understand Edward, but it is the way of the world."

"Uncle Richard is in heaven with Anne and his Edward now," Edward said as if that explained everything.

"Ah, the faith of the little children," Elizabeth said with a quiet laugh. "That he is, my darling." Many people said that Edward of Warwick was slow or stupid, but Elizabeth wondered if many people wouldn't be much happier if they shared his outlook.

"Daughter, I am going to lease the Cheneygates House for your younger sisters and I," Elizabeth's mother said.

"What? You will leave the castle?" Elizabeth couldn't hide her surprise. Her mother had always enjoyed being in the center of politics and activity.

"This is no longer my palace," admitted the former queen with a shrug. "Your sisters and I will be only across the river, but away from painful reminders."

"I understand, and I respect your decision," Elizabeth said. "I am sure that you will be quite happy there. It is a beautiful home. Thankfully, you will still be close at hand when I am in need of you."

Her mother waved the comment away. "There is little that you need me for anymore."

The evening continued on in family harmony, though Cecily

continued to keep to herself. Elizabeth was shocked that the loss of her common husband had affected her so strongly. She would remember to pray for peace and emotional healing for her sister when she said her prayers that night. When her family members filed out of the room, Elizabeth prepared for bed with a light, happy heart.

The next morning, Margaret ran into Elizabeth's room without waiting for permission to enter. Tears streamed down her narrow face and her auburn hair fell in a tangle around her shoulders. Before one of her ladies could admonish her cousin, Elizabeth ran to her and held her close.

"What is it, Margaret?"

Margaret could hardly speak through her sobbing. "They've taken Edward!"

"Taken him? Taken him where?"

"The Tower."

~ ~ ~ ~

The Christmas festivities carried on, but the joyful feeling in Elizabeth's heart was gone. She had not received any response to her note to Henry requesting an audience or information on her cousin. Margaret was crushed. The poor girl having already lost her mother and father was not prepared to be left without her younger brother. Elizabeth invited Margaret to share her rooms rather than staying in her own that seemed too empty, and they gave each other what comfort they could.

Elizabeth did not dare to share her private fears with her young cousin, but she couldn't dismiss the premonition of evil that filled her when she pictured innocent Edward sitting in a cell in the cold, dark Tower. She tried to tell herself that he would have royal rooms that would be comfortable and warmed by a cheery fire, but the vision of her brothers in similar rooms filled her with dread. Edward was the last in the direct male Plantagenet line. Would there be no more?

January 1486

"Elizabeth, you have been asking to speak to me."

Henry stood in the entrance to her rooms, and, though she had been hoping to have the opportunity to interrogate him about Edward for two weeks, she was flustered at his sudden appearance. She fell quickly and expertly into a low curtsey and her ladies followed suit.

"Your grace, please come in," she said, and a chair was placed for him near her own.

He strode across the room with so much more confidence than he had seemed to have when she first met him at Coldharbour. Her hand was in his, and he placed a lingering kiss upon it. Elizabeth's feelings were at war within her. She was touched by his affection but overwhelmed with concern for Edward. She could not go through what she had with her brothers again. She gestured toward the chair and waited for him to be seated before taking her own.

"I apologize that I have not been attentive," he began. "What concerns you, my lady?"

Elizabeth could not open the conversation with an accusation. "I wanted to speak to you of our wedding plans."

Henry's eyebrows rose, and she wasn't surprised. Certainly, his mother was the one to speak to about such a thing.

"I was under the impression that everything was well in hand," Henry said, once again taking up her delicate fingers in a gentle hold. "Does something concern you, my love."

Heat rushed into her face at his choice of words. Did he love her truly? How could he when they hardly knew each other? He must be putting himself through the motions of their courtship, as she was. She prayed that as she accepted Henry as her husband that her feelings for him would grow.

"I'm sure it is, your grace." Seeing the look on his face, she corrected herself. "Henry, I'm sorry. I suppose I am nervous and wanted to spend time with you."

This was the right thing to say as evinced by the way Henry's face lit up. "I am happy to oblige and only wish that I could have done so sooner." His hand moved up her arm in a more intimate gesture, which sent feelings through Elizabeth that left her confused.

"I do have one concern," she added, knowing that she must speak before she lost her nerve.

"What is it? Anything you need shall be yours."

She forced herself to look him directly in the eyes. "I am worried about my cousin, Edward."

He had the grace to appear embarrassed. "I am sorry about that, Elizabeth," he said as he removed his hand from her arm. "Surely, you understand that some York supporters are not content that we are to be married. They would fight to see the York heir on the throne."

"But that would be John," Elizabeth said without thinking. She hoped that she was not causing more of her cousins to be imprisoned.

"Ah, some would say so," Henry admitted. "But Edward is the last York of the male line, which is more important to some than the fact that your uncle named de la Pole as his heir." He said 'your uncle' with venom and accusation that told Elizabeth that she must chose her next words carefully.

"Henry, I mean no disrespect, of course. I am happy to be your future wife." She attempted to look demure. "I am simply concerned about my young cousin. His sister is beside herself with grief. He is all she has."

Henry sighed and tilted his head as if he were contemplating a puzzle with no solution. "She may visit him," he allowed. "But Edward must stay in the Tower for his own protection. What if the wrong people took custody of him?"

Elizabeth's insides twisted at his words that so closely mirrored those Richard had used regarding her brothers.

"Henry, have you discovered where Richard was keeping my brothers?"

Henry stood and began to pace.

"Leave us," he said with a flourish that included everyone in the room except the two of them.

Elizabeth nodded her consent to her ladies who looked to her for confirmation. It was a bold question, especially following the inquiry about her cousin, but she felt that it may be her only chance. When they were alone, Henry continued.

"Elizabeth, you must know the truth." He knelt before her, taking both of her hands in his.

She held her breath. "What truth?"

"Your brothers were killed at least a year ago on your uncle's command."

"No!" She pulled her hands away and found that it was not distance enough. She rose from her chair and ran to the window. It couldn't be possible. Her trust had been placed in Richard despite her mother's harsh words. Had she been wrong all along?

She sensed Henry stepping up behind, but not quite touching, her. She wasn't sure whether or not she wanted him to. Did he speak the truth?

"How do you know?"

He seemed surprised by the question. "Everyone knows it to be true," he said. "The boys have not been seen since shortly after your uncle's coronation."

She turned to look at him with tears filling her eyes. It frustrated her to appear weak, and she tried to blink them away. "That is not proof."

Henry raised his hand as if to touch her, but it fell back to his side. "My men have found nothing of them. Elizabeth, I'm very sorry, but I did not realize that you held out hope for them."

Her tears could be held back no longer. She was ashamed by both her tears and her naivety. Had she been so infatuated with Richard that she had believed empty lies? What of Anne? Had she too been deceived or a deceiver? Her mother had warned her, but she had refused to listen. It was inconceivable. How could she accept that little Edward and Richard were gone?

"I must go to my chapel," she said before rushing out of the room. She knew that it was unacceptably rude, especially in the company of the king, but she needed the solace of God's presence.

Henry found her before the altar on her knees, her tears slowed but not ceasing. He crossed himself and lowered himself next to her with his head bowed.

For a few moments, Elizabeth's prayers were a wordless jumble racing through her head. Then she whispered, "Lord, I am lost. Have you taken my brothers into their heavenly home? Forgive me for my foolishness, Lord, and guide me in your truth. Help me to be a pleasing wife to this man, who prays with me rather than being offended by my thoughtless behavior. Amen."

She peeked at Henry and saw that he was deep in prayer as well. Could she trust him after having it proven that she was a poor judge of character? She must. God was placing them together, and it must be right.

Henry opened his eyes to find Elizabeth studying him. They rose without speaking until they had crossed themselves and moved to a small bench.

Visions of her brothers as she had last seen them flashed through her mind. Many times she had pictured them at play on the grounds of Middleham or one of Richard's other estates, but now she felt certain that they had never been there. The entire time, had she been in love with their murderer? She remembered hearing the whispers about her father having Henry VI killed while he was a prisoner in the tower. Though she had told herself that it wasn't true, deep inside she had always known that it was. It had been the only way to stop the bloody conflict. Richard must have looked at her brothers in the same way.

"What would you have done if Richard had been captured at Bosworth rather than killed?" she blurted without thinking.

Henry's eyes widened but he did not scold her. Instead, he placed his thin arm around her shoulders and pulled her to him. She did not object or pull away. When seconds continued to pass, she wondered if he was going to respond to her impetuous inquiry.

"I would have had him executed," he said so quickly that the words ran together, as if it were a horrid truth that he would have admitted to none but her, and her only this once.

She only nodded, seeing that this was the way of her world. Thousands more would have died just as they had for more than twenty years before. Could Henry establish peace and unity for England with their marriage?

"And my cousin of Warwick?"

He took a deep breath and let it out slowly before answering. "He is kept for his own safety. I have no desire to make war upon ten-year-old boys."

But her uncle had. Her brother, Richard, had been only ten years old and Edward thirteen when they disappeared. Elizabeth's tears fell fresh again. They fell for her youngest brother who was so innocent, for Edward who had been raised to be king, and for her broken dreams and loss of innocence.

Henry pulled her closer. She heard his heart beating within his narrow chest. He was not the muscle-bound soldier that she had grown up expecting to see on England's throne. His voice still had a French lilt that was evidence of his exile, but she supposed that her own ancestors had spoken French at court as well. His hand brushed lightly up and down her arm, and she felt loved just for being herself for the first time since her father died.

She looked up into his hazel eyes, so different than the blue eyes she was so used to seeing in most of her family and thankfully different from Richard's startling green. He smiled slightly and hesitantly, he no more sure of the next move than she was. In that moment, in her private chapel before the altar of God, she decided that she could love this man.

That is when he kissed her.

~ ~ ~ ~

The gown was Lancaster red with the finest cloth-of-gold overlay and ermine trim at the cuffs and hem. It set off the red highlights in Elizabeth's hair that flowed down her back like a river of gold. Cecily had taken over the styling of her hair and Elizabeth laughed at the idea that her pampered sister would have a better hand at it than the woman who had been twisting and piling noble hair her entire life. The finished project was simple and lovely with tiny red and white roses mingling with the golden tresses. Everything about this wedding would emphasize the union of Lancaster and York in love, harmony, and especially in peace.

Margaret Stanley was sure to be supervising that all her arrangements were being carried out to perfection. Everything, from seating layout to the colors of her ladies' gowns, was carefully accounted for. Henry would be wearing York white to complement Elizabeth's gown. His mother had secured every diamond and ruby in London to bedeck her royal son. While Elizabeth was adorned simply and was a vision of beauty, Henry, in his white satin and cloth-of-gold with jewels glittering on every available surface, was almost gaudy. If Margaret had intended for him to outshine his bride, she would be disappointed.

Some of the guests might have been having these thoughts, but the bride and groom were not. Henry and Elizabeth saw beyond the Tudor roses that were freshly painted on the pews and pillars, past the carefully planned scattering of Tudor green, and had eyes only for each other as they said their vows and prayed that their marriage would bring lasting peace to their realm.

The celebration following mass was as uninhibited as the ceremony had been subdued. Wine flowed freely and all seemed to share the happy couple's hopes that the Tudor dynasty would be a blessing to England.

Edward Stafford, the seven-year-old duke of Buckingham, was embarrassed by the attentions of his mother. Katherine had made her home with Jasper Tudor, the husband of Henry's choosing for her, but she missed her little boy, who was now a ward in Margaret Stanley's household. The boy was the spitting image of his father and had been dressed as gloriously as Harry would have hoped for.

Despite his youth, noble woman across the country schemed to make him the husband of one of their daughters. When he came of age, he would be the largest landholder in England, and some would whisper that he also had a claim to the throne that was backed up by a few more drops of Plantagenet blood than ran through the current king's veins.

Others were in attendance whom Elizabeth had not spoken to since before her uncle's death. She was determined to see each person through new eyes. No judgment would be based on how one had behaved during Richard's reign. Could she blame the earl of Oxford, for instance, for not supporting Richard at Bosworth? How many had based their actions on what they felt was the truth about her brothers' deaths? She had been too stubborn to accept it and still wasn't sure of the truth, but was determined to move forward. She would not think of that today on this most happy occasion, but neither would she hold on to old opinions of the people surrounding her.

Cecily looked happier than she had since the annulment of her marriage, and Elizabeth was glad that her heart was healing. Though she would never say so, she was also pleased that Cecily had not become pregnant during the brief marriage. It would have only made the incident more painful and difficult.

"You are a gorgeous bride," Cecily slurred as she handed Elizabeth a goblet of wine though she already held one.

"Sister!" Elizabeth exclaimed, dismayed by the reason for Cecily's lifted spirits. "Please, sit with me," she begged and moved toward an alcove for relative privacy.

Cecily twirled one last time before collapsing on the bench almost in her sister's lap.

"This is not like you, Cecily. Would you like to lie down in my room?"

"Don't be ridiculous!" Cecily snapped. "I will not steal your spotlight, as if that were possible."

"Oh, Cecily, you cannot think that is what I meant," Elizabeth said and put an arm around her sister's shoulders, which were slumping as the false joy of the wine faded. "With whom were you dancing?" she asked in the hope that someone new had caught Cecily's eye.

"Your new husband, as a matter of fact."

Elizabeth was curious about the strange analysis Cecily had placed her under. "I am glad that you are making amends with Henry. He is doing his best to make good decisions for us all."

Cecily's laugh held a cruel note in it. "Especially for himself." She began lifting her cup, only to realize that it was empty. "Oh, get that look off your face, Bess. He dated his reign from the day before Bosworth to keep all the noblemen in fear. Our cousin, Edward, is in prison though he is a ten-year-old simpleton. If our brothers weren't dead before, they certainly are now. And I am to be the spare York princess until you prove fertile."

Cecily sobered instantly when she was faced with Elizabeth's wide, unbelieving eyes. "What did you say?" Elizabeth whispered.

Falling to her knees, Cecily begged Elizabeth's forgiveness. "I did not know what I was saying, Bess! You said yourself that I have had too much wine. I should have accepted the invitation to your room." She placed her head in Elizabeth's lap. "Please, Bess. Forget all I have said."

Absently laying a hand on her sister's head, Elizabeth was confronted with new doubts. How she had hoped to be happy and carefree for this one day, her wedding day. "I know the truth of most of what you have said. Why did you call yourself the spare York princess?"

Sobbing shook Cecily's shoulders and she swore that she would never imbibe again. "Bess, I am so thoughtless, on this of all days."

Elizabeth straightened her spine and demanded, "Tell me what you meant."

"It is not Henry's plan, of that I am sure," Cecily stuttered through her tears. Elizabeth's hand stopped the comforting motion in her hair and began to clench. "It is his mother, that horrid, controlling Margaret Stanley. You must be careful around her," Cecily warned her as she would if the devil were approaching.

"This is ridiculous," Elizabeth said, sure now that it was the wine that made Cecily speak foolishly. "We have known Lady Stanley our entire lives. She was a faithful lady-in-waiting to our mother."

"No," Cecily insisted. She lifted her head and moved back to the bench. "She was simply biding her time, waiting for the moment when she could place her son on the throne."

"But how could she have known? Henry has been in exile most of his life. He has never been heir to the crown."

"In her mind, he always has been. She is obsessed with him."

Cecily grabbed Elizabeth's arms and her eyes darted around almost as in fear. "Bess, be careful. It is not you she cares for but your royal blood."

"Of course, that is why our marriage was arranged in the first place." She was still in wonder of her sister's wildly swinging moods and bold accusations. "But now Henry and I are growing to love one another. We have been united in the eyes of God."

"I will tell you only because I have already spoken unwisely," Cecily continued. "She will not allow Henry to arrange a marriage for me until you have produced an heir. I am meant to be the spare."

Elizabeth looked into her sister's eyes and saw sincerity within them. She looked across the room at Henry. He seemed so happy to be her husband, but he kept her sister within his reach. Her head drooped and she closed her eyes. Cecily would not lie or purposely hurt her. There may be few that she could trust completely, but Cecily was one.

"I am very sorry that my husband has placed you in this awkward position," she whispered.

"Bess, you were so joyous a moment ago. It is quite possible that Henry does not even know of his mother's plan. It was she who told me when I inquired about betrothal arrangements." She grasped Elizabeth's hands as if they were a lifeline. "Please, be happy. If you love Henry, give him a son and all will be well."

The emotional blow had hurt, as had learning the truth about her brothers, but Elizabeth was learning that she must make the most of the information she gained. Rather than remaining a pawn on the royal chessboard, she would be a wise and empowered queen. She lifted her head and smiled at Cecily.

"You are right, Cecily. Margaret is not the queen. I am. I will give my husband a son, and I will make sure that he gives you a husband to your liking."

The sisters shared an embrace and a look of understanding before rejoining the party, each feeling like they were a few years older and wiser.

February 11, 1486

With her eyes still closed, Elizabeth relished the feeling of the feather mattress beneath her, heavy covers above, and little Margaret snuggled close for warmth. Since Edward's imprisonment, Margaret had clung to Elizabeth with ferocity. Elizabeth wished that Margaret's pain could be taken away, but Henry insisted that Edward must be held despite his obvious innocence.

Elizabeth opened her eyes and looked at Margaret with her russet colored hair and pale skin. While at rest she looked youthful and lovely with just the lightest sprinkling of freckles across her nose. When awake the stresses and tragedies of her life aged her beyond her fourteen years. What comfort she could provide, Elizabeth gladly and freely gave, but nothing could take away Margaret's loneliness over her lack of immediate family.

A wave of nausea overtook Elizabeth and distracted her from her thoughts of Margaret's situation. She sat up quickly, afraid that she would be sick. Cecily was awake and saw the look on her sister's face. She rushed across the room with a clean chamber pot and arrived at Elizabeth's bedside just in time.

After retching for a few minutes, Elizabeth weakly thanked her sister and climbed from the bed to avoid disturbing Margaret. Cecily sent the pot away with one of the ladies in the outer chamber so that Elizabeth would not be further sickened by the sour scent that was quickly filling the room. She opened a shutter and let in the frosty February air.

"Thank you, Cecily, for your quick reaction," Elizabeth had huddled in a chair before the fire and pulled a robe tightly around herself.

Cecily closed the shutter before the room grew too chilly and crossed to her sister. She was happier staying with Elizabeth than with their mother, so she had remained in Elizabeth's household after Christmas. Sitting down in the other chair before the fire, she looked knowingly at Elizabeth.

"You feel better now," she stated rather than asked.

"Yes, I think I do," Elizabeth said with some surprise. "It came and went rather quickly. I'm not even sure what brought it on."

"You're not?"

Seeing the skeptical look on Cecily's face, the truth dawned on Elizabeth. "Already? Could it be?"

"It is the only time our mother ever showed any sign of illness."

Elizabeth's eyes widened and she mentally counted the weeks. She and Henry had been married just over three weeks, but her last course had been about three weeks before that. She smiled triumphantly and placed a hand over her flat stomach that gave away no secrets.

"I believe you are correct, dear sister," she said with greater calm than she felt. She wanted to jump for joy and run to tell Henry.

"You must wait until you are certain," Cecily said as though reading Elizabeth's thoughts.

"Of course, I must wait," she said as she rose and went to Cecily. She took her hands and continued, "Don't you see? All will be well. Henry and I are content together. His mother will be happy with the promise of an heir, and you will be free to marry."

Cecily simply nodded, failing to be caught up in Elizabeth's enthusiasm. She was not sure that any marriage Margaret Stanley may arrange for her would be worth getting excited about. However, she was glad for her sister and gathered her in a loving embrace.

"Do you know what day it is?" Cecily asked, still holding firmly the thin figure that would soon round with new life.

"Oh, Cecily, you know that I am not one for keeping the

calendar."

"Happy birthday, sister dear. You are twenty years old today."

March 1486

Morning sickness continued to plague Elizabeth, so Margaret was included in her secret. Margaret was thrilled with the news and the fact that she was considered mature enough to be confided in. She waited on Elizabeth with increased enthusiasm and jumped up each time Elizabeth moved or muttered. Finally, Cecily had to take her aside and point out that the other ladies were certain to guess at Elizabeth's condition if she continued her exaggerated servitude.

Feeling confident at last, Elizabeth decided to tell Henry the happy news once she could count twelve weeks since her last course. A fluttering in her stomach completely unrelated to nausea filled her as she waited for him to come to her.

"Elizabeth, you look radiant," Henry said as he entered the room and pulled her into his arms.

"You also are looking well," Elizabeth said when he released her. She looked up at him and had to admit that he did appear more relaxed and healthy since their marriage. A smile brightened her face at the thought that she was such a blessing to him.

"I must thank you for asking me here," he said, and he led her to the chairs before the fire where she and Cecily had sat when she first discovered the news she was about to share with him. "Without your summons, I would have never been able to free myself from councilors and petitioners."

"Henry, you must remember that you are the one who is king," she said teasingly. Margaret Stanley may have always dreamed of her son wearing the crown, but she had not prepared him for the reality of doing so. "Send them from your rooms in a rage a couple of times, and they will cease their bullying."

Henry laughed. "Oh, Elizabeth. As if you have ever sent anyone away in a rage." He stood and moved his chair closer to hers.

Her laughter joined his. "Maybe not, but it seemed effective for my father." She discreetly examined his features. He seemed unperturbed, but she wasn't sure how he took mentions of her father being king.

They settled into comfortable silence for a few moments before Elizabeth could wait no longer.

"Henry, I wanted to speak with you about something very important."

He broke his gaze from the fire to look at her. "What is it, my love?"

"Who do you plan on marrying Cecily to?" She wasn't sure what had made her ask that at this moment. Since her wedding day, neither she nor Cecily had mentioned the spare princess theory.

If Henry was surprised or embarrassed by the question, he hid it well. He seemed to consider the question as though he had not thought much about it.

"Do you have someone in mind?" he asked, turning the question back to her.

Now Elizabeth wished she had spoken to Cecily about this. Was there a man that Cecily would want to have suggested? She was unsure. Cecily had been happy with Ralph Scrope, but Elizabeth knew that he was not someone she should mention.

"No. I simply recognize that my sister is lonely and desires a family."

"It seems curious that you ask if you do not have someone in mind," Henry pressed.

Elizabeth felt a flush rising in her face, so she determined to change the subject. "It is only that I am so happy in our marriage that I wish the same for my sister. She is my dearest friend, you know."

"I will spend some time considering her situation," he conceded, turning his attention back to the fire.

His lack of commitment to the subject discouraged Elizabeth

somewhat, but she moved closer to him with resolve. "Are you pleased with me as a wife, Henry?"

He slid from his seat and knelt in front of her. "I love you with all my heart," he said with his eyes fixed upon hers. "Have I given you reason to doubt it?"

"Not in the least," she insisted and pulled him up towards her and placed a light kiss upon his lips. "In fact, I couldn't be more pleased," she said with a secretive smile on her face.

"What is this about?" he asked as a worry line appeared between his brows.

"Oh, Henry," she sighed. "I believe that I am with child."

Elizabeth was not sure what she had expected, but certainly it had not been for the king of England to jump up and whoop with complete lack of royal dignity. He lifted Elizabeth from her seat and spun her around the room.

"You have made me the happiest man in England!"

She laughed and wondered how she had ever doubted him.

"When? When will my son be born?"

"Or your daughter," she said mischievously, the firelight causing her eyes to glitter.

"Do not tease," he said, pulling her close to his chest.

"I believe we can expect him, or her, in October. It is quite possible that I actually conceived on our wedding night," she admitted with a blush.

He kissed her ardently and buried his hands in her thick coppery hair. "Then our union is truly blessed by God."

"I believe it is," she agreed as she enthusiastically returned his kiss.

~ ~ ~ ~

As soon as Henry had been told, Elizabeth's pregnancy became public knowledge. Her belly seemed to have been waiting for it to be acceptable to expand because her dresses felt tight the very next day. Ladies were set to altering and sewing gowns to accommodate Elizabeth's figure as it filled out. Nobody was happier than Margaret Stanley about the news.

Elizabeth's relationship with her mother-in-law was precarious. At times, the older woman seemed fond of Elizabeth and they shared a common love for Henry. This was also their main point of contention as Lady Margaret seemed to be jealous of her own daughter-in-law if Henry spent what she considered too much time with his wife.

She insisted upon holding the queen's rooms of the palace rather than relinquishing them to Elizabeth. Henry justified this with the fact that he frequently discussed decisions of state with his mother late into the night. Elizabeth knew that she was seen as weak and insignificant because she did not insist on her rights, but the reward did not seem worth the fight. Lady Margaret would have been disappointed to know how frequently her son visited Elizabeth's rooms despite the fact that they were not connected to his own.

Elizabeth's mother was comfortably settled at Cheneygates House across the Thames from the palace. It was an ideal distance, close enough to be on hand when needed and far enough away to not be a daily burden. Elizabeth loved her mother but found herself too often on edge in her presence. They were too different in personality, with the older Elizabeth constantly in need of controlling the events and people around her, while the younger was more apt to trust in God and the people he had placed in her life.

Edward's imprisonment was the only part of Elizabeth's life that upset her and made her feel helpless. Whenever she attempted to bring the subject of her cousin up in conversation with Henry, he refused to discuss it. He was adamant that the boy remain in the Tower. Unlike her brothers, Edward did appear to be safe and relatively happy there. His sister, Margaret, visited him every few days and made sure that he had books and time in the courtyard. What future he was preparing for was anyone's guess.

The sweating sickness had finally dissipated, though Elizabeth still mourned the loss of Emma so soon after becoming her friend. People had returned to work, and the jobs left open had been quickly filled. Individuals continued to privately mourn, but the city of London was leaving death behind and moving toward a future that looked peaceful and bright.

Elizabeth strolled in the gardens that were beginning to swell with life just as she was. Her figure may not have revealed her condition too much yet, but the way her hand stayed protectively over her navel did. This was the baby that would end all division between Lancaster and York. No more war with its meaningless death and destruction would touch England's fields. Instead of trampled crops and rivers that ran red with blood, the people could enjoy safety and the bounty of their labors.

She reached out to touch the cherry blossoms. They were beautiful pink clouds for the few weeks that they appeared each year. Her eyes closed as her hands gently passed along the surface of the petals and she breathed deep of the fragrant air.

"Hello, my love."

Her eyes flashed open, and she smiled up at Henry. "Have your councilors given you an intermission?"

"Being king does still have some advantages." He wrapped his arms around her thickening waist. "For example, he has a beautiful wife."

He kissed her lightly and they stood in companionable quiet until Elizabeth spoke. "What are they concerned about today?"

"How do you know they are concerned about something?" Was

that a gleam of distrust in his eye?

She shrugged. "They are always worrying over something. I believe it is the utmost task of being a councilman."

His curious look passed as quickly as it had appeared, and he laughed lightly again. "In both statements you are correct," he admitted. "Men have arrived saying that Francis Lovell is gathering rebels to him."

"Francis Lovell, Richard's man? He is alive?"

"Apparently so, and he has not forgotten his former master but intends to continue the fight for him."

Elizabeth shook her head. "What can he hope to accomplish?" She was dismayed that Lovell would not be content with her as York queen. Why must men always find reasons to make war? She wondered if that would change once she gave birth to a son.

"Their intent was to attack when I leave on progress next month. I can only imagine that he had hoped to place a York prince on the throne in my place."

"But who?" Elizabeth asked without thinking. She realized her mistake when she saw the I-told-you-so look on Henry's face. "Edward," she said. Didn't these men realize the effect they had on her cousin's life when they fought in his name?

"Now you understand."

Elizabeth sighed as she leaned into him. "I understand. I do not like it and wish it was not the case, but I understand."

"You were young when your uncle George died, but surely you remember enough to know that all kings, even your father, have had to make decisions for the good of the country that they wish they did not have to make."

Elizabeth remembered little of George, duke of Clarence. He was Margaret and Edward's father, and he had been executed by her father, his brother, for treason. Would Elizabeth be able to pass such a judgment? She doubted it, and, seeing the mess it left for

Margaret and Edward, Elizabeth wished her father hadn't either.

"You know I support you in your decisions, Henry," she said, expressing none of her doubts.

"Publicly, yes. Privately, I know you wish I was more merciful."

"I wish your mother was more merciful," she said, allowing a little anger into her voice.

"My mother?" He had the audacity to seem surprised.

Elizabeth spun away from him. "Yes, your mother. I am fully aware that it is the Lady Margaret who desires to lock up every remaining York and throw away the keys. As your foremost advisor, she carries great power."

Henry would not be goaded into an argument. "No greater power than your own, I assure you," he said calmly. "I keep Edward because I think it is the right thing to do, not because my mother demands it."

Her eyes downcast, Elizabeth refused to say more on the topic and was disappointed in herself for ruining their few moments together.

He turned her toward him and put his hand on her chin and tilted it upwards. "You must concern yourself only with the health of our son," he said, placing his other hand on her belly. "Everything else, you may trust to me."

He placed a soft kiss on her lips and was gone before she could think of anything to say in response.

April 1486

Henry left on progress, and Elizabeth remained behind. The decision to stay in London had been a difficult one. Not only did she wish to be with her husband, but she felt certain that he would be better received in the north with her at his side. That was part of the reason that he was determined to go alone. He must establish his rule in his own right, not because a beloved York princess stood beside him. His main concern was her health and that of his unborn son. He never questioned that the baby would be a boy, but he prayed daily that he would be healthy.

Though she missed Henry, Elizabeth filled her time with sewing tiny clothes in the company of Margaret and Cecily, visiting her mother and younger sisters, and writing letters to be carried to her husband. Worry threatened to bubble up in her when she heard continued rumors of Francis Lovell drawing the discontented to him. Try as she might to focus on her growing baby and household duties, Elizabeth could not ignore the fact that those believing they were being loyal to her family may kill her husband.

She remembered how sure she had felt the last time Richard had rode away. His safety and victory were never in doubt. She forced herself to trust that God's plan for Henry was different. What else could she do?

For the first time in her life, her mother was a calming presence. Whether it was her advancing age or the coming of her grandchild, Elizabeth Woodville seemed to truly desire a quiet life free of politics and scheming. She shared stories with Elizabeth of when she was a young mother. Only when she mentioned her son, Richard Grey, did the tenseness around her eyes become visible. Guilt flooded through Elizabeth as she remembered that she had defended her uncle when he had put her half-brother to death.

"I know what you are thinking, Bess, and you should not," her mother said.

"I have been thinking about those years for some time now," Elizabeth admitted, "and I owe you an apology, mother. You were right about Richard."

Elizabeth's mother shook her head as if she would rather have been wrong.

"You also were right about Henry. I was wrong to doubt your choice of a husband for me. I truly was a foolish girl."

"Oh, Bess."

Elizabeth was enveloped in a hug that felt more sincere than any affection she remembered receiving from her mother before. She basked in it, refusing to be the one to let go first.

"I assure you that you are forgiven," her mother said. "I was no different at that age, and I am glad that you are able to think for yourself and stand up for what you believe to be right."

Elizabeth laughed. "Oh, no. I plan to be a submissive wife and dutiful mother. My time of headstrong willfulness is hopefully all behind me."

"Not all behind you, I hope," her mother said with a mischievous smile. "Sometimes the men do need us to stir them up and bring to light their faulty judgments."

"I will leave that to you then, mother, since your judgment has proven better than my own," Elizabeth said with a laugh, hoping her mother was joking.

A page arrived in the doorway and awaited Elizabeth's attention.

"You may approach," she said with a gesture to beckon him forward.

"A letter from the king, your grace," he said as he bowed low and held out the parchment bearing Henry's seal.

"Thank you." She uncharacteristically failed to offer him refreshment, her attention captured by the first news she had received since Henry had left London. Her mother and the ladies surrounding them were quiet while she read.

"Thank God!" she finally exclaimed.

"What is happening?" her mother leaned forward to ask.

"The Staffords, who had joined Lovell, have gone into sanctuary in Culham. Lovell has escaped, but Henry believes that he has left the country for Burgundy."

Elizabeth's mother sat back and quickly took up her work.

"I am surprised that Tom and Humphrey would join Lovell," Elizabeth went on still staring at Henry's writing. "Did they not rebel with Harry Stafford against Richard?" Elizabeth looked at her mother the way she had when she was a little girl, hoping that she held all the answers. "Why, even John de la Pole has accepted a position in Henry's government."

"Uniting with Francis now has nothing to do with Richard," Elizabeth's mother lectured. "You've lived through enough civil war to know that loyalties and alliances are forged and broken with every change that takes place. Richard is dead, and Henry is king. People will realign themselves."

Chills ran through Elizabeth's body as her mother coldly referred to a war that Elizabeth had assumed was over.

"But I am queen. If a York on the throne is what they are fighting for, why still fight?"

Her mother abandoned the work she was pretending to focus on. "You just said yourself that you will be a submissive wife and dutiful mother. Besides, Henry has placed no crown upon your head. Does that sound like a York on the throne? Of course they will still fight. They are men."

"But my son," Elizabeth said as her hand flew to her expanding abdomen. She ignored the reference to her lack of coronation.

"In fifteen years," the former queen guessed with a glance at her daughter's stomach, "men will be willing to fight for him. He is nothing but a future dream right now."

"A dream of a future for our country united in peace! How can the people not desire that?" Elizabeth cried.

Her mother sighed and seemed more like her old self. "You do not understand men or politics, Bess. It is what makes you a better person than the rest of us."

Later that spring, Elizabeth was relieved that her mother was not in attendance when she learned that Henry had pulled Humphrey and Thomas Stafford from sanctuary. She was shocked that he would violate the laws of the church in this way, though she knew that her father had done the same thing. Humphrey had been executed for his role in the treasonous plans, but Tom had been pardoned though heavily fined. By the fall of that year, Henry had obtained a papal bull excluding those accused of treason from the benefits of claiming sanctuary.

September 1486

The lingering summer heat lay upon the country like a blanket. Elizabeth sat in a shady spot in the gardens of Winchester Palace, where she had moved to be away from the disease infested city of London during her pregnancy. Henry had also been insistent that his son, for it could only be a boy, would be born at Winchester as the traditional location of King Arthur's Camelot. High expectations already existed for this unborn child.

Because she could not tolerate the stifling air inside, Elizabeth was often found under the arbors using a fan to stir the air into some semblance of a breeze. With her eyes closed, she forced herself to loosen her tight muscles. Beginning with her forehead that was lined with tension, she mentally moved down her body and released air from her lungs with each muscle relaxed. When she reached her abdomen, she smiled at the kicks and turns that were beyond her control.

She sighed and leaned back with both hands placed on the roundness of her baby that would be entering the world in the next six weeks or so. Something firm pressed up against her hand and she wondered if it were her son's little hand. She longed to hold his tiny fingers in her own. Soon the mysterious body part moved on as the baby rolled and turned within her womb. How miraculous that God could create this new life within her with no effort on her part.

The Lady Margaret had already prepared Elizabeth's lying in rooms and had been attempting to convince Elizabeth that she must enter them soon in order to be certain that six weeks would be spent there before the baby was born. Although Elizabeth appreciated her mother-in-law's attention and devotion to her unborn grandchild, she had no desire to spend a month and a half waiting alone in a dark room for her child to be born. Her mother had assured her that no such precautions were necessary. The mother of twelve was unable to convince the mother of one that she was knowledgeable on the topic. The fact that Lady Margaret's one child was king gave her all the authority she needed.

Elizabeth was delaying as long as she could but knew that by the end of September she would have to enter the luxurious but dull rooms. At least she would have her mother and cousin, Margaret, with her. She had insisted upon having those two present, as well as Marjory Cobbe, who had served as midwife for the birth of Elizabeth's two youngest sisters. Henry had mediated between his wife and mother and gained the Lady Margaret's acquiescence to these three attendants.

"Are you staying cool, my dear?"

Elizabeth smiled at the sound of Henry's voice. Throughout her pregnancy, his status as an only child had been clear. He was attentive and constantly concerned that Elizabeth was healthy and comfortable. She did not mind the attention but wished she was more able to calm his fears.

"I am perfectly well, my love." She opened her eyes and patted the bench next to her in invitation. He joined her and placed one of his hands between hers on her rounded belly. A smile lit his face when he was welcomed by a small protrusion pushing forth to meet his hand. He placed a lingering kiss on her cheek.

"I am glad you've found a cool spot to rest." He wiped sweat from his brow as he spoke.

Elizabeth laughed. "Well, relatively cool anyway. Can you remember a September so warm?"

"Well, having lived in France, yes."

"Of course, that was a silly question. The child robs me of my brain," she sighed. "I always wondered why my mother claimed that, but now I know it to be true."

A few locks of damp hair had escaped her pins and were

plastered to her face. Henry pushed them back and kissed her temple. "You are beautiful. Do you know that?"

She laughed again. "I do not feel very beautiful at the moment. I am swollen and red with heat, but I am happy that you are pleased, husband."

"I am," he said, kissing her again. "Very pleased."

"Pleased enough to celebrate even if I give you a daughter?" As her time approached, she became more concerned that the babe would not be the expected male heir.

He gazed into her eyes, and she was warmed by the emotion displayed. She knew that others saw caution, concern for the treasury, and even fear, but whenever his eyes found her she saw love.

"I will be more than content with a healthy daughter and wife," he assured her. "We will have plenty of time to have more sons and daughters whatever this one may be." He patted her stomach as if including the babe in the conversation.

"You put my mind at ease. Thank you, Henry."

"Thank you, my sweet Elizabeth, for being a wonderful wife and giving me what I know will be a beautiful child."

~ ~ ~ ~

The days at Winchester were more easy-going than those at Westminster had been. Fewer courtiers filled the hall, and Elizabeth felt more freedom to enjoy herself away from prying eyes. With Cecily, Margaret, and her mother, she held her own small, informal court and ignored her mother-in-law's requests that she enter her lying in rooms.

The weather finally began to cool toward the middle of the month and the women enjoyed the crisp air outside. Elizabeth brought puppies from the kennel into the gardens to play, though it reminded her of her time at Sherriff Hutton with Edward. She continued to pray daily for him because it was clear that speaking to Henry was not quickening his release. Maybe the birth of an heir would make him feel confident enough to give Edward his freedom.

Elizabeth watched as Margaret and Cecily ran and laughed together. Her desire to help them find husbands and happiness had driven her to bring up these topics with Henry as well. Although he was affectionate toward her as a husband, he made it evident that his word would be the last on matters of state.

The bulk of her midsection kept Elizabeth on the sidelines as the other women ran, threw sticks, and rolled in the grass with the dogs. It was amazing how young one could feel with a litter of puppies to play with. Elizabeth had begun to feel uncomfortable pressure in her abdomen and knew that she would not be allowed outside for much longer. Cecily came to sit next to her in the cool grass.

"Cecily, I am glad we are able to enjoy this day. I am afraid that I will not be able to delay entering confinement beyond this week."

Cecily nodded her agreement. "The king's mother does have a way of getting what she wants."

"Truly, she wanted me there at least a week ago, but I could not see the sense in spending six weeks in a dark, airless room." A stronger pain made her gasp and her hand flew to her stomach.

"Bess, are you alright?" Cecily turned to her with concern etched into her face.

"Quite." Elizabeth forced a small laugh through her grimace. "The babe is just getting large and making me more uncomfortable."

Cecily raised a doubtful eyebrow. "Discomfort? It looked like pain."

"Just a little. It is too early," Elizabeth insisted.

Her sister decided to take her at her word and relaxed in the soft grass. She too was considering the destiny of their cousins Margaret and Edward. What cruel twist of fate left them parentless and in the control of an inhospitable guardian. She also wondered when her own future would be determined. Henry had his wife and his heir. When would Margaret be content to release her spare princess?

Elizabeth gasped again next to her. This time, Cecily jumped to her feet and called to the other women.

"We must get Bess inside," she ordered. "She is having childbirth pains."

"But it is too early," Margaret pointed out unnecessarily as she stood with bits of grass and twigs stuck in her tangled hair. One look at Elizabeth's face caused her own to turn red. "I'm sorry, Cecily. What can I do?"

"Find our mother. Tell her we will meet her in the birthing room."

Cecily motioned for the other ladies to help her, and they pulled Elizabeth to her feet. As they did so, Cecily felt warm wetness surround their feet. She looked into Elizabeth's eyes and saw confirmation there. She also saw fear.

Her eyes fell on one of the ladies who was not helping support Elizabeth. "Have a messenger sent to the king immediately." Turning to her sister she softened her tone. "You will be fine, dear Bess. God is with you, and may he help us get you inside before the child is born."

By the time they arrived in the carefully laid out room, Elizabeth was panting and trying to resist the urge to bear down. Tears of relief flooded her eyes when she saw her mother hurrying toward her.

"Mama, you're here. It's too early." It was a ridiculous thing to say, but she felt her burden ease giving these problems over to her mother who had successfully given birth to a dozen children.

"There could be some miscalculation," her mother said soothingly, though they all knew that it wasn't true. Elizabeth and Henry had been married almost exactly eight months ago. Miscalculation wasn't a possibility. The baby was coming too soon. The dowager queen took charge of the room and ordered each person to complete a task, including the sending of Margaret to go into the chapel and pray for a safe delivery. Even the less pious Elizabeth Woodville was taking no chances with her eldest daughter and first grandchild.

Elizabeth was laid gently on the bed, but she insisted that she needed to be on the birthing stool.

"Not yet, my dear," her mother insisted. "You need to relax. It is the best way to keep the little one where he is for a little bit longer."

"I cannot!" Elizabeth cried.

Her mother appeared unaffected by her outburst. She gently pushed back Elizabeth's loosened hair and patted her face with a cool cloth. "You can, sweet Bess. Relax."

At that moment, the midwife entered the room.

"I will need to examine you," she said to Elizabeth without words of greeting.

Elizabeth's mother stood and looked down her nose at Marjory Cobbe. "You will remember that you address the queen."

Marjory bowed her head, "Yes, my lady. I was just told that it was an emergency."

Elizabeth's mother scanned the room for the culprit but addressed Mrs. Cobbe. "Young women always believe that labor is an emergency. My daughter is doing perfectly well, and you will show her due respect."

"Yes, my lady."

The atmosphere in the room quieted but also gained a level of peace with the confident arrogance of Elizabeth Woodville. The examination complete, she was reassured that her evaluation of the situation was correct. Elizabeth and her baby seemed to be doing fine, but the child would be born today.

Henry had yet to arrive at Winchester, so early in the morning of September 20th after a long night of labor, a second messenger was sent to him with the news that he was the proud father of a small but healthy baby boy.

Lady Margaret fussed over the fact that her carefully laid out birth plan had already been cast aside. To think, the king's wife going into labor while sitting in the garden! Now that the baby was born, the remainder of the schedule would be followed religiously. Elizabeth kept to the room, which was decorated with tapestries of subtle colors and calm scenes. Little air or sunlight was allowed in, at least when Lady Margaret was in the room. No men were allowed in the room for any reason.

This is why Henry was forced to sneak into his own wife's room. He arrived at Winchester as soon as he was able and was eager to see Elizabeth.

"It is out of the question," his mother stated. She held out the tiny infant to him as if for inspection. "She has presented you with a son. You can wait until she has been churched to be presented to you."

"Mother, she is my wife. She need not be presented to me." A grin split his face as he stared in wonder at the small bundle with a wisp of dark hair peeking out.

"For heaven's sake, Henry," Margaret continued. "You are the king, and you must behave as such. Do not be so enamored with this woman."

Henry looked at his mother, but could not find the desire to argue with her while he held his son. His tiny, perfect son. "This woman is the woman you insisted that I would marry for years before I actually determined to do so. I have married her upon your command, but I love her upon God's."

"You will wait," Margaret stated firmly as though she had forgotten that he was the king and not her little boy.

That very evening Henry was allowed into the room by a most unlikely ally, his mother-in-law.

"She has been eagerly awaiting your arrival," she said as she unlocked the door for him to enter. He chose not to notice that she did not call him 'your grace'.

"Elizabeth," he whispered as he entered the darkened room. He stepped carefully among the rushes, afraid of making a sound should he wake his wife or son. His eyes were still adjusting to the dimness when he was caught in an embrace that almost knocked him off his feet.

"Henry! You are here." Elizabeth held him tightly, and his arms wound around her waist. It felt strange to find her so much thinner than the last time he had held her. He kissed the top of her head until she turned her face toward him, and he covered her cheeks, eyes, and lips with his kisses. She returned them fervently.

"I am sorry I was not here sooner," he said. He ran his hands up and down her spine, reveling in the feel of her closeness.

"Do not apologize," she insisted. "I know you came as quickly as possible. More importantly, I have someone for you to meet."

Elizabeth guided Henry to an elaborate cradle with a tiny bundle inside.

"He was brought to me earlier," Henry said, certain that she must know this.

"Ah, but then he did not have a name. Can you truly meet someone if you do not know their name?"

He smiled and enjoyed the idea of the two of them sharing this private moment, stolen from the eyes of councilors and attendants.

"What is his name to be?"

"Surely that is for you to decide, as he is your son and heir. I have a feeling though, that you will like the name that has been placed upon my heart for him." She lifted the sleeping child and kissed his button of a nose. "I believe he will someday be King Arthur." She lifted him to his father in a private ceremony more moving to Henry than his own coronation.

"Prince Arthur," he murmured in agreement as he took his son and gazed into his cloudy eyes. "I am a very blessed man."

The three of them standing together with only faint light streaming around the edges of tapestries made a quiet picture resembling the holy family: father, son, and devoted mother.

~ ~ ~ ~

The next day, Elizabeth was allowed to sleep late. She would be kept in confinement until her churching, and her ladies understood her exhaustion. Her cousin, Margaret tiptoed to the side of the bed. Her adoration for Elizabeth was akin worship. She wondered that it never became jealousy. Though their fathers were brothers, Elizabeth was the one with the beauty, royal husband, love of the people, and now a perfect child. Margaret didn't mind. She did not desire to be put on display. Pursuing royal dreams had never gotten her father anywhere.

She watched Elizabeth sleep with the attentiveness of a mother watching her child. The gentle rise and fall of her chest was hypnotic, and Margaret shook her head to regain her focus. Her hand reached out to push Elizabeth's loosened hair into place. When she touched her face, Margaret gasped.

"Cecily, come right away," she said quietly but urgently.

Cecily quickly came from the connecting room. "What is it, cousin?"

Margaret looked up hopelessly with tears in her eyes. "It is a fever."

Color left Cecily's face and she touched her fingertips to Elizabeth's skin in hope of disproving Margaret's diagnosis. She pulled them back almost before making contact.

"She is burning up." Now that Cecily recognized the fever, other symptoms became clear. The flushed cheeks they had thought indicated radiant motherhood spoke a much more evil language. The steady breathing suddenly appeared too slow and shallow. No, God, please, Cecily thought.

"What can we do?" Margaret asked with tears streaming down her face. She had lost her mother to childbed fever and her father to death at his brother's orders. With her only brother imprisoned indefinitely, how much more could the girl be burdened with?

"Come, Margaret," Cecily said as she pulled the girl into her arms. "We will care for her to the best of our abilities. She is a strong woman. She is a York, as are you."

Margaret nodded and wiped shaking fingers across her tear-streaked face.

"Now, send Bess's most pious ladies to the chapel to pray and get that midwife back in here."

By the time the midwife rushed back into the room, Cecily was dabbing Elizabeth's face and neck with a cool, wet cloth. Elizabeth's eyes were closed but she did not seem to be asleep.

"What must we do?" Cecily demanded before Mistress Cobbe could speak.

"First thing is to warm it up in here," Marjory said as she walked awkwardly into the room. She had an uneven stride that was evidence of a childhood cart accident. "Her body is hot because it fights with itself," she continued, touching Elizabeth's flushed cheek. "Give it the heat it needs."

"The doctor wants to bleed her."

Marjory let out a harsh laugh. "And how many people do you

know have said they felt better after a bleeding?"

Cecily examined the woman's face. It was up to her to decide whose advice to take with her sister's life in the balance. She had not shared her concerns with Henry or his mother yet. Once they knew, they would take over Elizabeth's care. Cecily must take advantage of the time she had to do her best for Bess. She nodded, her decision made.

"Margaret," she said. "Cover the windows and have wood added to the fire." Margaret rushed to do as ordered when Cecily added, "And do not let that doctor step foot in this room again."

The eyes of Marjory and Cecily met with a new respect in each for the other.

"She also needs to eat," Marjory continued. "Broth is best."

Cecily looked to her cousin, who nodded. "I will see to it straight away," Margaret said before rushing from the room.

When she returned with the thin soup, Cecily was on her knees before the small altar that had been set up for Bess to use for her devotions during her confinement. Hearing the girl arrive, she crossed herself and stood. She took the bowl from Margaret's hands and they moved together to the bed.

"Bess, sweet sister," Cecily whispered. "You must wake and take some nourishment."

Elizabeth's eyelids fluttered but did not open.

"Come now, Bess. It is tasty broth," Margaret begged.

Elizabeth opened her eyes and seemed to struggle to focus them on the two women. It was all the opportunity Cecily required.

"Here you are," she said, forcing a spoonful into Elizabeth's mouth.

The warm liquid revived Elizabeth somewhat and she woke enough to hungrily finish the bowl. Cecily was pleased with this result and sent Margaret for more.

"You will get better," Cecily informed her sister.

Elizabeth nodded weakly, but Cecily was not discouraged.

"I had a peace come over me while at prayer. I believe God will heal you. You have not completed his plan for your life."

Elizabeth focused her eyes on Cecily for just a moment, smiled slightly, and fell back to sleep.

The next day, Henry stormed into the room careless of the noise or inappropriateness of his presence. He rushed to Elizabeth's bedside and kneeled before her.

"Elizabeth, you must wake."

"What are you doing?" Cecily demanded, not caring that she addressed the king.

Henry stood and strode across the room to her. "Why wasn't I informed of her illness?"

Cecily stepped back from him, surprised that he could become such a commanding presence. Still she was not afraid. She had grown up surrounded by larger than life, opinionated men. "I am caring for her with Margaret's assistance."

"Has the doctor been called?" The heat seemed to go out of his anger, and he centered on their common goal.

"I will not allow that man in the room again." Cecily could be a diplomatic princess, but she also had the ability to enforce her will. In some things, her mother's lessons were helpful.

"What? Why?"

"He recommended bleeding her."

"Then we shall." He moved as though he planned to bring the doctor back that very instant. Cecily put out a hand to stop him.

"Your grace," she said. "Henry, think about the bleedings that you have observed." She looked directly into his eyes. "My father was bled in the hope of healing him."

His hard gaze bore into her eyes, so much like Elizabeth's that it softened him. He let out the breath that he didn't realize he was holding and released the tension in his shoulders. Rubbing the nape of his neck, he struggled with the decision more than any other he had been forced to make.

"So be it," he said. "What can I do?"

Together they fed Elizabeth as much broth as they could get her to take. They talked to her and to each other for several hours. It felt surreal to Cecily to share such intimacy with the king. This was the man that Bess had raged about to their mother, and now he looked down upon her with unmistakable love. God's ways are definitely not our ways, Cecily thought wryly.

"What is going on in here?" asked the demanding voice of Lady Margaret from the sitting room.

Cecily almost laughed out loud when Henry straightened and a look of fear flitted across his face. Even the king can be made to feel like a naughty boy at the stern voice of his mother, it would seem. It had lasted only a moment though, before he stood and set his jaw. He met his mother at the door.

"What is the meaning of this intrusion, mother?"

Lady Margaret looked taken aback by his tone. "What are you doing in here?"

"I am caring for my wife, and you must lower your voice."

The expression on Lady Margaret's face left Cecily wondering if Henry had ever stood up to her before. She found she was clasping Elizabeth's hand firmly as if cheering for him.

"You should not be here," Lady Margaret insisted. "What if you should fall ill?"

"Because I am the king, and therefore less disposable than my wife?"

Lady Margaret shrugged, "Well, yes, to put it plainly."

Henry shook his head and moved back to Elizabeth's bedside opposite of Cecily.

"Henry, really. This is quite unheard of," Lady Margaret went on.

"I do not care if it is not heard of," Henry growled. "I will be with Elizabeth. This happened because she gave me a son. I will not leave her."

Lady Margaret looked from Henry to Cecily and back again. "Fine," she said before stomping from the room.

The next day, Elizabeth woke and was able to think and speak with more clarity than she had since giving birth. Cecily knelt at the small altar to offer up prayers of thanksgiving and was surprised when Henry went to his knees beside her.

As they crossed themselves and rose, they shared a smile of victory. Death would not claim their beloved Elizabeth. Cecily no longer wondered how Bess could love this man. The stern, quiet exterior housed a devoted soul. As they crossed the room to Elizabeth's bed, she held out her hands to them.

"Thank you for nursing me," she said. Though she was still pale and gaunt, her smile shone with promised health.

"Oh, Bess, I would nurse you if you came down with the plague," Cecily said.

"God forbid!" Henry said, crossing himself.

Elizabeth laughed. "You will have to excuse my sister's outspokenness. She seems to be trying to take the place of our beloved Mary." Enough time had passed that Mary's name could be spoken with the smile of memory and not the pain of mourning.

Cecily joined in Elizabeth's laughter. "I suppose I have become bolder in my old age."

Henry watched the two lovely sisters with a smile but could not join in their laughter with his fears for Elizabeth's life still so near the surface.

"Can we let in some air?" Elizabeth asked. "It is horribly stuffy in here."

"I'm sure that would be acceptable now that you are well enough to request it," Cecily said.

"Should we not wait and summon the doctor . . . . or Mistress Cobbe?" Henry amended when he saw the look on Cecily's face at the mention of the doctor.

Cecily was already throwing shutters aside. "My sister is a grown woman and capable of determining what her wishes are."

One side of Henry's mouth lifted in a wry smile. "She is the bold one," he whispered to Elizabeth. "I am thankful for my choice of York princess."

Elizabeth swatted his hand. "Are you certain? Cecily remains unmarried."

Now Henry did laugh out loud. It was a testament to how much their relationship had grown that they could joke about this once painful subject.

~ ~ ~ ~

Arthur filled Elizabeth's days with happiness. She no longer took note of evenings when Henry worked late into the night, though she was joyful when he appeared. Her heart was filled with love for the tiny human that had been created between them. Each gaze of his grey eyes and grasp of his tiny fingers bound her to him in a connection she had never felt with any other person. She now understood what the priest meant when he said that God loves people as his children. She would not hesitate to die for Arthur if it were to be required of her.

Winter 1486

Motherhood made Elizabeth's concerns fade away. Few things held the importance that they once had when she gazed upon her infant. Arthur would take after his father. This was already clear to her in his dark hair and serious eyes. Her only regret was that she could not nurse her own child. She understood the reasons why, of course. She was unlikely to conceive another child if she was nursing this one. Nobody needed to explain to her why it was so important for a king to have more than one heir. Still her heart ached every time she was forced to hand Arthur over to the round, buxom wet-nurse.

Arthur's rockers had little to do since his mother frequently held him or rocked him herself whenever he was not in the arms of the wet-nurse. They served more as company for Elizabeth than servants for her son and gave her tips on baby care. Not that she required much help. As the oldest of her father's ten children, she grew up watching and assisting with the care of younger siblings.

Although Henry was frequently kept away, he checked in with his wife and child at least once each day. Whether to take supper, walk in the garden, or simply sit by the fire, he made it a priority to spend time with them and ensure that they received all they needed. Elizabeth loved these moments when they were a family like any other in England, and they need not think about being king, queen, and prince.

Arthur did not seem to suffer from being born a month early. Though he was somewhat small, he was healthy in every way. Only a lack of baby fat attested to the fact that he had not spent quite the normally required amount of time in the womb. With the dedicated services of the wet-nurse, even this deficiency was soon taken care of. As his baby thighs obtained the customary rolls and cheerful belly laughs filled the nursery, concerns for his health dissipated entirely.

Little did Elizabeth know, this peace that they enjoyed as a loving family was the calm before the storm.

Spring 1487

Elizabeth was playing on the floor with a decidedly chunkier baby Arthur when Henry stormed into the room. She jumped to her feet and a nurse swooped in to remove the baby. Never had she seen Henry fuming this way.

"What is it, Henry?"

"Tell me why you did not believe your brothers to be dead," he ordered.

Elizabeth sucked in a breath. She had not thought of her brothers' deaths since Arthur was born. His birth had become a dividing line in her life, and she did not allow the ghosts of the past to cross it. She did not know what to say. Henry stepped closer.

"Why did you believe they were alive?" he asked more calmly.

"I'm not sure," she stuttered uncertainly. "I suppose that I believed what I wanted to believe, that my uncle would not do such a thing and that they were simply hidden away."

"What made you think that?" he pressed.

She took a deep breath to brace herself against this line of questioning. "Richard and Anne had assured me that they were safe. I believed them."

Henry shook his head and paced the room, rubbing the nape of his neck to relieve the tension found there. "But where could they have been?"

Elizabeth suddenly realized what Henry was asking. "Do you believe they are alive?" She couldn't keep the hope from her voice, but at the same time wondered what it would mean for her small son if it were true.

Henry stopped moving and looked carefully into her eyes as if he could discern the truth there. Giving up, he resumed pacing.

"Henry, what has brought this up again? You told me yourself that they died at my uncle's hand."

"Because that is what everyone believed," he said in exasperation. "For heaven's sake, Bess. They had not been seen in over a year. My men had searched everywhere for them in coordination with the hunt for traitors after my coronation."

"But now?"

"I don't know." He dropped into a chair and hung his head in his hands. "I just don't know, Bess."

"What makes you doubt?" she asked. "My mother always believed as you do and said I was naïve to believe Richard. What has made you change your mind?"

"I didn't say that I've changed my mind. There are rumors."

Tightness began in the center of Elizabeth's chest and spread out until she felt the need to sit down next to her husband. "What kind of rumors?"

He took a deep breath and slowly released it before answering. "In Ireland, our discontent York supporters are gathering around a boy."

Elizabeth clutched a hand to her breast. It could not be.

"Messages have brought conflicting information," Henry continued. "Some say he is claiming to be your younger brother, Richard. Others say he is Edward of Warwick."

"Who, of course, remains in the tower," Elizabeth said. The tightness lessened as she realized that there was no way this was her brother. This was a pretender being used to rally rebels. If they couldn't even decide who he was, he was certainly nobody. She placed a hand on Henry's, sorry that he was required to deal with this pointless uprising.

"Yes," Henry stated firmly. "For this precise reason."

Elizabeth nodded her assent. She would not debate the issue of Edward's ongoing imprisonment at this time. Her heart sank at the thought of men going to war once again, and this time with an unknown pretender leading the way.

"You do not believe it could be Richard either?" he asked, needing her reassurance.

"I do not," she admitted with dismay.

He leaned over and laid his head upon her breast. She combed her fingers through his thinning hair and comforted him as if he were her child.

~ ~ ~ ~

"Margaret, I would like to accompany you the next time you visit your brother."

Margaret looked somewhat taken aback by the unexpected request. Elizabeth's visits to Edward had become less frequent as his time of imprisonment lengthened. Assuming that her cousin was plagued by guilt, Margaret had ceased inviting her.

"Of course, Bess," Margaret replied, attempting to keep her voice neutral. "I was planning to visit Edward tomorrow and take him some new books."

"Is there anything else he needs?"

His freedom. Margaret wished that she could say it, but knew that it was not within Elizabeth's power. "He does require ways to fill his time. It is difficult for a boy his age to be alone without entertainment."

Elizabeth pursed her lips and fingered a fold of her skirt while she thought. "What of a dog?"

"I do not know what his gaolers would think of that," Margaret said doubtfully.

"But, Edward," Elizabeth pressed. "He would be delighted, would he not?"

Catching Elizabeth's excitement, Margaret smiled and agreed, "Yes, Bess. He undoubtedly would be."

The next day saw the cousins set out to visit Edward at the

Tower, carrying satchels of books and treats with a puppy nipping at their heels. Elizabeth chastised herself for staying away so long when she saw the way Edward's eyes lit up when she entered his room. It did not compare to his burst of joy when his new cellmate jumped into his arms.

"Edward, I have missed you," Elizabeth said, pulling him into a tight embrace.

"I miss you, too, Bess. I'm sure that you are busy being queen," he said without anger.

"I am blessed with a forgiving cousin," Elizabeth ruffled the hair of the boy and the dog in turn. "Are you kept well?"

"Yes, I have my books. Margaret is always nice to bring me things, and I get outside when I can."

"I will make sure that you are given adequate time in the courtyard." Edward was a boy, not a criminal. She saw little reason for him to be kept under close guard, or kept at all for that matter.

"Bess, remember when we built that fort out of branches and weeds?"

Edward did not have to remind her of their time in the north. It entered her mind whenever she was too weak to push it aside. It made her question whether she was doing the right thing, marrying Henry and allowing Edward to remain in the Tower, whenever she brought out those memories.

"It was great fun," she said in a low whisper that carried more emotion than Edward's question required.

Margaret's eyes flashed to Elizabeth, and she vowed that she would no longer let Henry's actions create a wall between them.

After spending the afternoon discussing happy memories, Elizabeth gave strict directions to Edward's guards that he was to have time outdoors each day. This would be in their interest as well, she had informed them, since he had a dog that would need to be exercised. The stern face she had put forth to them evaporated into a girlish smile when she turned to Margaret. They left the Tower with much lighter hearts than they had arrived with.

As they strolled through the gardens before returning to Elizabeth's rooms, Elizabeth was happy to have what she believed to be happy news to impart.

"Margaret, I believe that Henry has a match in mind for you."

Her forehead creased and eyes narrowed, Margaret seemed to take a moment to understand what Elizabeth was saying. The moment the truth dawned on her was obvious as her expression shifted to wide eyed wonder.

Elizabeth laughed as she pulled the younger woman to her side. "You know of Richard Pole, he is Henry's Constable of Harlech and Montgomery castles, and I believe I may have even seen you casting admiring glances his way."

Margaret blushed and turned her head away. She had not believed that Henry would think of a marriage for her with Edward in prison and Cecily still unmarried. She also had not thought her observations of Sir Richard Pole were so obvious.

"He is acceptable to you?"

"Quite, your grace," Margaret managed to mumble as conflicting emotions held her tongue captive. She felt Elizabeth's hand on her cheek and forced herself to look up.

"I believe that he will make you quite happy, and you deserve happiness and a loving household."

"Thank you, Bess. But what about Edward?"

Elizabeth released a sigh upon hearing the question she knew Margaret would ask. Gently pushing back a few strands of auburn hair that had strayed from Margaret's veil, she gave voice to her prepared response. "You cannot put your life on hold because of Edward's situation. I will continue to encourage Henry to release him, but, in the meantime, your future has been determined. The Welsh countryside will be a welcome change, and you can write to

Edward frequently. I will take over your visits to him."

Seeing the torn look on Margaret's face, Elizabeth continued. "You must look to the path that God has laid out for you until it becomes clear what his plans are for your brother. It is all either of us can do."

Finally, a hesitant smile reached Margaret's lips. "He is acceptable to me, Bess. Sir Richard, I mean. Quite acceptable."

~ ~ ~ ~

The next time Elizabeth spoke to her husband, the circumstances were more encouraging. Although rumors of rebels gathering in the north continued, Henry had not yet moved to put the revolt down. Soon he would be leaving to do so, and Elizabeth relished their time together before he must leave her again. They walked hand in hand through the garden enjoying the scents of spring.

"I have decided upon a husband for your sister," Henry said.

"For Cecily?"

He laughed. "Well, not for Catherine or Bridget, who are not yet ten years old."

"Of course," she said, laughing at herself. "I had just not thought about the subject for some time. She will be thrilled!"

"I do hope so. I have chosen John Welles, my mother's half-brother.

Elizabeth was thoughtful as she tried to remember what she could about Viscount Welles. He must be close to twenty years older than Cecily, but that was not necessarily a problem. He seemed healthy and successful. His close blood relationship to the king was a point in his favor, of course, but he also was not too highly ranked, which would please Cecily.

"I'm sure he is a wise choice."

"I am glad it pleases you," Henry said. "I will present the idea to John as soon as possible."

"You have not asked him?"

"No, I thought to ask your opinion first."

Elizabeth squeezed his hand. "I am honored, your grace."

He looked sideways at her to see the playful smile on her face.

"I would be certain that I have the approval of my queen," he said, turning toward her.

"Your queen?"

"Yes. Your coronation has been put off long enough as well. We shall have you crowned in November when travel to London is made easier by weather and crops are all put up for winter."

"Oh, Henry!" she exclaimed and flung herself into his arms. "This does mean so much to me," she gushed. Elizabeth refused to be hurt by the months that had gone by before her coronation was scheduled, but would be happy that planning would begin.

He kissed her ardently before replying. "It is about time," he admitted. "You are a patient and generous wife."

"I trust you, Henry."

She did not add that she was aware of his mother's conspiring to delay her coronation, most notably until she had proven that she could produce an heir. Let her be content with them both then. Henry had adhered to her wishes, and Elizabeth had given birth to a perfect baby boy. The Lady Margaret had no further reasons to put the occasion off.

Henry took her into his arms again, and no more words were spoken on the matter.

June 1487

Henry had left to put down the revolt in the north. Fervent York supporters gathered around the boy that they knew could not possibly be either Richard, duke of York, or Edward, earl of Warwick. Elizabeth still wasn't sure what their end goal was. A prince who combined the houses of Lancaster and York was heir to the throne. How could they not support him?

She was crushed when word started filtering back to her about who was involved in the rebellion. Her cousin, John de la Pole, the earl of Lincoln, began to appear as the leader of the revolt. He was son to her father's sister, Elizabeth, and had been named Richard's heir when his son died. Elizabeth wondered if he was fighting now in the name of this false prince in order to take the crown that had been once promised to him. She was stunned that he was willing to take it from her son's head in the process. Fighting against Henry was one thing, but Arthur had as much York blood as John did.

Surprising many die hard Yorkists, John had reconciled himself to Henry's reign after Richard's defeat. Rather than pressing his own claim as Richard's heir, he had served at Henry's court for over a year before disappearing. It was discovered that he had fled to Margaret of Burgundy, sister of Richard III and Edward IV. From there, he began his work as a rebel.

The young pretender had been crowned as Edward VI in Dublin on May 24th. Apparently they had decided that he was Edward of Warwick rather than claiming her brother's identity. The ridiculousness of it made anger rise in Elizabeth's chest. John certainly knew that the true earl of Warwick was held in the Tower of London, so what was his real goal? What had Henry done to drive him away?

The rebellion boiled over at Stoke on June 16th. The false Edward VI's troops were led by the earl of Lincoln. John de Vere, earl of Oxford and long time supporter of Henry Tudor, led the king's troops against Lincoln's Irish mercenary forces. The Yorkists did not stand a chance against the strength of the loyal Lancastrians and those Yorkists who had decided to support their queen and the united royal family.

When Elizabeth received word that John de la Pole had been one of the many killed in battle, she cried for him and for all the unnecessary losses she had experienced in her short life. He was one more good man gone far too early due to pride and the quest for glory. So many lives had been lost to the warring between Lancaster and York. It would end now because nobody remained to carry it on.

~ ~ ~ ~

When Henry returned to London, he was welcomed by joyful crowds and a grateful wife. She was surprised at the intense feelings that coursed through her body as he embraced her. Their marriage had begun with love that she gave in obedience. The love she felt for him now was full and freely given.

"Thank the Lord that you have returned victorious," she said when he held her at arm's length.

"He was with us," Henry agreed. "I am sorry about your cousin."

Elizabeth closed her eyes and pictured John, young, handsome, and impetuous. "He knew the path he was choosing when he rebelled against his rightful and anointed king."

Henry tilted her face upwards. "And I'm sure that knowing that makes his loss no less painful."

Elizabeth smiled through the tears threatening to spill. "You are an understanding husband, Henry. I thank God for placing us together."

"As do I," he said, pulling her more firmly against his body.

Henry left orders for horses to be cared for and men to be accommodated, so that he could retire with Elizabeth to her rooms. When they wanted to be alone, it was to her suite that they escaped since his rooms were still connected to his mother's. Margaret took a fierce amount of pleasure in having Henry at her beck and call. Elizabeth took some comfort in the number of times Margaret used the connecting door only to find that Henry had decided to sleep in Elizabeth's bed.

This would be one of those nights. Elizabeth arranged for a bath to be brought up and prepared for her husband. As she did, she smiled at the memory of her parents disappearing to bathe when her father had returned victorious from exile. She had been jealous that her father's love for her mother was greater than his love for her. Thankfulness overwhelmed her that she unexpectedly found herself in love in the same way. Henry was as completely different from her father as night from day, but Elizabeth had found that she appreciated some of these contrasts, though it did not make her love her father less.

After Henry had been bathed quite completely, they relaxed in Elizabeth's private sitting room with shutters opened to let in a cooling breeze. The sun shone in, and one could believe that all was right with the world, that hundreds of men had not just died fighting in a war that should have been over.

Elizabeth poured the wine and arranged a plate of bread and cheese herself to eliminate the need of allowing anyone into the room. She felt at peace. At this moment, she was just a wife welcoming home her husband. Soon she was reminded that he was also the king.

"Your mother will need to retire to Bermondsey," he said in the abrupt way of one who hopes that unpleasant information said quickly will be better received.

"A nunnery, why?"

"There is evidence of her involvement." Henry appeared to be speaking to his wine glass for his eyes refused to meet Elizabeth's.

"In what?" Before Henry answered, her heart dropped. She knew before he spoke.

"She was assisting John de la Pole. My informants believe she sent letters to Margaret in Burgundy, encouraging her to assist. She provided cash for the Irish mercenaries. It remains unclear exactly how deep her involvement went." After a pause within which Elizabeth remained silent, he added, "I will not have my mother-in-law tried for treason."

Elizabeth gasped. "She couldn't have!" But as she said it, she knew that her mother could and had.

Henry only shook his head. "I'm sorry, Elizabeth. I have tried to protect you from this, but she must be neutralized for the sake of our son."

"Her grandson," Elizabeth whispered. "How could she plot against her grandson?"

Henry wished that he had an answer when Elizabeth looked at him so pleadingly. Why indeed? Why was Elizabeth Woodville not pleased with her daughter on the throne and her grandson as heir?

"Perhaps she will be more content after your coronation, but I will not wait. She must go to Bermondsey immediately."

Elizabeth did not argue. She was still trying to process the fact that her own mother had plotted against her. Her mother had insisted that Elizabeth marry Henry and assured her that this was the way to keep the York family on the throne and then arranged to destroy them. Maybe it was not only men who needed a war to feel alive.

"Elizabeth, are you alright?" Henry placed a hand on her arm.

She nodded. "I am shocked. That is all. I thought my mother to be content with things as they are, but maybe she would never be content."

"Unless one of her sons wore the crown?" Henry asked. He knew that he shouldn't and that it would hurt Elizabeth more, but he must know the truth.

Elizabeth shook her head in bewilderment. "She has insisted that they are both dead time and time again. Would she have insisted upon our marriage if she believed one of them was alive?"

Henry sat back and squinted to better see his thoughts. "Maybe she would," he said. "If she believed that there was a good chance that both of her sons were dead, she would want her daughter married to the king." He moved his gaze to his wife. "But if she held out hope that a son was alive, she would want him to wear the crown."

"Did John give her hope that Edward or Richard was still alive?"

Henry shrugged. "Maybe. It took the rebels a few months to settle on Edward of Warwick as the name of their pretender. While they still considered naming him Richard IV, your mother may have been tempted to believe that it was true."

"Could they have provided that rumor to secure her support?"

Nodding, Henry agreed, "Her money and connections were vital."

Elizabeth seemed encouraged by the explanation for a moment, but then her face fell. "She still was willing to plot against me with only the glimmer of a hope that a son survived."

Henry went to her and gathered her in his arms. "This is why the Lord has a man and a woman leave their parents to cleave to one another." He kissed her. "I will never set anyone above you," he promised.

Almost as an afterthought, Elizabeth asked, "The boy, who was he really?"

Henry released her and returned to his chair with a shrug. "He is nobody. Lambert Simnel turns out to be his name. A simple baker's boy. A pawn."

"What happened to him?" Elizabeth asked, hoping that the young boy had not been sacrificed in battle to grown men's whims.

"I have brought him back to London with me." When Elizabeth turned her face away, he knew she believed the boy imprisoned. "I have put him to work in the kitchens."

Elizabeth's eyes lit up as she turned her face to Henry's. "Truly? He is not in the Tower? Will not be tried for treason?"

"I see no point. He appears to be no older than eleven and understood little of what was going on around him. He does, however, seem to have learned some more desirable skills from this baker."

"Thank you, Henry." Elizabeth went to him and put her arms around him. Maybe he did not understand that she could not bear the death of one more boy, but he had saved this one nonetheless. She loved him for it.

~ ~ ~ ~

The very next day, Elizabeth oversaw the packing of her mother's things and watched the carts roll down the road toward Bermondsey Abbey. Few words had been spoken between them for there was little to say. The truth stood between them like a wall that neither had the equipment to scale.

November 1487

Henry spared no expense on Elizabeth's coronation. If he had waited until an heir had been provided to have her crowned in order to please his Lancastrian supporters, he now gave an elaborate celebration in her honor to appease the Yorkists. Would he ever be able to unite the country under the Tudor banner and eliminate the white and red roses altogether?

Henry observed Elizabeth's sister, Cecily, now married to the faithful Lancastrian, John Welles. After thinking it, Henry shook his head ruefully. It wasn't just other people still dividing everyone into roses of red and white. He hoped that by the time little Arthur was king such distinctions would disappear and they could all just be Englishmen. As always, thoughts of his firstborn son brought a smile of pride to his face that made the lines of stress momentarily fade away.

November 25, St. Catherine's Day, was chosen for Elizabeth's coronation. It was no coincidence that St. Catherine was said to be a gentle daughter of a king. This day, Elizabeth would be put on display in pomp and ceremony, but the people were also reminded that she was a humble wife and mother first. Growing up in the royal family, Elizabeth was an expert at walking this fine line. She excelled at appearing both majestic and demure.

London had loved her father and transferred their love to her when he died. It was for her sake, and that of their pocketbooks, that they gave such loyalty to Henry Tudor. If they could not have a York king, they would settle for a York queen. Three days of celebration would solidify Henry's reign in the eyes of loyal Yorkists in a way that his marriage and his son had not yet done. As the crown was placed upon Elizabeth's Plantagenet red-gold hair, a communal sigh of relief was heard.

A procession of barges travelling down the Thames began the

days of ceremony. The floating pageant gave hundreds a coveted glance of the queen's rumored beauty. The shoreline was crowded with people, and they were not disappointed. Banners and streamers danced in the river breeze, the noise of musicians competed with the cheers of Englishmen, and a red dragon spewed flames. The dragon barge was meant to remind those watching that this was not simply a day to honor Elizabeth, but also the Arthurian legend brought to life in their son.

The barges that had set out from Greenwich came to a stop at the Tower, where Henry and Elizabeth would spend the night before Elizabeth's coronation according to tradition. She wanted to pass their time in the Tower's royal apartment in joyful anticipation of the following day's festivities, but she found that the ghosts of her brothers haunted her as soon as they crossed the threshold.

Henry noticed the cooling of Elizabeth's attitude, but waited until they were in their rooms before speaking of it.

"Are you feeling well, my love?"

"Of course." Smiling up at him, she was happy to be free of the ceremonial gown and robes. It was the simple private moments that meant the most to her.

"You seemed to hesitate as we entered the Tower grounds."

She sighed. "I suppose I did," she admitted. "It is difficult for me to detach this place from things that have happened here." That some things displeasing to her were still happening there, she did not say.

Henry put his arms around her. "Your brothers," he said.

She buried her head in his chest and simply nodded. And Edward, she silently added.

"I will do my best to distract you from such thoughts." He tilted her chin up to kiss her.

After spending a surprisingly pleasant night in the place she had least wanted to visit, Elizabeth was up with the sun with ladies buzzing around her to prepare her for her day. This was a day that would be long remembered in England. She hoped that when the crown was placed on her brow, the country would be united in peace between Lancaster and York. Her clothing alone had cost more than most people ever saw in their lifetimes. White cloth-of-gold was trimmed in silk and lace. A luxurious ermine mantle served to keep her warm and demonstrate her majesty. Her hair was topped with a gold circlet that held the place for the heavy crown that would be later set there.

Her litter was overflowing with more swathes of white cloth-of-gold and surrounded by guardsmen in York livery with white roses and yellow sunbursts embroidered on their chests. It made Elizabeth's heart swell to see the York emblems proudly displayed once again, and she was eager to thank Henry for his thoughtfulness. How much had he been forced to argue with his mother to secure this display of York pride, she wondered.

As the procession neared Westminster Abbey, the crowd pressed in. Everyone from the mayor of London to children living on the street was anxious for a close look at the queen. The chance to be near her, or the possibility of hearing her voice, was a strong incentive to the people, and her guards were forced to hold back in order for her litter to pass by. She tried to look toward each person for a moment that would touch each heart, but there were so many. She was moved by the people's devotion to her.

Once inside the cathedral, she gazed up at the soaring arches and was amazed once more by the beauty and wonder of this building. Though she had grown up with Westminster as part of her family's life, she never grew used to the splendor of the place. Before the noblemen of the land, she was anointed on her chest and head with blessed oil. She received the ring, scepter, and rod with all the dignity expected of her. Finally, the gold crown was placed on her head. She was no longer just the king's wife or the prince's mother. She was the Queen of England.

She thought of Henry watching from behind a lattice panel to ensure that the day's focus was kept on her. Was he proud of her at this moment? Was he hurt by the love shown for her by people who should love him? Would he be content with peace even if it did not include love? It was so difficult to obtain both.

The procession moved to Westminster's Great Hall to enjoy a banquet menu that included courses of food that were as carefully crafted as the clothes Elizabeth wore. Some of the pastries and marzipan were almost too beautiful to eat. The scent of roasted meat and sound of music filled the air to create a festive atmosphere. Elizabeth wished that Henry could share this moment with her rather than remain hidden away with his mother in their concealed balcony.

She was ready for the dancing to begin, having eaten more than her fill. Dance she did, with everyone from her sisters to the little duke of Buckingham. Cecily had shed her despondency when she gained a husband. Viscount Welles may not have been who she would have chosen for herself, but she was a woman made for married life and was relatively pleased with the king's choice for her.

"Cecily, you look radiant," Elizabeth said as they danced. The warmth of the hall and the dancing gave both women a rosy glow.

"Thank you, your grace," Cecily said with an elaborate curtsey.

They giggled like little girls as they spun around the room.

"You seem quite pleased with your husband," Elizabeth continued.

Cecily gave her a secret smile that acknowledged much more than what had been said. "I am pleased."

"I am glad to hear it. When Henry asked my opinion of John, I was not sure whether or not to recommend him." He was a staunch Lancastrian. Did this bother Cecily? Elizabeth laughed at herself. She was happily married to a Lancastrian king after all.

"I was not sure myself at first," Cecily said. "But he has been an attentive husband. I admit that his pleasure over having a young, attractive wife has resulted in numerous benefits for me," she said with a laugh.

How wonderful it felt to talk as wives rather than displaced princesses. Elizabeth thought ahead to Cecily having children and pictured their babies running and playing together. Even on her coronation day, Elizabeth found more pleasure in the simple aspects of life.

"How is little Arthur?" Cecily asked. The way the corners of her mouth upturned told Elizabeth that Cecily hoped to soon hold her own child.

"He is well. He thrives despite his early birth, for which I thank God."

"I include our young prince in my daily prayers as well," Cecily said. "You keep him with you?"

"As much as I can. It will not be many years before he will be taken from me to learn to govern and soldier. I baby him now while I can."

"As would I, sister. And a brother or sister for him?"

Elizabeth shook her head. Almost a year had passed since Arthur's birth and she had not yet conceived again. Arthur had been conceived so quickly that she had assumed that more children would arrive with similar ease.

"Henry was gone much of the summer," she offered as excuse.

"I have no doubt that you will conceive again in good time," Cecily said. "Do not rush God's plans, dear Bess. Too many women wear themselves out with new babies each year."

"You are right, of course. I do have hope that God will bless us with another child soon though."

They continued to dance for a few moments, each lost in their own thoughts.

"Do you miss mother today?" Cecily asked.

Elizabeth was too caught off guard by the question to completely hide her surprise.

"No?"

Elizabeth contemplated before answering. "Our mother has made it difficult to miss her."

Cecily laughed. "Well said, but it does seem like her presence is missing today."

Elizabeth swept her eyes across the room and agreed. "She was so frequently the center of attention at an event like this."

"She continues at Bermondsey?"

"Yes, but you need not worry. She is not kept like a nun."

"I would not have believed otherwise."

"She runs the abbey as though she has always been there and it is her own private kingdom."

Cecily nodded. "She is happy then."

"Who knows?" Elizabeth asked. "One would have thought she'd have been happy with a daughter on the throne and a grandson as heir to the crown."

Cecily took Elizabeth by the arms and pulled her aside, causing a momentary stumble on the part of the dancers surrounding them. "You are still sore over her plotting."

"I suppose I am," Elizabeth admitted. "It hurt enough that our cousins would plot against me, but our mother?"

Cecily wrapped her arms around her sister. "I know. I think that, despite the fact that she forced you into this marriage, she believes that you would be happy to be freed of it."

"Why would she believe that?"

"For some, being a York is all that matters."

Elizabeth shook her head. "It is insane! It will keep these petty rebellions going on for decades, until the last drop of Plantagenet blood has seeped into the ground."

Cecily said nothing, but the look on her face told Elizabeth that was exactly what she thought would happen.

Christmas 1487

Elizabeth and Henry retired to the palace at Greenwich to celebrate the Christmas festivities. Unlike all other occasions Henry had taken advantage of to demonstrate his majesty, this Christmas they spent together with Arthur in relative quiet. After the pomp and circumstance of the coronation, Elizabeth was content to spend time with her baby and took advantage of the extra time with Henry to attempt to conceive another. She hoped the sickness that she endured after Arthur's birth would not interfere with presenting Henry with future sons.

As she watched Arthur toddle about, she thought back to the previous Christmas spent in this same beautiful castle. Then he had been only a few months old and fears still hovered like dark clouds that his premature birth would cause sickness or death. A smile lifted her lips to look at him now, healthy and robust. His thin body had filled out with baby rolls and dimpled knuckles so that nobody would guess his surprising entry to the world.

Henry lay on the floor among the rushes in a most undignified manner to play with their son. He too seemed to have a healthier pallor after two years in England. Surely the air was healthier here than in France, Elizabeth thought. Though Henry was still rail thin, his cheeks weren't quite as sunken, and his skin had lost the yellow tint it had formerly held.

Despite the difficulties they had encountered in their short marriage, Elizabeth was sure that God was smiling on them now. With peace in the land, Elizabeth looked forward to her husband's prosperous reign and seeing additions to their family.

St. George's Day 1488

Elizabeth gazed out the window while preparations for St. George's Day went on around her. White flags blazing with St. George's cross were fluttering in the wind as far as the eye could see. This holiday, coming in the wake of Easter, would be filled with feasting and dancing. Wine would flow like water, leaving many wishing that they had not celebrated quite so enthusiastically the next morning.

The spring air carried the scent of new life and renewal after the cold winter. The warmth was welcome, and Elizabeth closed her eyes to bask in the sunlight. She prayed that the spring would bring new life to her womb as well.

"This dress is heavenly!" exclaimed Cecily as she held up the deep purple folds of fabric. Cloth-of-gold accents and embroidery punctuated the waistline, sleeves, and hem.

"Lady Margaret had it designed along with one for herself," Elizabeth said. She moved toward her sister and gently ran her hand down the full skirts.

"You will match the king's mother?" Cecily said with a raised eyebrow.

Elizabeth smiled at Cecily's skepticism. "Yes. It will show our unity and our support for Henry." Seeing Cecily's remaining doubt painted on her face, she shrugged. "We will show that we are loving daughter and mother-in-law."

It was Cecily's turn to smile. "You have the patience of a saint, Bess."

"Was St. George known for his patience?" Elizabeth asked in an effort to lighten the mood and change the subject.

With a laugh, Cecily said, "As much patience as any Plantagenet warrior, no doubt. You may be the only one in a long line of kings and queens to possess the trait, sister dear."

Elizabeth was still fingering the soft folds of her dress. She raised her eyes to meet her sister's and asked, "Do you remember when Anne and I wore matching dresses at Christmastime?"

"Of course," Cecily said. Both sisters retreated into thoughtful silence.

The days at the court of Richard and Anne seemed part of a different lifetime. Now that she was older, she wished that she had not paraded her health and beauty while Anne wore her matching gown. Poor Anne died believing that Richard would be soon married to Elizabeth. Instead, she had married his murderer. Murderer? Not exactly. It had been a long time since Elizabeth had thought of Henry in those terms or envisioned what it had been like for Richard to be killed in battle.

"Richard has been dead for almost three years."

Cecily nodded and examined her sister's features for a moment before replying. "Do you miss him?"

Elizabeth took a deep breath and shrugged. "I try not to think about it . . . . try not to doubt God's plan. If I think about it, I find myself filled with questions with no answers."

"What kinds of questions?"

Elizabeth let her eyes survey the room for eavesdroppers before answering. "I thought I loved him. Then I was convinced that he had our brothers murdered, and I was ashamed of having loved him. Now the only thing I am sure of is that he is dead."

Cecily's mouth formed a flat line while she bit her lips and considered her response. "Henry believes that our uncle killed our brothers."

"Sometimes, I am not sure that he is certain of it either, but it is easier for him if it is true."

They neared precarious ground. Cecily was not sure who Bess was loyal to before all others, her husband or her brothers. "If they are still alive, they are a threat to his crown."

"And mine," Elizabeth finished for her. "But if they are dead, our uncle is a murderer."

"Not necessarily."

Elizabeth was taken aback. "What do you mean?"

"I'm sure that anybody who has spoken to you on this matter would have you believe that the only possibilities are that our uncle had Edward and Richard killed or hidden, but what of others?"

"Who?" Elizabeth whispered. Part of her didn't want Cecily to answer. This was exactly why she chose not to think on this topic. Where would it lead?

"What of Henry Stafford?" Cecily asked, not because she believed the duke of Buckingham had killed her brothers but because she was not sure she could mention those suspects at the top of her list.

"Harry?" Elizabeth shook her head so furiously her hair began springing from its pins. "Surely not. Anne believed them to be alive."

"Maybe they were," Cecily agreed. "At the time."

"Then who . . . ." Elizabeth's voice trailed off as Cecily's implication became clear to her.

"Margaret," Cecily said quickly, before Elizabeth could let the thought form in her mind that her own husband could be the culprit. "Margaret Stanley would have done anything to clear the way for her son to take the throne." She saw relief flit across Elizabeth's face and was glad, but she wondered where her thoughts would wander later.

"Henry's mother," Bess shook her head more slowly, not wanting it to be true. "I don't know, Cecily. This way of thinking will only lead us to distrust those closest to us."

"They have never been found. They are your brothers and you are the queen."

"What can I do?" Elizabeth asked with tears in her eyes. "I have left matters of state to Henry and his mother."

"I'm sorry, Bess," Cecily reached for Elizabeth's hand and pressed it within her own. "I do not know what I hoped to gain by dragging this up."

"I miss them so," Elizabeth said as a single tear escaped and created a path through the light powder on her face.

"As do I," whispered Cecily as she embraced her sister, a queen with no power.

~ ~ ~ ~

That evening Elizabeth and Lady Margaret appeared in their coordinated gowns, and Elizabeth had further reason to be reminded of Anne. Though Lady Margaret was barely into her forties, her face was crossed with harsh lines of worry and conspiracy. Due to a pious lifestyle that included a minimalist diet, her figure was thin and sickly. Compared to Elizabeth's full figure and rosy complexion, Henry's mother appeared elderly and unhealthy.

"Don't you look lovely," Margaret said. She approached Elizabeth with outstretched arms while her eyes examined her figure.

Elizabeth knew that her mother-in-law was searching for signs that she was with child. Curtseying just enough to be respectful, Elizabeth responded, "As do you lady mother."

Lady Margaret waved the complement away. "Beauty has never been my gift. It is better left to girls of York." She had a way of saying it that made it sound like an insult, as if that was all the poor York women had. "I hope you are as healthy as you appear." It was what passed for subtlety with Margaret Stanley.

"I am, lady mother, though I do hope to find myself with child again soon." She had no patience for her mother-in-law's barely veiled questions and references, so she dashed her hopes directly.

A disappointed grunt escaped Margaret's throat. "Surely, the Lord our God will bless the king with another son in his own good and perfect time." She looked down her nose at Elizabeth to make clear that she knew who was standing in the way of God's plan.

"I have complete confidence in the Lord's plan," Elizabeth responded dutifully. Though she did, in fact, trust God in this, the words felt hollow when speaking them to her mother-in-law.

"Henry has learned patience through the hardships of his life," Lady Margaret said, and Elizabeth felt the inference that she was one of those hardships, comparable to exile in Brittany.

"Certainly he does not wish Arthur to remain an only child as he himself grew up with that burden to bear." Elizabeth could not stop the words from escaping, but then despised how Margaret brought out the worst in her.

Lady Margaret did not respond to this reference to her barrenness which followed giving birth to Henry at the early age of thirteen. She narrowed her eyes and examined Elizabeth, who refused to flinch or look away. Finally, it was Margaret who dipped her head to Elizabeth before walking away. Elizabeth had expected Margaret to react in anger or pride, but what she had seen in her mother-in-law's eyes before she turned away was unexpected: respect.

Summer 1488

The rose was white in the center and blood-red at the edges of the petals. A white York rose dipped in Lancastrian blood. The morbid thought came to Elizabeth's mind uninvited while she examined the new rosebushes that had been contracted by Henry. He would cement his reign even among the flowers which would no longer be allowed to display their loyalty in red and white. This beautiful hybrid was being planted around royal palaces as fast as they could be grown.

A bench hidden in climbing clematis vines became Elizabeth's sanctuary from the new Tudor roses and prying eyes, but the colorful blooms could not keep her own thoughts from her. How she wished God's plan was clearer to her. She had felt that he had led her to marry Henry. What else could she have done? Her womb remained empty since Arthur's birth, and she couldn't help but wonder if it were due to the disfavor of the Almighty. She placed her hand on her flat stomach and sighed. If the might of her will could create a flutter there, she would have carried and birthed another child by now.

Confusing thoughts flitted through her mind about the rumors that never failed to abound at court. Not only did she carry her personal sorrow over her seeming barrenness, but Henry's reign was far from peaceful. The uniting of the houses of Lancaster and York had not convinced all Englishmen to lay down their weapons. Edmund de la Pole, brother to the dead John de la Pole, remained on the Continent - plotting, they all knew. Whispers of another claimant had reached her but not in enough detail for her to determine the danger. Regardless of who Henry had married, a remnant existed that would never accept him.

Elizabeth prided herself on being a godly, submissive wife, but she was troubled by what she heard of Henry's methods of taxation.

The vile John Morton, who was now Archbishop of Canterbury, had created a process of extortion known as "Morton's Fork." If a man was well off, he had plenty to share with his king. If he had little, he was adept at getting along on less and could give to the king. Hatred was a feeling that Elizabeth rarely indulged in. For Morton, she made an exception. He had caused trouble for her father and uncle with his thinly veiled Lancastrian loyalties. Though he rejoiced in Henry as a Lancastrian king, Morton did little to gain for Henry the love of the people.

"You are adept at hiding."

At the sound of Henry's voice, Elizabeth's hand slid from her lap where it had been guarding her empty womb and she lifted her face to meet his gaze.

"I wish I could hide from the world sometimes," she admitted.

He moved toward her, his lithe muscles beneath velvet caused a stirring within her. When she did not move to make room for him, he was forced to sit with his body pressed against her side. It made her smile to exhibit some small level of power.

"You have not been yourself," he said.

"And who have I been?"

He snorted and nodded. "You sound like your sister."

Elizabeth thought of Mary, but she knew that he meant Cecily.

"I would be more like her, living in the country as a wife and mother rather than a queen."

Henry took her hand in his. With his other hand he caressed her cheek and turned her face to him. "Why are you so despondent?"

Though she could see concern in his eyes, Elizabeth could not deny the desire to snap at him. "I am a barren queen with murdered brothers, a cousin imprisoned for sharing my blood, and another in exile because he desires my husband's crown. Let's not forget that I am forced to give up my rooms to the king's mother."

The quick intake of breath she heard told her that she had succeeded in shocking Henry. So rarely had she allowed dark clouds to shadow her sunny disposition that he was not prepared to hear the burdens on her heart. He squeezed her hand and looked out toward his Tudor roses, and she wondered if he was sorry he had sat next to her.

"Elizabeth . . . ." he said and then faltered because no answer for her complaints that would ease her pain. "Do not call yourself barren. Arthur is such a joy to both of us." It was the safest course of action to speak of their son. Just as he brightened a room by entering it, mention of his name blew some of the storm clouds from his mother's face.

"You are right, of course," she whispered but her head remained hung over stooped shoulders. Was it the weight of the world pressing down upon them?

"Bess," Henry said as he lifted her chin once more. "We must travel to Sheen. It will lift your spirits to spend time with our son away from London."

She looked away from him because she wanted to ask if he would join them there but knew that she was supposed to be comforted by the thought of time away with Arthur. She did truly love the manor house at Sheen. It was more of a large family home than a royal palace, and she held many memories of times there with her father and mother. Back when the world was a different place. She could not reconcile the anger and depression she felt that made her want to lash out at Henry with the deep desire to be with him.

He pulled her to him, ignoring the weak resistance she offered. "We will go by Christmas and stay there together," he whispered in her ear with his mouth close enough to brush her skin. The warmth of his breath sent a shiver through her body and she let go of her ambivalence toward him. She would direct it at someone else and cling to Henry as her lifeline.

Easter 1489

By Easter of the following year, Elizabeth's spirits were lifted by the time spent at Sheen and the secret that she carried. Christmas had been spent at the relatively private manor house. After the requisite amount of pageantry and feasting, the cold winter months had been spent with the old moat separating the royal family from the cares of state. She knew that it had been a sacrifice for Henry to delegate duties in order to spend time with his wife and son. The smile that tugged at the corners of her mouth was proof that it had been worth it.

They had decided to celebrate Easter at Hertford Castle, and Elizabeth was content to avoid the city of London for a few more weeks. Henry's arrival would mean the descent of courtiers and petitioners, but not the level of chaos that would be found when they lodged at Westminster. She did not even regret that Lady Margaret would arrive with him now that she knew that she had news that would serve as both weapon and gift.

She had decided to welcome them in the great hall rather than waiting in her private rooms as she would normally do. Her confidence and optimistic disposition were renewed. The greeting would please her husband and remind her mother-in-law of who was the true queen. She had spent a ridiculous amount of time having her hair pinned and curled in an intricate design, her face lightly powdered, and an expensive blue cloth-of-gold gown arranged around her. Her hair was woven around a delicate gold circlet that was barely discernible among her copper locks. She was not a vain woman but was aware that her appearance would greatly please Henry. The majestic public greeting would be improved upon only by her ardent private welcome that would follow.

"His Majesty King Henry and Lady Margaret the King's Mother," declared a page. Elizabeth had instructed them to formally announce members of nobility as they arrived, including her husband. She straightened her back and felt a flush rise to her cheeks.

He entered with the dirt and sweat of the road still upon him. Rather than being offended, Elizabeth was attracted to the road-worn look and scent of horses that she subconsciously connected with her father. She thought men were more appealing in this state than in flowing court robes and glittering jewels. She held herself back from rushing to him and waited for him to approach.

"My lady," he said as he bowed before her, keeping up the standard of formality she had set.

Half a pace behind him, his mother was forced to follow suit and curtsey before her daughter-in-law.

Elizabeth smiled and beckoned Henry forward. "You are weary from your travels," she said. A barely perceptible movement of her hand brought a servant to her side. "Please show our lady mother to her rooms and see to her needs. I will tend to the king."

His mouth turned up only slightly, but she saw the desire in his eyes that matched her own. He turned to his mother. "I will see you this evening, mother," he said and kissed her hand. "Please, feel free to rest as long as you feel is necessary."

Lady Margaret looked from her son to Elizabeth, saw that she was being sent away, and was annoyed that there was little that she could do about it. She had wanted Henry to marry Elizabeth, but never thought that the York princess would replace her as first woman in his life. It was the way life should be, she knew, but that did not mean she had to like it. She tilted her head toward each of them before stalking out with the servant hurrying after her.

As the heavy oak door closed behind her, Elizabeth released her laugh and stood to embrace Henry. He kissed her hair, ear, and neck before pulling back to look into her eyes. "You tease poor mother."

"It was not my intention," she admitted. "But a happy coincidence." She looked up at him through her downcast lashes. "My intent was to tease you, your grace."

"That you have." He wrapped his arms around her waist to swing her around. Her carefully arranged skirts flowed around her before he set her back on her feet. "We should retire to your rooms," he said, placing a soft kiss on the corner of her mouth."

"Yes, we should," she agreed. "For we have much to celebrate."

"Do we?"

"I do believe that our time at Sheen was quite therapeutic," she said as she took his hand and began leading him from the hall.

"Good, it was intended to be so." He was still looking at her quizzically.

"I believe it was also rather . . . . productive."

She turned to face him while they stood before the door, and the look in her eyes told him the truth. His hands flew to her abdomen. "Truly, my love?"

"Yes, Henry. God has blessed us again. I believe that we will have another autumn baby." She smiled radiantly, all her previous cares diminished in her current joy.

"Praise the Lord!" Henry said and embraced her again. After a moment, he pulled away with a look of concern. "But if you are with child, I should have my own rooms."

Elizabeth laughed. "And we should not have relations on Fridays or during Lent." She mocked the rules of the church uncharacteristically. "My mother has assured me that it is no cause for concern." Her hand found its way underneath his tunic, and his objections died before reaching his lips.

~ ~ ~ ~

Elizabeth was pulling gowns from trunks when Henry walked

into her room a fortnight later. She smiled when she saw him standing in the doorway and held up a deep green gown for his approval.

"It appears that I have allowed my condition to remove my inhibitions about Easter feasting," she explained with a laugh. "I am getting clothing from storage with a little more room for expansion."

He chuckled with her and wrapped his arms around the waist that he could not perceive was any larger. "You have been a glutton, then? No matter, it is a softer, safer home for our child to grow."

"Henry!" she lightly smacked his arm. "How can you sit next to Archbishop Morton and call me a glutton?" she asked half-jokingly.

"Ha!" he laughed sharply. "Sometimes it is the princes of the church that are most vulnerable to temptations."

"Not princes of the realm?"

"I am strong as steel in the face of beckoning sins," he stated firmly. Only his wide grin gave away his lightheartedness.

Elizabeth looked at him as if to say she knew he could be tempted but she would show mercy at the moment. "Have you told your mother our happy news?"

"I have, and she is thrilled."

"Because she believes you will stop visiting my rooms," Elizabeth couldn't help saying.

Henry pulled her closer. "Then she will be sorely disappointed."

Just as he leaned to kiss her, a breathless servant appeared in the doorway. He hurriedly knelt and said, "Your grace, a messenger."

Henry silently cursed the man, kissed Elizabeth quickly on the tip of her nose, and turned away from her. "Have him sent to the hall," he said before following him from the room.

The messenger brought news that confirmed it was not just

Elizabeth who was displeased with Henry's taxes and Morton's justifications. The duke of Northumberland had been set upon by a mob while attempting to collect taxes in his region. While Percy was hacked at with the crude weapons of peasants, his retainers stood aside and refused to protect him. Henry was horrified at the news and couldn't help but wonder. Had the anger toward Northumberland been due to taxation or the fact that he had held back his troops from supporting Richard at Bosworth? Would the ghost of the last Plantagenet king ever cease to haunt him?

November 1489

The river Thames churned cold and grey with icy raindrops pelting its surface. From Elizabeth's perch within her warm confinement rooms, it was a beautiful sight displaying the wrath of nature upon the water. Elizabeth stood and crossed the room to enter the small attached chapel. She knelt before the altar with slow, clumsy movements in order to give thanks for her healthy pregnancy which seemed to be lasting a full term.

Arthur had not been pleased when he was told that his mother would be away from him for several weeks. He had stormed and stomped with all the fury of a spoiled three year old who is not getting his way for the first time. Elizabeth had soothed his hurt with hugs and kisses while wiping tears from his plump cheeks which were pink with frustration. He had sniffled and she wiped his runny nose with her handkerchief. She had worn a confident, reassuring face to hide her own lack of desire to be away from him.

Kneeling in her small, private chapel, she thanked God for Arthur and prayed that he would be pleased to be presented with a baby brother. Elizabeth would not allow herself to consider the reason Henry, Margaret, and the rest of England prayed for another boy. Surely, Henry would never find himself in need of a spare heir. Would any number of sons make him feel secure on his throne?

As she stood and crossed herself, the familiar pains gripped her, and she called for her mother. Despite some bad feelings between them, at this moment when her life and that of her child hung in the balance, her mother's presence was a balm to her worries.

Elizabeth Woodville rushed into the chapel without saying a word. The pain edged with fear on her daughter's face told her all she needed to know. As her mother approached, Elizabeth had a fleeting thought that the former queen seemed to have done all of her aging in the years since Edward had died. Was it due to the concerns and schemes or because she no longer had the king to retain her beauty for. Though fine lines etched the skin around her eyes and mouth, she remained lovely, and Elizabeth hoped that she was so well preserved at fifty-two years of age. Another pain broke through her thoughts and she leaned upon her mother to be guided to the bed.

The walls of the room were covered in tapestries featuring Biblical scenes, not pictures of battle or sacrifice, but peaceful mothers such as Elizabeth and Mary and one of the angel horde exclaiming halleluiahs over the shepherds. As pains continued to grip her in rapid succession, Elizabeth focused her eyes and thoughts upon these scenes. Her mother's words of comfort were soothing white noise without distinguishable words. How much fear did Mary feel when she brought our Savior into the world, Elizabeth wondered. Did she ever wonder if her life would be given in exchange for his? Though Elizabeth had hoped and prayed for the child about to be born, she could not help but utter a whispered prayer for herself.

The baby was coming quickly and the midwife had been sent for immediately after Elizabeth's mother had assessed her progress. She ordered prayers spoken as a part of the routine of delivery rather than piety. She may have retired to a nunnery, but Elizabeth Woodville would always be a woman who trusted first in herself and believed in creating your own destiny. If God was otherwise occupied, she would ensure that her daughter and grandchild were cared for that day.

"Mother," Elizabeth groaned. "It is happening too quickly!"

Rushing to her daughter's side, she gripped her hand and pushed damp hair from her face. "You are doing beautifully, Bess," she said in a calm, confident voice. "This child is just anxious to see you face to face." She smiled at her daughter and wondered, not for the first time, that this kind and obedient woman had been born of Edward and herself. A crooked smile lifted one side of her face. *God has lessons to teach each of us through our children,* she admitted only to herself.

"Pray for me mother," Elizabeth begged. "For I am afraid."

She knelt, not releasing Elizabeth's hand. "Heavenly father, send your angels to protect your obedient daughter, Elizabeth, and her child. Send her comfort and peace, I beg of you."

"I am not worthy, Lord," Elizabeth interrupted. "I am afraid. Increase my faith and forgive my unbelief," she moaned as she felt she was being torn in two.

"Amen," her mother whispered, ending the nontraditional prayer. She fixed her eyes on Elizabeth for a moment before conferring with the midwife.

"The child comes quickly, but there is nothing to be afraid of," the midwife reassured. "I know what to look for, you know."

Elizabeth Woodville's eyebrows arched in surprise. It had been years – decades? – since anyone had spoken to her that way. Then she laughed out loud. It was somewhat refreshing.

In the end, the midwife was correct. A squalling, chubby child was safely delivered within a few hours of Elizabeth's first pain. Both mother and child were well, and not one person expressed disappointment that the babe was a girl.

~ ~ ~ ~

Henry brought Arthur to meet his baby sister, who would soon be christened Margaret, and Elizabeth's heart soared to see them after her weeks in confinement. Was Arthur taller? Did she detect a few more grey hairs at Henry's temples? *Surely, the people we love do not change so quickly,* she assured herself.

A nurse laid Margaret in Elizabeth's arms before quietly leaving the room. Elizabeth savored this moment with her little family gathered around her. The fire cast a warm, orange glow about the room, and she could imagine that nothing else in the world existed.

"What do you think of your baby sister?" she asked Arthur, who was peering down at the bundle with a thoughtful wrinkle to his brow.

His eyes, which were hazel like Henry's, met his mother's. "Are you sure it's a girl?"

The disappointment on his face made Elizabeth laugh, and she put up a hand to keep Henry from saying the admonishment she could see on his lips. "When I was a little girl," she said. "My mother had three girls before my first brother was born." She kept the smile on her face and was determined to not think of the fate of that greatly celebrated baby boy.

Arthur looked horrified. "You will not have three girls, will you mother?"

"I will have whatever children the Lord chooses to give me," Elizabeth said with her hand cupping his soft, rosy cheek. "I am daily thankful that he chose to give me this little boy."

Finally, Arthur smiled. "I am too," he said, cuddling up to her side. "But next time, I do hope he gives you another boy."

Winter 1489-1490

Christmas festivities went by before Elizabeth's churching, not that she felt much disappointment. She enjoyed the quiet times with Henry and their children. Never did he make her feel that he was displeased with being presented with a daughter. Elizabeth would soon be twenty-four and hoped to have many more children. Her mother had brought life to ten children beyond Elizabeth's current age, so she was determined to be patient.

Margaret was a needy child and Elizabeth missed the immediate bond that she had felt with Arthur. Too often she found herself handing over the crying child to a wet-nurse after losing patience with her. Remarkably, Henry seemed more forgiving of the child's screaming. If he were in attendance when the crying began, he would pace the room, bouncing the baby gently, while crooning to her in a low voice. Elizabeth caught the surprised exchanges between Margaret's nurses and silenced them with a glare. Henry had the cares of a kingdom upon his shoulders. If he chose to take time to sooth a cranky child, nobody would be allowed to accuse him of behaving in an undignified manner.

A long awaited visit from Cecily broke through the winter gloom once Elizabeth had left confinement. The children were scrubbed and dressed in lavish fabric, and nurses stood by to take them away once they had been presented. Elizabeth adored her children, but looked forward to sharing a few precious days with her sister.

Sounds of hurried movement and footsteps informed Elizabeth of Cecily's arrival before the heavy door was forced open on its groaning hinges. She smiled at Arthur's rigid stance, so determined was he to be the perfect prince. If Margaret could get through introductions without squalling, it would be a minor victory.

Cecily swept into the room with a radiant smile on her face and a light blue gown swirling around her. Elizabeth smiled at the choice of color. Most noblewomen would not wear light colors for it gave the appearance of lack of wealth. Cecily would wear whatever color she liked and not concern herself with others' thoughts.

"Look at those gorgeous children!" Cecily exclaimed as soon as she laid eyes on them.

Arthur looked at his mother, at a loss of what to do in the face of such informality. Smiling, Elizabeth gave him a gentle shove. "You may greet your aunt Cecily," she whispered in his ear.

He performed a solemn bow and stated, "You are most welcome here, Lady Cecily."

"Isn't he just the most precious thing?" Cecily exclaimed as she pulled Arthur into her arms. He remained stiff only for a moment before giving in to his aunt's affections. He giggled when she messed up his carefully arranged hair and kissed him on the forehead. He was disappointed when she eventually set him aside to see baby Margaret.

"Well, the poor girl looks like our father!" she said when she looked down at Margaret's red face and auburn hair.

Though the comment would have rankled coming from someone else, Elizabeth laughed at Cecily's analysis. "She will be a lovely lady when she grows into her temper."

"Ah, you have your hands full, Bess," Cecily said knowingly. "If she has inherited the Plantagenet fury."

Elizabeth nodded. "She is very certain of herself already and will be a strong woman," she said. "A much stronger woman than her mother."

Cecily put an arm around her sister. "She is very blessed by the mother God has placed her with, one who can keep her temper in check."

While the sisters shared a moment of shared understanding and pleasure at each other's presence, Arthur stood on tiptoe in an effort to be part of the conversation.

"She doesn't really do anything," he insisted. "I can show you my soldiers."

"Well, now, commanding your own troops already?" Cecily asked as she crouched down to Arthur's level.

"The soldiers of England always beat the armies of France," Arthur observed quite seriously. "And I have books."

"That they do," Cecily solemnly agreed. "And I would love to see your books after I have seen to my luggage."

Arthur beamed at his ability to capture his pretty aunt's attention. He was not even upset when his nurse took his hand to lead him away, but he looked back to wave and found her smiling after him.

After the children and their nurses had filed out of the room, Cecily turned her brilliant smile on Elizabeth. "You look lovely, Bess. Did you suffer ill after Margaret's birth?"

Elizabeth shook her head, "Thank God, no. The child is more difficult but the recovery was free of complications."

"Praise God," Cecily echoed. "I regret that I was not with you."

Elizabeth laughed at the memory of her fear. "It was scary in its quickness. I was thankful for our mother's presence."

"Really?" Cecily's eyebrows shot up in surprise. "You are reconciled to her then?"

Considering her response before speaking, Elizabeth finally admitted, "I believe we have come to an understanding."

"An understanding that you will not ask any questions that would convict her," Cecily guessed.

"She was a comfort to me during my labor, and I do not know the extent of her involvement in the Simnel rebellion or under what understanding she participated. I feel it is better left that way."

"It is best to look forward rather than back," Cecily agreed.

"Even better to look up," Elizabeth amended. "You seem

radiant with happiness, Cecily."

"I am, Bess," Cecily sighed. "I cannot wait another moment to tell you my news."

Joy spread across Elizabeth's face as she guessed at the only news that would so enliven her sister.

"Yes," Cecily affirmed Elizabeth's unspoken thought. "I am with child."

Pulling Cecily into her arms, Elizabeth was ecstatic that her sister would soon have the quiet family life she longed for. She held her tightly, their blond locks – Elizabeth's more copper and Cecily's more silver – intertwining where they had slipped free of their arrangements.

"God's blessings on you and your child," Elizabeth whispered as she reluctantly released her sister.

"Thank you, my queen," Cecily said with a shallow curtsey that made Elizabeth laugh.

"And Viscount Wells, he must be happy."

"Oh, please call him John," Cecily insisted. "He is beside himself with joy, especially since I informed him that I saw no need to restrict nocturnal activities due to the baby."

The sisters exchanged smiles of shared secrets. "You do love him then," Elizabeth stated, happy that Henry's choice had given her sister joy.

"I do." If there was a small part of Cecily's heart that would always belong to Ralph Scrope, it was no greater burden than that carried my most noblewomen.

"Wonderful! Now, we can begin to obsess over grooms for our young sisters instead."

They both laughed, but neither mentioned that it would indeed be soon when Henry would choose a husband for Anne, who was now fourteen years old.

Elizabeth motioned for servants to see to Cecily's luggage and led her from the room. As they retired to a quiet library, Elizabeth decided to share news of her own.

"Henry has indeed been planning a wedding, but not our sweet sister's."

Elizabeth could almost see the names flashing before Cecily's eyes as she considered who was in need of a spouse.

"He has agreed upon a betrothal for Arthur." Elizabeth kept her voice void of emotion so that Cecily would be free to express her own. Though she knew child betrothals were common, she had been a part of them herself, she also knew that they could lead to betrayal and heartache.

"Who has he matched our prince to?" Cecily asked, her voice matching Elizabeth's in flatness.

"Catherine of Aragon, daughter of Ferdinand and Isabella of Spain."

Cecily allowed hesitant approval to appear on her face. "A good match," she admitted.

"It was part of the Treaty of Medina del Campo," said Elizabeth, struggling to work her mouth around the unfamiliar Spanish words. She had already spoken to Henry about adding the language to Arthur's tutoring schedule. "During my confinement, Henry dubbed him a Knight of Bath."

"Ah, is he growing up on us already?"

Elizabeth smiled wryly. "Well, he is quite mature for a three year old."

The sisters laughed together, enjoying the warmth of the fire and the feeling of camaraderie that enveloped them.

~ ~ ~ ~

The Christmas court was a subdued one despite the recent birth of the royal daughter. A measles epidemic raged through the city, reminding Elizabeth of the loyal Emma who had died after helping her minister to those in need in the wake of the plague that had followed Henry's men to London. This time, she sent what money and goods she could to be distributed, but she could not put herself in harm's way now that she had her children to think about. She prayed that God forgave her selfishness.

February 1490

Though a brisk wind whipped around her and snow threatened to fall, Elizabeth was glad to be returning to Westminster. The privacy and peace that existed outside of London's gates was a welcome refuge, but she could not forever ignore the fact that she was queen. Arthur had been returned to his own household at Farnham. Part of her heart ached for him, but she had grown accustomed to the fact that he would never stay with her as though she were nothing more than a merchant's wife.

Margaret's cries could be heard from where she was carried in a litter accompanied by her wet-nurse and attendants. Elizabeth closed her eyes and prayed for peace from, and affection for, this colicky child. It only made her desire Arthur's presence all the more. She would be reunited with him soon, when he came to London at the end of the month in order to be installed as the Prince of Wales. For just a moment, she allowed her mind to retrieve memories of the previous Prince of Wales. She must learn to give up to God this mystery that would not be solved.

The chilly air wound its way through her hair and under her mantle, cooling her nerves and temper. Soon she would be in her own rooms within the palace walls being welcomed by her husband, and Margaret would be sent to her own.

The vision of the city of London emerging through the fog allowed Elizabeth to sigh in relief. She was anxious for a bath and rest. How much more wearying was travel with a squalling child! Within minutes of their arrival, she had dismissed Margaret and her caregivers. She sought peace and quiet with the company of her ladies and prepared for her reunion with Henry.

"I wish to be with my sister when she enters her confinement chamber."

Henry was taken aback by the request. He turned his face away from the crackling fire, hiding his emotions in the shadows. Her chamber was warm and comfortable and revealed no evidence that its occupant had only just arrived.

She knelt before him. "Henry, I realize that it is an unusual request, but I would be such a comfort to her."

He smiled and wound a lock of her coppery blond hair around his hand. "You know that you may have anything, so long as you ask looking as fetching as you do now." She wore only her chemise, and her hair was unbound and spilling down to her waist.

"Thank you, Henry!" She sprang to her feet and embraced him fervently.

Laughing, he pulled her into his lap. "Some women would squeal over jewels. You desire only my permission to serve as an attendant. Do not be too easy to please, my queen."

Her eyes smoldered at him from beneath lowered lashes. "But, my lord, there is more that I require of you."

~ ~ ~ ~

A lump rose in Elizabeth's throat as she listened to the crowd of faithful Englishmen cheer for her son. Though Arthur looked more like his father than anyone in Elizabeth's family, she could not help but feel that things were being made right by another little boy being named Prince of Wales. Another Plantagenet prince, she thought but could never say. Outwardly, she embraced her role as the mother of the Tudor dynasty.

Though he was only three years old, Arthur bore the ceremony and attention as one born to it. He was already much more comfortable with the trappings of royalty than his father. Elizabeth loved Henry, but recognized that at times he appeared as though he were a merchant playing king for the day. Nobody would ever say that about Arthur.

King Arthur. Even his name left no room for doubt that he was born to rule and to rule well. She beamed at him, and he rewarded her with a tiny dignified smile. His self-control was more evidence of his Tudor ancestry. Elizabeth could admit to herself that a little less fiery temper and impetuousness would serve Arthur well as a ruler and save him some of the heartache that had plagued her family.

She would not think of her family today. She wouldn't picture her father, young and vibrant, making people love him just by walking into a room. She wouldn't think about her mother, at this very moment ruling her world that was now limited to Bermondsey Abbey. No little ghosts of her brothers would be allowed to march along in the procession. She certainly would not allow her mind to drift into the world of what-ifs where she saw Richard victorious at Bosworth instead of Henry. No, God had worked things out, and she would see only those he had left to her.

April 1490

"Bear down, Cecily!" Elizabeth pushed sweaty locks of hair from her sister's face and stared intently into her eyes. "You can do this, sister dear. Remember, you are a Plantagenet princess."

Cecily seemed to take a respite from her pain as she gazed back into her sister's face, soaking up the strength that Elizabeth offered. She said nothing, but lines of stress seemed to ease slightly on her forehead and around her eyes.

Elizabeth allowed nothing but confidence to emanate from her. As one who had lived her entire life at the royal court, she was an expert at only displaying those emotions that were fitting at the moment. The fear that Cecily's labor was taking too long, that she didn't seem to be making any progress, would not be found anywhere in her countenance.

"I will leave you for just a moment to offer up prayers of thanksgiving that the Lord will soon bless you with a hardy child," Elizabeth said, giving Cecily's clammy hand a reassuring squeeze before standing.

When she turned toward the small chapel that lay just off Cecily's lying in chamber, she exchanged a look with the midwife that bid her to attend.

Entering the chapel moments after Elizabeth, the midwife found her at prayer just as she had said, but the prayer was one that pleaded for the lives of Cecily and her unborn child rather than the platitudes of thanks she had expressed to her sister. The midwife waited as Elizabeth stood, crossed herself, and placed a kiss upon the small gold crucifix before turning to her.

"Tell me," Elizabeth said, wishing to waste no time or words.

"I believe the baby has not turned properly," admitted the midwife. She hoped the queen would be prepared for what must come. In either death or the solution she proposed, Cecily must endure more pain after the hours of anguish she had already faced. After she explained to Elizabeth what she felt must be done in an attempt to save both mother and baby, Elizabeth simply nodded.

"Let us see to our work with the help of God then," Elizabeth stated as she strode from the room.

Even in her weary, pain-laced state, Cecily had noted the disappearance of the two women. Her eyes asked the question that she couldn't bring her voice to express.

"You are going to get through this," Elizabeth assured her. "The midwife must turn the baby. It will be painful, but I am here with you. More importantly, God is here with you, my strong sister."

Worry pooled in Cecily's eyes, but she said, "Our mother has done this a dozen times. Certainly my Woodville blood will serve me as well as my royal blood does."

Elizabeth smiled. "You brave, wonderful girl," she whispered as she patted a cool cloth over Cecily's flushed face. She nodded to the midwife who was positioned over Cecily's abdomen with a look on her face that Elizabeth recognized from seeing men as they headed into battle. "Cecily. Look at me," she ordered.

Cecily screamed.

Over and over again, she screamed. Elizabeth forced herself to keep eye contact, to mumble prayers and words of strength, and to keep her fear and anguish from making an appearance. As the midwife stood from her labors with sweat dripping from the tip of her nose, Cecily fainted to escape the pain.

Elizabeth had no need to control her emotions with Cecily unconscious. "Will she be alright? Will she wake up?" She shook the poor woman in her distress as if she could make the answers fall out faster and in the form she desired.

"I believe so, with the help of God," was the exhausted reply of the thin form that had turned limp as a ragdoll in Elizabeth's grasp.

Releasing her with sudden awareness of her actions, Elizabeth said, "Forgive me." She rubbed her hands over her face, and the weariness that fear had been holding at bay washed over her like the tide coming in. "Forgive me, dear woman. You have saved my sister's life."

The midwife simply nodded and prayed that the words were true.

Cecily's respite did not last long. Her contractions awoke her with fierce intensity. She moaned, fighting the pain that drug her from her blissful unconsciousness. "No, I can't," she sleepily muttered.

Elizabeth was immediately at her side, taking up her hand. "Yes. You can."

Cecily's eyes opened at the sound of her sister's voice. She sounded so sure. Maybe she was right. She felt the midwife examining her and wondered at the complete loss of modesty and privacy that accompanied the birth of a child, royal or peasant.

"You will push now, and this time it is going to work. You did not go through that pain for naught," Elizabeth said, imbuing Cecily with courage and the will to continue.

"Push now, my lady!" ordered the midwife in uncharacteristic boldness.

Cecily took a deep breath, said a silent prayer, and pushed. She pushed and groaned until she was sure she could take no more. In her mind, she saw her father and Mary and was certain that they would soon be welcoming her into heaven.

Darkness overwhelmed her.

Had days passed or only seconds? Cecily looked around the room and saw attendants in a flurry of activity, a radiant smile on her sister's tired face, and a wiggly bundle that was letting its unhappiness be known in a very vociferous manner.

She had survived! As had her baby.

"Bess!" she urged her sister to come closer. Words of

appreciation simply would not be adequate, and she allowed tears to run down her face.

Elizabeth patted her hand and wiped away her tears. "You have a proud and perfect daughter," she said with a smile. "Cecily, you have demonstrated such strength and courage today. They are no doubt traits that you will instill in my lovely niece."

"What is to be her name?" asked one of Cecily's ladies. Elizabeth had an admonishment on her lips when Cecily offered her ready answer.

"Elizabeth," she said. The anguish and exhaustion had already been cleared away by maternal happiness as she held out her arms for the squalling bundle. "In honor of my queen, my sister, and my best friend."

November 1490

Elizabeth watched her children play with their nurses on the lawn at Westminster. She was beginning to long for the countryside and to be gone from the harsh, dirty air of London. Arthur kept running toward little Margaret and gesturing for her to follow him. She would take a few shaky steps before winding up on her bottom. After several attempts to keep up with her brother, she remained on the ground and screamed until she was red in the face and her nurse swept her away.

That determination will serve her well one day, Elizabeth thought. While Arthur had no trouble reaching Elizabeth's heart, Margaret had needed time to bond with her mother. Now that a year had passed, Elizabeth was able to appreciate the strong personality that made her young daughter so difficult at times.

As she watched the nurse carry away the flailing toddler, she saw that Henry was making his way toward her. Arthur also had noticed the approach of his father and flung himself into his arms. Henry, always somewhat uncomfortable with public displays of affection, gave Arthur a brief hug before telling him to run off and play.

"How are you, my dear?" Elizabeth asked as Henry relaxed next to her. She was glad that the cares of the world seemed to lift from his shoulders when he was with her, but she wished that he didn't have to carry them at all.

"I am well, of course," he said, but the way he fidgeted needlessly with his sleeves hinted at something that he did not want to tell her.

"What is it, Henry?"

He sighed and looked up to the sky. "Nothing of great import. My uncle Jasper has just sent word that Katherine has given birth, but to a stillborn babe."

"Poor Katherine!" Though she would not say so, she was thinking of Katherine's other children, the product of her long and loving marriage to Henry, duke of Buckingham. They had been made wards of the king upon Henry's accession. She couldn't imagine how her aunt must feel now to lose this child as well.

"It is to be expected of course," said Henry matter-of-factly, though Elizabeth knew that he would mourn for Jasper's lost heir.

"I know how much Jasper means to you," Elizabeth said. "I'm sure that his loss feels almost as painful as if it were your own." She placed a hesitant hand upon his arm. Would he wish to address his feelings or be embarrassed that she had mentioned them?

He closed his eyes and lowered his head to his hands. "Jasper is getting no younger, and it must pain him to lose his son."

Her hand grasped his arm more confidently. "It was a boy then? Surely, Katherine will provide him with another."

"Katherine also is getting no younger, but the Lord does work miracles in his own time." His voice expressed no confidence in the power or willingness of the Lord to work a miracle in this case.

Hesitating only a moment, Elizabeth decided to share news that was sure to bring Henry out of his melancholy mood.

"Henry, my love. I do not know God's plans for Jasper and Katherine, but I do know that he intends for you to have another son for your quiver."

For a few seconds, Henry did not move, and Elizabeth wondered if he had understood. Then he slowly raised his head from his hands and grasped her arms. Light returned to his eyes and a smile to his lips.

"Truly? You are certain to be with child again?"

"Quite," Elizabeth confirmed with a smile. "I wanted to be sure before I told you after the wait we endured between Arthur and Margaret."

She said no more because Henry was no longer listening. He

had jumped from his seat and was swinging Arthur around in the air.

"You're going to be a big brother!" he shouted as Arthur giggled in delight.

~ ~ ~ ~

A few days later, Elizabeth was pleased to have her sister, Bridget, visit her. A ten year old who seemed to have the soul of a mature adult, Bridget was expressing her desire to enter a convent.

"It was always our father and mother's plan for me," Bridget needlessly explained. "I am ready."

Any other young girl telling Elizabeth that she was ready to make a lifelong commitment would have been dismissed immediately, but Bridget had never been like other children. She had grown up through trying circumstances, which she believed God had seen her family through.

"If you wish to devote your life to God's work, I certainly will not stand in your way. However, it is Henry who must approve this plan. He may have a match in mind for you."

Bridget cringed visibly. "Bess, I have no desire for a life of public drama."

Elizabeth smiled rather than admonish her sister for her tactlessness. Was it really any different than the opinion expressed more eloquently by Cecily?

"I vow to speak to the king on your behalf," Elizabeth promised, and Bridget contented herself with that.

Luckily, Elizabeth had recently given Henry the news that made him willing to fulfill her heart's desire. When he came to visit her, she welcomed him enthusiastically to her rooms.

"Henry, do relax by the fire. You look absolutely careworn." She accepted a tray of cheese and wine from a servant before gesturing for them to be left in privacy.

Henry melted into the chair and gratefully accepted the food and drink. "Bess, you always see my needs before I see them myself."

"You really must make sure that you have time to rest," she said as she took her place next to him. "Surely, you cannot be efficient in your work or clear-minded in your decisions if you are plagued by constant weariness."

He just nodded with his eyes closed. He was soaking in the warmth from the fire and enjoying the one place where he was free to relax. Elizabeth sat back, content to allow him a moment's peace. She was surprised when he sprang up after just a few moments.

"I almost forgot," he said with a smile brightening his face and making him look years younger than just a moment before. "I have brought you a gift."

He took a small package from beneath his robes and held it out to her. She smiled up at him as she took it.

"What is this?" she asked as she opened the small wooden box. Inside, a gold ring glimmered with diamonds and rubies that had been painstakingly formed into the design of a perfect Tudor rose. Elizabeth gasped at the perfection in the intricate design. "It is the most beautiful thing I have ever seen! Oh Henry, where did you find a jeweler with such skill?"

"I am happy that it pleases you," he said as he pulled her into his arms. "Only the best is acceptable for my lovely queen, especially now that you are going to give me another son.

"Thank you," she whispered.

"Anything you need. You need only ask."

She chose her moment well. "There is one thing I have been meaning to discuss with you."

Henry looked shocked to be taken up on his generous offer. "Yes?"

Elizabeth laughed. "Do not worry, my husband. I will not be

requesting half of your kingdom."

He also chuckled at the idea that Elizabeth would ever ask for more than he could give. "What is it then?"

"I would like you to send Bridget to join the Sisters of the Order of St. Augustine." She did not give him a chance to interrupt. "She is simply set upon the idea of going to Dartford, as my parents always intended for her. I know that she is young, but this is her calling, of that I am sure."

Any argument Henry may have posed died on his lips. "Very well, my queen. You may give her my word that she may retire to the Dominican priory."

June 1491

Elizabeth's sister, Anne, had become her attendant when Cecily left court for marriage. She was more reserved than anyone else in their family but was pleased to serve her royal sister. Anne quietly closed the door to the lying in chamber behind her. "It is a robust, young prince, your grace," she said with a humble curtsey.

"Thank God!" exclaimed Henry. "And Bess, she is well?"

Still not raising her eyes to meet his, Anne replied, "Of course, your grace. The queen is resting but is in perfect health."

"Praise the Lord," he mumbled without thought or much praise. His mother was striding down the hall toward him.

"Henry," she said as if she was still addressing an undisciplined youth rather than the king of England. "The baby?"

"A boy."

Margaret hastily crossed herself and murmured the required thanks. "I must speak to you."

"Yes," Henry agreed. "Another boy."

Anne, who seemed to have been forgotten as she often was, wondered at Henry repeating himself. Apparently even those welcoming their third child could have new father fears and confusion.

"We must discuss him at once," Margaret demanded. "He is claiming to be Richard of York."

The two of them turned as one and walked away without so much of a glance at Anne. Her eyes widened at the mention of her brother's name, the brother she barely remembered and had long thought lost. She rushed back into the room to tell Elizabeth that their brother had been found.

September 1491

"Do you truly believe it is him?" Elizabeth asked. She was bouncing her newest son, named Henry after his father and the long line of Lancastrian kings before him, on her knee as her husband ranted about the man who the Irish were calling Richard of York. While Henry paced, she considered this possibility and what it would mean to her - and her sons - if her father's heirs were still alive. Where had he been all these years?

"Of course, I do not believe it is him!" Henry's nervous fidgeting and obsession with obtaining information about the pretender spoke louder than his angry words. "Do you?"

Elizabeth pondered this question, which deserved a careful answer. Could this be her youngest brother? It was possible since her brothers had not been seen since September of 1483. Did she believe it was? It would mean her sons were disinherited, her husband a usurper, and she a fraudulent queen. Once again she asked herself if she believed that Richard could have killed them. Mixed messages swarmed her memories. She didn't know, but she had to support her husband.

"No," she stated firmly, offering no explanation for her certainty.

It was the right decision. She could see the tension leave Henry's face and shoulders as he ended his pacing and eased himself onto the bench next to her.

"He has landed in Ireland," he said in a more controlled voice, as if they were discussing a merchant bringing an interesting load of goods. "They are going to crown him Richard IV."

Elizabeth turned her face away and closed her eyes. Richard IV. Could it really be? No, Arthur was England's next king.

"Ludicrous," she said.

"Quite," agreed Henry, and they said no more.

February 1492

"I believe we should visit our mother," Anne said in her soft, hesitant voice.

Elizabeth lifted her eyes from the altar cloth she was embroidering with tiny green leaves. Her sister rarely made a request, having none of Mary or Cecily's boldness. "You miss her?"

"Of course," Anne replied as she fidgeted with her own sewing. It appeared she was doing the fabric more harm than good.

Elizabeth took her nervous fingers in her hands. "Anne, please stop punishing the cloth. You may speak to me as a sister, not always as a queen."

Anne took a deep breath and forced herself to look into her older sister's eyes. "I know that our mother has caused you – all of us – some hardship in the past, but her health is failing, Bess. She is more ill than she wishes for us to know. Before you go into your confinement . . ." she trailed off as her courage ran dry.

"You are right," Elizabeth admitted as she rested her hand on her stomach that was once again rounded with new life. I have not honored our mother as I should. All past mistakes should be forgiven as I hope that my children will forgive me for my own faults." And I pray my brothers forgive me for denying them if one of them is truly still alive, she thought to herself. "Is her condition as severe as that?"

Anne's slender shoulders lifted in a shrug. "I cannot say for certain. She puts on her most regal façade when I visit, but I feel it, Bess. She will soon join our father . . . and brothers, in Heaven."

Elizabeth searched Anne's face looking for explanation of the hesitation before adding Edward and Richard to the inhabitants of Heaven. Did she believe that the young man in Ireland was Richard? Not surprisingly, Anne broke eye contact first and focused on her thin hands in her lap without saying more.

"We shall visit Bermondsey tomorrow," Elizabeth stated. "Please inform the ladies and attendants who will need to prepare."

Anne jumped up to see that Elizabeth's orders were carried out before any awkward questions could be asked of her.

The next day, Anne and Elizabeth set out with the minimum number of attendants to visit their mother, former queen of England, who now presided over the nuns of Bermondsey. During her morning prayers, Elizabeth had asked forgiveness for having neglected her mother and thanked the Heavenly Father for Anne's intercession. She silently repeated these prayers when she stepped into her mother's room.

Elizabeth Woodville had aged into a shadow of her former self since Elizabeth had last seen her. The hardships of her husband's death and disappearance of her sons had added fine lines to her face, but she had still been beautiful. Little remained of her famous beauty as her daughters gathered around her. The shimmering blond hair that had captured the attention of a young king was thin and cropped short to avoid the difficulty of maintaining it. The skin, kept smooth through creams and constant attention, had been allowed to fall into dry haggardness. A plain dress hung loosely on her bony frame. Still, she smiled brightly as her daughters surrounded her.

"You have even brought my little Cat!" their mother exclaimed with more motherly affection than they remembered her expressing before. Their youngest sister, Catherine, in her twelve years, had experienced almost constant political upheaval and considered the gossip and questions that flew through Henry Tudor's court to be perfectly normal.

"Do you know that they believe our brother, Richard, has landed in Ireland to reclaim his crown?" she blurted.

Elizabeth's eyes widened at this, but her mother didn't even blink.

"Likely only fools believe that," she said calmly. "How are you, Bess? I hear that you are expecting another child." She firmly closed any discussion of her lost sons.

"Yes, mother," Elizabeth took up a thin hand and noted the blue veins that coursed close to the surface. "I hope for another son of course."

"Be careful how many sons you pray for," her mother said harshly. "Edward III's quiver of sons has caused heartache for generations after his passing."

Elizabeth tried to imagine her little Arthur and Henry fighting each other for the throne or forcing abdication on each other's children. Had the great King Edward ever envisioned the fighting that might break out between cousins?

"I pray that my children and their descendants will be protected from such a fate," she whispered. She did miss Arthur now that he was master of his own household, but was consoled by the fact that her cousin Margaret would be with him as Sir Richard Pole had been named the Chamberlain of Ludlow Castle. Margaret was sure to shower Arthur with affection while maintaining the necessary discipline.

"As do I," the former queen said nonchalantly, patting her daughter's hand. "And Cecily, she also has added another daughter to her household."

"Yes," Anne said, seeing that Bess required a moment to put out of her mind the disturbing visions her mother had placed there. "I was hoping we would be the bearers of good news, but clearly you have already heard."

The older woman laughed. "I still have my informants, but in this case Cecily wrote to me after the birth of little Anne. Named for you?"

Anne blushed. "I'm sure not," she said. "More likely, the babe is named for our lovely queen, Anne Neville."

Elizabeth Woodville grunted at that but chose not to comment on the virtues or lack thereof of Richard's frail queen.

"I had hoped to attend her once again," Elizabeth added. "But Henry did not wish for me to travel in my condition."

"I am sure that Viscount Welles arranged for her to be well attended. He does dote upon her," Anne reassured Elizabeth with a wistful look in her eyes.

I must ask Henry about his plans for sweet Anne, Elizabeth thought, suddenly realizing that her quiet little sister was ready to begin her own family. She removed one of her hands from her mother's in order to take up one of Anne's small but capable hands. "I'm sure you are right. Cecily has done well and made her husband very happy." Anne's blush deepened at the attention that she was receiving, but she warmed at her sister's praise.

After an hour of pleasant small talk, Elizabeth could see that her mother was tiring. It saddened her to see this woman who had served her husband so competently, sometimes scheming more than she should have, looking so worn. Maybe it was better to be taken in relative youth as her father had been. He would always be remembered as a strong, golden warrior.

"We must allow you to rest, mother," Elizabeth said as she stood. Her sisters and attendants rose with her. She half expected her mother to argue and claim unending energy, but she acquiesced with a sigh.

"Your mother is an old woman," she said with chagrin. "I have appreciated this visit more than you know."

Were there tears in Elizabeth Woodville's eyes? Certainly not.

"I love you, mother," Elizabeth whispered as she leaned to embrace her. She couldn't remember the last time she had said it. Had she ever said it and meant it as sincerely?

"And I love you, my daughter. I am so proud of the queen you have become. I am happy to see that you have learned from my mistakes."

Elizabeth had an argument on her lips that her mother waved away.

"I am old enough to admit that I did indeed make some mistakes, though they may not be the same ones that you see," she said with a wry grin. "You are a beautiful, kind, and thoughtful woman, Bess. How you are the product of Edward and myself I am not at all certain, but I am glad that you are."

Speechless, Elizabeth simply embraced her mother once more and then stepped back for her sisters to do the same.

As they rode the barge back across the Thames, Elizabeth approached Anne. "Thank you for suggesting this visit, sister dear. I had put it off for too long and it was more enjoyable than I anticipated."

Anne simply smiled and leaned into her sister's side. They enjoyed the companionable silence for the remainder of the trip.

June 1492

Lady Margaret had recently visited the confinement rooms. Cecily did not need to ask when she entered. The closed shutters and snuffed candles told her that her sister's mother-in-law had been present. Though Margaret had no children besides Henry, and he had been born when she was only thirteen, she considered herself an expert on childbearing. Surveying her sister's calm face, Cecily wondered how she had the patience for such an overbearing presence in her life. Then she smiled to herself, thinking that their mother wasn't much different, except that in this area she truly was an expert.

Cecily threw open the shutters without needing to be told. Elizabeth allowed them closed and the room darkened to please Henry's mother, but she drew the line at leaving them that way once Margaret had made her departure. Taking a deep breath of warm, grass-scented air, she turned a smiling face toward Elizabeth, who returned the grin in full.

"Thank you, Cecily. I know she means well, but it was starting to feel a bit stifling in here."

Cecily allowed a small laugh. Margaret's very presence was stifling, but she would attempt to be as kind and graceful as her sister in this case. If Elizabeth could bear it in her condition, then Cecily could too.

"How are you feeling?" Cecily asked as she sat at the edge of her sister's bed. It was far too large for one small woman with a giant mattress stuffed with expensive feathers. At least Margaret made sure that Elizabeth was accommodated in royal fashion.

"I have nothing to complain about," Elizabeth said with a content sigh and a hand placed upon her rounded belly.

"And even if you did, you would not."

Cecily fluffed Elizabeth's cushions and fetched her a cup of wine. Then she noticed their younger sister, Anne standing near the door looking as though the doctors had bled her, so white was her face. Glancing toward Elizabeth to ensure that she had not noticed, Cecily rushed to Anne and pulled her into the hallway. A guard sat half dozing just outside the door, another requirement of Margaret's that seemed completely unnecessary to Cecily. She was once again thankful that it was her sister, and not her, who was queen. They moved down the hall to a small alcove that offered some privacy.

"What is it, Anne?" Cecily asked impatiently. "You should not enter Bess's room looking as though you have seen a ghost."

Anne blushed and struggled to speak, stopping then starting to mumble so that Cecily did not catch a word she said.

Cecily sighed and took Anne's hands in her own. "Anne, my dear sister, I am not angry with you. I only wish to help Bess have as easy of a time as possible. What has upset you?"

Tears streamed down Anne's face and she looked to the floor rather than her sister's face. Cecily cursed her impatience and wiped Anne's face.

"Hush, Annie. Surely things are not as bad as all that. Tell me."

Cecily's arms went around her younger sister who sniffled and wiped at her eyes.

"It is mother," Anne sobbed. "She is gone."

Gone? Dead? The news was not completely unexpected. Elizabeth Woodville had been in declining health for months, but still it was difficult for Cecily to believe it. She remembered her mother as such a strong presence, full of life and vitality, and now she was no more.

Anne continued to sob freely in her sister's arms. She was a young woman who was close to few but held those few very close to the heart.

"There now," Cecily crooned, wondering how her own eyes

remained dry. "Mother was looking forward to the glory of heaven that she now enjoys. Imagine the greeting she will give our father."

Anne released a choked laugh at that. Young as she was, she remembered the passion that had flamed between their parents.

"I am sorry that I could not control myself better within Bess's room. Do you think she noticed?"

"I do not, but we must decide how to tell her."

"Oh, Cecily! Surely not until after the birth."

Cecily shook her head. "She would be unhappy with us if we were to keep it from her or if she were to learn of it through gossip. Do not worry yourself. I will tell her when I think it best."

"Thank you, Cecily. I do not think that I could do it."

"You have a tender heart, and that is nothing to be ashamed of," Cecily assured her and then held her until her tears had run dry.

Later that evening, Elizabeth and Cecily had sat down to a supper carefully created to include the queen's favorite dishes.

"Bess, I have something I must tell you."

"Finally," Bess said with a sigh. "I have felt the tension in the air since this morning and was hoping you had cleared the room of all others in order to share with me what everyone else already clearly knows."

"We have underestimated your ability to read us, I see," Cecily said with a half-hearted grin. "I'm afraid the news may upset you, but I would have you hear it nonetheless."

Elizabeth placed her cup on the table and let her hands rest in her lap. "And I would hear it."

Cecily rose from her seat and knelt in the fragrant rushes by her sister's chair. "It is our mother."

Elizabeth closed her eyes and drew in a long breath before nodding. "She has died."

"Yes," Cecily whispered. "I am sorry that it has happened this way and at this time." She reached for the small white hands lying in Bess's lap.

"She did not call for us."

"No. She would not have wanted us to remember her that way, and, of course, she knew that you were unable. She would not have wanted you to feel guilt in not being able to attend her. More likely she was saddened by the fact that she could not attend you."

Elizabeth smiled. "She was a mountain of strength when I labored to bring Arthur and Margaret into this world. I pray that she is now at peace with herself and with God."

Cecily stood and put an arm around Elizabeth's shoulders. "Then you can bear it?"

"I can. Our mother has been joyously welcomed into our Savior's arms, not to mention our father's. What could make her happier?"

"Oh, Bess, how I do sometimes envy your faith. I believe you are right. Our mother's earthly time lasted longer than her pleasure in it. Thank you for reminding me of that. I will be happy for her and try not to mourn."

"There is nothing wrong with mourning, dear Cecily. I will miss our mother and will be forever grateful that Anne convinced me to make that last visit, but I am also thankful that she has received her heavenly reward."

Cecily gave Elizabeth one last squeeze before returning to her seat, wondering if either of them would be able to eat now. She had forgotten that the hunger of a pregnant woman is lessened by few things of this world. Elizabeth had taken up her spoon before her sister had retaken her seat.

"I will name this babe for our parents," Elizabeth said after a few silent moments. "Edward if it is a son and Elizabeth if it is a girl."

"That is a wonderful idea," Cecily agreed. "But did you not

grow weary of the confusion of two Elizabeths in the house as a child?"

Elizabeth grinned. "It has its advantages and disadvantages. My daughter will be called Eliza."

She said it with such certainty that Cecily was not surprised when her sister gave birth to a perfect little girl less than a month later.

July 1492

"She is beautiful, just like her mother," Henry said while holding tiny, copper-haired Eliza.

"You are not disappointed in another daughter?" Elizabeth asked. Henry had not shown dismay, but she knew how important sons were to a king. She remembered her father's joy upon meeting little Edward for the first time.

No, she would not allow herself to think about that.

"Disappointed? Of course not! You have provided me with two healthy sons. More would only cause rivalries. Remember Edward III."

"How could I forget?" Elizabeth's entire life had centered on the debate concerning which of Edward III's descendants had the best claim to the throne of England. Maybe two sons were sufficient.

She had invited Henry to join her in the gardens, so happy was she to be released from her luxurious but confining birthing chamber. With a wave of her hand, attendants rushed in to scoop up baby Eliza and carry her inside. Those who remained put a respectful distance between themselves and the royal couple.

"I have heard that my grandmother Neville refused to attend my mother's funeral."

Henry took a deep breath and sighed, confirming Elizabeth's belief that he was hoping that she would not hear this particular bit of rumor.

"It is true. I wish that I could tell you that she was ill or feeling her age, but she would certainly tell you the truth were you to speak to her. Cecily Neville never forgave your mother for ensnaring your father."

"I know," Elizabeth agreed. "I just wish that she could have at least forgiven her in death. My grandmother is a pious woman. I am surprised that she has overlooked the virtue of forgiving others their trespasses."

"Forgiving and mourning are two different things, Bess. I'm sure that the duchess of York forgave your mother and even loves the children she bore her son, but to publicly mourn her is much to ask."

"You're right, of course. Maybe I expect too much of an old woman rather set in her ways. I thank you for allowing a quiet funeral as my mother requested. She would not want people to think about her as she was in her last years but to remember her at my father's side."

Henry said nothing but took his wife's hand. All else was left unspoken as they watched the sunset splash across the canopy of the sky. A few tears streaked down Elizabeth's face as she considered the fact that her mother would never enjoy this sight again, but then she smiled when she marveled at just how glorious it must appear from heaven.

October 1492

The scene in the bailey was no less familiar than it was unwelcome. Men examining their horses a final time while squires scurried to ensure that everything was packed for their masters correctly. Though their armor was not necessary at this point, many wore it, for it made a memorable spectacle for an army to march out fully armed even if it were only to march onto waiting boats. When they stepped foot onto French soil, the helms and hauberks would serve for more than ceremony.

Elizabeth surveyed the scene from her chamber window. Autumn leaves scattered in the wind and the trees beyond the castle walls were a masterpiece of reds and golds. She wondered how many of these men were looking upon the autumn splendor for the last time. Would Henry be one of them? She could not ponder that type of thought, with Arthur only six years old. As much as she cherished her husband, it was England that would suffer most if left once again in the hands of a child king.

She allowed herself to follow this path in her mind for only a moment. If Henry were to fall in France, would the English accept her rule as regent more affably than they had her mother's? Would Arthur's kingship succeed where her brother's had failed? Elizabeth wondered who would race to her side in support and who would act in rebellion against her. Her cousin Edmund de la Pole, possibly. They were fond of each other, but it was said that her ancestress Matilda had been fond of Stephen, too, and it did not keep him from stealing her crown.

Shaking negative and unnecessary thoughts from her head, Elizabeth spotted Henry among his household knights and milling crowd below her window. Pride filled her heart as she gazed down at this man she had learned to love unashamedly. How interesting are the ways of the Lord, she reflected. Her memories of ranting at her mother in hatred for the exile she had never met were replaced with feelings stronger than any she had for any other person. Only God could have brought that about, of that she was certain. Henry would never look the ideal soldier as her father had, but he looked lean and strong in his finely tailored livery today.

They had agreed to say a private farewell before Elizabeth appeared for the formal send-off. When Henry disappeared from her window view, she knew that he was coming to her for that purpose. Feelings raged inside her, fighting for prominence. Worry slithered through her veins making her want to hold onto Henry and beg him not to go. Love of her husband tended to agree with worry, but love of her country wished him health and good hunting. Pride in the king Henry had become and knowledge that he needed to see that to encourage him today was what she allowed to the forefront. By the time she had arranged her skirts and her face, he had arrived.

He knelt before her. "I desire your blessing, my lady queen."

"In Our Father's name, you may have it. May he bless you and your mission." She lightly touched his forehead as she said it the way she did when she blessed her children.

He stayed on his knee head bowed for a moment longer than necessary, and Elizabeth knew that he was saying one last silent prayer before leaving her for what they both knew could be forever. When his eyes were lifted to meet hers, she said, "The Lord will keep you, Henry. Of that I am sure." Once again, she had reason to be glad that she was capable of infusing her voice with more confidence than she felt.

"With your blessing and continued prayers, I believe that you will be proven right." He stood, without the slowness that some men his age displayed.

"You will certainly look more fine than Charles," Elizabeth said, holding her arms out to draw him in. "I am almost tempted to keep you here for one more hour for a proper farewell."

Henry leaned down. With his forehead and nose lightly touching hers, he said, "Do not tempt me, woman. I may never again find the strength to leave your bed if I give in now."

"Very well," she said, lightly kissing his lips before growing more serious. "Do be careful, Henry."

"You needn't be concerned, my love. I will be back with the pretender in hand before our babe's birthday."

Elizabeth wished that she could send Henry with the knowledge that she was again with child, but it was not the case. With little Eliza just five months old, she could hardly be disappointed. However, she did wonder how long Henry would be gone, how long before her womb would have the opportunity to quicken again.

"You do believe that King Charles will turn over . . . the pretender?" Who was he? She wished she had a name for him as she was not about to call him what he had begun calling himself, Richard IV.

Henry nodded firmly. "He has nothing to gain by protecting this supposed king. As much as the French king may enjoy needling me with his presence, he will not be worth fighting for."

"Go with God then, my love."

They joined hands and exited the room. With each step, Elizabeth held her head a little higher and her back a little straighter. When she appeared before the rows of mounted men, she was no longer a worried wife but a stately queen. The men marched off, ready to die for her.

~ ~ ~ ~

Henry was disappointed to not bring his rival back to England in chains. Instead, he brought home a chest of Charles' money and a signed treaty that exiled the sometime Richard IV into Burgundy.

July 1493

"Perkin Warbeck."

"I'm sorry?" Elizabeth's eyebrow shot up as she curiously looked at her husband.

"The pretender, he is Perkin Warbeck. He is Flemish and certainly not your brother."

"Well, that much we knew to be true."

"I will ruin him. Nobody will believe that he could be Richard of York when they hear the true story. My spies have located a father, a simple fisherman in Flanders."

A father, Henry had said. Not his father. Elizabeth mentally filed this away.

"Henry, what will the French king say to this?" It mattered not whether she believed him, but whether their royal peers did.

"He has already sent him into exile. He should be thankful that he has and does not have to deal with the embarrassment of harboring a common fishmonger as a king."

"But he is welcomed to the Burgundian court as the English king," she risked pointing out.

"Bess, your aunt Margaret would welcome Satan himself to her court if she believed that he may rebel against me."

Elizabeth crossed herself but said nothing.

"The fact of the matter is that your father's sister is not content that you, her niece, are queen of England. She will not rest until a male York heir has taken my place, even if she has to create one."

It was true. Elizabeth did not understand it, but the duchess of Burgundy was not content to leave England in peace with Henry as king. The sons of Elizabeth and Henry were not Yorks in her mind, but Tudors not fit to wear the crown.

"But this man is not a York heir, why would she give him her support?"

Henry poured himself a cup of wine before shrugging and saying, "Who knows? She hopes to replace him with someone more suitable after removing me. She believes that he is one of your father's illegitimate sons and figures one of his by-blows is better than his daughter. Her mind is an enigma to me, Bess."

"Do you believe he is my father's son?"

Another shrug. "I have no idea. It is said that he resembles your father in looks and character. He is charming and is blessed with that red-gold hair you all seem to have. While your father does not have quite the reputation for spreading his seed as Henry I, it would not come as a surprise if Warbeck is the result of one of his trips to the continent."

This gave Elizabeth pause for thought. While she couldn't bring up any real hope that this Perkin was her brother, Richard, she was only slightly less uncomfortable making war upon a man who may be her half-brother. Feelings of mercy were sometimes better left to God. This man had started the battle, not her, but she would fight for her son's inheritance.

September 1494

"Your grace, I would speak to you."

Elizabeth recognized both the formal greeting and the voice that held no respect for the title that she must use.

"Yes, Lady Margaret," she said in response, knowing that Margaret preferred a more stately honorific.

The two women took measure of each other, Elizabeth's face calm and giving away nothing, Margaret's heavily lined with a sourly puckered mouth.

"We can use my chambers."

Elizabeth had little choice but to follow as her mother-in-law strode quickly in the direction of her rooms that connected with Henry's. Theirs was a fragile peace. Elizabeth chose not to speak up about the times her husband's mother attempted to usurp her position, but Margaret understood that if she pushed too far it was Henry who would be enraged rather than his wife.

Margaret's rooms were lavishly decorated with tapestries detailing the life of Christ and his saints upon each wall. A thick Turkish carpet covered most of the floor, and cushioned chairs were pulled close to the hearth. A flagon of wine with finely engraved silver cups stood on a small table and informed Elizabeth that this meeting had been planned in advance.

Elizabeth did not wait for Margaret to give her permission before claiming the seat she preferred and waited to be handed a cup of fine wine from Burgundy before speaking.

"What do we have need to discuss?"

Margaret, for her own part, sat upon the other chair as though it were a throne and dismissed her attendant before favoring Elizabeth with a glance, let alone an answer.

"I am in the process of planning Harry's installment as duke of York, and Henry insisted that I enquire as to whether you had any desires regarding the ceremony."

Elizabeth lifted her cup to give herself time to think. She was somewhat hurt that Henry had not even shared his intentions with her, hated it when she learned something from her mother-in-law. Then there was the idea of her little Harry as duke of York, a position that had last been held by her brother, Richard. The man exiled to her aunt's court in Burgundy claimed to currently bear this title when he was not calling himself Richard IV.

"I trust your judgment on this, of course," she said, her feelings too jumbled to think of anything else.

"It is to take place as soon as possible, now that your aunt has pushed Henry beyond even his saintly patience."

Elizabeth didn't want to ask, knowing that it was exactly what Henry's mother was baiting her to do, but her curiosity got the best of her. "What has the duchess of Burgundy done?"

The smile that lit up Margaret's haggard face told Elizabeth that she was mentally scoring herself a point in a game that only she kept track of. She took her time before answering.

"Surely, you heard. No? The Flemish pretender was paraded at the funeral of the Holy Roman Emperor as Richard IV."

Elizabeth allowed herself no reaction to this news, and Margaret was forced to carry on.

"Phillip of Burgundy, now the heir, has been providing him with men, money, and the title of king of England. Henry has decided that naming his son duke of York will send a confident message that we do not believe anyone else alive holds that particular title."

Elizabeth closed her eyes for a moment before responding. She was sure that Margaret never considered the fact that she was speaking of Elizabeth's little brother when she tactlessly referred to his death.

"Maximilian is maintaining his support of the pretender now

that he has been named Emperor in his father's place then?"

"Maximilian allows Phillip free reign to do whatever he will," Margaret said with a dismissive wave of her hand. "Whatever is allowed in Burgundy, it will no longer be accepted in Henry's kingdom. Harry is to be duke of York and no other."

Elizabeth nodded. "I agree. I ask only that in the planning of festivities it be kept in mind that the prince is only three years old. He will tire easily and his temper will be demonstrated publicly if too much is required of him."

"I am well aware of Harry's age and abilities," Margaret snapped.

"Then I leave it in your capable hands," Elizabeth said as she stood to leave. She knew that she should be happy to see her young son honored as duke of York, but it felt too much like the final strand of hope that she would ever see her brother again was fraying and about to snap.

~ ~ ~ ~

By the end of October, England had a new duke of York. Prince Henry had charmed and exceeded everyone's expectations during the lengthy ceremony, games, and meals that had been deemed necessary components of the festivities. Only one thing marred the occasion. Henry and his mother had agreed that men should be carefully placed throughout the crowd, listening for whispers of discontent or faith in another duke of York.

January 1495

Elizabeth was mentally packing for the move to Sheen, calculating certain items to be left here at Greenwich and others that she could not do without. How she longed to be gone from this palace, not due to any particular fault that it had but because Sheen would always feel more like home. As she sat absent-mindedly toiling at her embroidery which was always close to avoid idleness of hands, Henry stormed into the room.

It was unlike him not to follow accepted etiquette even when entering his own wife's chambers. Almost as if he believed that following royal procedure would help people accept his kingship, he would remain formal until they were alone. Whatever had upset him, took up enough space in his mind to force these expectations from the forefront. He looked more furious than she had ever seen him, and the thought flitted through her head that he did indeed have a few drops of Plantagenet blood.

"Clear the room!" he ordered, sending servants and ladies-in-waiting scurrying from the path of his wrath.

Elizabeth stood slowly and watched her attendants for signs of disobedience. Any, who may have considered questioning Henry's command, withered under her calm gaze. While his temper was all the more terrifying for its infrequency, Elizabeth had been dealing with fiery tempers her entire life and was able to be an island of peace.

"What is it?" she asked quietly when the door had shut behind the last bowed page. She placed her hand on his arm and could feel his pulse racing through a vein that always popped up near the surface of his skin. Her cool fingers gently massaged in an absent-minded fashion, as though to slow the beating of his heart.

"Stanley," he grunted as if the word was a curse, and maybe it was.

Elizabeth would have cursed William Stanley straight to hell had it been within her capabilities after the battle of Bosworth. She mentally shoved aside the conflicting thoughts and feelings that threatened to surface whenever she allowed herself to dwell for too long upon the brief time between her father's death and her uncle's. William's brother, Thomas Stanley, Henry's stepfather, was not much better, but surely he was not opportunistic enough to plot against his wife's son. Elizabeth waited in silence, knowing it was the best way to draw Henry out.

He stormed to the table holding a flagon and wine glasses. Though he normally ate and drank only as minimally required, he took a huge gulp before refilling the cup and handing the other to Elizabeth. She gestured for him to sit, and he took another long drink before accepting the offered seat.

Elizabeth watched his face, which was focused on the low fire that served to keep the winter chill from her chambers. Severe lines were etched into his forehead and around his mouth. He seemed not to move even to breathe, taking on the appearance of a gargoyle frozen forever in anger. She was beginning to wonder if she would have to drag his story from him when he made a quick movement.

She leaned over to extract from the rushes the small item that Henry had tossed angrily in her direction. It was a badge in the shape of a white Yorkist rose, the type she remembered men in her father's household affixing to their hauberks. Her fingers caressed the emblem, almost lovingly, before she was pulled back into the present.

"It was found among dear uncle William's belongings, along with many other trappings of York livery and enough cash to fund a well-armed contingency of men."

Instead of loud anger, there was now quiet fury in his voice. Elizabeth found the latter had much more effect on her nerves. She swallowed the lump that had formed in her throat.

"I don't understand," she said, though she was afraid that she did very much understand. Stanley had decided that he might benefit from playing kingmaker again. How much would the man claiming to be her brother reward Stanley for turning on his brother's stepson?

The look Henry gave Elizabeth told her that he was not convinced of her ignorance but that he would humor her.

"Clifford assures me that Stanley intended to give generous support to your Perkin once he managed to land on our shores," he said while intently watching her face. She kept it carefully arranged in neutrality.

"Henry? My Perkin? Certainly, you do not mean to accuse me of having anything to do with encouraging others to take away the throne of my son."

His eyes narrowed. "You concern yourself not with the crown of your husband?"

She was tempted to stand and walk to the window. She wanted to remove herself from his suspicious glare but knew that it would only work to convince him of her guilt.

"I meant only that I have no reason whatsoever to ally myself with the likes of William Stanley." She spat the name out with more venom than he had ever heard direct toward for any man. It was enough to shock him from his anger and into curiosity.

"But you have allied yourself with him before." At her upraised eyebrow, he continued. "Before I came to claim the crown from the usurper, Richard, the Stanleys assured me of your encouragement – your desire to become my wife."

Elizabeth felt heat rising to her cheeks. Though she thanked God for the love she now felt for Henry, she had not had anything of the desire Henry referred to before they met. Her daily life now centered on her children and striving to be a God pleasing queen. She rarely allowed herself to consider her torn feelings over how her marriage had begun. How much could she say about that to Henry?

"I assure you that I am not now and have never conspired with any Stanleys."

Again, Henry's hazel eyes attempted to look deep into her soul. She liked it not. Thoughts and feelings resided in her soul that she wanted nobody to examine, not even herself. She forced herself to sit with her back straight and her face confident.

"You did not wish to marry me," he said. It was not a question.

"I did not know you," Elizabeth whispered.

"But you knew that I would save you from your uncle. Was it not enough?" he pleaded.

Elizabeth sighed, but would not lie to salve his bruised ego. "Why should any of this matter now?"

He shifted in his seat, leaning back as if to consider her from another angle. "Were you in love with Richard?"

"I thought you came to tell me about the treasonous William Stanley. Do you prefer to speak about my uncle who has been dead these past ten years while I have been warming your bed and bearing your children?" she said with more anger than she felt as if it could hide her secret guilt.

It was Henry's turn to look surprised. Elizabeth was infrequently anything other than docile and submissive. He had hit a chord, but did he want to continue to play it? He leaned forward in his seat and decided that he did not have patience for more doubts and puzzles.

"Sir William has been arrested and has been given accommodations in the Tower." He went back to looking at the fire.

"I'm so sorry, Henry." Elizabeth moved her chair closer to his and placed her hand on his arm. This time, the blood was not racing with the same intensity. The lines were not as deep in his face, but neither had they disappeared. "I know it must be a severe blow to you that William would betray one of his family for a pretender." She bit her tongue to keep from saying anything more about how she felt about the Stanley brothers, who had always seemed to end on the winning side of any fight. She thought that she would need to speak to her confessor about the feeling of joy that rose within her breast when she envisioned William Stanley as a desperate Tower prisoner.

Henry sipped wine from his cup before responding. "I can trust nobody. Except Jasper." He fixed his gaze on her as he said it, leaving no doubt that she had been purposely excluded.

"Jasper has been your greatest supporter and confidant," she agreed, refusing to join in a battle that was sure to wound on both sides. He looked disappointed.

"Perkin will attempt to land."

Elizabeth nodded. "It seems likely."

"He will not win."

The confidence in Henry's eyes was proof that, while many in England still thought of him only as Elizabeth's husband, he considered himself king in his own right and was willing to prove it on the battlefield once again.

"Of course he will not," she agreed. They stood together as if by silent agreement. This threat and newfound confidence made him seem taller, broader. She felt a familiar stir at the hunger that replaced the suspiciousness in his eyes. When he roughly claimed her mouth with his own, she gladly allowed herself to be conquered.

Later, when the heat from the fire and their passion no longer heated the room, they burrowed into the thick covers on the bed. With Henry more at peace, Elizabeth dared to question him.

"What will you do next?"

"Next? Good God, woman! Are you not satisfied?"

Elizabeth smacked at him playfully. "You know that is not what I meant."

He instantly became more serious. "Stanley will be brought before me tomorrow to answer the charge of treason."

Pressing her lips together into a firm line, Elizabeth nodded. Though it did not give her joy to hear it, she also could not bring herself to feel an ounce of sympathy for the man who had betrayed more than one king.

"You will defeat the pretender without him," she stated firmly. While she could not bring herself to use the name that she was certain her husband had created for him, she also would never call this man Richard of York. Who was he, really, she frequently wondered on nights when sleep failed to claim her.

Henry pulled her into his arms. "You do not know what it means to me to have you at my side."

She refrained from pointing out that he had accused her of untrustworthiness not an hour ago and decided that the unspoken accusation was better left forgiven and forgotten. Before her mind could wander into the swamps of the unanswered questions and unspoken concerns, Henry spoke again.

"I would see your remaining sisters married."

Elizabeth gasped but quickly controlled herself. "Who do you have in mind for them, if I may ask?"

A smile tugged at one side of his mouth. "You may."

"Henry, do not tease me."

"I have spoken to Sir Thomas Howard regarding Anne, she being the older of the two. Cat, I am still considering options for."

"What about William Courtenay?" Elizabeth blurted before she had considered whether her suggestion would work for or against the young man who made little Cat blush each time he spoke. She hoped that he would dismiss the idea that had been put forth to marry her to James Stewart, duke of Ross and brother of the Scots king. As unrealistic as it may be, she hoped to keep her sisters in England.

Henry frowned thoughtfully, but would give up nothing. "I will think on it," was all he would promise.

February 1495

Thomas Howard had proved willing to wait for Anne of York to become his bride. Originally betrothed to her in 1484, he finally took her as his bride in 1495. Quiet Anne glowed in her wedding finery and blushed each time comments regarding the upcoming bedding reached her ears. Never straying far from her new husband's side, she attempted to shyly avoid the spotlight at her own wedding feast.

Elizabeth smiled seeing her sister so content with the man who had been chosen for her long ago. Observing her simple joy and submissive attitude, few who did not know her would have guessed that she was a princess born of Edward IV and Elizabeth Woodville. Though she had her share of blond, sapphire-eyed beauty, she had none of the arrogance or even confidence of her parents. This seemed to suit Thomas just fine. Elizabeth was happy that Anne had been married to someone who seemed capable of finding contentment in the type of quiet family life that would please her. The last thing Anne needed was a husband who would put politicking over his family.

As Elizabeth was envisioning Anne's future full of children and country manors, Henry stepped up to her side and pressed close to her. She caught the scent of wine in the air as he handed her a cup. She accepted it gladly, thankful that this was an occasion for them to enjoy without being the center of attention. Of course, there were those who took this opportunity to press Henry with their ideas and desires, but he brushed them aside with good-natured invitations to join him in a toast to the bride and groom.

"Henry, it pleases me to see you so lighthearted," Elizabeth whispered as they watched dancers take the floor.

"What is not to be happy about?" he asked rhetorically, pulling her closer to him. "I have the most beautiful wife in England, two healthy sons, and matters are working themselves out nicely."

Elizabeth did not wish to ask what those matters might be and shatter the pleasantness of the moment. Instead, she gestured to her sister, Cat, flirting mercilessly with the handsome William Courtenay.

Cat was sixteen and beautiful. She shared Elizabeth's reddish blond coloring as opposed to Cecily's more silvery blond. A light dusting of freckles that would have made a lesser beauty appear low-class, only added to her playfulness. Poor William was no match for this vixen who had watched each of her older sisters snatch men's hearts. For her own part, Cat did not notice the other men looking enviously at Courtenay as her eyes never left his deep brown ones.

Elizabeth looked at Henry in eagerness for his acquiescence. How could anyone watch the young couple and not wish them well? Courtenay was the close friend of Elizabeth's cousin, Edmund de la Pole, which made him even more suitable in her eyes. Henry, who looked at Edmund as a possible rival with his copper hair and Plantagenet blood, may not see it as a credit to William. He was ready to pose his argument when he looked down at his wife, who clearly had dreams of romance and happily ever after on her mind.

"Very well," he said gruffly. "She may wed Courtenay."

October 1495

Though the path was worn fairly smooth by thousands of feet that had trod it before her, Elizabeth could still feel the edges of small stones press uncomfortably into her bare feet. She knew that others would feel that it was unnecessary for her, as a queen and mother of three healthy children, to make this pilgrimage to Walsingham, but she had felt drawn to it. The recent loss of her three year-old daughter, Eliza, had forced her to acknowledge that a crown did not protect her from death. It reached out its ugly talons to snatch away peasant and princess alike. There was no better place than Walsingham to appeal to the Lord for more children and give him thanks for those he had trusted to her.

She had refused to wear anything on this last stretch of the journey that would identify her as a queen, but even bare of accessories and in her simple shift, her regal bearing and beauty gave her away. She was almost thirty, and childbearing and overflowing royal tables had caused the lithe figure of her younger years to disappear under a body that was more voluptuous, and Henry claimed more pleasing. Her face was slightly more round but had yet to bear any fine lines that would give away her age. A few of her rings had needed to be expanded to accommodate fingers that were no longer as slender, but her hair, let loose for this visit with God, shone like new copper in the bright sun.

Some would notice the bulge beneath the loose flowing fabric that indicated that Elizabeth had already been blessed in the way most supplicants to the Virgin at Walsingham prayed for. It was another reason for people to wonder why she made this holy walk, but she did not care what people thought. She had lived so much of her life concerning herself with what people would think, but today was between her and her God. She would beg him for the serenity required to accept the death of her daughter and ask for his hand upon the child she could feel fluttering in her womb.

Her mind focused on just how to express her requests to God when she entered the chapel, she failed to notice the crowd that grew around her or the quiet conversation that praised her beauty and piety. Unlike some, even among those who worked within the church, Elizabeth's faith was as real and important to her. She did not walk this path for show, and she took little note of those quietly gathering to get a glimpse of her.

A cool autumn wind blew through her hair, lifting it as though it were her banner. The folds of fabric gave her little protection against the cold, but she did not feel it. Her eyes were focused upon the intricate stonework that soared toward heaven. She tried to force the scene before her to replace the images of her lifeless child that kept trespassing into her thoughts.

A child's death was nothing new or infrequent, but it did not keep it from being any less tragic when it was your own. Elizabeth's hand moved to her throat in an automatic motion to finger the locket that she had begun wearing, within it hid a tiny lock of little Eliza's pure white blonde hair. With a slight shake of her head, she dropped her arm back to her side. The locket was back in her borrowed rooms, along with all other jewels and fine clothes. She must be thankful that she would see her beautiful daughter one day when they met in heaven and stopped longing for her earthly presence. Oh, how it tested her faith.

She was thankful that Eliza had been taken quickly. Though it meant that Henry and Elizabeth had not been able to reach Eltham in time to sit at her bedside, it also meant that Eliza had not suffered the pain of dying that others were often forced to face. A fever had raged like a fire through her small body for only a few days before she succumbed. By the time Elizabeth had reached her and laid a shaking hand on her waxen cheek, Eliza was strangely cool and at peace.

The new life Elizabeth carried kicked and rolled, drawing her back into the present and away from her daughter's deathbed. "Are you attempting to console me, my little one?" Elizabeth whispered. She was careful not to look down at her growing belly as she spoke, not wanting quite yet to make her condition public. Some would guess anyway, but the recent reminder of the stealthiness of death made her wish to keep her pregnancy unknown. Maybe she could shield the new life from harm if its existence were secret.

As she entered the chapel, the stones under her feet became smoother but not warmer. She closed her eyes as she shuffled forward, taking in the scent of incense and fresh rushes. Surely, God was in this sacred place and would hear her more clearly from here. When she opened her eyes, she spotted the altar holding the vial of the Holy Mother's milk and a beautifully jeweled image of Mary herself. Kneeling before these sacred artifacts, Elizabeth poured her heart out to the Lord of all and listened intently for his voice.

~ ~ ~ ~

Henry sat before an untended fire, looking every one of his thirty-eight years. His spine curved, the weight of the world seeming to become too heavy for him. Though he must have heard Elizabeth's approach, he did not lift his head or move a muscle.

"Henry?" Elizabeth paused before him wondering if he was lost in mourning for their little Eliza. She slowly moved forward and knelt before him.

"Henry."

His body twitched as if waking from sleep and his eyes moved to seek her face.

"What is it, my love?" she asked.

He took a deep breath and leaned back in the chair.

"Warbeck."

It took Elizabeth a moment to switch gears in her mind. Her thoughts had been only of her children, the one lost and the one on the way. She searched her memory for recent developments regarding the man everyone now referred to as Perkin Warbeck.

She remembered that he was in Scotland being treated as a royal guest. Elizabeth assumed that this was more to annoy Henry than because King James actually believed Warbeck's story about being her brother. It was revenge for the several English princesses who had been offered as Scottish brides but had never set foot in that rugged northern land. Or so Elizabeth had assumed.

"What news is there of him?" she asked when it was clear that Henry was going to offer nothing more.

An ironic smile formed on his lips but did not reach his eyes. "He has been given a noble bride." Henry shook his head as he spoke as though he thought he must surely be mistaken.

Elizabeth's eyes widened in surprise. This was more than a game to torment England's king. For James to have offered Warbeck such a prize was to recognize his claim to the throne.

"Who?" she whispered.

"Kathryn Gordon," Henry said with a great exhale of breath. "She is supposedly a great favorite of the Scots king. It is rumored that he would not have given her up if she had agreed to become his mistress instead. Unfortunately for James, the lovely lady also has high moral standards."

"But to give her to Warbeck is to support his claim. It is a notice to all that James believes him to be . . ." She couldn't bring herself to say Richard IV or Richard of York. "Who he says he is."

Henry looked at her like a tutor humoring a slow student. "Yes, it is."

Shrugging, Henry reached for his goblet of wine. "He undoubtedly does not believe that Warbeck is your brother, but is willing to sacrifice the fair Kathryn to give me headaches in all foreign relations." He had stood and began to restlessly pace, leaving Elizabeth kneeling before an empty chair. Now he spun on her. "Do you know what this is going to do to our negotiations with Ferdinand and Isabella?"

Sliding into the chair that Henry had vacated, Elizabeth did not answer immediately. They had been attempting to forge a marriage contract between their son Arthur and the Spanish princess, Catherine of Aragon. Would they be hesitant when they learned that Henry's rival had gained the support of Scotland?

"Surely, they will not be greatly affected by the actions of James Stewart. They know him to be rash and short-sighted," she soothed.

Henry shook his head again, wondering if the peace that currently reigned in England would ever envelope him or if he would always feel that he was fighting for his right to wear the crown. "They may know that in their hearts but still not be willing to give up their daughter in show of support. How much easier it will be for them to simply find her another husband while we work out our own struggles."

The mother's heart took over in the queen. "If that is so, then we will find a more appropriate bride for our son. He is to be the king of England – how dare they look down their noses at him!"

This finally brought an authentic smile from her husband. He approached her and pulled her up from the chair. "Of course, you are correct," he said once she was firmly in his arms. "But I do not intend to let this pretender determine who my son can and cannot marry." He released her to resume his pacing. "I am beginning to wish that his landing in Kent had been successful, so that I may have defeated him once and for all."

Even after the beheading of William Stanley, Warbeck and a small force paid for by Maximilian of Burgundy had attempted to invade the previous June. At Deal Beach, Henry's men had butchered an advance party, sending Warbeck, who had never left his ship, back to sea. At the time, it had seemed a great victory, but as this phantom enemy continued to flit about the edges of their lives and coastlines, Elizabeth wondered if they wouldn't have been better off letting them land, as Henry now seemed to wish for.

"When he does, you will be ready. How can he expect to stand up to you," she said. "If men could not be raised against you at Stoke, they certainly will not run to this known fraud now." She was glad that her voice sounded more confident than she felt.

Henry seemed convinced by her words. He once again held her close, but there was no passion in his embrace. She could almost see the wheels that were still spinning in his head.

December 1495

The great hall at Sheen was filled with people, music, and laughter. It was difficult to remember that outside the wind blew and snow fell. The glow of candlelight and aroma of appetizing food completed the cozy scene. Elizabeth especially was enjoying watching her children interact and dance. It seemed like it had been too long since they had all been together as a family.

Before she had much opportunity to appreciate the idyllic setting, she felt Henry tense beside her. She turned and saw that his face had gone ghostly pale and his hand was tightly clenching a piece of parchment.

"Henry, what is it?" she asked, laying a hand upon his arm.

He looked at her and she was reminded of the look upon Arthur's face when she had told him that he would not see his favorite hound again. It was the look of a wounded little boy looking for comfort.

"Henry?" She felt fear rising within her but reminded herself that all of her children were present, so the worst could not have happened. "What is it?" she repeated.

He shook his head incredulously. "It is Jasper. He is dying."

Jasper Tudor was by no measure a young man, but he was Henry's mentor and most strident supporter. His death would be a crushing blow to the king, who saw traitors surrounding him at every turn since William Stanley had plotted against him.

"I'm so sorry," Elizabeth said as she took the hand that Henry was using to mangle the unwelcome missive. "I know Jasper has been like a father to you."

"I will have nobody left in whom I can put my complete trust."

Elizabeth was used to these comments that inadvertently insulted her but was surprised that he did not make an exception for his mother either.

"What ails him?" she asked. "Is there time to go to him?"

"He made his will on the fifteenth."

Four days ago.

"Will you ride to Thornbury tomorrow?" All visions of a family Christmas shattered, but she admitted that she could not take away Henry's opportunity to see Jasper one last time.

Henry stood, leaving his untouched food on the table before him. The revelries going on around them suddenly seemed incongruous with the feelings coursing through them. He looked down at Elizabeth who was trying to decide if she should leave with him and said, "If I cannot find a way to leave yet tonight."

~ ~ ~ ~

Henry arrived at Jasper's manor at Thornbury on December twenty-first, just in time to say good-bye.

February 1496

A light blanket of snow covered Sheen Palace's lawns and gardens. A chill breeze snuck in through the window that Elizabeth sat near, but she took no notice of it. Her mind was looking ahead to the coming season that would melt the snow, moistening the ground for the new life that would soon spring from it. In the meantime, the snow was beautiful, at least from a distance. She had no desire to run outside to play in it as her children did. The way it covered the ugly dead leaves and scarred ground served to remind her of the purity that covered the sins of all who believe in the Savior.

She had ordered the children's attendants not to allow them outside for too long. Illnesses that seemed of no consequence could quickly turn deadly, even in the royal nursery, as Eliza's death had proven. Arthur was away at his own household at Ludlow, attended by her cousin Margaret and Sir Richard Pole, and would likely be too concerned about maintaining his dignity to play outside. She was glad to not have to worry about him, so important was he as Henry's heir.

Harry's hair shone particularly red against the white of the snow, and Elizabeth couldn't help but allow a smile to turn up the corners of her mouth as she watched him allow his sister to pelt him with snowballs. Already learning the rules of chivalry, he dared not toss any her way, but instead focused his attack on the king's ward, Charles Brandon.

Charles was the son of one of Henry's most staunch supporters, William Brandon. William had been killed by King Richard at Bosworth, and, therefore, never saw his friend take the throne. In return for this loyalty, Henry raised Charles at court and allowed him almost the same advantages given his own sons. Harry, at five, adored Charles, who was a very worldly eleven year-old. Charles seemed to enjoy having the king's son follow him about and was more than happy to humor him and teach him things that Elizabeth would rather he did not know quite yet. They were nearly inseparable.

Charles displayed his budding skills of flirtation as he helped little Margaret up when she slipped on the ice. Though she was only six, a red flush covered her cheeks when she looked up at the handsome boy. Elizabeth told herself that the flush was caused by the cold but also made a note to watch young Brandon around the girls at court.

Clasping her cloak more tightly around her, Elizabeth wondered that the children seemed perfectly comfortable outside while she was cold in her window seat. She sent an attendant for mulled wine to warm her from within but was surprised when the door to her chamber opened again almost as it closed. She looked up to see not the servant she had just sent, but a page from the hall. He knelt before her and did not deliver her message until she had granted him permission to rise.

"The dowager duchess of Buckingham requests an audience with your grace," he said with the formality of one new to the position and very nervous about performing it perfectly.

"Katherine?" Elizabeth asked. "Of course, I will receive her."

She assigned the tasks of arranging chairs and refreshments near the fire to the closest of her ladies and asked another to ensure that her hair and dress were acceptable. By the time her mother's sister entered the room, Elizabeth looked as though she had been waiting all day for her to arrive.

Elizabeth stood and embraced Katherine as she entered the room, immediately removing any formality from the visit. She noticed that Katherine was not wearing widow's weeds though Jasper was not two months gone. Instead of appearing sad or weepy, her aunt looked rosy, content, and more vivacious than most women of thirty-eight.

"Aunt, you look stunning," Elizabeth said, holding her at arm's length. "I was so sorry to hear about Jasper. Henry was thankful that God allowed him a last visit before his passing."

"Jasper was a good man," Katherine said without much emotion, the way one might comment on an old tutor or distant relative, not a husband.

Elizabeth guided Katherine to the arranged seats near the hearth by a hand on her arm and nodded to the attending lady to pour the wine.

"Your marriage was happy?" she inquired quietly once the attendant had left them in semi-privacy.

Katherine smiled slightly. "It was not unhappy. Jasper was indeed a good man, but he was also a man who had been single until he was fifty-five years old. Besides the obvious, he had little idea what to do with me."

Elizabeth laughed and Katherine was encouraged to continue.

"Though I did mourn Jasper, I must tell you, Bess, that I have found happiness."

A cold heaviness centered in Elizabeth's chest as she wondered what her aunt meant by this. She was afraid she knew. Saying nothing, her eyes widened and indicated that Katherine should continue.

"Please forgive me, Bess," Katherine said, setting aside her wine cup and taking up Elizabeth's hands. "I know that Henry will be wroth with me, but I need you at least to understand."

Forcing a smile, Elizabeth said, "I do not know what it is you wish me to understand."

Katherine shook her head. "You are right. I am nervous and not making any sense." She took a deep breath and reminded herself that this was her niece she was talking to. "I am married."

The truth of this statement knocked the wind out of Elizabeth.

She wasn't sure which was worse, the fact that her aunt had remarried within weeks of her husband's death or that she had done so without the king's permission.

"Before you say anything, let me explain," Katherine begged.

Elizabeth was more than content to let her do so. She nodded.

"I have been married twice, both times to the man that a king chose for me. My Harry and I grew up together and it felt like it was meant to be. I never questioned that he should be my husband. It never occurred to me that I might marry someone else. When he died . . ."

The fact that Harry had been executed by Richard, Elizabeth's uncle, hung in the air.

"When he died, I truly mourned him. I still miss him."

Elizabeth remained quiet as Katherine mentally took a short trip into the past.

"I married Jasper without complaints and was not altogether unhappy to do so," she continued. "But since then, I have met someone who makes me truly happy."

"Go on."

"I was faithful to Jasper, you can assure Henry of that, but once he died I saw no reason to not grasp at happiness while I could."

"No reason other than the king's permission which you were lacking," Elizabeth pointed out.

"He would not have given it," Katherine said matter-of-factly. "So I did not request it."

"What man was worth this?" Elizabeth wondered.

"Sir Richard Wingfield, a man that you would not likely remember if you have ever had occasion to meet him. The king has no need for concern. I am not likely to provide Richard with an heir since I was not capable of providing Jasper with one. It appears that I did not inherit the Woodville fertility."

"But you do seem to have been blessed with your mother's skill for making a scandalous marriage," Elizabeth pointed out wryly. Elizabeth's own mother's marriage had been no less a scandal, though in that case it had been she considered too common compared to the king. Elizabeth's grandmother, Jacquetta had married a squire in her late husband's household.

"Will you tell Henry for me, Bess? Honestly, will he be furious?"

Elizabeth tried to put herself in Henry's place and imagine how this news would filter through is mind.

"There is sure to be a fine," Elizabeth said. Angry or not, Henry would impose any fine that he felt he was owed.

"I expected that," Katherine agreed with a nod. "But do you think he will have it annulled?"

Elizabeth almost reacted with an immediate denial, but then she remembered her sister, Cecily, who had been forced from the arms of the Ralph Scrope and into a marriage to one of Henry's choosing. She more carefully considered her words.

"I do not believe so." She knew it wasn't the reassurance her aunt was looking for, but she also did not wish to give her false hope. "I will speak to him as soon as I am able. How long will you stay?"

"I had planned on being here a fortnight," Katherine said, her tone despondent. She had clearly hoped for greater promised from her niece.

Elizabeth nodded. "We will see this settled then, and I will do my best for you."

~ ~ ~ ~

Henry was furious.

"How could she defy me this way?" he said in a low voice, but Elizabeth wished he would just shout.

She let possible responses flash before her mind's eye, but none she found would have the effect of calming him so she remained silent.

"What is it with Woodville women who they think they can just marry whomever they please?"

Again, she discerned this to be a rhetorical question. Without speaking, she glided across the room to fetch a flagon of wine. Her womb was heavy with the child that would soon be entering the world. Of course, Henry's mother had been urging her to go into confinement. Apparently the idea of being locked away from the world for weeks at a time was much more appealing to Margaret than it was to Elizabeth. Henry took the wine from her hand and moved toward the hearth.

As he stood near the fire, leaning against the wall, Elizabeth thought he looked more worn than she had ever seen him. The grey at his temples seemed to spread daily, and this late in the day there was a hunch to his back that did not exist when he first rose in the morning. The burdens of running a kingdom slowly caused him to stoop until he could get another night of rejuvenating sleep.

Still, she could not bring herself to curse her aunt for grasping at love while she could. She wondered what it would be like to marry for love. Shaking her head to rid it of wanderings, she approached her husband.

"Henry, I do not quite know how to say this, but I do not believe that she was thinking of you at all. She did not do this to anger you, but was following her heart."

"Rubbish!" he exclaimed, shaking off the tentative hand she had lain on his arm and crossing the room. He glared out the window before stomping back to the fire. Sitting heavily in a chair, he gulped down his wine and held the cup out to her.

She took the cup but did not immediately move to refill it. "Did you have plans for her, Henry?" She couldn't believe that he would have already chosen a groom for Jasper's widow, but, until

Katherine had confessed, she wouldn't have believed that she was already remarried.

"Of course not," he denied unconvincingly. Sitting back in the chair, he stretched his legs toward the fire and held out his hand for a cup.

Elizabeth hurried to refill it. Weariness washed over her and she decided that she would indeed enter her confinement chamber next week. Quiet solitude seemed quite attractive at the moment. Handing the cup into his waiting hand, she said, "Surely the marriage market can spare one barren Woodville bride."

"Yes, I am sure you are correct," he reluctantly agreed.

The anger had drained from him, and she should have been happy. Somehow, she sensed that he had replaced Katherine's potential marriage with another scheme.

When Henry announced that the young duke of Buckingham, Katherine's son, would be fined for his mother's impetuous nuptials, Elizabeth was, for the first time, embarrassed to be Henry's wife.

March 1496

On the 18th of March, Elizabeth gave birth to a daughter, who was named Mary for the Virgin Mother. As she stroked the cheek of her newborn babe, she thought of Eliza and a single tear traced a path down her face.

She was thirty years old and not certain she wanted more children. Each confinement brought greater fears of the sickness and death that can arrive in the wake of new life, but she trusted that God knew the time he planned to call her.

As she had spent the two weeks before the birth in the quiet company of her ladies, she had found peace in not bearing Henry's problems for him. She had also heard of his continued insults to the duke of Buckingham, Edward Stafford, that he deserved simply for having more royal blood than Henry did. John Morton was out collecting taxes for Henry with his scandalous greed and manipulative practices. Whispers were growing more outspoken that Henry was all but obsessed with the man he called Perkin Warbeck, who was in Scotland with his noble bride.

Elizabeth sighed as she looked down at the innocent babe attempting to focus milky blue eyes on her mother. She did not want to reenter the world where she battled to win Henry's trust and mediated for those who did not wish to approach him. Though she would never share it, even with Cecily, she was no longer sure if she desired her husband in her bed.

She dared not voice this thought. It was the occupation of all women, and especially queens, to bear children, sons as heirs and daughters as tools for alliances. Despite the love that swelled in her heart when she gazed down at her tiny daughter, she felt in her heart that this should be her last one. Surely, Henry would see the reason in that. Four children were sufficient for their purposes without the fear of fighting among them as they grew. She desperately wanted to make sure that a better life was left for her children and her kingdom than what had existed through the bloody battles of her father's generation.

As her head spun with these new ideas, she kept her conversation to the topic of little Mary. Elizabeth had not ordered windows opened and candles lit as she usually did once her labor was complete. She desired sleep and quiet time with the new baby. The outside world was not beckoning to her despite the fact that she had been isolated from it for three weeks. Her ladies shared looks that quietly acknowledged the difference, but none spoke of it.

Four days after the birth, it was Cecily who attacked Elizabeth's moroseness head-on. Throwing open the shutters and ordering a bright fire to counter the refreshing breeze, she did not look to her sister for approval until the deeds were done.

"Bess, you need some sun and spring air. Why have you kept closed up?"

Elizabeth just sighed. She didn't really know what to say or how to explain that she felt content alone in the dark room with her baby. Cecily brushed hair from Elizabeth's forehead as she examined her face.

"Why don't you let me brush your hair? You will feel better sitting near the window."

With a shrug, Elizabeth began rising from the bed. Cecily jumped up and moved a chair near the window with a flourish. "Your grace," she said, giving her sister a curtsey as she sat.

A smile flitted across Elizabeth's face so quickly that Cecily was not sure that it had ever been there, but she refused to be discouraged. Elizabeth was always there for others, and she was determined to return that generosity of spirit. Cecily's hands ran through Elizabeth's golden tresses that seemed to grow more red than gold with the passing of years. She chatted about inane topics as the comb eased out tangles and took no offense when Elizabeth did not respond.

With slight resentment at being drawn from her bed, Elizabeth had given in to her sister's request because it was easier than denying it. Cecily's voice droned on, but Elizabeth closed her eyes and concentrated on the sensation of the cool air moving in through the window contrasting with the warmth from the fire. The scents of fresh buds and wet ground were carried on the breeze, and Elizabeth was reminded of how much she enjoyed walking in the garden this time of year.

She remembered walking in the gardens at Westminster with Richard. The memory could be reviewed without stabs of regret or anger now that over ten years had passed. As long as she kept the memory separate from the question of her brothers' disappearance, she could recollect her feelings for her uncle as if looking at someone else's life and being slightly amused by it. God had ordained that Henry should be her husband, and she could be content with that at thirty as she had not been at twenty.

Elizabeth thought about interrupting Cecily in her story about one of her ladies being discovered in an indiscreet situation in order to ask her about their brothers. Did she think they were alive? Did she believe that Perkin Warbeck was really Richard? No, she could not handle such a conversation right now. Better to enjoy the spring air and the feel of her sister's hands in her hair.

"Bess, are you asleep?"

Cecily's voice roused her from what had indeed been a slight doze. "Of course not," she objected. "I was simply relaxing."

Patting the intricate braids one last time, Cecily moved to face Elizabeth. "Soon you will be churched and we can be outside again rather than just at the window."

A smile that did not reach her eyes formed on Elizabeth's lips for a moment as she rose to return to bed.

"Bess, what is it? You do want to leave this room don't you?"

"Don't be ridiculous, Cecily. Of course, I want to leave the room."

"Fine. I will not push. Maybe your spirits will be raised by Henry's visit."

"What?" Elizabeth paused half in and half out of her bed. "He is here?"

"He rode in moments ago. I am sure that he will be here as soon as he can be made presentable. I will bring Mary to you."

With that she spun to leave before Elizabeth could object to her plan.

When Henry entered the room, Elizabeth was not prepared for the feelings that exploded in her chest. Far from the feelings she had been having since Mary's birth, joy rose within her at the sight of him. How did she think that she was going to treat him only as a partner in raising their children and governing their kingdom? Keep him from her bed? What an absurd thought! She willingly rose from bed for the first time since entering the chamber to go to him.

"Bess, you look beautiful. Praise be to God for your health and that of our new daughter."

She buried her face in his chest and choked on the words that she should have been saying. He held her firmly, not understanding why she clung and heaved with silent sobs. His eyes searched for Cecily's, and she looked as pleased as a mother watching her child accomplish something they had been pushing them toward. He kissed the top of Elizabeth's head and moved his hands along her back letting her be the first to leave space between them.

"Henry, I am so happy to see you," Elizabeth whispered when she finally found herself able to speak.

He kissed her forehead, cheeks, and finally her mouth. "I have missed you more than I can say," he admitted. When she said nothing more but burrowed deeper into his arms, he felt that somehow a pending disaster had been avoided, though he knew neither what nor why.

September 1496

"Kathryn has given him a son."

The tone in which the simple statement was made told Elizabeth all she needed to know. This was no child to rejoice over. Perkin Warbeck, who claimed to be Richard IV, would now claim to have in his hands the heir to the throne as well. Anger rose within Elizabeth at the thought of someone replacing her Arthur as it never had when rebels tried to replace her husband. A flush burned across her face. This must be stopped.

"What are you going to do, Henry?" she demanded.

"I have been told that he and James are preparing to raid in the north. Warbeck believes that James is going to fight his battle for the throne for him. More likely, the Scots have their eyes on Berwick. I am going to negotiate a peace with James that will entice him to abandon his ties to his little pet. He will see that it is better to have me as an ally than an enemy."

"You will fight him?"

"I will offer Margaret to him."

Elizabeth forced her features to stay neutral as comprehension dawned. Margaret, her daughter, would be offered as a bride to the Scottish king. She had always knows that would be the fate of her daughters, but James was known for his sinful living and many mistresses. How could Henry so calmly plan to give his own daughter to such a life?

"He will accept," she hesitantly agreed. "As you said, the alliance with Warbeck is costing him more than he is worth. Margaret and your friendship are valuable assets." She couldn't help emphasizing the word 'assets', hoping that he would understand that she thought he was treating their flesh and blood no more kindly than he would cattle. If he noticed, he gave no indication.

May 1497

England moaned under the burden of the taxes that Henry's parliament enacted in order to fund the raising of troops and purchase of weapons and supplies. Elizabeth did not fare the spring any better as she was driven to bed by illness. Though never in fear for her life, she had missed seeing her children and husband while abed at Greenwich for several weeks. Finally, she felt well enough to make plans to return to court.

Henry's mother had been surprisingly accommodating. Whether it was for love of Elizabeth herself or for Henry's sake, Margaret had sent her own physician to see to her daughter-in-law, personally visited, and brought exotic foods to tempt her appetite. Elizabeth thanked God for Margaret's resourcefulness and kindness while asking him to forgive her for being so judgmental of her in the past.

Looking forward to an unhurried progress to Eltham to visit the children before joining Henry in London, Elizabeth was unprepared for Henry's message. The man arrived looking as though he had ridden hard the entire distance from Westminster to Greenwich.

"Your grace," he said wearily as he knelt at Elizabeth's feet.

"You have a message from my husband?"

"Yes, your grace. He would have you travel to Sheen in all possible haste. An uprising in Cornwall demands the king's attention. He would have you join him before things escalate."

"I will leave with the dawn," she assured him, gesturing to Jayne, who promptly left the hall to organize the packing. "You may find refreshment in the kitchen. Do you intend to return to the city today?"

"I must, for I will ride with the king's troops when they march on Cornwall."

His pride was evident and brought a smile to Elizabeth's face. It was a fine reminder that some men did see Henry as the true king and served him loyally.

~ ~ ~ ~

The trip, though short, had left Elizabeth worn and weary. Her illness had sapped her of strength that had clearly not been completely regained. She was ready to collapse into bed, but Henry, after a brief formal greeting, had whisked her into his chambers rather than hers. Rolls of parchment were stacked on every flat surface; Henry left so little to underlings and insisted on personally attending to each task. Forcing away her feeling of exhaustion, she joined him at the table where a map of his domains was flattened and weighed down.

"Peace has not yet been finalized with the Scots," he said, gesturing toward the north. "And these Cornish malcontents are taking advantage of the fact that my troops are occupied." This time the gesture was more angrily directed at the southwest.

"What would you have me do?" Elizabeth asked, unsure why he had chosen to have this discussion with her rather than one of his advisors.

"You are to collect the children from Eltham and continue on to the Tower, Bess."

"The Tower?" She tried to avoid it if possible, unable to separate it from the memory of her brothers.

"Yes, the Tower," he confirmed. The look in his eyes told her that he knew of her hesitancy, but this was not the time to make sentimental decisions. "It is the safest place."

"Yes, Henry."

"The rebels will be surprised to learn that my armies have, for the most part, gathered in Lambeth. With the Percys defending the border, I have not been required to send as many north as has been assumed." He paused to smile at her, pleased with his minor victory. "They will run into a wall before making it to London, but I will take no chances with your safety or that of our children."

"And your mother?"

"She will join you."

Elizabeth nodded in acknowledgement. Henry continued to examine the map as one who desires to watch the drama unfold immediately before his eyes rather than wait for it. His brow furrowed in concentration, while Elizabeth scanned the chamber for a chair or stool. After a few moments, Henry looked at her as though he was noticing her for the first time.

"Bess, you have pushed yourself to the brink." He circled the table and took her into his arms. She leaned against him. "Your chambers have been prepared. Let me escort you."

She allowed herself to be led to the rooms that she always occupied when staying at Sheen, as she often did. Henry usually stayed with her, his own rooms turned into more of a workroom, as she had just seen evidence of. Her chambers by contrast were a welcome sight. While she had been with Henry, Jayne had seen to it that candles were lit and food was delivered.

Elizabeth sighed deeply as she fell into the window seat. She closed her eyes and basked in the warmth of the sun until Henry handed her a goblet of wine.

"Thank you."

"I am glad you were able to come so quickly, Bess. I know that you have not been well and see that you remain not fully healed."

She took a grateful gulp of the sweet red wine before answering. "I tire more easily, but you need not fear. I am no longer suffering the illness, just the effects of spending weeks in bed."

"Praise God," he said, squeezing onto the narrow window seat next to her. "I will leave in the morning and you must as well. I am sorry to ask it of you, but I must see to our army and you must see to our children."

"Of course, my king."

June 1497

Henry had departed to contend the Cornishmen. After growing up with her father continuously riding off to take someone in hand, Elizabeth could not trudge up much concern for this minor rebellion. Still, she had set out for Eltham, if at a more leisurely pace than Henry had intended for her to take. The towers of Eltham were spotted in the distance, and Elizabeth smiled as she thought of the reunion she would soon have with her youngest children.

Arthur, who resided at Ludlow, was almost eleven, practically a man in his own right. Henry continued to negotiate a marriage contract for him with Catherine of Aragon, the daughter of Ferdinand and Isabella of Castile. Elizabeth had long ago accepted the fact that Arthur had a life separate from her own now that he was old enough to spend his days learning to be the next king. He would not be with his brother and sisters when Elizabeth arrived at Eltham.

Margaret, already a beauty though not quite eight years old, would be overjoyed to see her mother. She had outgrown the fussiness that Elizabeth had struggled with when Margaret had been an infant. She was still strong in opinion and spirit, but had gained self-control and the manners of a princess. She doted on her younger sister Mary, who had celebrated her first birthday in March.

Ruling over the household and his sisters, in practice if not in name, was Henry's namesake, Prince Harry. At almost six, Harry was the spitting image of Elizabeth's father. Were he the one to be king after his father, it would be as if the Plantagenets had never given way to the Tudors, Elizabeth thought ruefully. Instead of the robust reincarnation of Edward IV, Arthur, who took much more after his father, would rule England, a true Tudor in name and appearance.

Riding into the bailey, Elizabeth was surprised to see that another person had seemed to arrive just before them. As the man approached her, she saw that he wore the livery of Henry's household knights, and her concern grew.

"Your grace," he said, bowing before her. "The king has sent me to ensure that you move with all haste to London. The rebel force is approaching with more speed than originally anticipated. He would have you safe within the city."

A blush of embarrassment flared across Elizabeth's face, and she hoped nobody noticed. She had been lazily travelling as if on progress while an army bore down on her children. "We will leave within the hour," she stated loudly enough for all to hear as if it had been her plan all along. "Lady Denton, you will see that the children's necessities are packed as quickly as possible." Beth Denton had been in charge of the nursery at Eltham since it had been established, and Elizabeth was grateful that she could count on the woman being capable of taking this sudden upheaval in stride.

Ignoring those who would push forward to attend to the queen, Elizabeth rushed into the palace to find her children and see that they were comfortably gathered into the waiting litter.

"I want to ride my pony!" Harry objected. He stood with his sturdy little legs shoulder width apart and his chubby fists on his hips, looking like a miniature king. The fleeting thought crossed Elizabeth's mind that she and Henry may be making a mistake in considering the dedication of this son to the church, but it was not the time to think about it.

"Harry, we must travel quickly and far. You will obey me in this."

His freckled face fell and his posture stooped, and she was reminded that he was only six years old. She squatted down to look into his eyes that were as blue as her own. "Harry, I will see if there is time to have your pony ready to go with us, but you will begin in the litter." A wide grin was her reward, and she tousled his red-gold hair. "That's a good boy. Now where are your sisters?"

Before he had time to answer, Margaret was walking toward them with baby Mary in her arms. A nursemaid was a step behind them carrying a large basket of the items that were considered vital to have in the litter with the little ones during the trip.

"Margaret, aren't you a lovely little lady!" Elizabeth exclaimed. She regretted that she was not always with her children and was amazed each time she saw her daughter and another transformation had taken place.

Margaret did her best to curtsey with the bundle in her arms. "My lady mother," she said in formal greeting.

"God bless you, my daughter," Elizabeth said, rising her up in recognition of her well-learned manners before pulling her into a more casual embrace. "Thank you for helping your nurses prepare for the journey, Margaret. I look forward to spending time with each of you, and you can tell me what you have been learning."

"Yes, mother. I have been learning French and the history of the Plantagenet kings. I also have my embroidery to show you."

"Wonderful, I cannot wait to see it. We will speak in French at supper to practice your skills." Elizabeth's own French was impeccable due to her lessons as the future queen of France when she had been betrothed to the Dauphin so many years ago. She gestured to her daughters and their nurse to continue on to the bailey and be settled in the waiting litter.

True to her word, Elizabeth and the children, along with their attendants were setting a fast pace for London.

"Keep nothing from me," Elizabeth insisted when Henry's man sidled up next to her.

He nodded, respecting her for her quiet strength and her

heritage. "The rebel army has swelled to include over 18,000 men. They collect more malcontents as they march."

Eighteen thousand! Were Englishmen still so discontent with Henry as their king? Her face showed nothing. "May God bless the king and his armies as they crush this rebellion." She said what was expected of her as calmly as possible.

They arrived in London with no pageantry or welcoming crowds. Wearily, the small procession made its way to Coldharbour House. Though the Tower was the safer stronghold and Lady Margaret not the most welcoming host, Elizabeth would camp with Henry in his army tent before entering the Tower.

Six days were spent in the incongruent activities of playing with the children and receiving increasingly alarming reports from Henry. The rebel army continued to receive more support than he had dreamed was possible and was marching on Farnham in Surrey. With the promise of battle taking place so near the city walls, Elizabeth realized that she had no option but to move her family to the safety of the Tower.

Approaching by barge, she gazed up at the whitewashed stone with conflicting feelings warring within her. She had happy childhood memories of this place, of another life when she thought her father was a god and would reign over England long into her own adulthood. So much had fallen apart when he died. Now the Tower was a stark reminder of her brothers, who had last been seen here in the autumn of 1483. Had it truly been almost fifteen years? Her brothers would be twenty-seven and twenty-three if they were alive today. Were they?

She shook her head, hoping that her brothers' spirits would someday stop haunting her. It was not likely to cease as she took up residence in the fortress where many believed they had died.

~ ~ ~ ~

"What is that sound, mother?" Harry asked. The booming sounds reminded him of thunder though it was sunny and clear.

"That is the sound of battle, my son," Elizabeth said, taking advantage of his brief willingness to be pulled onto her lap. They sat together looking out the window though they could not see the source of the noise. "I was the same age as you when I was closed up here while my father took on rebel forces. Kentish rebels took advantage of his absence to attack London, but my Uncle Anthony repelled them and executed their leader." She gazed out the window as she spoke, missing the enraptured look on her son's face. If she allowed herself, she could forget what year she was in the situation was so similar.

"What happened to your uncle? Why have I never met him?"

His question brought her back to the present as completely as if she had been doused with a bucket of icy water. She was uncertain how to answer him about events that had taken place during that part of her life that she didn't fully understand either. She wondered if anyone would ever piece together her family's story in complete accuracy. If she couldn't, how could anyone else?

"He was executed for treason," she stated flatly.

"What?" Harry's head spun around to fix his icy stare at her. "A soldier hero was executed for treason?"

"They were confusing times, Harry. I pray that you will never encounter in your life the type of events that occurred after the death of my father."

A flash of comprehension crossed his face. "Your evil uncle killed him, like he did your brothers."

He stated it like it was a fact, and, even though she had wondered if it were true, it angered her to hear her six year old say it. He had been taught to say it, she realized, for how else would he know if someone had not put it into his head. She made a mental note to speak to Lady Denton. Not all of the Plantagenets were gone. They had forgotten about her.

"No. He did not." In that moment, she was certain that she spoke the truth.

Harry looked confused, but said nothing. He looked as if he was searching his memory for the proper lesson. Surely he had remembered correctly. He remembered being astounded by the story of his grandfather's brother who had stolen the crown and ruled England with a heavy hand. He even would have married Harry's mother if his father had not rescued her. Yes, he knew that he remembered that part. He looked at his mother, doubting himself. Surely she would know what had happened.

"He did not," she repeated, but Harry would be disappointed if he thought she would say more.

~ ~ ~ ~

The next time a disheveled knight was presented to Elizabeth, fear did not accompany him. Though he looked as worn and dirty as their last messenger, he also exuded the joy of victory as he knelt before his queen.

"Please, stand," Elizabeth said with a smile. "And tell me of my husband's triumph."

He rose and gladly accepted the wine that was offered to him. Elizabeth waited patiently while he took thirsty gulps. He had earned the privilege of a few moments respite before sharing his story.

"Not one will doubt your husband's skill as a soldier now, your grace." He took a drink from the cup that had been refilled for him, and Elizabeth ignored the implication that Henry's prowess had been previously questioned. "The rebels did not expect us to have a force of 25,000, your grace. We were able to surround them and,"

He paused realizing that the queen would not need nor desire the gory details of battle. "The king led us bravely and competently. He will present himself to you after he has given thanks at Saint Paul's."

"Thank you for your report and thank God that the enemy has been delivered into the king's hands," Elizabeth said as she gestured to servants to attend to her husband's faithful household knight.

September - October 1497

Following his victory over the Cornish rebels, Henry turned his attention to the north. The peace negotiations had been going back and forth for months, but it was time to finalize the terms and put an end to the border raiding. He would give James his daughter, Margaret, but in return he wanted Warbeck. With the thrill of success in the south fueling his ambition, he was certain that James was ready to come to terms.

Henry's luck seemed to be fleeting. Though the Treaty of Ayton was indeed signed, James informed Henry that Warbeck and his noble wife had already been sent away on a ship fittingly named the *Cuckoo*. Henry was not amused. So close to having the pretender in hand, Warbeck managed to slip through his fingers again. The feeling of not being in complete control was a way of life Henry had been forced to accept as an exile. It was not something he relished as a king.

Elizabeth attempted to comfort her husband as he fumed over the news of Warbeck's most recent escape, but he refused to be distracted. He would have his reign secure so that he could turn to the task of seeing Arthur properly married to the woman who would be England's next queen.

An agreement had been reached over the summer regarding Arthur's betrothed. Catherine, the Spanish Infanta, would be sent to reside at the English court in December 1499 upon reaching age fourteen. Arthur had presented himself well at the formal betrothal that had taken place in August. Tall, graceful, and intelligent, Henry thought that his son would be the man that he himself would have been if not forced to endure exile during his formative years. The betrothal ceremony was one of the few events that had given Henry any joy since the rebellion, but he also knew just how easily betrothals could be broken.

It was in this state of mind that Henry received news that Perkin Warbeck had landed at Whitesand Bay near Land's End in Cornwall. Not wishing to underestimate the malcontents in the southwest a second time, he was quick to assemble his men and arms. He was uncertain whether the Englishmen would join Warbeck, seeing this as a chance to have their revenge, or if their recent defeat would leave them hesitant to join him. He intended to be prepared for either eventuality.

Once again, Elizabeth watched as the man she loved rode away. She would never get used to the feeling of not knowing if she would see him again as his army marched off. Her father had led men away many times and always returned, but Richard had not, though she had fully expected him to. As she lost sight of Henry among the dust and crowd of horses and armor, she wondered if she'd had her last glimpse of him.

~ ~ ~ ~

When Henry left to hunt Perkin Warbeck, Elizabeth left with her mother-in-law and younger son on a progress meant to remind Englishmen that they had a duke of York, and he was the spitting image of his royal grandfather, Edward IV. This man claiming to be the rightful king could not be supported by anyone who laid eyes on little Harry, or so Elizabeth hoped.

They rode at a pace slow enough for Harry to ride a horse that Elizabeth felt was altogether too large for him, but she had been assured that his presence must be royal in every way. She had to admit that few would guess that the boy was only six years old. Sturdily built and confident, he sat upon that glossy gelding with his head held high and red-gold hair shining like a second sun. Elizabeth remained always a step behind to keep the crowds eyes on the young duke of York, and he performed his role beautifully.

Waving to old men, blowing kisses to young girls, Harry looked as though he always rode stallions through city streets. His cloth-of-gold shimmered in the sunlight as his cloak was fluttering in the autumn breeze. Elizabeth had to turn away when tears threatened and pride closed her throat. How she wished her father could see his grandson today. She squinted in order to search the sky questioningly. Maybe he could. It made her smile, and that brought another cheer from the friendly crowd.

Their route brought them to Walsingham, far from the forces of Warbeck or pockets of rebels, and Elizabeth was glad to enter the chapel there as she had before with praises on her lips for the warm welcome Harry had received everywhere they had gone. She also surprised herself by finding that she was able to once again pray for the gift of more children, should it be the Holy Father's will. The fear and depression that had assaulted her after Mary's birth had truly left her.

As her prayers turned to Henry and his army, she heard a faint shuffling behind her. Taking a moment longer to finish her prayers, she stood, crossed herself, and turned to the waiting page. He shifted from foot to foot in impatience, but did not speak until Elizabeth nodded to him.

"A messenger from the king," he announced, excitement bubbling in his voice.

Good news then, Elizabeth thought. The messenger should not have whispered of his news, but it was possible that the page had deduced positively based on the man's appearance and attitude. It was easy to tell those bringing news of a defeat from those bearing news of a triumph. She simply gestured for the page to lead the way to the hall where the man, who Elizabeth recognized from Henry's household, awaited her while people gathered to hear what he would say.

Elizabeth considered clearing the room to hear word of her

husband in private, but she shared the page's opinion that this was not a man bringing an unwelcome message based on his relaxed posture and easy smile. She would share the happy news with those who had come to hear it. Seating herself in a large chair that had been placed at the head of the hall for her use, she gestured for the man to come forward. He did, and knelt before her.

"Please, rise. You have come far and bring news we are eager for you to impart."

"Yes, your grace," he said in a deep, silky voice that caused the women listening to give each other appreciative looks. "Your husband has had another great victory. This time he has the pretender Warbeck in hand."

Gasps went through the crowd. Warbeck's name had been whispered for so long without him setting foot in England that he had become something of a myth. Now he was reduced to being a man, a prisoner of the king.

"Praise God!" Elizabeth said, her eyes scanning the hall and quieting the whisperers. "Please, tell me all."

The messenger stood tall and proud, enjoying his moment as the center of attention. "The pretender and his disorganized force of mercenaries and discontented Cornishmen made their way to Exeter. He was proclaiming himself Richard IV as he went, which drew a few, who did not know enough to know better, to his banner. Their attempt at a siege at Exeter was a pathetic failure, which should prove that this man is no son of our great Edward if nothing else does." He paused to allow quiet agreement to move like a wave through those listening. "He was greatly deserted after this failure, but he pushed on toward Taunton until the king's army drew near. Then the coward deserted the few men who had been willing to stay with him until the end in order to attempt an escape in Southampton. Not able to make his way through our king's coastal defenses, he took sanctuary in Beaulieu Abbey."

Elizabeth sent up a silent prayer that Henry had not dragged Warbeck from sanctuary as her father had done to his enemies in the past. She did not think his reputation could afford such as act against God. She need not have worried.

"The king, being as merciful as he is great," the messenger continued. "Promised the boy a pardon in return for his surrender, and he had the sense to accept."

Elizabeth realized that she had been leaning further and further forward. She sat back in her chair, taking a deep breath. This man, who had been claiming for six years that he was her brother, was in her husband's custody. She was eager for the day that she would lay eyes on him and be able to judge him for herself. She also dreaded it.

"What else happened in the aftermath?" she asked, knowing that there were always messy items to wrap up after an event such as this.

Less willingly than before, Henry's man went on. "King Henry went back to Exeter where some of the rebels were hung. It would have done no good for him to show too much mercy, your grace."

Elizabeth simply nodded for him to go on. She was more than familiar with the concept. Why did men seem to forget that the women had grown up in the same war-torn times that they had?

"When confronted with men who would have known . . . Prince Richard." He felt his face go red at the reference to the queen's brother. "The pretender did not know them, and he confessed to his grace, the king, that he had lied about being the duke of York."

Arranging her face carefully to not show emotion at this, Elizabeth nodded for him to continue.

"When the king found out that the pretender's wife had been left at St. Michael's Mount, he sent some men there to take her into custody as well. I heard that she was in black of mourning when taken for she had lost a babe while she waited there for her treacherous husband."

"Thank you and God bless you for your loyalty and fine service," Elizabeth said as she gestured to servants to see to his comfort. Those indicated eagerly responded, hoping to hear more details from this man who had been in the thick of the action. Surely, there were parts of his story that had not been appropriate for royal feminine ears.

Taking Jayne aside, Elizabeth said low enough only for her ears to hear, "Prepare our things. We will leave for London with the dawn."

~ ~ ~ ~

Word reached Elizabeth upon entering the city that her husband was not in London. She fought back disappointment and made arrangements to stay just one night before travelling on to Sheen. By the time they arrived the next day, even Harry was tired of riding.

"Will my father be there?"

"Yes, Harry, that is why we have come." Elizabeth snapped, lacking her normal patience.

"I'm sorry, my lady mother."

She sighed and smiled at him. His freckles stood out dark against his pale skin after so many days in the sun, and his hair displayed streaks of strawberry blond. "It is I who should apologize," she said. "I am weary of travel and ready for a bath and a warm bed."

"My own bed would be nice," Harry agreed though he wrinkled his nose at the idea of a bath.

When they finally entered the bailey at Sheen, Elizabeth had never been happier to be at the end of a journey. She was also overjoyed to be greeted by her husband, who waited to personally help her from her horse. They held each other close for a moment, neither uttering a word.

"Bess," he whispered into her hair, taking deep breaths to soak in her scent.

"Henry." She looked up at him. "Thank God for your victories and that you are free from injury."

"Amen," he agreed and then kissed her, a quick, sweet kiss that was more than he usually would allow in front of the watching attendants but held promise of more.

"Father, I rode all the way to Walsingham and back!" shouted Harry.

Henry smiled and released his wife in order to squat down to his son's level. "Did you now?"

Harry puffed out his chest and a broad smile split his face. "I certainly did! Tell him, mother."

"I believe you, my fine prince," Henry said, ruffling Harry's ever unruly hair. "And a wonderful job you have done of watching over your mother in my absence."

If it were possible, Harry's smile increased.

"I heard that you killed the rebels and took Perkin Warbeck as prisoner," Harry said before he could lose his father's attention.

Henry raised an eyebrow, wondering who had been sharing war stories with a six year old. "It is true that the rebellion was quelled and the leader is in my custody. It is a king's duty to protect peace within his realm, and his family's job to support him, as someday you will support your brother, Arthur."

Harry's face fell a little at this. He understood that Arthur was to be king, while he would likely become an archbishop, but it seemed horribly unfair. "Of course, father."

"We can talk more later, after I have cleaned up and had some rest," Elizabeth interrupted. "Harry, why don't you join your father and I in my chambers after supper?"

This grown-up invitation had the desired effect, and Harry's face lit up again. He skipped along as his nurse led him away. Both parents watched him, wishing that they again had that kind of unbound energy.

"When you are ready, Bess, I will also have the lady Kathryn Gordon presented to you."

"She is here?"

Henry nodded. "She was in an awful state when my men found her. Apparently, she had been with child when they landed but lost the babe after Warbeck left her at St. Michael's Mount. Of course, it was also a terrible shock when her husband confessed to her that he was not who she believed him to be."

They had begun walking into the palace as Henry spoke, Elizabeth grasping tightly onto Henry's arm.

"She believed him to be Richard then?"

"I'm afraid so," Henry confirmed. "She wept and raged when Warbeck told her the truth, but I have tried to show her every kindness as the cousin of our daughter's betrothed."

"Poor woman," Elizabeth sighed.

A large tub had been lugged into Elizabeth's chambers and filled with buckets of hot water. It felt like the height of luxury to settle into the rose scented liquid and close her eyes while Jayne washed her hair. She would have been lulled to sleep if it were not for the thoughts of Kathryn Gordon that flashed irritatingly through her mind.

Apparently, Lady Gordon had not been part of the deception but one of the many fooled by this man claiming to be her brother. Henry showed no doubt that the man was not Richard, and his wife seemed to have believed his confession, as little as she liked it. Elizabeth didn't know whether to be sad or relieved. Soon she would meet his wife. Had Kathryn been looking forward to the time when they would meet? Did she believe that they would be rival queens? Loving sisters-in-law? Certainly, she expected neither of these extremes now. Elizabeth decided to delay this delicate introduction until the next day. It would give them both more time to decide what they should expect from the other.

Henry entered the chamber as Elizabeth's ladies finished dressing her. He dismissed them with a wave of his hand, and Elizabeth nodded her consent.

"I will not be able to let Harry stay long. I am eager for bed," she said wearily.

"As am I, my lady."

Elizabeth swatted playfully at her husband with a laugh. "You are welcome in my bed, but be warned that I may be asleep as soon as my head hits the pillow."

He gathered her into his arms, and she gratefully leaned into him, feeling the stress of the past weeks draining from her as she soaked in his strength.

"How was our son welcomed in the east?" Henry asked as he kissed the top of her head.

Elizabeth put enough space between them to look up into his face. "He was marvelous, Henry. You would have been so proud. Nobody who saw Harry would guess that he was anything less than a prince."

Henry simply nodded as if he had expected no less. Summoned by the sound of his name, Harry came running into the room until a stern throat clearing from his attendant slowed him down and he bowed before his parents.

"Please stand, fine prince," Henry said formally. "I have been informed that you performed the duties of the duke of York to the queen's complete satisfaction."

"Thank you, your grace!" Harry's words joined in the game of formality though his tone held too much enthusiasm for a courtier.

Elizabeth smiled at the happy picture made by father and son. Harry was chattering about the trip, his new horse, and the little gifts that people had handed him as he rode through the crowds. Elizabeth half listened while her mind wandered. Did all princes of the Church start out as rambunctious little boys? She was brought back to the present by the sound of her husband's voice.

"Harry, I believe that you will need to get yourself off to bed before your mother falls asleep in her chair."

"But I haven't yet told you about . . . ."

"There will be plenty of time for that tomorrow," Henry stated firmly before Harry could race into the next topic.

Harry pouted but knew better than to argue with his father. The hours on horseback had also worn him out more than he cared to admit, and he was looking forward to his soft mattress and goose-feather pillow. He placed a kiss on the cheek of each parent before accepting their blessing and leaving for the nursery.

"Ah, that boy will make us proud, Bess. I am certain of it."

"Yes, he is a good boy," Elizabeth agreed.

"Let's get you to bed as well," Henry said, standing and extending his hand to her. She took it and let him pull her up and lead her to the bed.

Once they were settled under the covers, she found that she did have a little more energy to expend before falling asleep.

~ ~ ~ ~

The next day, Elizabeth was more nervous than she cared to admit. She was not pleased with the selection of dresses she had with her, all either too formal or too plain for the sensitive meeting with the woman who had hoped to usurp her position.

"No, not this one either!" she exclaimed with uncharacteristic anger toward her ladies.

"Alright, your grace," Jayne said, calmly laying the fifth gown aside. "This one then, for the blue brings out the beauty of your eyes and the red in your hair."

"Yes, it will have to do," Elizabeth grumbled.

As she tied and adjusted the dress, Jayne tried to sooth her queen's nerves. "This was the best choice after all. You were right to reject the others. I apologize, your grace, for not thinking of this one first."

Elizabeth sighed. "Jayne, you have a dear heart, for you know it is not your fault that my nerves are on edge. In all honesty, I am not quite sure why either."

Jayne continued the final touches on Elizabeth's hair while humming a hymn. She guessed that Elizabeth was nervous about meeting a woman whose beauty was as legendary as her own but was ten years younger, but she was not going to voice anything of the sort.

"There. You are beautiful, your grace," Jayne said as she took a step back to admire the product of her labors.

"Thank you," Elizabeth then put steel into her spine, lifted her chin, and gestured for her page to go before her to the great hall.

She was so accustomed to the appreciative looks and murmurs as she entered a gathering that she took no note of them now. Taking her place at Henry's side, she nodded to him and he signaled to one of his attendants. Within moments, a lovely young woman, who could be none other than Kathryn Gordon, was led into the hall. Gasps were heard throughout the hall and the murmuring rose in pitch. Elizabeth felt her cheeks go hot.

Kathryn was willowy, though she had recently born a child. The black mourning gown that Henry had provided her with accentuated her alabaster skin and made her red hair seem as bright as a fire at midnight. Her smooth skin was not marred by anything more than a few freckles and slight darkening under her eyes. She looked like a fragile wood sprite with its wings clipped. Her face was carefully controlled, showing no reaction to the whispering surrounding her or the queen's careful examination.

Elizabeth was hit with the realization that lines had formed at the corners of her own eyes. She forced herself not to glance down at the waistline that had expanded slightly each year since her marriage. As she gazed at this sad, yet beautiful woman before her, Elizabeth experienced feelings of jealousy and envy that had never assailed before. Scriptures said that there was a time for everything, and clearly her own time had passed.

Lady Kathryn curtseyed low before the king and queen, and Elizabeth looked to her husband. He was enraptured. With heat of anger and embarrassment threatening to burn her from within, Elizabeth forced herself to take a deep breath. This woman before her had lost a child and all but lost her husband. Elizabeth would not allow herself to treat her cruelly simply for the crime of being beautiful.

Once Kathryn had made humble obeisance to the king and queen and Henry had formally welcomed her to court, Elizabeth stood and approached her. Dipping into another graceful curtsey, Kathryn waited for Elizabeth to raise her up.

"Lady Gordon, I am happy to welcome you as one of my ladies in waiting."

"I am pleased to serve you, your grace." Kathryn's voice was soft and put Elizabeth in mind of a songbird.

"I look forward to becoming better acquainted," Elizabeth said as she guided the younger woman to a more private corner. "You can tell me about James, my daughter's future husband." She favored Kathryn with a smile that she hoped was friendly and encouraged camaraderie.

"I am sure that your daughter will be quite happy at the Scottish court, your grace," Kathryn replied blandly with her head downturned.

"Please, in private call me Elizabeth." She patted Kathryn's hand and decided to address head-on the wall built between them. "I understand that you have been through a horrid ordeal. I pray that you know that you may confide in me. It will earn you neither judgment nor contempt."

Lady Gordon blinked, taken aback by the queen's kindness. She decided to return the forthrightness with her own. "I did not expect for us to be meeting like this. My husband did not describe you this way."

"Your husband does not know me," Elizabeth countered.

Kathryn dropped her head in shame. "Yes, I know that now."

"You are innocent of his crimes," Elizabeth assured her. "You will not be judged for them."

"It is not that," Kathryn said, raising her head so that the tears in her eyes glistened. "I still love him, despite it all. I still love him."

She shook her head, silently berating herself for her naivety, but Elizabeth stopped her with a hand on her cheek.

"Of course, you do. What a treasure of a wife he has in you, even if his name is not the one you believed it to be, the man still is the one you married."

The tears were released in full force now, streaming down Kathryn's pale cheeks. Elizabeth caught Jayne's eye before leading Kathryn from the public hall toward her own chambers. No longer jealous, Elizabeth saw not a beautiful rival, but a broken heart.

Kathryn could not believe that she was in the queen's chambers, crying her heart out, with Elizabeth murmuring soothing words and rubbing her back. Richard, who was not Richard, had filled her head with visions of triumphant processions into London and an older sister who needed to be put in her place. Never had she considered that he would fail or that he had lied. She was still trying to get her head around the fact that this was not even his sister. Yet, she had welcomed the woman who had hoped to take her throne.

"You poor thing," Elizabeth said after a few moments had passed. "Can I pray for you?"

This new kindness renewed Kathryn's sobbing, but she nodded her appreciation. Elizabeth pressed a wine cup into Kathryn's hand before kneeling at her private altar. She was unaware that Kathryn's wine remained untouched and her eyes stayed fixed on the praying queen.

"Thank you, your grace," Kathryn whispered when Elizabeth returned to her side. "Elizabeth," she corrected herself, catching her encouraging smile.

"May God bless you, Kathryn. May he be with us all as this web of deception and betrayal is unraveled."

December 1497

"He has sent my son away!"

This exclamation was filled with all the pain wrenched from Kathryn's heart. She was sobbing as she hadn't since the day she and Elizabeth had first met and had melted to the floor in a puddle of silk skirts. Elizabeth ran to her side.

"What is it, my dear?" She was afraid that she knew.

"Hen . . . the king. He has sent my son away. I am never to see him again."

Elizabeth put her arm around Kathryn's slender shoulders and begged God to give her words of comfort. She was not surprised that Henry had taken this step to remove the boy who had potential to be the center of rebellion. After all, her poor cousin, Edward, still languished in the Tower. She had given up on pleading Henry for his release and kept her requests for God's ear alone.

"God will watch over him when you cannot," Elizabeth whispered.

"I don't want God to watch over him!" Kathryn shouted as she sprung to her feet. "I want to watch him! Is it not enough that my husband has been taken from me and I lost our babe before it was given breath? Must he take my son?"

Elizabeth knew that Kathryn blamed Henry, rather than God, for her losses, but she would not disparage her husband whether she believed him in the right or not.

"But you will see your husband, as Henry is releasing him and allowing him to remain at court." She did not add that she was certain he would be under heavy guard.

"Truly?" Kathryn grabbed Elizabeth's hands with greater strength than she would have guessed the smaller woman to possess.

"I have just received word," Elizabeth said, happy to be able to bring some joy to the shattered woman's life. "He has been released from the Tower. When Henry travels back to Sheen for his Christmas court, he will bring your husband with him."

"Praise to God and all his saints," Kathryn said in a whisper.

Elizabeth hoped that she had not raised her hopes too high.

~ ~ ~ ~

Christmas at Sheen was becoming one of Elizabeth's favorite times of year. Her children and husband would all be present, something that only happened a few times each year. She loved the smell of evergreen boughs and mistletoe, the warmth of the Yule log that would burn throughout the days of Christmas, and the smell of the savory foods that the cooks would labor over in an effort to spotlight their greatest achievements. Only one thing gave her reservation, the promised presence of Perkin Warbeck.

Elizabeth had not yet met the man who had claimed for six years that he was her younger brother. She was confident that Henry was correct in his assessment of him as a pretender, for he had been paraded in London and presented to men who had knowledge of the prince. He had recognized none of them. Though he looked enough like Edward IV to be one of his by-blows, it seemed that his greatest weapon was his charisma. How did this man, whom Henry had cursed and despised from afar for all those years, convince the king to allow him to spend Christmas with his wife at the royal court, Elizabeth wondered.

The women were in the hall when the sounds of a commotion in the courtyard alerted them of Henry's arrival. Elizabeth had been playing cards with Jayne, but the game was forgotten as she gave orders for wine and food to be brought for the king and his men. Then Henry entered the room, speaking jovially with a man who made Elizabeth's breath catch in her throat.

He looked like her father had looked when he was a young king, tall with copper hair and far too much confidence for a man who was supposed to be a prisoner. As they entered the hall, Warbeck's attention toward Henry waned as his eyes swept the hall for the only person he desired to see. Kathryn ran to him and would have thrown herself into his arms if she had not perceived the look of outrage that was forming on Henry's face. She turned from her original course and demurely curtseyed to the king.

Henry raised her up and kissed her hand before leading Warbeck to Elizabeth, leaving Kathryn looking longingly after him. For his part, Warbeck had covered his feelings as quickly as they had crossed his face, replacing desire for his wife with charm for the queen. He bowed deeply before her.

"Your grace."

Elizabeth felt odd addressing him, no more comfortable with the name Perkin Warbeck now that it seemed to be his true one. She usually referred to him as Kathryn's husband, but now was forced to speak, "Warbeck."

There was an amused glint in his eye as he unbent, as if he somehow understood how difficult this was for Elizabeth. His wife had quietly fallen into rank behind the queen, and Warbeck chose to bridge the moment's awkwardness by next speaking to her.

"My beautiful bride," he said, bowing more deeply before her than he had the queen.

A blush rose to Kathryn's face, making her look younger and even more desirable. "Husband," she replied as he lingered with his lips on her palm. He could feel her blood pulsing through the vein in her wrist and was anxious to feel it elsewhere. The king coughed.

"I apologize, my liege," Warbeck said, dropping Kathryn's hand. "I had almost forgotten the greatness of my wife's beauty . . . and yours," he added with a quick look at Elizabeth. Had he dared to wink at her?

Henry took up Elizabeth's hand, appearing clumsy and nervous compared to his suave prisoner.

"I have ordered refreshments for you and your men," Elizabeth said, collecting herself from the shock of the introduction. This man certainly had the skill to unnerve people. "Would you like to change and rid yourself of the dust of the road?"

Warbeck was gazing at Kathryn, clearly not listening, but Henry answered for them both. "Yes, I trust you've arranged for my guest's lodging as requested. I would take a moment to clean up before the evening entertainment."

Henry had requested that a room be prepared for Warbeck that was comfortable but inaccessible from the outside. It was to be well guarded. He was not about to take a chance that his prisoner would escape or that Kathryn would be found with child. Elizabeth wondered if Kathryn realized that she and her husband would be afforded no private moments. Part of her felt sorry, for the two of them were ogling each other in obvious desire. On this point, though, she was forced to agree with her husband. One son between Lady Gordon and Warbeck was more than enough.

Henry and those who had accompanied him left to find their lodgings. Elizabeth watched her husband leave the hall before turning to Kathryn. She looked more radiant than Elizabeth had ever seen her, though her hair and dress were just as they had been a few minutes earlier. No matter whether his name was Richard or Perkin, he held Kathryn's heart in the palm of his hand.

"I am glad to see you reunited with your husband, Kathryn. You are glowing in his presence," she observed.

Kathryn blushed and lowered her eyes to the floor. She had been raised to act properly and not wear her feelings on her sleeve, but he had an effect on her that she could not deny.

"What has he told you of his past?" Elizabeth asked, the vision of her father as a young man still fresh in her mind.

Kathryn seemed surprised by the inquiry. "Before or after his capture?"

Pressing her lips together, Elizabeth regretted asking the question. "Both. I know that he is said to be from Tournai, the son of a boatman. Has he mentioned his boyhood?"

Before answering, the younger woman examined Elizabeth's face in open curiosity. "Do you believe he may be Richard of York?"

"No," Elizabeth was quick to answer though it caused Kathryn's face to fall in disappointment. "But I do wonder if he is my father's son."

It took a moment for Elizabeth's meaning to form in her mind, but, when it did, Kathryn's eyes widened. "You believe he is a bastard child of the king!"

Treating the subject with nonchalance, Elizabeth said, "It is certainly possible. I loved my father dearly, but he was not known to be strong against the temptation of lust." She shrugged. "I simply wondered if Perkin," she used the name purposely here for the first time, "had ever mentioned being adopted or taken in."

"Well, I suppose he did, since he said that he had been hidden by family loyal to the York cause after being rescued from the Tower. I haven't had a chance to speak with him about his true background. I know only of the same confession that has been made public."

"It matters not," Elizabeth said, closing the subject to discussion. "He is not who he claimed to be. That is all that is important."

Kathryn knew better than to say more, but her face did not hide her feeling that it was not the only thing that was important to her as her gaze once again found the doorway where she had last caught sight of him. Elizabeth sighed. Maybe Henry's clemency would not be the mercy that she had originally thought it would be.

~ ~ ~ ~

Throughout the Christmas revelries, Elizabeth watched her friend's eyes follow Warbeck in longing. Though he was better at hiding behind his façade of friendliness and flirtations, his desire for his wife was burning just under the surface. One catching a glimpse of what the couple thought was a private moment was likely to be burned by the flames of their passion.

Elizabeth had caught them in an intimate embrace that surely would have progressed into more. Upon questioning, Kathryn admitted that Warbeck had been able to convince his guards that he deserved a few moments with his own wife. The fact that these men could be so easily manipulated worried Elizabeth, and she wondered how much to tell Henry. That he needed to be aware of Warbeck's skills of coercion was clear, but if he knew the full truth, that Elizabeth believed that the moment had lasted long enough to possibly result in pregnancy, his fury would know no bounds.

She lay in bed, awake though it was well past the hour she usually retired, trying to decide what should be done about Kathryn and her overly enticing husband. Henry seemed surprised that she still desired Warbeck after learning the truth about his birth. He had been certain that once Kathryn, a woman of noble birth, knew that she had been given to a pretender – a commoner – that she would be disgusted. How shocked he was to find that he was still fighting to keep them apart.

Tossing and turning, Elizabeth cursed her brain for choosing the late night hours to attempt to work out unsolvable problems. She was certain that the only way to keep Warbeck from his wife was to lock him in the Tower with helpless Edward of Warwick. She, however, would not be the one to suggest a step of that magnitude.

The air around her seemed too thick. Was it smoke? She sat up to peek through the bed hangings and confirm that the fire in her hearth had been properly attended. Swirls of smoke squeezed their way through the curtains as she parted them, but it did not come from her fireplace. It seemed to be seeping through the cracks around her door. Fear tightened like a fist around her heart.

"Fire!"

She didn't realize that she had said it out loud until her ladies started mumbling and sleepily shifting.

"Wake up! There is a fire!" she screamed.

This time, the lighter sleepers came fully awake as they realized the danger they were in.

"The children," she grabbed the woman closest to her. It was Jayne. "See to the children." Suddenly, having her entire family gathered in one household seemed most ominous. Jayne rushed from the room, trusting that her queen could see to herself. Smoke billowed in and filled the room when she opened the door.

As soon as Jayne disappeared, the doorway was filled with men who had been sent to escort the women to safety. Elizabeth was able to breathe her first sigh of relief because their presence indicated that Henry was aware of the fire and would have made it outside himself. At least she would have sighed in relief if she could breathe. The air in the room had become opaque and she choked on the hot, thick smoke.

"My children," she said to the man who took her arm. She recognized him as one of Henry's household knights.

"They are outside," he reassured her, carefully keeping his eyes straight ahead. His honor would not allow him to look upon his queen in her nightshift, even if she was one of the most beautiful women he had ever seen.

"Praise God!" she sighed.

"He is good, but he expects us to do our part," the knight said, propelling her forward. He seemed to have a sixth sense that allowed him to navigate the corridors in the darkness of night and confusion of smoke and fumes. "We must get you to the courtyard."

They were almost there. Elizabeth could almost taste the cool, fresh night air on her tongue. The gallery was in flames that appeared impassable and Elizabeth prayed nobody was trapped within it. Before she could complete the thought, she saw that someone was making their way through the hungry flames that licked at every surface. A figure, their identity hidden by the tapestry that was thrown over them as poor protection against the blaze, jogged along the gallery, dodging falling timbers and plaster. Elizabeth felt remorse for this man, who would likely die though he was making a valiant effort. Then the tapestry slipped for a moment from his head. It was Henry.

The ceiling of the gallery collapsed with a roaring crash.

~ ~ ~ ~

When Elizabeth awoke, she thought she had been having a nightmare. The smell of smoke was still within her nostrils, so realistic was the dreadful dream. Then she realized that she heard crying, and she looked around to see that she was lying on the grass of the courtyard. The palace of Sheen was nothing more than a pile of smoldering embers with a few brave pillars still reaching for a roof that no longer existed.

Henry. She thought that she would cry, but her eyes were too dry. They burned from exposure to the smoke and her skin felt raw like after too long in the summer sun. It wasn't just a dream. She had watched her husband die.

A cup was suddenly at her lips. "Drink, my lady." It was Jayne. Thank the Lord that she was safe. Elizabeth knew that meant that her children were also free from danger for Jayne would have died before leaving them.

"Thank you," Elizabeth rasped, surprised at the rawness of her throat. The smoke seemed to have invaded every part of her body.

"The children were outside before the fire reached their chambers," Jayne assured her, knowing that Elizabeth would want to know but that speaking would be painful for days. The queen smiled, her eyes still closed.

"Bess?"

Her eyes flew open. It couldn't be, but she would not mistake the voice that had often whispered endearments into her ear as they embraced.

"Henry!" She would have shouted, but it came out only as a whisper. Now a few tears did manage to escape her scorched eyes. "But I saw . . ." she could say no more. Her throat throbbed with pain, but her heart filled with joy. He pulled her into his arms. She had thought that she would never touch him again, never hear his voice. "The gallery," she managed.

"Yes, I am singed a bit," he laughed ruefully, and she gaped at him in surprise. He was not normally one to joke so lightly about his life. To be able to jest about his near death experience, he must be in shock. She didn't care. He was alive and that was all that mattered. She clung tightly to him while he explained that the children were quite snug in the stables and felt that they were on a great adventure. This made her laugh, but that lead to painful coughing. Henry piled blankets on and around them to protect them from the chilled December air and held her until she fell into an exhausted but peaceful sleep.

~ ~ ~ ~

The next time Elizabeth awoke, it was not with the horror that had filled her the first time her eyes had opened to take in the

Sheen courtyard scene, but with sadness for the home she had lost. She was thankful beyond measure that everyone from the king to the youngest kitchen boy had escaped, but mourned the loss of her favorite manor.

Smoke still rose from the remains of this place that held so many memories for her. Wagons were being packed up with what belongings had not been destroyed so that the royal family could be moved to London. Elizabeth saw that Kathryn was snug in her husband's arms, oblivious to the guards surrounding them. It seemed like a lifetime ago that Elizabeth had been lying in bed attempting to decide what to do about the two of them. She need not have concerned herself. Henry was watching the happy couple from across the lawn, and he did not look pleased.

As if reading her mind, Henry mumbled, "It seems that our guest needs to be kept under closer guard."

Elizabeth nodded since speaking was still painful. She was content to look upon her husband. She had been so sure that she had lost him. He had never been strikingly handsome, but now his hair was thin and held more than a little grey. His teeth, which had always given him trouble, were few and in poor condition. However, she saw him only as the man who loved her and had brought peace into her life. After all, who was she to judge when her youthful beauty was now hidden behind a double chin and fine lines?

The children came running across the lawn toward their parents, stopping short to bow and curtsey as they had been taught. A memory of properly presenting herself to her own parents flashed through Elizabeth's mind.

"Mother, we are to go to London," Harry said with no attempt to conceal his excitement.

"Sorry about your house, mama," Margaret said as she subtly elbowed her brother's ribs.

"Yes, sorry, mother," Harry added with his eyes on the ground.

Mary did not speak much yet but took full advantage of the older siblings who were more than willing to speak for her. She climbed into her mother's lap instead and circled her chubby arms around Elizabeth's neck.

"We will be on our way soon," Henry said as he tousled each child's hair.

"Who started the fire?" Harry asked.

Elizabeth's eyes flashed toward her husband. She had not yet considered that the fire may have been purposely set, had assumed that a fireplace had not been properly tended.

"We do not know . . . yet," Henry said, but his eyes were focused across the courtyard. Elizabeth followed his gaze to find Perkin Warbeck.

January 1498

"Jayne, please see that Anna comes to see me."

"Yes, my lady," Jayne said with a quick curtsey. She went in search of the young woman who was a recent addition to Elizabeth's household. In a few moments, she returned with young Anna a few steps behind. The hesitant woman had to be gently pushed forward by Jayne before she approached the queen.

"Your grace," she said in a shaky voice.

"You need not worry," Elizabeth gently assured her. "You have not displeased me."

Relief flooded Anna's face, but she said nothing.

"It has come to my attention that you lost something very valuable to you in the fire at Sheen, Anna."

The girl nodded. "My mum's locket," she said. "She gave it to me before she passed on, your grace."

"Just as I thought. Though I understand that it cannot take the place in your heart that your mother's possession held, I hope that this will be some small consolation to you." Elizabeth took Anna's hand and placed a silver chain in her palm.

Anna gasped and looked down in disbelief. Hanging from the finely wrought chain was a sapphire the color of her queen's eyes. "Your grace, I couldn't," she stammered, holding the gift out to hand it back to her benefactress.

"You can and you will," Elizabeth insisted, closing Anna's fingers around the necklace. "I insist."

"Thank you, your grace, and God bless you," Anna mumbled as she dropped into a clumsy curtsey. She glanced at Elizabeth, who nodded, and then rushed from the room.

"That was very kind of you," Jayne said after they watched Anna leave with wry smiles on their faces. "She will never forget this moment and will be loyal to your house until the day she dies."

"It is no more than she deserves," Elizabeth said. "Now please send in the page boy, Stephen."

"Yes, your grace."

~ ~ ~ ~

"I have something to show you," Henrys said as he spread a large sheet of parchment out on the table, weighing down the edges with anything at hand as he spoke.

"What is it?" Elizabeth asked. She had not seen this kind of excitement in her husband for months and was glad he had a project that was bringing him joy.

"Richmond."

Elizabeth looked down at the rough sketches. A gorgeous palace was taking shape though it was not yet a detailed drawing.

"I will tear down what remains of Sheen and build a new castle in its place. We will name it Richmond in honor of my title before ascending the throne."

"How grand, Henry! It will be beautiful, but you will not keep the chapel?"

Henry shook his head. "No. The stone walls saved it from the worst of the fire, but it will be better to start fresh. This palace will be part of my legacy."

Built on the ashes of her family's legacy.

"I cannot wait to see it take shape," she said.

Hurriedly, he rolled up the parchment and was preparing to leave. "Sorry, I had but a moment."

"I am glad you shared that with me," she said as she placed a kiss on his cheek. "Do not work too hard, my love."

He grinned at her and left her chamber as Kathryn walked in.

"Shall we work on our altar cloth?" Elizabeth had been about to go visit her children, but she tried not to mention them in front of this poor woman who had been forced to give her only son over to Henry. Nobody knew where the boy had been placed. Henry simply said he would be raised by a loving family and Kathryn needed to forget about him.

"We can, your grace."

Elizabeth raised her eyebrows. They had long since dispensed with formalities in private. "What is wrong, Kathryn?"

The younger woman looked angry at herself for allowing tears to spring into her eyes, and she furiously swiped them from her cheeks.

"It is my husband," Kathryn cried. She avoided using his new name even more than Elizabeth did. The queen wondered if they still used the name Richard in private. Not that they were supposed to meet in private.

"The king has shut him away, your grace. I cannot bear it!"

Tears ran freely down her lovely face, but there was little Elizabeth could do.

"I am afraid the king saw and heard too much over Christmas."

Kathryn nodded. "I know. We could not help ourselves." She scrubbed at her face again before seeming to find her courage. "He is my husband!"

Elizabeth set aside the embroidery silks that she had been sorting and turned to face Kathryn. "I have the greatest sorrow for you. I truly do, but you must understand that Henry intends to keep you apart. He will not have another pretender's son questioning his position, and you would not want another child only to see it taken away."

A flush quickly rose to Kathryn's face and Elizabeth prepared herself for an angry outburst, but Kathryn's self-control overcame the sense of injustice that had almost overwhelmed her.

Elizabeth continued, "At least your husband is relatively free, if not free to do as he pleased." At least he is not in the Tower, she left unspoken.

"Very well," Kathryn softly acquiesced. "I will pray that God gives me strength to give him thanks in these trying circumstances, for I know that you would help me if you could."

Would she? Elizabeth was not so sure. Though she took joy from helping the less fortunate, she did not believe that would extend to assisting the man who tried to take the crown from her husband – from her son – in fathering an heir.

June 1498

Throughout the spring months, Warbeck kept his guards on their toes as he attempted to arrange a conjugal visit with his wife. The men assigned to keep him out of trouble found him charming, even enjoyed playing cards or dice with him, but they were not going to bring the wrath of their king down upon themselves in order to help him collect on the marital debt. Kathryn continued to be friendly toward Elizabeth, but her building frustration was evident to all who spent time with her. She was a cousin to the Scottish king and was not even allowed private time with her husband. Part of her wished that she and Richard, for that is the only name she would ever call him, had run away and lived in obscurity rather than landing at Whitesand Bay. Better to be poor than apart.

Elizabeth quietly observed the changes in these royal guests. Kathryn hid her feelings with the skill of one who had grown up at court. She was more withdrawn and quiet, but that could go unnoticed. Warbeck's charm was failing him. So used to getting what he wanted because of his good looks and ability to make people want to please him, the months of being kept a pampered prisoner were wearing on his nerves. No longer did passion enflame when the two of them locked eyes. It was desperation.

When Elizabeth heard the commotion of shouting voices and stomping horses on the morning of June tenth, she did not need anyone to tell her what it was. Warbeck had escaped. Surely, it had only been a matter of time before the bird decided to fly from its gilded cage.

She rose and quickly dressed. As soon as her eyes fell upon Kathryn, she knew that her suspicions were correct. Kathryn kept her head down, but Elizabeth could see the blush rising along her neck. To her surprise, Henry burst into her chamber, sending her partially dressed ladies scurrying to make themselves proper for the king.

"I will be leaving soon," he said to his wife, ignoring all others. "Warbeck escaped last night and has taken sanctuary at the Charterhouse."

Elizabeth heard Kathryn gasp and was sure that Henry did, too, but neither of them glanced her way.

"You will be safe?" Elizabeth worried.

Henry laughed. "He is on the run with nobody's assistance unless you count the Charterhouse prior who has begged me to spare his life. I will be safer than in my own bed."

"Very well," said Elizabeth, unnecessarily adjusting Henry's cloak. "Come to me when your task is complete." And how would it end, she wondered. With Kathryn in misery, that was the only certainty.

"I will, my love." He kissed her and was gone.

Kathryn was on her knees in front of her queen before the door had shut behind Henry.

"Please, your grace," she cried. "You must beg for my husband's life!"

Though torn with conflicting feelings, the Elizabeth would always stand firmly at her husband's side.

"I will do no such thing," she stated quietly but firmly. "Your husband has rebelled, lied, and snubbed his grace's mercy. It is out of my hands."

"No, please! I swear, he was not running to followers but to exile. We simply wish to live together in peace. Please, Elizabeth!"

The personal plea tore at her heart, but it was too late. "I do not know what the two of you hoped to achieve, but this escape attempt was ill-conceived. Henry will not show him the mercy of the past few months in the future."

Kathryn stood, her face contorted with rage. "Mercy! Forcing us to see each other every day, but not live as husband and wife – you call that mercy? And I suppose it was grace that led him to abduct my child? The king," she infused Henry's title with venomous contempt, "will not even call my husband by his name. Richard."

Gasps and murmurings spread throughout Elizabeth's chambers.

"Leave!" Elizabeth ordered in uncharacteristic sternness. She said nothing more until the room was cleared but fixed her face, which was pinched with anger, on Kathryn.

"Your husband is not my brother."

"You said yourself that he is the image of your father. I do not believe you. You are simply protecting your own position and that of your children."

"You believe that I would disinherit my own brother for the sake of myself?" Elizabeth's lips pursed, exposing fine lines around them that she normally tried to conceal.

"I do, but Richard is willing to withdraw his claim if we are allowed to leave England in peace."

"Do not ever call him that again! Do you understand the pain it causes each time someone uses the name of my little brother to call upon a pretender? I do not deny that Warbeck may be my father's son, but, if he is, he is a by-blow..."

Kathryn cut her off. "You mean no more legitimate than yourself?"

Elizabeth sucked in her breath and was struck speechless. Those months of wondering if it were true that her parents were not married in the eyes of the church. She had left that pain behind when she married Henry. With her right of blood and his right of conquest, they had put the past behind them. But here stood this woman, ready to excavate it for reexamination. Elizabeth forced herself to take a moment to calm herself before responding.

"I understand that this is not the life you thought you would have when you married Warbeck, but those who plot against the king are not normally allowed to live at court in relative luxury. You need to prepare yourself for the consequences of this escape attempt," Elizabeth insisted.

"And what will happen to the guards who assisted him?" Kathryn asked. Her tone inferred that she felt that she had laid down a trump card.

"What do you mean?" Elizabeth asked as her brow furrowed.

"Sir William Smith and Sir James Baybroke, they plotted with my husband to gain his freedom."

Elizabeth focused on her facial features in an effort to give nothing away. She would not allow her eyes to widen, her lips to part, or her cheeks to redden. Henry's trusted men had allowed Warbeck to escape. When Kathryn had time to calm herself, she would regret sharing this information that would prove to Henry that Warbeck was still capable to winning people's loyalty away from their king. Elizabeth would not speak on the matter.

"Kathryn, I believe I will return to my bed this morning. Please have a tray sent up to break my fast," she said, closing the discussion.

Without waiting for a response, Elizabeth turned and entered her private chamber and closed the door behind her.

~ ~ ~ ~

Henry accepted Warbeck's surrender at Charterhouse, and assured the prior that his life would not be forfeit. But when they returned to London, Warbeck was lodged, not at Westminster, but in the Tower.

338

August 1498

Rodrigo de Puebla stood before Elizabeth and Henry with a strained look on his suntanned face. He was a Spanish diplomat who had been an ambassador for Ferdinand and Isabella in the marriage negotiations with the Tudors for several years. He enjoyed speaking of the promised marriage between Arthur and Catherine much more than the marriage that Henry was proposing for Rodrigo himself.

"I am honored," Rodrigo said with an eloquent bow, "But you would not expect me to accept such a proposal without the approval of my own king and queen."

"Certainly not," Henry agreed. He placed a high value on loyalty and would not undermine that of another monarch's subjects. "I will leave it to you to discuss with them as you see fit."

"We would love to have you on English soil more often, Rodrigo. You would be tempted to stay longer if you had an English bride," Elizabeth teased.

"Nothing could be more of an incentive to stay as long as possible than your own beauty, your grace," he said with another perfect bow.

"Ah, we will not pressure him, Bess. What of the plans to bring Princess Catherine to court?" Henry asked, changing the subject to one that Rodrigo was much more comfortable with, though there was an issue with this long discussed topic as well.

"Catherine longs to learn English customs and meet her betrothed, of course," Rodrigo said in the perfectly pronounced English of those who have learned it as a second language. "There remains, however, one concern."

"What concern might that be?" Henry asked, his temper already rising.

Rodrigo was used to dealing with royal anger and continued

politely but firmly. "Concern remains regarding the rebel claimant to your throne. It is said that he resides at court with his wife."

"He is imprisoned in the Tower and has not been allowed privacy with his wife since his capture in October of last year," Henry corrected. "He is no threat whatsoever. In the six years that he trounced around the Continent attempting to gain support for his claim, he failed miserably, just as he did when he landed on England's shore."

"True, but he still lives," Rodrigo pointed out as if it were a minor problem to solve.

Elizabeth gasped. "He is kept in a prison that none has ever escaped from."

"Well, few, anyway," Rodrigo said in an off-hand manner that allowed him to correct the queen without sounding insubordinate. This also allowed him to segue into his masters' other complaint. "There is another Plantagenet prince held within the Tower with a strong claim to the crown, is there not?"

"My cousin has been under guard since his tenth year. He has never shown any sign that he is a threat to my husband's reign," Elizabeth said calmly. She was practiced at keeping her anger hidden, but Edward's imprisonment was a topic that still unnerved her, and now Rodrigo was implying that it was not enough.

"The earl of Warwick is a simpleton, kept in comfortable confinement for his own protection," Henry said lazily, as if Edward were of no consequence.

Elizabeth took a deep breath. Of course Edward was a simpleton. Henry had allowed him only the most minimal of tutoring or interaction with anyone other than his guards. Elizabeth remembered the innocent little boy who wondered if he would get his turn to be king. Did he still wonder about crowns or would he be happy simply to be free? She shook herself from her internal meanderings to listen to the Spanish envoy.

"Be that as it may, Catherine's parents must be assured that their daughter's ascendancy to the English throne would be secure as Arthur's wife. With two men in London ready to take the young prince's place, you can understand their apprehension."

"No, Rodrigo, I do not," Henry bellowed. "Do you believe that they are more concerned than I am about the security of my kingdom and my son's inheritance? I can assure you that neither of these men you have mentioned are a threat in the least. You are welcome to meet them and judge for yourself."

Rodrigo's eyes lit up at this invitation. So few men were accepted into the company of Edward of Warwick, many had forgotten that he existed. Perkin Warbeck, on the other hand, had charmed half of the monarchs of Europe before being captured by Henry, who had stunned them all by welcoming him to court rather than executing him. He tried to hide the excitement he felt, already envisioning the report he would be able to give to his king and queen.

"That would be favorable," he said calmly. "I will meet with the earl and the pretender as soon as is convenient." He bowed and left the hall before Henry could backtrack on his offer.

~ ~ ~ ~

Elizabeth was surprised to get a request for an audience from the Spanish envoy a few days later. She rarely met with him without Henry, but this made her curious rather than concerned. Eager to finalize the alliance with Spain, she asked that he be brought to her immediately.

"Your grace," he said, bowing before her within her chamber as gracefully as if they were before an audience in the great hall.

Elizabeth rose from the window seat and gestured for him to join her at a small table she had set up with wine and her favorite tarts and cheese.

"You are too kind," Rodrigo said as he took a seat.

"I am intrigued, Rodrigo. What would cause you to ask to meet me specifically, not Henry?"

Rodrigo took a long drink from his cup. "Ah, sweet Rhenish red, not one I often taste while in London." He set the cup down, while Elizabeth neither lowered her eyes nor broke the silence left by her inquiry. "You cut quickly to the heart of the matter, your grace. I thought you may be interested in my observations at the Tower."

Elizabeth furrowed her brow. Whenever she visited Edward he was well treated, if isolated. She sent him books and letters as often as she was able, as did Margaret, but she could not deny the fact that life went on while Edward became a man without one. "Edward was well, was he not?"

"Oh yes," he said, nodding like one who is happy to have some good news to impart. "Edward is not so much a simpleton as an uneducated young man who has not experienced much. He certainly maintains strong devotion to you, your grace, and through you to your husband."

"As we said," Elizabeth pointed out. "He is no threat."

"Probably not," Rodrigo agreed, yet a frown settled on his face. "What is it?"

"I had hoped to observe for myself the similarities between Warbeck and the great king Edward."

Elizabeth blushed. "He resembles my father, that would be difficult for me to deny, but I can assure you that he is not Richard."

"That is just the thing," Rodrigo said, leaning toward her in his intensity. "I could not see the resemblance."

"I am confused, Rodrigo. I hide nothing from you. Truthfully, he is closer in appearance to my brother, Edward, than to Richard, but I, their sister, would know if he were either. Between you and

I, I suspect that he is a product of one of my father's dalliances."
She knew that it was dangerous to confess so much to a man with
the ear of the Spanish monarchs, but he would have observed the
truth for himself.

"You do not understand, your grace," Rodrigo made a motion
to take her hand before regaining possession of himself. "He would
be unrecognizable to his own mother. Warbeck has been severely
beaten, possibly tortured. He resembles no Plantagenet prince in
his current condition."

"No!" It came out as a whisper, and Elizabeth's eyes bulged in
shock. What she had to say about this revelation needed to be said
to Henry, though, not Rodrigo. "I have no knowledge of this."

"That is why I am here," he said, sitting back in his chair and
reclaiming his cup of wine.

"Did you speak to him?" she asked.

"As much as he was able. His face is disfigured and he is missing
several teeth. Speech was difficult and painful for him."

"And what did he say?" she hesitantly inquired.

"He claimed to be Richard of York."

~ ~ ~ ~

Elizabeth stormed into Henry's chambers, something she had
never done before. "Leave!" She ordered away his attendants and
scribes with a wave of her hand.

Henry's eyebrows shot up in surprise, but he did not
countermand her. Whatever had upset her must be serious for her
to overcome her natural docility. When the room had emptied, he
cleared his throat and asked, "What has upset you, Bess?"

Elizabeth ignored his outstretched hand and his attentive tone.
"You have upset me," she stated with her feet planted and hands
on her hips. She saw his face tighten and his hand fall back to his

side, but he forced himself to remain calm. "What has been done to Warbeck and why is he claiming again to be my brother?"

"Warbeck escaped and incurred some injuries upon his capture."

She cut him off before he could say more. "You are lying. He has been beaten. Have you tortured him as well?"

"Bess, he took the mercy that had been shown him and threw it in my face. Why would he try to escape when he was allowed free movement at court?"

Elizabeth sighed and shook her head then used the tone she employed when explaining something to a child. "It is because you kept him from his wife, from his child. You are a man, Henry. Is it so difficult for you to imagine what you might do in his situation?"

"I had to keep him from his wife. Any children of his could be the source of rebellion," Henry calmly explained.

"Because he is my brother," Elizabeth blurted.

They stared at each other, each waiting for the other to contradict this statement.

"He is not Richard," Henry stated.

Elizabeth's eyes narrowed as she examined her husband in a new light. She knew that Warbeck was not Richard because she knew her brother. While Warbeck had the look of a Plantagenet, he did not look like Richard. But how did Henry, who had lived in exile throughout Richard's life, know that?

"I have admitted that I believe him to be my brother," she said again. Pressuring him to reveal more.

Henry vigorously shook his head. "He may be the result of your father's famously wandering eye, but he is not heir to the throne."

She agreed, but asked insistently, "How do you know?" Her eyes were piercing, more angry and accusatory than Henry had ever seen them. He was first to look away.

"We have discussed this. It is common knowledge that your

uncle killed both of your legitimate brothers," he lamely mumbled.

"Yet you are threatened by this Warbeck, but not my bastard half-brother, Arthur, who is a member of your household," Elizabeth pointed out, moving to force him to look at her.

"Arthur is not a threat and has no ambition. Warbeck is and does. It is not important what I believe to be true about him, but what he can convince others of," said Henry more firmly.

"Yet, you seem certain that his story is false, despite the fact that he has taken it up again."

"He knows he has nothing to lose, Bess. He is grasping at straws, hoping someone will believe him and come to his aid."

"I have no doubt that you are correct," Elizabeth agreed before pressing, "but you are not answering my question."

Henry gave her a hard look. "What do you want from me, Bess? Everyone has known that they are dead for fifteen years."

The whispers of gossip that had reached her ears naming Henry as her brothers' murderer spun through her head. She had pushed him this far. Had she the courage go farther? The air sizzled with the words that neither of them dared to say. As they stared into each other's eyes, her anger deflated and he knew that she would not ask the one question she had really meant to ask.

"What happened to Baybroke and Smith?" She settled for a safer inquiry.

"Warbeck's gaolers?" Henry blinked at the sudden change in topic and intensity. "Nothing. Why?"

"They allowed a treasonous prisoner to escape. Is there no punishment for permitting rebels to run free?"

Henry's face went blank and slightly pale. Then she knew that she had caught him in a scheme, though not the one she had thought to accuse him of. "He was released on purpose," she said with dread. She did not realize that her husband was capable of this type of treachery. "The guards were told to let him escape so that you had the means to justify his harsher treatment and isolation."

Henry said nothing, and Elizabeth turned and strode from the chamber.

~ ~ ~ ~

Elizabeth was thankful for a visit from her sister, Cecily. She wasn't sure what to do with the information she had obtained about Warbeck. Or if she should do anything. Cecily listened without comment as Elizabeth described how Warbeck had been trapped into having more crimes heaped upon him and the severe treatment he had been receiving.

"Why do you think Henry allowed him to be at court in the first place?" Cecily asked. She looked at the ceiling and twirled a loose strand of hair as she considered the situation.

"I suppose so that all would see that he was no true threat." Elizabeth had not thought to question Henry's mercy. It was not more than he had done for Lambert Simnel, who was still a member of Henry's household caring for his falcons. "It could have been for the sake of his wife."

Cecily's eyes lowered to take in her sister. "He is fond of Kathryn?"

Elizabeth shrugged. "Everyone is fond of her. She is devout, kind, young, and beautiful."

"Hmmm..." Cecily's eyes strayed upwards to search the roof beams for more ideas. "But something made him change his mind."

"Warbeck was becoming quite popular, and there was the difficulty of keeping him from his wife's bed."

"Ah, Bess. There you may have it. Henry believed that a noble woman would disavow her husband upon learning that he was, at best, a king's son born on the wrong side of the sheets."

"Yes," Elizabeth agreed, nodding. "I think that is true."

"He wants no more little rebel Warbecks running around, but he could not justify a more severe sentence when Warbeck was making friends at court. So, he convinced him he could escape."

Hanging her head in shame of her husband's deeds, Elizabeth mumbled a positive response.

"He will not wish to stop with imprisonment," Cecily predicted.

Elizabeth's head shot up. "What do you mean?"

"Warbeck will not be content to waste away in the Tower quietly the way our poor cousin has. Henry will look for a way to have him eliminated."

Elizabeth was about to contradict her sister, but then she remembered bits of gossip from when she was a child. The sixth king Henry had been locked up in the Tower when he died, supposedly of misery. Her father had executed rebels time after time to protect his crown, and his brother had done no less. Somebody had killed her brothers, but was it to protect Richard's crown . . . . or Henry's?

"Yes, I believe you are correct. What should I do?" she asked, her eyes imploring Cecily for the answers she could not conceive.

"You should do nothing," Cecily stated firmly. "Henry is the king, and it is not only his own crown that he protects."

February 1499

"If Henry was displeased with the friendly welcome Warbeck received at court, he must be gnashing his teeth over Ralph Wilford."

Cecily and Elizabeth sat together in Elizabeth's confinement chambers at Greenwich. A cozy fire burned in the hearth, and the windows were covered with tapestries to keep out the winter chill. The sisters felt as though they were in their own private world, away from that place where schemes unfolded and people died. John Welles, Cecily's husband had gone to God earlier in the month, but she thwarted each of Elizabeth's efforts to discuss the loss. After losing her husband and both of their daughters, Cecily needed to think about something other than what God had taken from her.

Elizabeth closed her eyes and soaked in the fire's heat. She recognized Cecily's statement for what it was: an effort to avoid her own tragedy. "He has run out of mercy," Elizabeth admitted. "The man who put Lambert Simnel in the kitchens rather than the executioner's block no longer exists."

"I don't understand it, Bess. Why would this man claim to be Edward? Have people forgotten that he is still in the Tower?"

"Maybe they have," Elizabeth said sadly, thinking of all that Edward had never been allowed to experience. "Whatever the reason for the impersonation, Wilford was quickly executed for claiming to be the earl of Warwick. It seems that people must be content with Henry's rule."

"I do not believe that." Cecily paused to pour more wine into their cups before settling back into her seat. "When it is Arthur ruling and more time has passed, the people will embrace him. Our brothers and uncle will be forgotten as our cousin has been."

"I pray that you are right," Elizabeth sighed. "I would have Arthur enjoy peace during his reign as neither my father nor husband was allowed to do."

"He will be known as Good King Arthur, with no remnants of our cousins' war to besmirch his long and peaceful reign."

"Amen."

The sisters sat silently before the fire for a few moments, each lost in their own thoughts. Would they see the glorious era of Good King Arthur? The wine and warmth comforted them each and made their troubles seem far away. It was easy to believe for a moment that they were just two sisters, not princesses with a lifetime of worries, deaths, and betrayals between them.

"The baby will arrive soon," Cecily said. "Do you wish for a girl or boy this time?"

Without opening her eyes, Elizabeth replied, "A queen is required to wish for boys." A small smile touched her lips. "Too many boys served as the third Edward's curse. I believe I desire another girl, who can help Arthur build his peace through marriage alliances."

"A wise choice, sister," Cecily agreed. "How is your backup prince? Any more suited to the church than before?"

Elizabeth laughed out loud. "Oh, Cecily, nobody else would dare speak of Harry that way! But you are perceptive. He enjoys riding his horse more than learning his verses, though he excels at both. Surely, no priest seemed suited to that profession when they were not quite eight years old."

Cecily thought that she could think of a few examples to fit that bill but did not press. "He keeps his tutors on their toes, I am certain."

More laughter. "That he does," Elizabeth agreed. "I see so much of our father in him," she added in a softer voice.

"Yes, he is a perfect little Plantagenet prince."

"Do not let Henry hear you call him that!"

"I only give voice to what you were thinking, Bess."

"Be that as it may, it would hurt his pride. He has plenty of others to do that," Elizabeth sadly murmured.

"And what of little Margaret and Mary," Cecily asked, steering the conversation back to the happier topic of the children though it hurt to think of her own little ones swept up to heaven.

"Margaret will be married to James, though when she should be sent to him is a matter of some debate."

"His reputation does not paint him as the ideal husband to a child bride," Cecily agreed. "Is it that you are afraid that his womanizing will hurt Margaret's feelings or that he will take her to bed too soon?

"Both," Elizabeth confessed.

Cecily snorted. "In that you are likely justified in your fear."

"I have my mother-in-law to thank for this victory," Elizabeth admitted and smiled at the shock on Cecily's face. "She was a strong voice in the argument that girls should not be expected to be wives in the full meaning of the word until they are at least fourteen."

Cecily nodded. "Having given birth to Henry when barely thirteen certainly qualifies her to speak on that topic."

"Yes, there was no need for her to point out that she had never been able to conceive again. Of course, Henry takes his mother's advice to heart on all matters, but on this she is indeed an expert."

"And James is content to wait on his young bride?" Cecily asked with one eyebrow raised.

"He has agreed not to demand that she be sent to him before September 1503. By then I will have to form a new argument for her delay."

They shared a knowing smile.

"Mary is a sweet, little beauty, who can wrap anyone around her smallest finger," Elizabeth continued. "Even Harry will take a break from his vigorous activity to take refreshment with his youngest sister. I believe he will see himself as her protector throughout their lives."

"You have done well, Bess. And this little one," Cecily patted her sister's large, rounded stomach, "will be no less blessed."

~ ~ ~ ~

Edmund entered the world just a few days later, and Elizabeth prayed that she had not cursed him by not desiring another boy. She also prayed that this set of brothers would grow up in peace with each other to live long and happy lives that had been denied to so many other sets of Plantagenet brothers.

June 1499

"The Spaniards are not going to accept anything less than execution," Henry said as he paced the room. His hair was disheveled and greyer than ever. He worked his jaw in a nervous motion that let Elizabeth know that he also had a toothache. The yellowish tinge to his skin and the way it hung loosely on his frame did not speak well toward his state of health.

"Please, Henry" she said, directing him toward a bench. "Sit down."

He followed her command like a child. "I'm sorry, Bess. I know that it will be difficult for you, but I must do this to secure Arthur's future."

Taking a deep breath to give her time to consider her words, Elizabeth sat next to her husband. "I do not wish for Warbeck's death, but he is a traitor. Your decision would be legally justified."

Henry gave her an odd look. "You don't understand, Bess. Not just Warbeck."

Elizabeth's eyebrows drew together. "You're right. I don't understand."

He took her hands and kept his eyes on them rather than her face. "It is not only Warbeck that they insist must be executed for treason. They want no rival claimants to their daughter's position."

"But, Henry, who?" Elizabeth asked in confusion.

He forced himself to look her in the eye. He was a king not a coward.

"Warwick."

Elizabeth sprung to her feet, her hands fisted tightly at her sides.

"No! You have kept Edward in prison for over half his life despite the fact that his only crime is possessing royal blood in his veins. I will not stand for this. He is innocent!"

She paced across the room while Henry silently watched her fume.

"I have begged you to make a place for him, Henry. Pleaded for you to give him some minor position, but you have left him only with the title of rebel. Lambert Simnel, who rode with an army against you, cares for your falcons, but my cousin you would kill?"

"It is not my wish," he said quietly in contrast to her rage.

"You are the king! If it is not your wish, do not do it," she shouted.

Henry stood and made his way toward the door. "We will talk about this more when you have had time to calm yourself. Think about our son."

He left as the tears began to stream down Elizabeth's face.

~ ~ ~ ~

"What is going on, Jayne?"

Elizabeth was bouncing little Edmund on her knee, casually wondering if he would be her last child. She would have had to have been blind to fail to notice the way servants were huddling together whispering the latest rumors.

"It is news from the city, your grace," Jayne said hesitantly.

"London? What news?"

Elizabeth was only half listening as she admired her youngest son's strength and obvious charm. He was delighting her with his toothless grin when Jayne's next words chilled her to the bone.

"An escape from the Tower, my lady."

Elizabeth's knee became still, and she locked her gaze on Jayne. The look on her closest companion's face told her that they shared the same thoughts. Nobody escapes from the Tower . . . . unless they have help.

"Warbeck?"

Jayne nodded before adding softly, "With a conspirator."

"No, he wouldn't!" Elizabeth gasped, almost allowing Edmund to wriggle from her grasp.

Jayne didn't ask if Elizabeth meant Henry or Edward of Warwick. She wasn't sure that she wanted to know.

~ ~ ~ ~

Elizabeth did not go to London, refused to beg for the life of her cousin when she knew it had already been forfeited. Edward would not have partnered with Warbeck to escape from the Tower. Even if he had, it would have been impossible for them to do so without the collaboration of a guard or servant. Henry had arranged it, she had no doubt, and she would not look him in the eye as he attempted to deny it.

She was at Greenwich with her children gathered around her, remembering Edward as a child. He had enjoyed such simple things in life, things that had been denied him for over a decade. What would this do to his poor sister, Margaret? She surely would not believe the story of the two prisoners managing to communicate from separate cells and coming up with a plan to escape. Only those who did not know him would be tempted to believe, they and the people who wanted him dead. It was easier than believing the king of England was a cold-blooded murderer.

Little Mary ran through the grass on short, sturdy legs, and Elizabeth wondered when was the last time that Edward had been allowed outside, let alone to run free. He was a man grown now at twenty-four and had spent more years in the Tower than out of it. Elizabeth closed her eyes so that only the orange of the bright sun was visible. How many more times would Edward be allowed to feel the warmth of the sun upon his face?

A tear rolled down her cheek, and a little voice said, "Why are you crying, mama?"

Elizabeth blinked back her tears and wiped her face. Harry was standing in front of her, hair and clothes in complete disarray, but concern on his face.

"Who has made you cry, mother?" he demanded, and she could imagine him placing his hand on a sword hilt at his side if he were old enough to carry one.

"It is nothing," she insisted, pulling him into her arms. He would have patience for his mother's embrace for only a moment, so she cherished the feel of his warm body. "Sometimes mothers just get sad."

He looked at her while deciding if this explanation satisfied him. "Sometimes Mary and Margaret cry, but I don't."

Elizabeth laughed. "It is because you are a strong little man, Harry. We soft-hearted women need strong boys like you to care for us and protect us."

Harry pulled from her arms, as she knew he would. He put his hands on his hips and said, "I will protect you, my lady mother."

"And your sisters?" she asked.

He looked across the lawn at them for a moment as if considering before promising, "And my sisters."

"Thank you, Harry. God bless you," Elizabeth managed around the lump in her throat.

Harry, certain that he had made his mother feel better so that she would no longer have to cry, strode proudly back to his sisters.

November 1499

Warbeck was executed after a vague statement about not being who men thought him to be. Those who believed him to be Richard wondered if they had been following a pretender. Others, who had been sure that he was not their prince, worried that they may have just watched the execution of Edward IV's son.

Edward of Warwick, son of George of Clarence, who had himself been executed by his brother for treason, was executed for treason on the twenty-eighth of November. Some were struck by the youthful innocence of his appearance as he strode slowly but steadily to the gallows. Before placing his neck on the block, he looked up toward the sky with his arms outstretched, collecting the crisp autumn air and heat from the sun into his embrace before kneeling to never feel it again.

A plague tore through London with damning speed. With a third of the city's population dead, including Henry's oldest supporter and advisor, John Morton, there were whispers that the wrath of God had fallen on the king for the killing of England's true king. Whether that true king was Richard or Edward, could not be agreed upon.

Early in the new year 1500, Henry and Elizabeth travelled to Calais to visit Archduke Philip and remove themselves from the path of the plague. Though they went together, they were far from one another in spirit for the first time in their marriage.

June 1500

Elizabeth had played her part as the dutiful wife and proper queen during their stay in Calais. She wished that her first trip abroad had been under different circumstances so that she could have enjoyed visiting the lands of her Angevin ancestors. They had left the children, besides Arthur, at Hatfield in Hertfordshire, where they were sequestered from the pestilence of the city. Far from London at Ludlow, Arthur should have been safe as well, but word had reached them that he was ailing. Elizabeth prayed without ceasing that he would be healed, could not imagine what would happen if he succumbed as so many others had.

With the wind whipping around her and pulling her hair from its pins, she squinted over the water for the first glimpse of land. Henry kept trying to convince her to rest in the tent that was set up for them, but she felt closer to her children if she stood in the prow of the ship.

"Land ho!" shouted the sailor keeping watch in the crow's nest.

Elizabeth turned her head to look at him. He was peering in the same direction as she but must have better vision. She leaned out as far as she could without fear of falling and narrowed her eyes. Was that green in the distance? It must be the shores of Dover. She smiled as the shoreline grew into existence before her eyes.

She thought of each of her children in turn and longed to hold them in her arms. How much little Edmund would have changed in the weeks since she had left him. She prayed again for Arthur and hoped that she had not cursed him with her comments about kings with too many sons. Her oldest was almost fourteen years old and would soon be ready for marriage to the Spanish princess his father had chosen for him. The last time Elizabeth had seen him, he had been able to rest his chin on the top of her head. He was no longer her little boy, but she could not help but worry about him as if he was.

He must be cured. God would see to it. Henry had been through so much already in his attempt to secure his hold on England's throne. Her lips thinned as she pressed them together thinking of the sacrifices that had been made to guarantee his son's rights.

Jayne made her way to Elizabeth's side. "Glad I am to see these shores," she exclaimed. Jayne had not enjoyed being aboard the ship or the forwardness of the men of Calais.

Elizabeth took her hand. Besides her sisters, Jayne was Elizabeth's most beloved confidant and was always with her even when her sisters could not be. "Praise the Lord, we have safely arrived. I am anxious for news about Arthur."

Giving Elizabeth's hand a squeeze, Jayne nodded. "He is a strong boy with a legion of prayers being sent the Lord's way for him. When we arrive, we will hear that he has been back out hunting for the past week."

Elizabeth laughed and took comfort in Jayne's optimistic attitude. "I pray that your prophecy comes true."

As they disembarked, a man that Elizabeth recognized from her children's household approached. The look on his face gave her a sinking feeling, but she forced herself to stand tall and await his message. He knelt before her and waited for her to give him leave to speak.

"God bless you for greeting me with news of my children," she said, raising him up. She was astounded that her voice did not shake.

"Do not bless me, your grace, for I bring tidings that will bring you grief," he said with a curious amount of moisture in his eyes.

Elizabeth closed her eyes and said a brief silent prayer for strength. "Tell me."

"It is your son."

"No." She shook her head and would have backed away had Jayne not put an arm out for support. "Not Arthur!"

Confusion briefly clouded the messenger's face. "No, your grace!" he cried out. "It is not the heir whom I bring news of, though I have heard that he was recently cured of an illness."

Elizabeth sighed in relief, but Jayne held fast.

"I come from Hatfield," he continued. "It is your youngest son," he sputtered quickly before any more confusion could ensue. "Prince Edmund died three days ago of the plague."

Elizabeth's eyes widened and she sucked in her breath. She prayed it would be her last. How could she go on after the death of the little boy she had said she did not want? "No," she whispered. It was not the overwhelming grief that she would have felt over the death of her firstborn but a wave of guilt that washed over her.

Edmund had just been learning to walk when she had seen him before leaving for France. Now he would never toddle toward her again, holding out chubby, dimpled hands for her to catch him. He had joined his sister, Eliza, in heaven. Elizabeth hoped that their first meeting had been a joyous one.

Henry, just noticing the scene on the dock, made his way to his wife's side. "What is it, Bess?"

Elizabeth shook her head, unable to speak. Henry looked to the messenger, who was dismayed at having to repeat his sad news. He knelt once again, and said, "Your grace, it is your son, Edmund. He died three days past, may God assoil him. Forgive me for being the cause of the queen's grief."

The lines on Henry's face deepened as he tightened his face to gain control of his emotions. "God bless you as forgiveness is unnecessary," he said after a moment. "I pray that he did not suffer."

"No, not for long," the messenger said, though he did not know if it were true. He would not be the one to inform his king and queen that their son had died after days of crying and anguish, too young to understand what was happening to his feverish body.

"Thank you," Henry said. He placed his arm around Elizabeth's shoulders and steered her away from the onlookers that were beginning to gather. "Bess, I am so sorry," he whispered in her ear.

"As you should be," she said, angrily shaking free of his embrace and swiping at the tears on her face. "You have cursed our family with murder, and now the plague brought upon our kingdom has taken our son!"

Henry stood on the dock, speechless, as Elizabeth hurried to the waiting litter with her women scurrying to follow.

November 1501

Catherine of Aragon had landed on English soil with her Spanish retinue. After over a decade of negotiations, and more concessions than Elizabeth cared to think about, she would see her firstborn married. Her heart swelled with pride to imagine her son taking a wife, fathering children, and wearing his father's crown. She prayed that God would allow her to witness each of these milestones in his life.

Relations with Henry had been strained ever since the deaths of Edward and Edmund. When Elizabeth had been a little girl, she had been able to look the other way and stop her ears from hearing rumors of her father's ruthlessness. She was no longer a little girl, and Henry's actions repulsed her in a way that her father's never had. She wondered if her cousin, Margaret, would ever forgive her for not being able to save Edward. Maybe she should have made more of an effort years ago. She had never foreseen the length to which Henry would go.

In order to plan an elaborate twelve day celebration for the wedding of the heir to the throne, Elizabeth had been spending more time with her mother-in-law than her husband. Lady Margaret did not comment on the marital division that she was no doubt aware of. Since Henry had the sons he needed, she probably did not care. The two women were able to be united over their common excitement concerning the upcoming nuptials and did not discuss Elizabeth's marriage problems.

"They should stay at Baynard during the festivities," Margaret said in the tone that she always used, one that allowed for no other opinion than her own.

"That would be suitable," Elizabeth agreed. She had learned long ago that it was easiest to let Margaret have her way unless a detail was worth a battle.

Fabric samples and documents were scattered around the room as the women planned for the most important event of their lives the way the men planned for battle. The path of the procession was charted, and they had ridden it several times to note any problems that may crop up. Enough fabric had been ordered to carpet the entire trail so that the royal wedding party would arrive at St. Paul's undefiled by dirt or any less desirable substances that frequented the London streets.

Wine would flow freely in the streets for the entertainment of the people whose involvement would be limited to catching a glimpse of the prince and his Spanish bride as they rode past. Extra guards would be on duty to keep the crowd from becoming overly enthusiastic in their celebrations.

Elizabeth sat back and stretched to ease the pain in her lower back. Remembering her own bridal procession, she hoped Arthur and Catherine would find lasting love and contentment in their marriage. For a long time, she had believed that she and Henry had. Now, she was not quite so sure.

As if her thoughts had commanded his presence, Henry entered the chamber. He surveyed the mess with an upraised eyebrow and dismissed the servants with a silent gesture. His mother remained seated, certain that anything he would say to Elizabeth could be said to her. He did not seem to mind.

"I would speak to you about the wedding," he said.

"I can assure you that we are more than capable of handling this while you take care of the rest of the country," Margaret said without looking up from the samples she was examining.

"I have complete faith in that," Henry assured her with a smile. He never seemed to notice her rudeness. "There is one request that I would make though."

"What is it?" Elizabeth asked. She felt the need to remind them that she was in the room.

Henry rubbed his hands over his face. He looked weary, as if speaking to his wife was one more offensive task that he was forced to perform. "I do not believe that the marriage should be consummated."

"What?" Margaret shouted. Elizabeth said nothing but her eyes grew wide. "Arthur is fifteen years old, Henry," Margaret continued as if speaking to a child. "He is ready to be a husband in every sense of the word. Surely you would like him to beget an heir as soon as possible."

Henry poured himself a cup of wine and drank half of it before responding. "I am not certain that his health allows it."

"What are you talking about?" This time it was Elizabeth's turn to go on the attack. "You did not tell me that our son was ailing."

"I'm sure it is nothing, Bess. Some weakness and difficulty eating. I would just like him to have a chance to fully recover before taking part in the physical demands of the marriage bed."

"The Spanish will not be happy," Margaret pointed out.

"The Spanish do not have to know," Elizabeth said, surprising herself by taking Henry's side. "If it is a matter of my son's health, we will take every precaution."

Henry looked at her and she could read the silent thanks on his face. She turned away, angry that this was the first she had heard of Arthur's symptoms. Please, God, she prayed. Do not take this son, the hope of the kingdom, from us.

~ ~ ~ ~

When Arthur arrived in London later in the month, Elizabeth was reassured that her fears had been for naught. Riding into the city at his father's side, the prince was a vision of elegance and grace. He had the slender, wiry build of a young man, but he would fill out as he grew. It wasn't until she beheld him up close that

Elizabeth noticed the shadows under his eyes and hollowness of his cheeks.

"You have not been eating enough," she chastised him. "Have you a case of the marriage jitters?" She joked to lighten the weight that was building and threatening to crush her heart. She shoved a plate in front of him and pretended not to notice that he spent much more time moving the food around than placing it in his mouth.

"I am fine, mother," he said wearily. "The trip has been tiresome. I simply need some rest."

"Very well," Elizabeth said, caressing his face with her hand. No fever. "Your chamber has been prepared." She motioned for a servant to assist Arthur into bed. "We will talk more tomorrow."

"Yes, mother," he agreed, kissing her on the cheek. "God bless you."

"May he bless and keep you, my son," she whispered as he walked away.

~ ~ ~ ~

Catherine of Aragon rode into London amidst cheers from a pressing crowd. Every man, woman, and child hoped for a glimpse of the woman who would be the next queen of England. She did not disappoint. Perched upon a highly decorated mule, Catherine could have been an angel from heaven with her white skirts spread out around her and her light auburn hair flowing down to veil her small body from view. It would not be easy to follow in the footsteps of the popular and beautiful Queen Elizabeth, but most agreed that Catherine looked like she may be up to the task.

Elizabeth welcomed Catherine to Baynard's Castle to prepare for the wedding taking place the next day. She was delighted by the lovely, quiet girl who seemed perfectly suited to her serious and solemn son. Since they both spoke Latin, that is the language that they chose to communicate in.

Catherine curtseyed deeply before her soon to be mother-in-law. "Your grace, I am pleased to finally meet you."

"I feel as though I already know you," said Elizabeth, pulling Catherine into an embrace. "Your letters have brightened many of my days, and I look forward to seeing you and Arthur wed on the morrow."

Catherine blushed and looked down at her hands. "Prince Arthur has written many fine letters that I keep with me always."

"I believe the two of you will find great happiness together."

Elizabeth directed Catherine to a small table with two chairs that she had prepared for them before the hearth. "Let us sit and get to know each other better. You must be hungry," she said, indicating the plate of cheese and wafers.

"Thank you, your grace."

"Please, call me Elizabeth."

"Thank you, Elizabeth," Catherine said and blushed again at the informality.

"Have you found England to your liking?"

"Oh, yes. It is beautiful." Catherine could have said nothing else. How could she point out that it seemed rather rainy and cold. The people seemed rather improper. The king had even demanded to see her face before he would allow the wedding to take place!

"I hope you have been made to feel welcome here." Elizabeth poured two cups of wine, and she placed one in front of the nervous young woman before taking a sip from her own.

"Quite," Catherine said. She would not admit that she felt like a displayed trophy more than a welcomed princess.

"Good," Elizabeth said taking another sip. She waved away her attendant and turned back to Catherine. "And now you may tell me how you truly feel."

Catherine's eyes widened in fear and surprise. Could the queen discern her disappointment? She tried to mumble an assurance that she could not be happier but stopped when she finally looked up from her lap to see the queen's face. Elizabeth looked as friendly as any merchant's wife with her eyebrows upraised and a twitch of a smile on her lips.

"I have been a paraded princess all of my life, dear Catherine," she said, patting the girl's cold, clammy hands. "I do know what it feels like. I have not however had to leave my country and be paraded in front of complete strangers who do not share my language. It must be awful. Praise God for bringing you through it for you have more trials to come."

Catherine's jaw dropped and her mouth worked to come up with a response. Then they were both laughing, and Catherine's fears melted away.

"Thank you, your grace. I feel that I have a friend here."

"The first of many, I am sure," Elizabeth said, taking a few morsels from the table. She shouldn't, she needed to fit into her gown specially made for the wedding festivities. "Arthur will be an attentive husband, and I do not say that simply because he is my son. I think the two of you are well suited and will be happy together."

"I pray that God blesses us with happiness and many children," Catherine said, almost keeping another furious blush from covering her face.

"That is my prayer as well. Is there anything else that I can do for you? Do not be afraid to ask," Elizabeth insisted.

Her hands twisted in her lap and she had to force herself to look up. "I do have one concern," Catherine admitted.

"What is it?"

"A motto," Catherine said almost in a whisper. "I am told that queens of England have a motto."

"That is true. Mine is 'Humble and Reverent,' though sometimes I must work to personify these qualities," Elizabeth said thoughtfully.

"That is lovely, your grace . . . . Elizabeth. I do not know what mine should be," Catherine said as a worry line creased her brow.

Elizabeth did not allow the smile that threatened to creep up to her face. She could see that, to Catherine, this was a serious dilemma indeed. Examining the girl thoughtfully, she could see that she embodied humbleness more than herself. What would be a fitting motto for the wife of her son?

"Humble and Loyal."

Catherine tilted up her chin and smiled. She was not one to notice her own strengths but was pleased by what the queen had seen within her. "Humble and Loyal. Yes, I do like that. Thank you, your grace."

The next day, Arthur and Catherine said their vows in St. Paul's Cathedral, and the festivities that would last for the next twelve days began.

On the morning following the wedding, Arthur boasted of spending the night in Spain.

December 1501

It was time for Arthur and Catherine to make their way to Ludlow, where they would rule as the Prince and Princess of Wales. Arthur was anxious to return to what he considered his home. The festivities had exhausted him and he was weary of keeping up appearances. Catherine was fond of her new husband but was fearful of another move and leaving those she was just growing to love.

"Catherine, my dear," Elizabeth said, embracing the younger woman. "Thank you for the time we have spent together. I know that you will make my son very happy."

"Thank you, Elizabeth. I mean to." She no longer felt that she needed to keep her eyes down when she spoke to her mother-in-law and would miss her greatly in the days to come.

"Keep him on the straight and narrow," Henry joked, knowing that nobody held Arthur to a higher standard than himself.

Catherine laughed and said, "I will, your majesty, and thank you for all you have done for me." She was no longer appalled by Henry forcing his way into her lodgings to see for himself what his son's Spanish bride looked like. Now he was the caring father-in-law who had showered her with jewels and shared his library with her when she was morose over the return of her attendants to Spain.

Henry spoke with Arthur off to one side where the women could not overhear. Arthur seemed to be assuring his father of something, but Elizabeth couldn't be sure what.

"Do let me know when you find yourself with child," Elizabeth whispered conspiratorially to her daughter-in-law and was surprised by the deep blush it raised.

"Of course, I will, and I pray that it will be soon."

"God bless you and keep you, my dear daughter."

"And you," Catherine said with a small curtsey.

Their procession began its journey, and Elizabeth stood watching until they were out of sight. It made her sadder than ever to watch Arthur return to his own estates.

January 1502

Elizabeth found it difficult to believe that it was time to lose another of her children to marriage. She still missed Arthur and Catherine more than she admitted to anyone other than Jayne, but it was time to sign the long negotiated treaty with the king of Scotland.

Princess Margaret was formally betrothed to James IV in an elaborate ceremony that emphasized the solidity of the Tudor monarchy and its unity with its neighbor to the north. With this treaty in place and Arthur married to the Spanish princess, few could doubt Henry's permanence.

Elizabeth sat beneath a canopy wrapped in warm furs with her youngest children, Harry and Mary, at her feet. She looked at them and longed to tousle their hair and pull them into her arms. Their day would come too soon. Though she longed for an advantageous marriage for Mary and a prominent church position for Harry, she hoped that both could be put off for several more years.

Elizabeth found that she was holding her breath when the Archbishop of Glasgow asked Margaret if she entered into this agreement of her own free will. Ten-year-old Margaret knew plenty about free will, but she played the part of the dutiful daughter on this day and answered in the affirmative. The marriage by proxy was quickly completed and Margaret was officially the Queen of Scots.

The agreement was that Margaret would be sent to her husband next year, but Elizabeth hoped to delay further when that day approached. Though she could not express it publicly, she still had concerns about her womanizing son-in-law. She knew that September 1503 would come far too soon to please her, but she made up her mind to enjoy the wedding festivities and her daughters' company rather than concern herself with tomorrow's troubles.

February 1502

"Henry, I must speak to you," Elizabeth said, catching him between petitioners in the great hall at Westminster.

"Of course," he said, and he rose to lead her into a more private chamber.

"I have received a letter from our daughter-in-law."

"News?" He knew it must be important for her to seek him out. She continued to speak to him only when necessary since the earl of Warwick's execution. She never outwardly opposed him, so he said nothing but prayed for healing between them.

Elizabeth nodded. "I am afraid that Arthur has fallen ill."

Henry's lips pursed into a thin line. He had warned his son about waiting to consummate the marriage, though he was as eager as any new husband. His health was the first concern, for the sake of the kingdom.

"Catherine writes that he is bound to his bed, and she struggles to get him to eat."

"She is a good and devoted wife, and he is a young man. He was probably out of bed before you received the message."

"I do hope so," Elizabeth said doubtfully. She remembered Arthur's pale complexion and weariness that he had tried to hide over the weeks that he had been in London. Ignoring the signs of consumption, she acknowledged that there was nothing to be done if that was what Arthur suffered anyway. "I would like to pay for prayers to be said for him."

Henry shook his head. "We cannot allow doubts and rumors to spread. I already have my hands full dealing with another one of your troublesome cousins."

"Edmund?"

"Of course, Edmund." He began to pace, a sure signal of his anxiety. "Your de la Pole relatives insist that they are not content with my rule even without Edward as their figurehead. Maybe it is Edmund himself who believes he should take his place."

Elizabeth said nothing. She would not rise to his bait. Besides, she knew nothing of her cousin's plans. She was not surprised that Edmund and his brother, William, were not deterred by Edward's execution but infuriated by it.

"I am in the process of revealing the conspiracy supporting him, which, of course, will include William Courtenay. I am sorry, Bess. They may be your extended family, but they continue to plot against me."

Elizabeth forced herself to take a deep breath and unclench her fists. "I will have the masses said for both Arthur and Catherine. Everyone will assume that we pray for them to be blessed with a child." Then she turned and walked away.

~ ~ ~ ~

William Courtenay, Cat's husband, and William de la Pole were arrested and put into the Tower, as was James Tyrell, a former follower of Richard III, who had been convinced to leave the relative safety of Calais and return to England. Edmund de la Pole remained at large, though Henry managed to have him excommunicated.

Elizabeth sent care packages to her cousins in the Tower, much to her husband's chagrin.

April 1502

"Your grace, wake up. It is the king. He has sent for you." Jayne had been the only one of Elizabeth's ladies willing to disturb her when the king's page arrived at her chambers. She could not remember the king calling for her at such an hour, or rarely ever, for he would simply come to her chambers if he wished to see her. That had not occurred for some time either.

"What is it, Jayne?" Elizabeth mumbled sleepily.

"I'm not sure, your grace. The king requests that you attend him."

A feeling of foreboding coursed through Elizabeth's body. Her mind immediately brought up words from Catherine's letters of Arthur's failing health. He had been able to spend some time out of bed, but would quickly grow weary and return to it. She was immediately awake and had Jayne assist her with her closest dress. "Pray for Arthur," she whispered in Jayne's ear before rushing out the door.

Henry was waiting for her, seated upon a bench with his confessor before him. Elizabeth looked from one to the other but could not discern the reason for her being yanked from her bed. She took the seat next to her husband when he offered it.

"Your majesties," the aged friar began, "I regret to be the one to bring you tidings of the worst sort."

Elizabeth's heart plummeted and she grasped Henry's hand. Forgotten were all of the crimes that she had held against him. He was no longer the murderer of her cousin but the father of her son.

"Three days ago, on the second day of April, your dearest son, Prince Arthur, was departed to God."

Elizabeth closed her eyes as tears began to stream down her face. Henry was squeezing her hand so hard that it hurt, but she didn't care. She wanted to kick and scream. Arthur, the mingling of Tudor and Plantagenet blood named after the golden king of legend, was dead before reaching the age of sixteen. Images of him as an infant, toddler, and small boy flashed before her mind's eye. She had been so full of hope for him. He had been as serious and contemplative as his father, but with enough of his mother's charm and piety to earn the love of the people that eluded Henry. Now, he was gone.

She realized that Henry's confessor was again speaking.

"If we receive good things at the hands of God, why may we not endure evil things?"

It was true, but it was not what the grieving couple needed to hear at this moment.

"Please," Henry said with a catch in his throat. "Give us a moment of privacy before we offer up prayers for the soul of our beloved son."

"Of course, your majesties," the friar bowed as much as his hunched back allowed and shuffled from the room.

As soon as the door closed behind the old man, Henry took Elizabeth into his arms. She no longer had the strength or desire to fight him.

"Our son! Conceived on our wedding night and gone before both of us. Why, God? Why?" she cried.

"Bess," Henry whispered in her ear. "I'm so sorry, Bess. Sorry for everything that has hurt you. It was all for naught."

"No! No!" She could say nothing more. She pounded her small fist into his chest to emphasize each repetition of the word. They held each other as their tears mingled and neither could find the words to comfort the other.

After a few moments, Elizabeth pulled back and dragged her hand across her swollen eyes. "We must pray," she said.

Henry nodded and took her hand. He led her to his private altar where they prayed together for the soul of their firstborn son to be welcomed into heaven without suffering the punishments of purgatory.

They had worn themselves out with weeping, but Henry would have to make the announcement, send messengers, and see that Harry, who was now the king's heir, was brought to court.

Elizabeth returned to her own chambers and fell upon her bed. Was it only a few short hours since she was at peaceful sleep here, not realizing that her son lay cold in death? Her tears started anew, and for the first time she felt anger toward God. She had endured so much and the loss of so many. Why had he needed to take Arthur? She punched her pillow and tore at her bedcoverings. She did not realize that she was screaming.

"Bess, Bess, hush my love." Henry was there with his arms around her, pulling her fingers from the shredded cloth. He made shushing noises as he rocked her back and forth like a child, and she cried again, thinking fleetingly that tears must eventually run dry.

When she had calmed herself, she whispered to him with her head rested on his shoulder. "I am sorry, Henry. My faith was tested, but God will comfort us."

"As he always does in his perfect wisdom," Henry agreed.

"I also need to apologize for not being a good wife to you of late." Henry made to stop her, but she placed a finger upon his lips. "It is true," she insisted. "I have been polite, but not loving nor submissive. In the future, I will be the type of wife the Lord intends for me to be."

"Oh, Bess," Henry sighed, squeezing her more tightly. "I have prayed that you would forgive me. I love you so."

"And I love you, Henry," she said. "And I will give you another son."

Henry took her face in her hands. "No, Bess. It would not be safe for you to enter the birthing chamber again."

"Nonsense," she insisted, taking his hands into her own. "I am thirty-six and my mother was forty-three when she gave birth to my youngest sister."

"I feel that we should pray before making a decision of this magnitude," he said, still slowly shaking his head.

"We will pray," she agreed. "We will also remember that the Lord our God has also blessed us with two fair princesses and our dear son, Harry. They will be a comfort to us in the coming days."

"Yes. Harry," Henry said thoughtfully. "Thank you for your comfort, my wife," he said, reluctantly leaving her embrace and rising from her bed.

"It is you who came to comfort me," she reminded him.

"Yes, it was Jayne who came for me."

"I am glad that she did and will thank her."

"I will come to see you again as soon as I may," he said kissing her forehead. "Get some rest, my love, and be in prayer."

Elizabeth compressed her lips and answered him with a slight nod before he left her alone with her thoughts and memories.

~ ~ ~ ~

Elizabeth felt ill the next day, but she could not be certain if it were the effect of too many tears or true sickness. She rose only long enough to send a messenger to her sister, Cat. It was her hope that they could be a comfort to each other since Cat's husband, William Courtenay, remained imprisoned in the Tower.

She was pleased when Cat arrived within the week. Still not feeling well herself, Cat's youthful energy seemed to increase her own vigor.

"Bess, we must get outside. It is fresh spring air that you require," Cat insisted once she and her things were adequately settled.

"I don't know," Elizabeth said, pulling a coverlet more firmly around her.

"Yes, you do," her sister insisted. "You love the outdoors, your gardens, and the scent of springtime." She pulled the cover from Elizabeth's grasp and snapped her fingers at Elizabeth's women. "A wool cloak for the queen," she insisted with confident authority.

Before Elizabeth knew it, she was strolling along the garden paths with Cat beside her and a few attendants trailing behind. Elizabeth tired quickly and asked that they rest on a bench beneath an arbor of Tudor rose vines, though they were not yet in bloom.

"I am so thankful for your presence, Cat." She took a deep breath to soak up the scents of another spring. She refused to think about memories of those past spring gardens or future ones that would not include her son. Right now, she needed to live in the moment.

"It is beautiful here." Cat's eyes were wide open in contrast to her sister's closed ones. The gardens at Greenwich were her sister's pride and joy, and it showed even early in the year before many of the plants had risen to their full glory. "It will be soothing for our souls."

Opening her eyes just a crack, Elizabeth peeked at her sister. She saw no anger in her countenance and was thankful for that. "I am sorry about William. I have sent him items to ease his troubles, but I know that is little comfort to you."

"Oh, Bess. I never doubted you in the least! I am as sure that Will's imprisonment was Henry's decision, not yours, as I am certain that Will and Edmund have, in fact, had treasonous conversations."

At this, Elizabeth's eyes were fully opened. "They schemed against Henry?"

Cat shook her head and waved a hand dismissively. "They are no rebels," she said. "They are young men who are all talk about family honor. Leading an army against Henry is completely different than claiming a more royal bloodline than his."

Elizabeth didn't need to remind her sister that the supposedly innocent talk that she referred to was treasonous. "Please, do not say more. I do not wish to know anything that would be wrong for me to keep from my husband."

"And I do not wish to put you in that situation, Bess. But, don't you see? If Henry simply ignored the arrogant talk of young men, it would melt away like winter snow. It is his campaign against all with Plantagenet blood that raises men's ire."

"You speak with a maturity that is deep for your years," Elizabeth admitted. Did Henry make his own trouble when he disallowed her cousins their pride? What could he do but protect his crown? No matter how many years passed, there were times like this when she wished she could be advised by her parents. "I have tried to cool the flames of Henry's temper on these matters and urge him toward mercy, but he is a king defending his realm."

"I'm sure that is what he believes, and we need talk on it no further. You have greater concerns at this time than the method your husband employs to rule his kingdom."

"Thank you, Cat."

They sat back in companionable silence broken only by the songs of the birds.

May 1502

"Henry, will you come to me tonight?"

A blush rose on Elizabeth cheeks and she cursed her silliness. Thankful for the low light in the hall and the conversations that distracted the people around her, she willed herself to be calm. She and Henry were sixteen years married, but it had been quite some time since she had made this request. Surprise was evident on his face as well, but he eagerly consented.

Regardless of anything else going on or her own personal feelings, which were still confused and conflicted, Elizabeth felt that she must bear Henry another son. Harry was robust and athletic, and to think of him dying young was almost laughable. Almost. She would take no chances with the succession of the kingdom. Harry would need a brother to stand by him in difficult times when he was king and his sisters had been sent away to husbands.

Jayne and Cat helped her prepare for him that evening, neither casting judgment upon Elizabeth's decision but trying to lighten the mood with girlish talk and bawdy jokes. Elizabeth smiled at the two women who showed her such devotion and thanked God for them. When they left the room and Elizabeth was alone and waiting, she prayed quietly that God would restore feelings of desire for her husband. She may not agree with everything he had done, but she still owed him that much.

When he entered the chamber with a boyish look of expectation and happiness on his face, Elizabeth laughed with joy and took him into her arms without hesitation. Henry had conflicting feelings of his own. Still uncertain that Elizabeth should attempt bearing another child, he was nonetheless thrilled that she wanted him again. He would leave it in God's hands.

Later that night, as they lay exhausted but satisfied in each other's arms, Elizabeth was certain that seed was taking root.

~ ~ ~ ~

In the meantime, few were considering any pregnancy of the queen's but were quite concerned regarding another possibility. Catherine of Aragon, Arthur's poor wife of only three months was travelling to London to be with her husband's parents. Despite her mourning, she would need to attend to questions from all sides about her relations with her young husband. Had the marriage been consummated? Was it possible that the heir to England's throne was not Harry after all, but Catherine's unborn babe?

Elizabeth did not believe that it was possible. Their marriage had been brief, not that it took more than one night, as Arthur's birth had proven. However, Elizabeth was also aware that Henry had encouraged Arthur to wait until his health had improved before having relations with his beautiful bride. The question remained whether or not Arthur had obeyed.

Catherine arrived in a small procession swathed in black. It was a grim reminder of the joyous ceremony that had welcomed her just months earlier. Then the blushing bride, now the sixteen year old widow. She rode in a litter rather than on horseback, partly to avoid prying eyes but also because she had been struck ill at the same time as Arthur and was still healing.

Elizabeth had made sure that no crowd was in the courtyard when Catherine arrived. This was not a moment to be shared with the public as the mother received the daughter-in-law in their common grief. Catherine was assisted from the litter, and Elizabeth immediately took her into her arms, ignoring formality. When they separated, both had fresh tear tracks on their cheeks but a smile on their face.

"I am so happy to be with you. It was so difficult to be at Ludlow once Arthur was gone."

"You poor girl! That must have been a terrible blow to you, mourning your husband on your own."

Catherine nodded. "I had the comfort that God gives, of course, but a listening ear and soothing arms would have been appreciated as well."

"You will have them now, my daughter," Elizabeth assured her.

They went inside, leaving the luggage to Catherine's attendants, many of whom wondered what the future held for their mistress. Once they had settled in Elizabeth's private chambers, Catherine was eager to speak.

"I want you to know that you need not fear that I am pregnant. Harry is his father's heir; there should be no doubt."

Elizabeth looked up in surprise, not at the news but Catherine's boldness in saying it. "You have come a long way from our first meeting, when a blush burned across your cheeks."

Both women smiled at the memory. "It seems in some ways so long ago." Catherine said wistfully. "Caring for an ailing husband was a quick lesson in maturity. Arthur and I knew each other well from our letters, but it did not prepare us for what we went through." She paused. "If this is too difficult for you to hear . . . ."

"Not at all," Elizabeth encouraged her. "I would hear of the comfort my son received in his last weeks."

"He was not always ill, and we had some delightful outings. Our friendship grew, but not our intimacy. Arthur confided in me that it was not his father's will, nor did he feel physically well enough, to consummate our marriage. We were both content to wait, not realizing that he would not get better."

A single tear ran down Catherine's face, but she had cried herself out many times before this day. She could speak of Arthur now and knew that her heart had begun its healing. Elizabeth sat silent for a few moments, picturing her son and his wife walking through the Ludlow grounds. She tried to stay away from the vision of him thin and weak in bed, but at least that image also included Catherine devotedly attending him.

"Thank you," she finally whispered. "It gives me peace to hear of your time together. Know that I would have rejoiced if a grandchild was a possibility."

"I know you would have, but it will be better for the kingdom if it can rally behind Harry."

"That is generous of you."

Catherine shrugged. "Maybe it is, but it is also the way it is. I will support my brother-in-law as my husband's successor and wait upon he and your husband for what they would decide upon my own fate."

That was something that Elizabeth had not yet considered. With Harry confirmed as heir, what would be Catherine's place in England? "What is your desire?" she asked.

With a sigh, Catherine shook her head. "I am not sure and am almost thankful that others will decide for me. I have practically been raised believing that England would be my home. Part of me wishes to stay, but I am unsure what my place would be. The other half of me desires nothing more than running home to my mother and father."

"Your confusion and your feelings are completely understandable," Elizabeth assured her as she rose to get them wine. "We will deal with this decision as necessary. For now, you are my welcome guest that we may take comfort in each other."

Later that day, other concerns would require Elizabeth's attention. The whispers and diverted eyes of servants alerted her that something was going on unrelated to mourning for England's prince. She took Jayne aside the first chance she had and insisted that she be told what was going on.

"Your grace, it is nothing that you should concern yourself with under the circumstances."

"I am a grieving mother, but I am also a queen. Tell me."

"Very well," Jayne gave in, taking a deep breath. "Sir James Tyrell has been sentenced to death for treason along with several others said to be involved in conspiracy with him."

Elizabeth was taken aback. Though she was not closely acquainted with him, James Tyrell had served her father, uncle, and husband, seeming to be able to please each of them without drawing accusations of unfaithfulness for serving the others.

"I heard that he had been brought from Calais."

"Tricked into coming, they say." Jayne was warming up to her storytelling. "It is said that he was ready to come out in support of Edmund de la Pole. That is the charge he dies for, but there are whispers that there is more."

"More?" Elizabeth asked. Her mind was too fogged with grief to understand what Jayne referred to.

"I do not really know, your grace." Jayne faltered but Elizabeth could see that more remained unsaid.

"Jayne. A man is to die," she pressed.

Nodding, Jayne continued. "I have heard that the man had information about your brothers, the little princes."

Elizabeth sucked in her breath and took a step back. She had been unprepared to have the specters of Edward and Richard raised again. "What information?" she demanded.

Jayne shrugged and looked apologetic. "That he murdered them, your grace."

~ ~ ~ ~

After hearing the news about James Tyrell, Elizabeth had raced to her private chapel and knelt before the altar. God give me wisdom, she prayed over and over again. She had given her brothers up for dead long ago. Well, she mostly had. Something deep within her had still held onto hope, had closely examined the face of Perkin Warbeck to see if it was that of Richard. If Tyrell had confessed to murdering him all those years ago, then all her hope had been in vain. Had he named the man who ordered them killed? Almost two decades later, she could not quite believe it.

"I must speak to him," she spoke aloud though none were in the room to hear her.

Henry was not in favor of sending his queen to speak to the killer of her little brothers, but she had never been so adamant about anything and he did not want to destroy the trust that was again growing between them. On a sunny May afternoon, with butterflies wandering through the air and signs of new life sprouting all around, Elizabeth arrived at the Tower to speak to the man who claimed to have killed her brothers there.

The warmth of the sun dissipated as soon as she entered the stone walls. The heat could not penetrate the thick, cold rock, and the chill tried to seep its way into her heart. One glance toward the tower where her brothers had been held before they disappeared was all she allowed herself. Today, she would deal only in facts. Plenty of time had been given over in the past to sentiment and dreams. Truth was what she would have before she left these haunted walls for what she hoped would be the last time.

She paused in an empty passageway to calm her breathing and say a silent prayer. Whatever she learned today, the fate of her brothers needed to be left in the past. If James Tyrell could not enlighten her with the truth, then she must accept that she just would not know this side of heaven. After a few moments of mental preparation, Elizabeth stood proudly to her full height, shoulders back and head held high, and marched toward Tyrell's cell.

Elizabeth nodded to the guards to give her entrance. They shared a hesitant glance before unlocking the heavy oak door. Far be it from them to say no to the Queen. When they made to stand in the doorway for her protection, she spoke for the first time since entering the nightmarish castle. "Leave us."

Her voice echoed around the bare walls, and she could have sworn that she heard other voices mingled with her own as if ghosts called out to her. The guards were more hesitant to follow this order. After all, it would be the wrath of the king brought down upon them if something happened to Queen Elizabeth. In the end, they quailed under her imperial glare and returned to their post on the other side of the heavy door.

Elizabeth was pleasantly surprised to see that Tyrell seemed relatively unharmed, unlike Warbeck, who had been unrecognizable to those who saw him after his death. She shivered and flung that thought aside. She could not be distracted from her purpose, for she was certain that this would be her only opportunity to speak with the man who claimed to have killed her brothers.

If James Tyrell was shocked to be receiving the Queen of England as his visitor, he did not show it. His face was grim and resolute. It was the face of a man who knew that he was going to die and was determined to make it a good death. He stood to give up his stool to Elizabeth, as it was the only seat in the small, dark chamber, but Elizabeth waved away this effort and remained standing before him.

"You served my father, fighting with him at Tewkesbury, and loyally served my uncle as a member of his household."

With a slight dip of his head, Tyrell said, "That is correct, your grace."

"Though your father was executed for treason, you have supported the York cause." Even to the extent of rallying behind her cousin, Edmund de la Pole, most recently. She was not interested in exploring that path. "If what I am told about your confession is true, you committed a heinous crime against the family you have continuously served." She paused and narrowed her eyes to examine his face, which gave away nothing. "If you killed my brothers, it was done on the order of my uncle, in whose service you were at that time employed. I need you to tell me if that is true."

Tyrell was not intimidated, though Elizabeth did her best to put on the most regal manner she had ever seen displayed by her own mother. After considering her for a moment, he said, "That is the manner of my confession."

Elizabeth smiled at him. "Ah, but I have read your confession. I am interested in what you would say that could not be put to parchment."

Rubbing his face in an effort to wash away the conflict within him, Tyrell took more than a minute to form his response again. "My confession is complete."

Elizabeth began to feel that this visit was pointless, and she would go to her grave not learning the truth.

"You have a son, Sir Tyrell."

"I do, your grace. He is enjoying similar accommodations as myself . . . . for now."

It was a clue, and she knew he would not give her many.

"He will inherit your lands and titles, despite your confession," she guessed.

Tyrell only nodded once.

"Or because of it," Elizabeth said, closely watching his face. His answering nod was almost imperceptible. "You did not kill my brothers," she concluded.

An almost imperceptible flicker of fear flashed across his face, and he leaned forward to furiously whisper, "You must say nothing," he ordered her, as though he spoke to a serving maid rather than his queen. "My death will have been in vain if the king believes that there are doubts about my guilt. My reputation will mean nothing, but I can secure my son's place." He quickly sat back and arranged his face, leaving Elizabeth to wonder if the whispered declaration had been imagined.

Elizabeth looked toward the door, reassuring herself that they could not be overheard. Leaning closer than was proper, she asked the question that had plagued her for almost two decades. "Did Richard order the murder of my brothers?"

Tyrell peered into Elizabeth's eyes, knowing that he was closer to her than anyone other than the king was allowed. Had he been that type of man, it would have been easy to kiss her and more long before the guards realized what was going on. Could he trust this woman with his son's future? He whispered as if they were lovers.

"He did not." He hoped and prayed that he had not just made a horrible mistake.

Elizabeth did not immediately move. She took in every detail of Tyrell's craggy face, for she must decide which version of his truth to believe: the one Henry forced from him upon threat of death to ensure his son's inheritance, or the one hesitantly given for the peace of mind of the queen. She straightened, pulling away from him. "That is what I have always hoped and believed. You may trust that I will not use this information to the detriment of your son."

She moved toward the door, but halted when Tyrell unexpectedly spoke once more. "For your brothers' murderer, you may wish to look closer to home, your grace." Fingers of dread ran up and down her spine at his words. She did not turn or respond, but pushed her way through the door and away from James Tyrell for the last time.

Elizabeth returned to her chamber just in time to bring up her breakfast into a pot held by Jayne. Sweat beaded up on her forehead as the queasiness threatened to knock her off her feet.

"Are you alright, my lady?" Jayne asked softly when Elizabeth seemed to have nothing left to bring up.

Leaning back and slowly nodding, Elizabeth cursed her own

impetuous decision, made in the wake of losing her firstborn child. She had convinced Henry that it was a good idea. Of course they should have another child. They were young enough, and Harry needed a brother, just in case.

"I believe I am with child," she admitted to Jayne. And his father might be a murderer, she thought only to herself.

"The king will be so pleased!" Jayne said with false enthusiasm. "You will also be pleased to hear, your grace, that your sister, Cecily, arrived and requested an audience just after you left for the Tower."

Elizabeth closed her eyes, wishing that she could take a moment to think before anything else was piled upon her weary shoulders. "Once you have disposed of that, you may attend me and send someone to escort my sister to my private chamber."

"Yes, your grace," Jayne murmured before leaving the room.

As soon as Cecily entered the room, Elizabeth knew that she had news to share for her sister was not accomplished at hiding her feelings. Apparently, neither was Elizabeth.

"Bess, my poor dear! Are you feeling well?" Cecily hugged her warmly before holding her at arm's length.

"I am quite fine," Elizabeth laughed without disclosing more. "Tell me what it is you have come to share before you burst with it." She gestured toward a window seat where they sat close to each other.

"I do hope that you can understand, for I know that I have been disobedient," Cecily began. She looked out the window rather than at her sister's face. "Bess, I am married."

Elizabeth gasped. It was the scene with her aunt Katherine being repeated before her eyes. It took her a moment in her current mental state to recover enough to respond. "God's blessings to you and your husband. Who is he?"

"Oh, thank you, Bess! He is wonderful, and I hope that the king will agree. His name is Thomas Kyme, and he is . . . . well, he is a squire."

Elizabeth smiled her first real smile of the day. Cecily may have had poor Ralph Scrope torn away from her, but she would have her common husband. "And you are in love?"

"Madly!" Cecily's glowing face and wide grin attested to the truth of it.

"I will, of course, speak to Henry on your behalf, though he may curse the Woodville women's habit of marrying for love. I would suggest that we also speak to my mother-in-law that she may take up your part. She has always been somewhat partial to you, respecting you for your boldness." At the mention of the lady Margaret, another thought occurred to Elizabeth, one that made her blood run cold but she had to push it aside for the moment.

"Thank you, Bess! And God bless England's most wonderful queen!"

Elizabeth waved away Cecily's exuberant appreciation. "Henry may not be in the mood to be overly generous, mind you."

"I do not care," Cecily said firmly. "As long as my marriage is left intact, he may take whatever he desires."

Henry did. Though Cecily was allowed her Lincolnshire squire, he confiscated her estates.

June 1502

Elizabeth had moved her household to Richmond following her visit to the Tower. She had not shared her suspicion that she may again be with child with Henry before leaving London because it was far too early to be certain. Her feelings toward her husband were such chaos within her. She had believed that healing was taking place between them after the loss of Arthur, but Tyrell's words to her had again turned her cold toward him. She must learn the truth. If Henry was responsible for her brothers' deaths and had lied to her for seventeen years of marriage, she would maintain a separate household from him for the remainder of her days. She would not endanger her children's future by making a public scene of it, but they could no longer live as husband and wife.

"Jayne, I am planning a progress."

"Is that wise in your condition, your grace?" Jayne spoke softly and made sure that they were not observed, for few guessed Elizabeth's condition.

"Whether it is wise or not, it is something I must do. I have put off discovering the truth for too many years. It can be delayed no longer," Elizabeth insisted.

"As you wish, my lady," Jayne demurred.

"Please send my sister, Cat. I would speak to her about my plans."

Moments later, Cat joined her sister and they huddled close together as partners in crime.

"I have visited the Abbess of the Minories," Elizabeth said in a low voice.

"She is cousin to Tyrell?" Cat asked.

Elizabeth nodded. "She does not believe that James, God rest his soul, committed this crime against our family."

Cat had expected no less. "Now what?"

"I informed Jayne that I would like to prepare to go on progress."

"You really intend to do this!" Cat looked at her eldest sister with new respect. "We will find the truth, Bess." Cat did not remember her brothers, something that she would not admit to her sister. However, her husband, Will Courtenay, remained in the Tower for supporting their de la Pole cousins. The least Cat could do was to help her sister in her quest for truth. If Henry was found to be the boys' killer, would Edmund become king? She shook her head. She must focus on the present.

"Once I have Princess Catherine settled at Croydon Palace, we will be free to set out," Elizabeth said. "The poor girl is beside herself with grief and fear for her future."

"And is she with child?" Cat asked, though not out of concern for the Spanish princess whom she barely knew.

Elizabeth frowned and shook her head. "Catherine confided in me that Arthur had never felt well enough to consummate the marriage, though he gave the impression that he had to avoid embarrassment. Even if I did not believe her, which I do, her ladies have observed her monthly flux since his death."

"It is for the best that Harry is secure as heir," Cat said because it was the proper thing to say. She was not at all certain who the next king would be. If Henry died before Harry was of age, she doubted that he would be any more successful than her own young brothers had been.

"God has his hand in this," Elizabeth said softly. "Though I will never stop mourning for Arthur, Harry was not meant for a life devoted to the church. He will make a king in the very image of our father, and for that I am grateful."

Cat made no response and the women sat in their own private thoughts for a few moments.

Elizabeth broke the silence. "I have sent some goods and money to our sister."

Cat pursed her lips. She must guard her words carefully when it came to the king's actions. "Henry has not forgiven her."

Shaking her head sadly, Elizabeth regrettably admitted, "No, he will not annul the marriage, but neither will he restore her estates. Cecily was prepared for punishment, but I do not think she expected this. She is learning what it means to live without luxuries that we have always taken for granted."

"I hope that the love of her husband is recompense enough."

"As do I," Elizabeth agreed, but she wondered if it could be for a woman who had grown up a pampered princess.

July 1502

Wagons and litters were lined up with horses stamping the ground and pulling at their reigns. Elizabeth was nervous about setting out on her own, but whether it was the pregnancy that she was now sure of or the information she was afraid she would gain that caused her anxiety, she was not certain. Cat was full of enthusiasm and a sense of adventure, and Elizabeth wished that she shared her energy and optimism. As they climbed into a litter together, Elizabeth was glad that she had such an upbeat travelling companion.

At Colnbrook, they made offerings at St. Mary's Chapel for safe travels and good health in addition to prayers for Arthur's soul, though Elizabeth was doubtless that he would have been welcomed immediately into heaven.

By mid-July they were at Notley Abbey when they received a messenger from Havering bearing the news of the death of little Lord Edward Courtenay.

Cat received the news of her son's death without a crack to her composure. Her husband imprisoned, his heir dead, she refused to allow others to see her wail in pain like a commoner. After releasing the messenger to find refreshment, she rose and ordered her attendants to prepare her things to return to Havering.

"I'm sorry that I must leave you, Bess."

"Cat, I can accompany you." Elizabeth was disturbed by the lack of tears in her sister's eyes. "The truth about our brothers has waited this long to be revealed. It will hold a little longer. Let me be with you and comfort you."

"I do not need comfort. Find the truth, Bess, for the number who know it are dwindling as the years go by. If our family is to have justice, you must continue while I go to bury my son."

When Cat rode away with her small, sad group of attendants,

Elizabeth was more determined than ever to complete her quest before any more sons of York could die.

Unfortunately, she made it only as far as Woodstock when she was forced to halt for the sake of her health. Those with her by now were all aware of her pregnancy, but they hid their concern in her presence. Not only was the queen thirty-six years old, but she had suffered during her last pregnancy as well. Some were bold enough to question why she would risk this journey as she struggled with fatigue and nausea, but all loved her well enough to care for her without bringing these doubts to her.

It was August before Elizabeth felt well enough to move on, this time to the hunting lodge at Langley.

August 1502

Elizabeth felt lost not having Cat with her but then felt selfish for wishing her sister there rather than mourning for her son. Elizabeth had not known Cat's little Edward, who was not more than a toddler when he died. To assuage her feelings of guilt, she sent Cat money for funeral expenses and began including masses for Edward Courtenay's soul with Arthur Tudor's.

Jayne was forced to attempt to fill the gap left by Cat's absence, and it was she who accompanied Elizabeth to pray and give offerings at St. Anne in the Wood near Bristol. The queen seemed to be pushing herself despite obvious fatigue and dizziness. Jayne did not understand why Elizabeth did not delay her progress until after the child had been born and wondered what the goal of this progress could be.

The chapel of St. Anne's was a vision of beauty that belonged in a myth. Trees towered over the low stone building, which was covered in flowering vines making it look like the building itself had sprouted up out of the earth. Jayne and Elizabeth lit candles for Arthur and Edward before kneeling to pray before the altar. Elizabeth spent an unusually short amount of time on her knees before pulling herself up by grasping the prie-dieu rail and crossing herself.

It was the holy well that interested her. Leaving the chapel, the women followed a worn path through the thick woods to a stone well. A well of holy water, enough to bathe in, would certainly have healing powers. While her guards ensured their privacy, Elizabeth and Jayne undressed to their shifts and submerged themselves in the surprisingly cool water. Though neither said anything, both knew that prayers were being sent to the Heavenly Father for the health of the babe and his mother.

As they rose from the water, feeling refreshed and at peace,

Jayne spoke first. "Will we be carrying on to Ludlow, your grace?" She assumed that part of the reason for Elizabeth's ill-timed progress was to visit her son's household and grave, so she was surprised when Elizabeth answered without meeting her eye.

"No, we will not be stopping at Ludlow. I must get to Raglan Castle."

Elizabeth was already walking away with a more confident stride than the tired shuffle that had brought her to the well, leaving Jayne to wonder what on earth was at Raglan Castle.

After a brief trip into Wales, where they visited the Monmouth Priory and again made donations and gave alms, the royal procession carried on to Raglan, home of Charles Somerset, the last of the male Beauforts.

~ ~ ~ ~

Though Jayne was not as comfortable asking Elizabeth about her choice of destinations as one of her sisters would have been, she was able to discover more about the man Elizabeth was determined to visit. Charles Somerset, illegitimate son of Henry Beaufort, duke of Somerset, had loyally served Henry, who he probably considered some sort of distant cousin. He was also married to Elizabeth Herbert, daughter of William Herbert and Mary Woodville.

Jayne was certain that it was not this familial link that drove her queen but a more distant one. After Mary, Elizabeth's aunt, had died, William Herbert had married Katherine Plantagenet, the illegitimate daughter of Richard III. Jayne had long ago guessed that her mistress had conflicting feelings regarding her uncle Richard, but why was she trying to unravel the mysteries surrounding him now?

When they arrived at Raglan Castle and Elizabeth welcomed

Liz Somerset as graciously as a favored friend, Jayne knew that she was right.

That evening, Liz was basking in the attention of her queen and cared not to question what she had done to deserve it. They had dismissed their attendants and enjoyed a small fire to take of the evening chill.

Picking up her cup of wine, Elizabeth casually asked her host, "Did your step-mother ever talk about her father?"

The younger woman, who was incapable of subterfuge, shrugged without wondering why the question was asked. "She did not speak of him much. I believe the subject was painful to her for she often heard the rumors put forth against him."

"Then she did not believe them?" Elizabeth asked, attempting to sound casual.

Worry flashed across Liz's face. "Of course, she could not know the truth," she hedged, hoping that she had not caused offense.

Elizabeth leaned closer. "I do not speak in anger, dear cousin. I am trying to solve a little family mystery, and you are just the person to help me."

Brightening again, the young woman went on, "Well, she loved him endlessly, of course, she being a bastard and he arranged an advantageous marriage for her anyway. So many girls claim dukes and earls as fathers and don't receive a second glance let alone recognition from a king."

"He was a generous and pious man," Elizabeth said in encouragement.

"It was Buckingham she hated," Liz stated as her face darkened.

Elizabeth leaned back, her brow furrowed. "Buckingham?"

"Of course, your grace. She blamed him for everything - his rebellion that turned men against Richard after everything he had done for him. Well, then he had no choice but to execute him, but men said that Richard should have let the duke have his say. Forgive me, your grace, but, of course, there is the case of your dear brothers as well. God rest their souls."

Elizabeth had been raised to keep her face arranged, be polite in all circumstances, and not be shocked by anything. Those lessons were forgotten now as she stared at her hostess with lips parted and eyes wide. "Buckingham?" she repeated.

"Well, of course, your grace. Who did you think did it?"

~ ~ ~ ~

Elizabeth and her party remained at Raglan for enough days to not seem that they were hurrying away, but Elizabeth never uncovered more information than she had that first night. Richard's daughter had blamed Harry Stafford, not only for her father's downfall but for the death of his nephews.

It made some kind of sense, Elizabeth reflected, though she still could not imagine handsome, well-mannered Harry killing his own cousins. She smiled sadly to herself. If men could not kill their cousins, there would be many more men alive today. But she had loved Harry . . . . and Richard. She loved Henry, too, and did not want any of them to be guilty.

September 1502

The lazy days at Raglan had been easier for Elizabeth to bear. Back on the road, she realized that her health was not as improved as she had hoped, but she insisted upon one more stop before returning to Langley to convalesce.

At Berkeley Castle, she was forced to be discreet with her inquiries. She was not likely to find many people who were as well informed and willing to talk as Liz Somerset. The elderly Maurice, Lord Berkeley, had served as Knight of the Body to Elizabeth's father, Edward IV. The task of having private word with the master of Berkeley Castle proved much more difficult than it had with the mistress of Raglan. Though Lord Berkeley was effuse with his praise of Elizabeth's father and what he called the "good old days," he became tight-lipped on the topic of Elizabeth's uncle.

Elizabeth spent a few days resting to recover from the stress of traveling. She was surprised at the weariness she felt and the way her heart felt as though it would burst out of her chest with any physical exertion. She was frequently found kneeling in the small Berkeley chapel.

Jayne was packing Elizabeth's things. After a week at Berkeley, her mistress seemed ready to travel again and disappointed that she had not found whatever it was she was looking for. Elizabeth was taking a slow stroll around the garden, enjoying the warm sun and sound of birds singing. Soon an autumn chill would be in the air, and some leaves were just beginning to turn color.

"Your grace, I hope that you have enjoyed your stay."

It was Lord Berkeley, examining some plants and bushes that would need pruning before the cold set in. Elizabeth sent a silent prayer of thanks for this opportunity that she had been waiting for.

"It is lovely here," she said with a friendly smile. "I must apologize for my poor health. I would have enjoyed the opportunity to speak with you more."

Not one to mince words, Berkeley asked, "And what would the queen like to talk to an old knight about?"

"My brothers." She knew that she was being too direct, but time was running out and she had the impression that Maurice was one who appreciated directness.

He took a deep breath and stretched his back. "What do you mean?"

"I think you know what I mean," Elizabeth said, watching his face. "What do you think happened to them?"

"You do not still hold out hope that they are alive?" he asked in astonishment.

"No," Elizabeth admitted, eyes downcast.

"May I ask you a question, your grace. If you forgive an old man for being too forward."

"Of course."

"The Warbeck boy . . . . was he . . . ."

"No," she said firmly. "I saw him with my own eyes and spoke to him several times. He was not Richard."

Maurice's jaw tightened, but he nodded as if he had expected as much. "Then he really did it."

"Who?" Elizabeth asked breathlessly.

He took in her eager face and made a decision. Best leave deeds nobody should want to claim to those who are already gone. "Your uncle."

Elizabeth's face fell and her shoulders stooped. "You believe that Richard killed them."

"Well, not personally, of course," he said, looking away from her, supposedly to examine more plants. "Someone would have done it for him."

After a moment, Elizabeth asked, "Buckingham?"

Berkeley's head jerked. He was clearly surprised by this theory.

"Well, now, I have no reason to believe that. It is James Tyrell who has been executed for the crime after all."

"Ah," Elizabeth understood. She would not be gaining personal insight from Maurice of Berkeley. It was probably a habit that had enabled him to live a long, happy life. "Thank you, Lord Berkeley."

She did not see him again until he assisted her into her litter. She would spend the rest of the month at Langley, praying that she would not lose the child that had just began making its presence known through the fluttering in her womb.

~ ~ ~ ~

"Please, my lady," Jayne begged. "You must allow me to send for an apothecary."

"I do not want word to reach Henry that I am ailing."

"But you are, your grace."

Elizabeth gave a faint smile. "I would write to my sister, Bridget. The prayers of one closer to God would do me well."

"Yes, your grace." Jayne sent the message to Bridget, but also instructed the messenger to return with an apothecary.

Elizabeth fixed an angry glare on Jayne when the man entered her chambers, but she was too weak to make any further protest. Clearly, Jayne had already filled him in on the details of Elizabeth's symptoms: nausea, fatigue, dizziness, racing heartbeat. He left her with a few toxic looking potions and vowed to return in a few days. When he returned, Henry arrived as well.

"My love, why did you not let me know that you needed me?" Henry asked as he rubbed her cold hands and he ordered a cup of wine brought with nothing more than a glance.

"I am just not as young as I used to be, Henry. The babe is sapping me of energy, but he will be strong and that is what is important."

She could not decide how she felt about his presence. On one hand, she had not discovered any other evidence that it was Henry who had killed her brothers. On the other, only the flighty Liz Somerset had dared to share a theory that opposed the confession of James Tyrell. She could not evade her husband based on unfounded rumor forever.

"I am glad you are here, Henry."

She was rewarded by seeing his face light up, which only served to confuse her more.

October 1502

"Why Minster Lovell?" Henry asked. He had been as attentive as any husband could be for the past fortnight, but Elizabeth insisted that she felt well enough to continue on her progress. Henry was just as adamant that he would join her. It would make it trickier to ask her questions, but she could do nothing other than thank him for being so thoughtful.

"I would see that it is being cared for as it should be since it is now in our son's hands."

It was a lame excuse, and she knew it. Lovell Hall had been the estate of Richard's most loyal companion, Francis Lovell. They had grown up together, both trained in Warwick's household at Middleham. After Richard's death, Francis had fought for the fake Edward of Warwick at Stoke. Elizabeth knew that Francis would have realized that Lambert Simnell was not Edward, so she assumed that his loyalty had truly been with John de la Pole, Richard's heir who died fighting that day. Francis had not been seen since.

Henry only looked at her with a bemused expression before apparently chalking it up to the insane whim of a breeding woman.

Henry and Elizabeth gave offerings and handed out alms at every church and chapel along their path. They had so many things to place at the feet of God, including the soul of their firstborn child and the life of the one yet unborn.

Once they arrived at Lovell Hall, Elizabeth knew that she would not be able to carry out her own investigation. A skeleton crew kept the Hall in operation since it was rarely used, so it would be too noticeable for the queen to interview the servants looking for those who knew Francis. Jayne would have to do it for her.

Jayne was thankful to finally be brought completely into Elizabeth's confidence. "I knew that you must be up to something of this sort, your grace," she said when Elizabeth had explained her mission to solve the mystery of her brothers' murder. "I will do everything that I can."

When she reported back, Elizabeth cursed herself for not involving Jayne to a greater extent earlier.

"The cook, she was here and served Lord Lovell," she said as she ticked people off on her fingers. "And the master of the horse, though he's not master of much now. The gardener and one of the footmen both remember him well also."

"Good work, Jayne! And did you ask them about the princes?"

"Eventually, my lady. I have spoken to the cook as she will sing of the glory of days past to anyone who dares enter her kitchen, but the others may take more time to warm up to me."

"As you see fit," Elizabeth agreed remembering Berkeley's refusal to speak.

"The cook does not believe for one second that Richard had anything to do with the deaths of the boys," Jayne stated, hoping that would be enough to please her mistress. It was not.

"But who does she think did?"

"Your grace, Lovell was devoted to Richard, unable to believe anything bad about him. Those of his household are likely to believe the same," Jayne pointed out.

"That is why we are here. I need to know what those who remain loyal think."

Jayne looked down at her hands, twisting them together nervously. "She believes that it was at the hands of your husband, your grace." She was surprised when the queen simply nodded. "She has never left this estate, your grace. She has no way of knowing," Jayne soothed.

"But she does," Elizabeth interrupted. "For she would have heard it from Francis."

"If I may, your grace." Jayne hesitated, and Elizabeth urged her on. "Your husband was not in England until 1485. How could he have done it?"

Elizabeth had never tried to work out the how of Henry's guilt, but Jayne was right. It was something to consider. "Let me know when the others speak."

Jayne heard the unspoken dismissal and returned to her new position as royal spy.

~ ~ ~ ~

Elizabeth sat in a window seat looking over the gardens of Lovell Hall. They were compelled to remain because she was, once again, not well enough to travel. She was forced to admit that the routine of rising from bed, breaking her fast, and being clothed for the day, was exhausting for her. Her breath came in short bursts and she could feel her heart beating a quick cadence, so she had sat down to rest.

One of her attendants handed her some watered wine which she graciously took. It seemed to help settle the never ending nausea. With her previous pregnancies, the sickness had lasted only a few weeks. She was well into her pregnancy now with her belly rounded enough to leave nobody guessing, but still was sick into her pot every day. Her baby grew, but she felt herself getting thinner and weaker.

The sight of Jayne out on the lawn brightened her up a little. She was walking with Francis Lovell's former horse master, who was little more than a stable boy to an empty stable. Elizabeth hoped that Jayne would find out why he remained here on an abandoned estate rather than serving another nobleman. Maybe he knew something that the rest of them did not.

Elizabeth could not help but smile as she watched her conservative, respectable lady-in-waiting turn in to a coquettish flirt with the man who was easily twice her age. If the man suspected that he was being harvested for information, he gave no sign of it. Jayne even allowed him to kiss her on the cheek before walking away with much more sway to her hips than normal.

"Leave us," Elizabeth commanded as soon as Jayne entered the room. She ignored the knowing smiles that passed between her ladies who assumed that the prissy Jayne was about to be taken to task for her improper behavior.

When they were alone, Elizabeth patted the seat next to her, which Jayne hurriedly took.

"He has spent much time with Lord Lovell, your grace. Apparently, Francis – as he calls him – had no quandary with fraternizing with those beneath him and considered master Roland one of his greatest confidants."

"No," said Elizabeth, not believing her luck. "Is that why he remains here?"

Jayne nodded. "He does not believe that Francis is dead and asked me, 'How would he know how to find me if I were to leave?'"

Elizabeth leaned forward in expectation, forgetting her weariness for a moment.

"He is a staunch supporter of your uncle, too, of course, with Lord Lovell being such a good friend of King Richard. He believes that the intention was to send your brothers to safe homes where they could have a normal life and not be the figureheads of rebellions the way your poor cousin, Edward, was."

"That is what Richard told me," Elizabeth said with enthusiasm. "He even had us write to them, though we never received letters back. Does he know where they were sent?"

Jayne took a lingering drink from her wine cup, trying Elizabeth's patience. "Forgive me, your grace, but I said that was what he believes Richard intended. He does not believe that it ever came to pass."

Drained of the hope that had fueled her energy, Elizabeth

leaned back in her seat. "Why not."

"Because they disappeared before he had an opportunity to put his plan into place."

"Jayne, tell me. Did he use the word 'disappeared'?"

"No, your grace. He did not."

Elizabeth allowed her gaze to move back to the window and the overgrown gardens that had not been properly cared for since Francis Lovell's disappearance. Was he still alive? Oh, how she longed to speak to someone like him, who would be the owner of so many answers she searched for. Looking back at Jayne, she said, "Continue."

"He believes that they were murdered before Richard could move them by somebody who was close enough to know of his plans."

"Buckingham?" Elizabeth asked. She was no longer shocked when people suspected the handsome, fun-loving uncle she remembered of murdering his nephews.

"No, your grace. He believes that the duke of Buckingham made an ill-advised decision to press his own claim to the throne because he was led by the same person who arranged the death of the princes."

This was a new theory, and Elizabeth's face was filled with expectation.

"Buckingham's rebellion was nothing but a distraction and ploy to blacken Richard's reputation, according to master Roland. Henry Stafford was a tool in the hands of one more crafty and clever than himself, and he was drawn in by the vision of a golden crown upon his head. His head was filled with lies and promises that would not be fulfilled so that the way could be cleared for another to take Richard's place."

Elizabeth had gone cold and wished she had her wool cloak. This was the theory of Henry being behind the death of her brothers, but in much more detail and from a source who would have reason to know whether or not it was true. Had she married and had children with the man who killed her brothers and replaced them on the throne?

"That is not what my mother believed. She was fully supportive of my marriage to Henry." Elizabeth felt like she needed to defend herself.

"You misunderstand me, your grace," Jayne said softly, patting Elizabeth's icy hands. "He does not accuse King Henry, but the one who would pave the way for him."

Furrowing her brow and frowning, Elizabeth tried to force her weary mind to think. Jayne seemed to be urging her to come to the conclusion without needing to be told. She had the open and encouraging countenance of a tutor waiting for their student to give them the right answer. Then Elizabeth's mouth fell open and the wrinkles cleared from her forehead.

"Margaret."

"Just so, my lady."

"She was a lady-in-waiting," Elizabeth said, searching her memory for facts about the woman she had paid very little attention to at the time.

"She also attended to the princes' needs, so master Roland tells me," Jayne added.

"Truly? She had access to them in the Tower?" Elizabeth cursed her younger self for not paying more attention to what had gone on during those years. She had been young and selfish, thinking only of her own future as her brothers' was snuffed out.

"That is what he said, your grace. She saw to their care and visited them regularly. And then they were gone."

"But master Roland does not believe that they were moved."

She was shaking her head. "I'm sorry, your grace. No, he does not. He believes that they were killed and their bodies hidden, making it difficult for Richard, a man who many already believed the worst of, to investigate or make public the truth about them."

"Clearly, he felt that he could not tell me," Elizabeth admitted, wondering if Richard had ever felt as close to her as she had felt to him.

"I am sorry, your grace," Jayne said as she rose and fetched Elizabeth's cloak and wrapped it around her shoulders.

"Do not be, Jayne. Your help has been invaluable. I did not hold out hope, well not much hope, that my brothers had survived the year 1483. My desire is to find truth, not comfort."

"Your grace, if I may ask a question," Jayne faltered.

"Of course, it may be a question that I should be asking myself."

"Do you think the king knows?"

~ ~ ~ ~

Once Elizabeth felt up to moving, her procession travelled to Ewelme, which had been in the hands of her de la Pole relatives until their recent activities had put it in Henry's hands. If she had hoped to find a similarly vociferous and well-informed servant remaining there as she had found in Francis Lovell's master Roland, she was disappointed. After giving alms and offerings, she gave in to her body's demands and returned to Westminster, where she called upon Catherine of Aragon to join her.

January 1503

Elizabeth had passed the two months since returning from her progress in relative quiet and inactivity. Catherine was a great comfort to her and assisted with Elizabeth's charitable work and preparing the confinement chamber. Elizabeth was sure that this was the last time she would bear a child and looked forward to the time when her energy would return and she could feel like herself again. Catherine frequently joined her, kneeling at the altar rail to pray for a son.

If anyone questioned why the queen was not seen in the presence of her mother-in-law, nobody gave voice to it in Elizabeth's presence.

Splitting their time between Westminster and Richmond, Catherine and Elizabeth built the type of relationship that Elizabeth looked forward to having with her daughters, Margaret and Mary, once they were older. Catherine was happy to arrange for packages to be sent to William Courtenay, who still languished in the Tower, unable to mourn for his son with his wife. Without commenting on the family politics at work in the situation, Catherine attended to the tasks Elizabeth set for her.

The Christmas festivities had been too much for the ailing queen, and she had made only the necessary public appearances. She tried to make up for her lack of enthusiasm through generous gifts, which Catherine helped her arrange and have delivered. Elizabeth was thankful that the revelries were concluded, and she hoped that she could focus on preparing for her confinement at Richmond.

As the month wore on, Elizabeth had difficulty getting out of bed. Fears began to assail her that she would not be strong enough to bear Henry this final son. In her weakness of body and spirit, she requested to be attended by an astrologer.

"You can't be serious," Catherine exclaimed. "Your grace, we must go before the throne of the Lord our God not to men who would claim to have power."

"I have prayed to God, Catherine," Elizabeth moaned, tears gathering in her eyes. "My dear, you are like a daughter to me, and I am thankful for the consolation that you have given me. Please, allow me this reassurance."

"It is not right," Catherine continued to shake her head. "I will call back the doctors that they may bleed you again. It is bad humors in your blood that we must rid you of."

"No," Elizabeth stated firmly. "I can't explain it, but I feel even worse after the blood-letting. I cannot go through it again."

Catherine watched the tears flow over the gaunt cheeks of this woman she had grown to love, the woman she should have been presenting with grandchildren, and gave in. "Very well, sweet Bess. I will call upon Doctor Parron."

He was a surprisingly diminutive man, who would have been shorter than Elizabeth if she could stand. With his shuffling gait, he approached the queen's bedside without allowing his shock at her appearance to reach his face.

Elizabeth was propped up on pillows with her red-gold braids falling down either side of her. She was painfully thin except for the large mound of her belly lifting the bed coverings. Without energy for small talk, she said, "Tell me what you see in the stars, doctor."

"Yes, your grace," he said, bowing repeatedly and never straightening to his full height. "I have been watching the night skies for mentions of your name."

Elizabeth ignored the look of disdain Doctor Perron was receiving from Catherine, who refused to leave her mother-in-law alone with this man she considered evil.

"And what have you discovered?" Elizabeth pressed.

"I have seen your future in the stars," he said with a gesture that made Elizabeth look up to see if the stars were in the room. "I can foresee, your grace, great wealth . . . ."

Elizabeth felt herself losing patience. Maybe Catherine had been right. "Doctor, my child?" she said, sliding her hands up the rise in the covers.

"Of course, your grace," he said, bowing a few more times in rapid succession. "Your son will be a strong prince, one of many, of course."

"A son," Elizabeth said, a smile upon her lips.

"And the queen?" Catherine surprised them by asking from her perch in the corner. "What of the queen's health?"

"Yes, my lady," the doctor said with more bowing. "The queen will go on to bear more sons before going to her God when she is of a great age, not less than eighty years."

Catherine allowed herself a half smile, met Elizabeth's eyes, and nodded.

"Thank you, doctor," Elizabeth said as Catherine handed him a pouch of coins.

~ ~ ~ ~

Cat returned to Elizabeth's side to serve her in her confinement. She still mourned for her small son, but hoped to be in a better position to serve her husband at her sister's side. It was not possible for her to hide her surprise upon seeing Elizabeth's wasted condition.

"Sister dear," we must not travel for Candlemas. "You should be abed and surrounded by tempting foods."

"The babe is not due for another three weeks," Elizabeth insisted. "I will enter the confinement chamber upon our return."

Cat pressed her lips together, but conceded. On January 26,

the pair of sisters arrived at the Tower.

Upon their arrival, Elizabeth was whisked away to bed on the orders of her younger sister. She did not argue. In truth, she had to admit that Cat was right, and she should not have attempted the journey. Elizabeth was determined to travel only in order to enter her carefully prepared confinement chamber as soon as she could.

February 2, 1503

"Cat, you must forgive me," Elizabeth groaned. "This baby will not be waiting!"

The color drained from Cat's face, but she took charge with only a second of hesitation. The luxurious chamber at Richmond that had been prepared would go unused, and Elizabeth's child would be born within a cold, damp Tower chamber just like the one her brothers had died in.

Cat had never had any doubt that her brothers were dead and had not greatly concerned herself with who had been responsible. Her thoughts had always been for the future, a future in which William Courtenay and Edmund de la Pole would play a greater part.

Elizabeth groaned again and Cat was brought back to the present where she wondered if the future would include her eldest sister. She sent her sister's ladies scurrying to fulfill her commands as Elizabeth writhed upon the bed.

The midwife arrived just in time to deliver the queen of a thin, weakly crying baby girl. Named Catherine for the several wonderful women of that name that Elizabeth cherished in her life, the baby was quickly placed in the care of nurses as doctors were called upon to see to the queen. Despite their best efforts and the prayers of many, Elizabeth's health seemed to fail further.

February 11, 1503

Through half opened eyes, Elizabeth surveyed the room around her wondering why it did not seem familiar. The tapestries and darkness seemed subdued and gloomy. This was not her chambers at Richmond or Westminster. The Tower. A chill ran through her as reality flooded into her weary mind. She was in the Tower, the last place she had wanted to bear her child, but it had all happened so fast. As when Margaret had been born, this child had come with painful ferocity.

The child, had it been a girl or a boy? Why could she not remember? How much time had passed? Clouds seemed to move slowly across her thoughts making it difficult to focus on the memory beyond the pain that still lingered in her body.

A figure rushed to her side. One of her attendants had realized that she was awake. Thirst suddenly assailed her and she was grateful for the quick movements of the woman she could not yet identify, but she took eager gulps from the goblet as it was held to her lips.

"Slowly, sister dear. You will sicken."

Cecily. Of course, it was loyal, sweet Cecily. Elizabeth was overwhelmed with gladness that this person, who had served as a confidant practically since birth, was here beside her. Elizabeth knew that she would understand the request that she must make.

"My confessor. Please, Cecily."

Cecily pressed her lips together and blinked quickly to clear the tears from her eyes. Denying the request would not keep her sister with her but endanger her eternal salvation, but how she wished to say no. Without a word, she nodded curtly and turned from the bed.

Elizabeth heard only the rustling of skirts and hushed tones before the door opened and shut, leaving silence once more. Again, her sister was at her side. Cecily's hand in hers felt warm and smooth while her own seemed papery, cool, and almost as if it were not attached to her body.

Before too many minutes had passed, a tall figure burst into the room. The words of protest died on the lips of the women in attendance as they fell into low curtseys. Only Cecily stood and approached the king. They exchanged quick, quiet words before she stepped aside, and Henry rushed to the bed.

"Henry," Elizabeth whispered. "Then my instincts tell me the truth." There was only one reason her women would allow a man into the birthing chamber, king or not. How many breaths remained to her? It had never occurred to her to consider them finite.

"My beloved," Henry wept freely, showing more emotion to the ladies in the room than most had seen from him in the last twenty years. "Elizabeth, forgive me," he whispered.

Her hand raised from the bed to reach out to him but fell back before reaching its destination. "What would I forgive?" she asked.

He shook his head, remembering that the chamber was full of eager ears. Even his farewell to his wife would have to be controlled and carefully considered.

"Forgive me any time I have not loved you as fully as you deserved," he said more evenly. How he wished to say more. He was sorry for the grief he had caused her and her family, but he could not regret snatching the crown from her uncle's head.

She closed her eyes and nodded slightly, sensing that there was more he would say. A queen could not have privacy though, even in death. Were her breaths remaining now only one hundred? Fifty?

Her confessor was ushered in. He moved slowly and solemnly to Elizabeth's bedside, assured that death would wait for him to perform his duties at their proper pace.

Words coursed through Elizabeth's mind. Sins she would

confess. Questions she would ask. But she had the strength for none of them. "Pray Lord, forgive and receive me," was all she had the strength to say.

The priest made the sign of the cross over her and placed the tiniest portion of a communion wafer on her tongue. He stood, his duties complete.

She sighed, ready for her journey.

Images of her children raced through her mind. Harry would be king, though she would never see the crown placed on his russet head. Henry VIII. What kind of king would he be? He was a bright boy, and she hoped he would not make the mistakes that his ancestors had made. A prayer for him and the future of England floated like a mist through her mind. He looked so much like his grandfather. A smile flitted across her lips as she thought about this future king, who would be called a Tudor, but was thoroughly Plantagenet.

She opened her eyes to see Cecily and Henry, each holding one of her hands. Funny that she couldn't feel the pressure of their skin against hers. The energy to keep her eyes open was more than she contained. They closed. Was it now twenty? Ten?

"Happy birthday, my queen," Henry whispered. She was thirty-seven.

All went dark and quiet, and for a moment she was afraid. Then it was as though she had been miraculously healed. Pain lifted from her as if a bird carried it away. Strength flowed into her limbs, and she felt the urge to run through a meadow of wildflowers. Beautiful, yet indefinable, music filled her ears. More than one song played at a time, but her mind could snag each one from the cacophony. Then she opened her eyes.

Tears of joy ran in streams down her face as she ran to meet those waiting to greet her. Into the arms of her father she fell, and she took deep gulps of breath. He still smelled slightly of sweat and horses, but his body was not as she had seen it last. Instead, when she looked up at him, she was reminded of the day he had victoriously rode into London and saved them from sanctuary when she was just a girl.

That was when Edward, her brother, had been born. She turned quickly, her unbound hair flying around her. Her brothers. Of course they were there. They surrounded her, but she felt only happiness at their reunion. The doubt and curiosity that had plagued so many of her hours now dissipated in their presence. Only love and grace filled their eyes, not anger or condemnation.

Richard and Anne. The love between them was still clear, and she wondered if it hadn't been God's plan to not separate them for long.

Just when she thought her joy could not be greater, Eliza and Edmund threw themselves into her arms, and she saw Arthur awaiting his turn.

So many waited to greet her, but the crowd did not press. She saw no sign of impatience, only joy and happiness as they welcomed her into their presence. It was as if they had all eternity.

Then she heard the voice that did not need to be defined for her. It was a voice that she had never heard aloud though it had spoken to her heart, and she recognized it now as it beckoned her forward. Her family, friends, and those she instinctively knew to be her ancestors stepped aside leaving a path for her to follow as the voice gently commanded her.

"Come, my good and faithful servant."

Epilogue – February 1503

Henry left his wife's chambers for the last time. He would not cry until he was alone, so his mother's presence outside the confinement chamber kept him from breaking down. His face still gave away enough that she knew that the queen was dead.

"I am so sorry, Henry," she said, not because she cared all that much about her daughter-in-law, but because of the pain that it would cause her son.

Henry pressed his lips together, attempting to maintain control. It was easier to attack than mourn. "You need not worry, mother dear. She never discovered your secret."

Margaret watched her son stride away with her mouth agape and her eyes wide. They had agreed never again to mention those boys. She would have killed a dozen princes to ensure that her son sat on the throne of England.

Afterword

A lavish funeral was planned for Queen Elizabeth. If he had not always demonstrated it during her life, Henry Tudor left no doubt upon her death that he had truly loved Elizabeth. He never remarried, and his own health quickly failed.

Henry never entered the Tower again before his death on April 21, 1509. By this time, the fortress held as many bad memories for him as it had for his wife. Their son, Harry, who would become Henry VIII, would add to the blood soaked ground surrounding the Tower, but that is a story for another day.

Additional Reading

For those interested in reading more about the historical figures featured in this novel, I recommend the following sources:

Elizabeth of York: A Tudor Queen and her World by Alison Weir

Elizabeth of York: The Forgotten Tudor Queen by Amy Licence

Winter King: Henry VII and the Dawn of Tudor England by Thomas Penn

Last White Rose: The Secret Wars of the Tudors by Desmond Seward

Royal Blood: Richard III and the Mystery of the Princes by Bertram Fields

Richard III by Charles Ross

Author's Note

I decided to write about Elizabeth of York on April 12, 2013, my thirty-seventh birthday. Therefore, every day that I spent researching and writing about this captivating woman used one more day than she had been granted on earth. It was difficult but rewarding to enter the mind of this Tudor queen who I still prefer to think of as a Plantagenet princess. Though everyone recognizes the name of Henry VIII, few know that Elizabeth of York was his mother. I felt that it was high time that she receive some credit for bridging the gap between the Plantagenet and Tudor dynasties. What did she really think about her uncle and the fate of her brothers? Was she in love with Henry? I have tried to answer these questions to the best of my ability, but understand that it took as much imagination as research. Unfortunately, only so much information exists on this daughter, sister, niece, wife, and mother of Kings of England. I hope you have enjoyed my version of her story.

Connect with Samantha at
samanthawilcoxson.blogspot.com
or on Twitter @carpe_librum